Absolute
Darkness

Cynthia,
Don't Hold Your Breath!!
Thanks!

Tina A. O'Hailey

Black Rose Writing | Texas

The final approval for this literary material is granted by the author.

First printing

This is a work of fiction. Names, characters, businesses, places, events and incidents are either the products of the author's imagination or used in a fictitious manner. Any resemblance to actual persons, living or dead, or actual events is purely coincidental.

ISBN: 978-1-68433-030-0
PUBLISHED BY BLACK ROSE WRITING
www.blackrosewriting.com

Printed in the United States of America
Suggested Retail Price (SRP) $21.95

Absolute Darkness is printed in Garamond

DEDICATION

To the Shitty Writer's Club

Also by Tina O'Hailey
Published by Focal Press:

Rig it Right:
Maya Animation Rigging Concepts
1ˢᵗ and 2ⁿᵈ Editions

Hybrid Animation:
Integrating 2D and 3D Assets 1st and 2nd editions.

Absolute Darkness

ACKNOWLEDGEMENTS

Thanks go to the many people that helped and encouraged me along the way.

The Shitty Writer's Club: Matt Maloney, Kent Knowles, Pat Quinn. You helped me shape Alexander and keep this manuscript from being put on a pyre with the previous six. The release for each of us, accomplished in our own areas, to finish something, no matter how horrible, was the best approval to be bad one could ever have.

Thanks especially to my family of lovely enablers—John, JT, Danny; my caving family, in particular Mark Ostrander; my work family, Dr. Denise Smith and Dr. Teresa Griffis. You all put up with me, brought wine, listened while I droned on, and Mark knocked his head on the table in despair when I told him it had vampires.

My editor extraordinaire: Sherron Ostrander, who ignored Mark knocking his head on the table and became the best fiction editor I have ever worked with. Thank you for everything. You have taught me so much.

Thank you to Wendy Shirah for cave diving consultation. Any errors are absolutely my fault where I ignored good advice for the sake of dramatic concepts.

My apologies, I did not intend to write a romance novel. Alexander met my characters, Brandy and Susan, from other manuscripts; though I fought it, I could not make this anything but a love story.

PROLOGUE

"So you're telling me that it took seven tries?" Susan tested the roasting marshmallow by pinching it; blood red fingernails contrasting against the white flesh. Not satisfied with the doneness, she replaced it over the fiery coals.

Brandy's marshmallow was in flames, charred black. She blew on it, grinned. "Well, three of the tries were very unsuccessful for me, it seems." The blackened marshmallow flames were finally extinguished. "Many more were failures either due to you drinking, me dying or you getting knocked out. Or both. Seriously, you are a wreck."

"But you love me anyway." Susan popped the marshmallow in her mouth and immediately regretted it, fanning her mouth and whooping in gulps of air.

"That I do." Brandy pulled off a gooey melted bit of marshmallow and blew on it carefully then licked it off her fingers. "Who else would believe me?"

Brandy pulled a pocket watch from her pocket, eyed it, began to close it.

"What does that say?" Susan reached for the watch. "I don't remember you having that."

Brandy offered it to her friend and looked unseeing into the flames. The fire cast pulsing shadows across her face. "I got that, like, about ten thousand years ago."

Susan tilted the watch to the fire so she could read the inscription.

"The only reason for time is so that everything doesn't happen at once.

—R.C."

Susan made a sound between a grunt and a "hmmph."

Brandy grunted a response.

The friends fell silent and watched the flames dwindle to coals.

1 THE TIME WATCHER.
10,000 YEARS AGO.

"She's still there," he thought to himself. He glanced her way as he slid effortlessly through time and across the room. He batted absently at the wisps of spider webs. one moment only a strand, the next a full web, then it was gone. Dank, dead air pressed against his skin.

It was the look in her eyes that perplexed him most: sad, lost, empty. He sat next to her, followed her gaze into the pit's depths. She stared into the dark, seeing nothing but memory. He could see through all of time and regarded the pit in its infancy, as it enlarged, and the recent past. There, only a few days ago from the world's current time, a broken figure lay a hundred feet below. He could see the rock that had caused the fall, the look of horror on her face as she had watched her friend disappear, an outstretched hand grasping. He sat, watched the emotions on their faces. Surprise on the face of the one who fell. Horror and anguish on the face of the one who lived. Simple mortality. Why did she mourn the loss of her friend? What freedom to die. What joy to know you could end so easily. Why did she mourn? What did it matter? They all die; linears all die, so very easily. Linears, the outcast species spawned from his own ancestors: genetically malformed, weak, enslaved by time, oblivious.

His body, nearly immortal, had held his consciousness to this earth since the landmass had emerged as one continent from the sea. Time stretched behind him; his name lost, found, recreated, lost again over the endless existence. The last name he had claimed had been Alexander. He had forgotten the others, perhaps, or simply preferred to not remember them.

Alexander sat still, movements slow and thoughtful. He did not experience time, did not feel its pull upon his body's metabolism. Yet, he could see all of time from the moment he had become a man until now. It appeared and danced before him as ghosts. At will he could focus on a given moment in time and dial back the rest of the clouded ghosts before him. He crouched before the pit near the entrance of the cave, his cave. He took comfort in how slowly this cave had changed. The quiet of it: peace. The lack of visual clutter: bliss. Until now.

Like a healing bruise, a yellow stain smeared across the images of her as she mourned her friend's death. Yellow tinted the ghostly images of her friend falling then broken at the bottom of the pit, the color of puss. Ignoring the obvious stain in time was easier than ignoring the pain it caused him: a slow ache in his bones. The rock that had caused the fall stood out as the brightest tint of a ghastly yellow. This rock had been changed, altered. The accident had been caused. A manipulator had entered his sanctum and dared to alter events here. Alexander tried to muster the anger and indignity he knew he should feel. His heart felt too cold, too weary.

Looking up again, he could see misty visions of her throughout time, always coming here to sit and gaze. She didn't cry. It would have been a relief to see tears. Instead the sadness seemed to him as infinite as the universe.

He fell in love with her. How else could Alexander explain his procrastination to do what he should, to fix the error in time, to erase the yellow tinge that seeped into his body and across all the time he could see? To fix time would be to lose her. She would not visit the memory of her lost friend. He would not see her continuous trek span out before him as she progressed through her time. How long would she continue to visit and sit at the pit and mourn her lost friend? If he fixed time, he would not be able to sit near her, be with her, study the emotions on her face. Why mourn? He could wait; the pain was bearable. The universe was only mildly off its time track, a river with only a few divergent streams. Eventually, he would fix it, change it back. He had all of eternity, until the ache turned into agony, until the stream of time was too altered and threatened to leave its streambed.

The universe moved forward in time, slowly, for years. He entered his cave, welcoming the dark peace there and looked to the alcove where she sat.

Still there.

Still sad, still looking, never moving. She would be there in his vision forever. Her time had happened, she was there in that space and he could always see her, could focus on that moment or any of the other moments she had crawled, climbed or walked through his dark home. He studied them, all of her times spent there in the dark, until he knew her smile, how she touched her chin when talking, and the silly faces she made at her friend—before her friend had plunged to her death. He always returned to when she sat at the pit's edge and gazed mournfully.

From Alexander's frozen moment in time he began to anxiously watch for the ghost visions of her to appear as global time moved forward. Year after year, she returned, sat at the pit, mourned, then left. He sat with her. He cherished watching the new ghostly images of her appear in front of him while he viewed from his frozen moment, his time. He never dared to go close to her moment in time and risk being seen. He longed to. Alexander considered synching with time and waiting for her when she visited. He rejected the thought with a sudden, intense burst of anger. Hadn't he learned?

Eventually the visits were less often. Alexander waited and watched, having grown content with the ghost images of her. He spoke to the images of her upon his waking as he moved about his cave. First he spoke to her as a friend, confided in her image his secrets. He asked her questions. She did not answer them. Eventually he spoke to her ghost as a beloved companion. Then she did not visit anymore. No new images of her appeared. He watched. Alexander waited longer. How long do linears live? He looked towards the entrance of the cave. She did not appear again; only the ghostly images of her remained. It would be useless to find her. He considered the darkness outside his cave.

His bones ached as time struggled forward in its altered state. Alexander weakened, having forgotten to eat, for how long? He couldn't remember. Elsewhere he could feel other instances of time being altered, molested. He did not want to leave his static vigil here by her ghostly side. What if he stayed, let time slip, let the universe go? Would his inattentiveness to the keeping of time be enough to tear the universe apart?

Probably not. He sighed, slowly, soundlessly—air molecules disturbed and sent through time to collide and slide into unseen dimensions.

Somewhere, something, someone else was being altered, more streams of time being sent off course. Pain made his vision swim, tinged yellow then orange. No, he alone could not bring the destruction to the universe, but it would list and tear at him until he wished he could end it all. What if the others of his kind felt the same way? What if they all just stopped and allowed the manipulators to push time off its course until it had ripped apart at the seams and rendered everyone into…what? Death? Another existence? Energy? Nothing? Alexander felt the weight of his own eternal enslavement: heavy, all encompassing.

He sat again at the pit. His foot overlapped hers. His foot solid, her foot translucent. After all these years he had grown so accustomed to her. An eternal frown tugged at her mouth. Darkness obscured the color of her eyes.

A simple, nagging question burned through the darkness of his mood. The question refused to surface at first; it haunted and teased him until he could think of nothing other. He could not see the color of her eyes. What color were they? He couldn't see. No matter how he tried. How ridiculous it seemed to him that he had to know. Her sadness was even more profound in some way, heavier, more wrong for the fact he did not know whether blue, brown or green eyes held back tears.

His home. His cave: darker than night. No light had ever existed in this space. Not anywhere, not in any time. Alexander slowly and meticulously followed her movements through the cave on every visit she had ever made. She had crawled through this tunnel on her first visit. She had stood there with her friend that same visit. She had only sat at the pit a dozen more times, never venturing any further into the cave on the remaining visits. Only on the first trip did she smile, Alexander realized, a beacon in the dark. He could see frozen laughs shared between her and her friend. He dared to come close to her time, trying to see her eyes. She had used a head lamp when she explored. Long shadows tore across her face. He hurt to see the color of her eyes, always hidden from him.

A hundred years had passed and Alexander came to accept that he was holding onto something he could not have. A memory, a ghost, a linear who had been. For what? Why? The thought occurred to him that he could go find her, hear her laugh. He had never seen her laugh after her friend had died. Did she mourn only inside this cave or when she was outside as well? He had to let go of this. How do you let go of a thing that you see for all eternity? Forever visible? Forever part of your life.

The universe threatened to pull from its course, time had been altered in too many places. What if all others had stopped as well and this was the end he was looking for? He could hope. His vision was tinged with red as the time stream pulled over its banks and rushed towards entropy. He didn't see the red in his vision. He didn't feel the pain that pulsed through his body. Instead, he sat opposite of her. How could he let it end and not know the color of her eyes? She was beautiful to him. A linear. Hadn't he learned not to love them?

A new thought encompassed him. It was slow, deliberate and drowned out all pain. He could end her sorrow, release her. Enough with this self indulgence, a weakness. Remorsefully, he reached forward and back in time to when the rock still rested on the ledge.

He wasn't going to look at her, but his eyes betrayed him.

He saw her sad face.

He touched the rock in the past.

He didn't say good bye.

He loved her.

He pushed the rock into the pit.

It fell to the bottom where now no broken body lay. It would not be there to fall when his love and her friend would come to climb out of the pit. It would not be there to cause the death. No death, no broken body at the bottom of the pit, no sad look to haunt him, no yellow altered time pulling the universe towards chaos, no pain tearing through his body. He watched as the vision of her sitting, always sitting, disappeared. The air where she had been was no longer tinged that awful, sick yellow hemorrhaged with red.

She and her friend had left the cave into the sunlight where he could not go. Fifty feet before the entrance, she had stepped from the dark into the first twilight rays of light then had turned, as if she had heard something.

In the dim light he could see her grey eyes look back towards the dark of the cave.

He would not see those grey eyes again in his dark home. She was gone. He sat at the pit alone and stared into the darkness at the rock, a hundred feet below, where once a broken body would have been. Pain no longer gripped his body. He did not care. He would have cherished everlasting pain in place of the emptiness that now echoed in his soul.

2 THE MANIPULATOR.
THURSDAY AFTERNOON.

Yindi had to hurry. He didn't want to get caught. Then he would miss the moment and now, now was the moment. Grass stuck to his feet as he ran. He whistled to himself, tunelessly. Birds, startled, fled his path. Fidgety and hopping on one foot he paused to look around. Where would she go? There, there! She was going to cross this field and go into that cave. He searched through the future to see where his best chance would be. He had to hurry before she got there. He couldn't get caught.

There, right inside, he could feel the moment. It was simple. She would be here soon. Yindi paused again. Oh, she had a friend. Good, good. He searched again. Unable to see the particulars of what happened in time, he could only feel what would best sate his need. The feeling drew him to the opening of the cave. He cast about, nearly frantic, touching and feeling the air and walls around him. Where was it? What was it? When was it? The moment. The thing.

He ventured further into the darkness, groping. Pebbles.

Grit. Cave crickets skittered from his fingers. A lustful warmth engulfed him when his fingers grazed the rock. Willing himself to see into the darkness, he tensed: muscles bunched, heart pounding. A moan escaped when he grasped the rock and the full impact of the thing spread through his veins.

Quick, quick, he had to see the best way to adjust time before she got here. He lay on his belly in the dirt, both hands outstretched around the rock. A pit gaped in front of him. He didn't look into it. It didn't matter, he could not see into the darkness. His eyes looked into nothing and everything. It wasn't a decision that moved his hands; instinct and raw need showed him what to do. He loosened the rock and felt the rush of elation. That was it. Yes. He could see the time shift, turn yellow. No longer green. Altered. It caught his breath. It felt good.

He scrabbled back and sat on his haunches, rocking slightly and chewing the nail of his right hand. That was fine. Just a small shift. He could go do more elsewhere. This was good here. He felt time unraveling and slipping in this future. Intoxicating. He couldn't stay to watch. He had to keep moving, find the next thing. The things were everywhere. Had to keep looking and pushing. He itched to go, already anticipating the next rush when he found the next moment. Yindi chewed his lip and let out a snort through his nose. This was good. This was…

He paused. Looked into the darkness ahead of him. Was this…

Yindi tipped backwards, his feet going in front of him, and landed painfully on the pebbled ground. He giggled and hugged himself. How amazing, he had never been here before, never seen this place before. Smirking, he hastened his efforts to retreat from the cave, slightly panicked. Dust rose on the cool air. The draft carried the dust from the cave entrance to the dark passages beyond.

Already the pull to go somewhere else, to find the next thing, beckoned him. A siren song that never ended. A thirst unquenched. Yindi looked back, one foot scratching the other ankle. The thing, the rock Yindi had manipulated, was here in his place: the watcher's place. It was day, though the manipulated thing was in the dark. Could the watcher change it? The need to find the next thing itched. Curiosity is a need too. It cried louder. Yindi scurried, ran, jogged, fell and nearly crawled on all fours through the grass and into the woods to watch.

Two women walked casually across the grass towards the cave. Yindi hid behind a tree, biting his lip nervously. Drops of blood fell unheeded to his filthy shirt. The women both wore backpacks. One carried a rope coiled and draped across her shoulder. They clanked as they walked, harnesses and gear hung from their hips. Each paused at the entrance, turned her headlamp on, then walked into the darkness. Someone laughed. A small sound, then Yindi could not hear them.

Yindi's breath came in short bursts while he waited. Would the watcher be able to change it? It was day. But the thing was in the dark, a dark that has always been. No sun has ever shone there. Yindi's eyes darted to the sky, the sun, the trees, the cave opening. Yindi picked at his nubbed fingernails.

He could still feel the slight unwinding of time. It still felt good and washed through him. The watcher was not aware and had not changed anything back. Yet. The world would turn yellow then slide to orange and red and with it satisfaction. Peace for Yindi. Chaos for all. Yindi's eyes fluttered and rolled to the back of his head momentarily overcome by ecstasy.

A mental snap, a jolt of lighting to his stomach. Yindi doubled over and wretched dry heaves. His moment, his thing, was gone. He had changed it. He was there. Yindi tried to see a shape, an indication of someone there, but could not find anything in the darkness of the cave's entrance. Suddenly afraid, Yindi straightened. Waives of nausea threatened to double him again. He calmed himself visibly. It was day. The watcher couldn't come out here. Yindi knew he was safe, for now.

The need to find the next thing intensified. Where would it be? When? What was it? Who would be the one altered. Already excited to find it, Yindi turned and did not look back. Squirrels chittered at being disturbed. Yindi jogged, walked, ran at an uneven pace into the woods and away from the cave.

***

Yindi was not there when the two women exited the cave, just at sunset. One turned and looked back towards the entrance. A whip-o-will whistled from the trees. After a while the taller of the woman grabbed the shorter one's sleeve and tugged her away. Reluctantly, the shorter woman turned, glanced back again, then turned and walked away. The two muddy figures traipsed through the field and disappeared.

3 THREE DOOMED TO DIE.

"You should have seen it, Brandy. There he was, crawling in the passage in front of me." Susan hunched over and mimicked someone crawling. "Butt naked, with only a helmet and a pack."

Brandy nodded silently over her cup of coffee and did not look up.

Susan continued, "That wasn't the worst of it." She paused and leaned back in her lounge chair. "He got stuck between two rocks." Susan burst into high-pitched laughter.

Long shadows from the sunset tortured the grass under their feet. Someone drug another folding chair close to the two women: one still laughing, the other peering into her coffee mug.

"You made that up. Didn't he get cold?" The newcomer took his seat, gave Susan a bottle of Rolling Rock; he opened hers, opened his, drank.

"Swear, Mark." Susan turned towards Mark and raised her beer in a small toast. "Stuck between two rocks and stopped so suddenly I almost, you know." She took a sip. "Almost ran right into his ass." Susan erupted into laughter again.

Brandy looked from the cup, to Susan, to Mark without moving a muscle. She raised an eyebrow of hello to Mark and smirked a just shoot me grin.

Mark leaned in close to Susan and in a stage whisper said, "I think Brandy has heard this one before."

Just then, over the intercom loudspeaker, a voice announced, "No smoking, no lighters. We're going to light the bonfire in ten minutes."

Brandy, Susan, Mark and many others from their group were camped quite a ways from the fifteen-foot stack of wood that would soon be ablaze. Even from where they sat they could smell the kerosene that had been poured on the neatly stacked tower of corded pine and oak. Hundreds of cavers and enthusiasts were strewn about the five-acre field. It was Thursday evening, one day into a five day, four night annual camping event.

"That means you, Rock Muncher," Susan called out to a nearby group. The accused person stood unsteadily from his perch and came towards Susan, a grin on his face, a red Solo cup in hand.

"I can see it big as ol' day. You are sittin' here tellin' tall tales about me." Rock Muncher, no one could remember his real name, squatted on the ground near Susan. He wore what seemed to be a loincloth, cowboy boots, a beaded necklace and a baseball cap. "She's tellin' lies about that crawl to the Junction Room back in Blue Springs Cave. I did not get stuck."

Blaine, tall and with a perpetual smile, idled to the group. "He got stuck. Don't let him fool ya."

Rock Muncher stayed squatted on his haunches and rocked

a bit. The sun was gone and twilight fading. "Didn't. Got pinched is all," His voice lowered and he pouted.

Susan burst into gales of laughter and was joined by Mark and Blaine. Rock Muncher's voice tightened as he tried to defend his honor, "I dislodged a rock with my knee and it fell over and pinched me to another rock." He smiled and regained some confidence, "Not everybody would have that problem."

Susan snorted a laugh. Brandy had resumed staring at her coffee.

Mark grimaced and replied, "I don't think I can picture caving naked. I'll have to pass."

A few others, attracted by the laughter, gathered around the group until seven bodies garbed in an array of t-shirts depicting logos and illustrations from caving gatherings gone by, sat in mismatched folding chairs and laughed together. One of the group waited until the laughter had died down and interjected, "That ain't nothin'. You went into that cave naked. I had a cave take the pants right off me."

The older caver leaned forward in his chair, wild grey beard, pale blue eyes. "I was crawling out of some god-forsaken damn hole in the ground, which, by the way I was tricked into going into."

Another older fellow walking by bellowed, "I thought it was the right entrance."

"Anyway, I was crawling out of this tight little birth canal of a tunnel and got to this spot where I couldn't do nothing but go forward." The old caver, who could probably out cave anyone in the group, looked around to make sure he had everyone's attention. Brandy met his gaze briefly. "I wrenched and I wriggled, my arms stuck with one forward and one back so I could fit. When I popped through the tight spot, my pants got caught on the rocks and pulled down around my ankles. Well, there was still a hundred or more feet of belly crawl to go and I didn't have enough room to bring my legs up and reach the pants." Brandy smiled slightly and returned to contemplative study of her coffee cup. "What else was I to do? I had exit fever and had to get out. So I kept going, damn the pants and rocks and such. I pulled 'em up when I got out."

Rock Muncher, not wanting to give up the stage, added, "See, he had no trouble getting pinched on rocks. Not all are as blessed."

"Not to support your case, but belly crawl, son. Had a hell of a road rash."

Blaine stretched and looked towards the tower of wood. "Oooooh." The sound was the exhale in the shape of a large O. He stretched his long 6' 4" frame so that he slouched low, his feet sticking out in front of his lounge chair. "Some are blessed more than most."

Susan, lacking a member to measure, changed the subject. "I think the tightest spot I ever got in was in the Slim Chance slot of Jewel Cave. I had to let all my breath out and squeeze in, my head cocked to one side. Had to take my helmet off to fit. It was only about four feet in length. Maybe the width was seven inches. You could touch air with both hands stretched out to the side once you got in. But right in the very center, I had to breathe and couldn't take more than a shallow breath cause my rib cage was crunched in so. Almost panicked."

She reached out her thin arms in display and turned her head to the side; blonde hair fell over her shoulder. "I kinda just leaned to one side like I was going to do a cartwheel until I could get my head out of there. Then it was OK."

"Have you ever gotten into a tight squeeze cave-diving?"

Mark asked the group. He reached into a cooler for another beer. "I heard Carrey, this gal from Florida, talking about it. Having to navigate tunnels where she had to take off her tank and pull it through with her or push it ahead of her. You thought pushing a pack through a crawl was bad. Do that in water where one misstep could end your air supply. That's scary."

Blaine eyed his empty bottle by staring down its neck, "No, not me. I don't try that cave diving thing. Gotta worry about compression and air mixtures. All that math." Someone handed the retired accountant another beer. He continued, "Besides, I don't like fish."

"We do. Cave-dive, I mean. I like fish too." Susan waved a hand as if someone was interrupting her. No one was. She continued, "Got a couple of entrances we've been trying to connect for years. Connected them with a dye trace but can't find the passage." Susan motioned to Brandy with her beer. A burst of laughter and singing nearby drew everyone's attention.

"Yet," Brandy said quietly, more to her coffee than to anyone else. She looked up and met Susan's gaze, raised one eyebrow.

"Where?" Blaine looked around the group to see if anyone knew.

Mark looked down at his drink.

Susan answered, eyeing the bottom of her empty bottle, "Near Brandy's grandma's place in…"

Brandy cut her off. "It's no big deal. We go out there on weekends and plinker."

"How deep?" Blaine asked.

Mark opened another beer and handed it to Susan.

Susan answered, distracted. "Under a hundred feet. When

we do find the connecting passage it's going to be a bitch if it is tight. Not so deep that it would take a lot of staging of tanks." Susan looked over her shoulder. "I wonder if the bonfire is going to be lit soon. Do you think it's too big this year?"

Many in the group gave their opinions of bonfires and sizes. Others only murmured, studied their drinks or fell to silent contemplation.

Brandy suddenly leaned forward. "OK. I got one for you. Has anyone ever seen a ghost in a cave?" She fiddled with her necklace, placing the charm on her chin and stretching her jaw forward. The bat charm dangled from its taught chain.

Before any could answer, the loudspeaker announced, "Five, four…" All eyes turned to the pile of wood.

"Three."

Brandy looked to Susan and shrugged.

"Two."

Susan gave a quizzical glance but could not hold it for long. She turned to face the stack of wood.

"One."

With a whoosh the pile was alight. Cheers and claps rose around the crowded field. Hundreds had gathered to see the bonfire. There was an instant shift in the crowd as it moved away from the blazing heat.

From the makeshift stage at the end of the field, guitar licks sounded and a band kicked into action.

The old timer got up from his tattered chair, covered with yellow and black bat stickers. "Well, that's my cue to boogie." With a spry step he left the group. A few others followed.

Mark, Susan, Brandy and Blaine remained. The quiet group, who preferred to watch the dancing and mayhem comfortably from the sidelines. They surveyed the crowd of cavers in various forms of party mode between the towering bonfire and the stage. The October night was crisp and cold on Lookout Mountain. The crowd was bundled; many wore hats to cover their ears. Cavers, who make a hobby out of crawling in cold, wet caves are well versed at wearing layers to stay warm. Many wore Chili-Heads hats and shirts, a brand of outdoor wear created for cavers. The shape of the hats caused the wearers to look like court jesters in silhouette. Some, oblivious to the cold due either to stamina or inebriation, wore less; their flesh stood out in the crowd, bare pinkish white patches in the dark mass of flannel, camouflage and generally faded clothing. The shadow of the crowd writhed and churned with the blazing fire. A few broke from the crowd brandishing marshmallows on sticks as if they would try to roast them on the inferno. They could not get close to the flame and ended up sword fighting with the wooden sticks, brazenly calling taunts out to one another.

"Did you see something?" Mark eyed Brandy.

Brandy screwed up her face tightly as if the word was difficult to speak. "Yes." A squeak, not even a word. She blinked and looked from Susan to Mark and then finally to Blaine. Wincing, she dropped her gaze to her coffee and sloshed the cooling liquid around in the cup.

"You want a beer?" Blaine offered, trying to help.

"I don't drink, usually, but thanks." Brandy tried to smile; it refused to emerge. She lifted her coffee cup and tipped it towards Blaine in a salute. "You guys will think I've lost it."

"Implying you had it to begin with," Blaine interjected.

Susan came to Brandy's rescue. "Don't mind him. Tell us. We won't laugh. Honest." Then she settled into her folding chair like a child waiting to hear a story.

"Susan and I went ridge walking last night when we first got here, right after we pitched our tents." Brandy looked around to see everyone waiting for more. Her story bolted from her like a horse released from a starting gate. "It was a bright full moon and easy to see in the dark. There's this place over in Payne cove that we've had our eye on for a couple of years." She looked mournfully at her cold coffee again, snorted, poured the brown liquid on the ground, then continued. "We went there this morning. Little horizontal entrance that has a smallish crawl then opens up and all of a sudden there's a pit. You wouldn't expect to see a pit there, but there is one. About thirty feet or so deep. You can go around, there's more horizontal passage into all sorts of dome rooms and crystals. We dropped the pit on the way out, just to see where it went."

Susan handed a well-worn thermos to Brandy. She poured herself a cup. The steam curled and stretched towards her face. Brandy continued, "The pit ended at this small water crawl and neither of us felt like going in it. It looked like it went quite a bit, but icky. So we turned to climb back out. There was only room for one to climb out; the other had to duck into the crawl to stay out of the fall zone in case of rocks."

Susan jumped in, unable to be quiet any longer. "There was this huge rock at the bottom that must have fallen from the lip of the pit. It was cracked in two. Had to weigh two hundred pounds. It looked like it had just fallen recently. The wear on it didn't match the rest of the rocks on the ground"

Brandy sipped quietly, her eyes wide over the rim of her coffee cup. Then she added, "I climbed out first while Susan waited below. As I climbed over the lip of the pit, I could feel some of the rocks there in the wall give a little bit. I could see where that big rock had just fallen. It left a big hole in the side of the pit. I told Susan about it, to be careful, and she climbed out next."

Susan, being the one any loose rocks would have fallen on, took up the story, "Can you imagine what would have happened if that big rock had fallen on me while I was climbing out?"

"End of Susan," Brandy grunted.

"That would have hurt. Two hundred pound rock to the head. Sheesh," Mark winced.

Brandy continued, "While she was climbing, I had the strangest feeling that we weren't alone. Now I don't get all goofy or anything, but I trust my instincts." She rubbed her arms and continued, "The hairs on the back of my neck stood up and it was like we were being watched. I've never felt that ever. Weird, you know. The dark is usually so peaceful."

All were quiet for a moment, regarding the peace they all felt when in the tomb-like darkness of the cave. The dark there held nothing to cause them fear. Indeed, they all had enjoyed sitting still, turning off their headlamps and seeing nothing. Absolute and pure darkness with nothing but their heartbeats and the distant sound of dripping water to convince them they existed.

"Just as we were leaving the cave, I turned back to see if we had left any rope or gear and for a split second, someone was standing there at the edge of the pit." Brandy's voice became a whisper.

"You're shitting me," Blaine blurted.

"No, swear. He was looking at me." Brandy looked at each friend in turn, her eyes pleading for them to believe.

Given that no one was completely sober except for Brandy, they were her rapt pupils and firm believers. "What did he look like?" Mark asked.

Brandy considered the question. "It was such a quick glimpse. Pale white, ghostly. Dark hair, I think, messy or curly, short. Sharp nose and chin. Dark eyebrows."

"What was he wearing?" Susan asked breathlessly.

"I didn't really get a good look. Not a caver. No helmet or anything. Dark clothing, maybe just jeans and a t-shirt." Brandy closed her eyes to try to remember. "I don't know. I just saw his face. Then, he was gone." She opened her wide, grey orbs. "He was there. I swear it."

No one answered at first. Then all at once they tried to give their explanation for what it might have been. Mark's voice won out over the turmoil. "I absolutely believe in ghosts."

A loud ruckus at the bonfire interrupted him. Someone had decided now was the appropriate time for all to do their turkey call imitations. It started with one call then was answered by another. Those unable to speak the language, answered in suitable calls: wolf howls, dog barks, cat meows and a joyful monkey.

Susan raised her voice to join the din, a well done turkey call. Mark continued once the zoo noises had abated. "There's all sorts of things we can't see. All around us, all the time. Dark matter, infra-red, colors in the spectrum that our eyeballs can't see." He held his hands up to encompass the universe as a whole. "Just because we can't see it, doesn't mean it isn't there. There's a lot that is there that we aren't aware of. That doesn't mean it isn't real."

Susan shivered. "And it doesn't mean that it can't see us."

Mark gave a whistle and all watched as a spotted mongrel

came towards him, licked his bare knee, and sat, still slobbering. "Like Rusty here. Just because she can't see colors doesn't mean they don't exist. "

Blaine grinned and nodded. "I think we just go on as energy. Just move to other places. Could be your ghost is some old caver."

Brandy thought on it for a moment, then mused, "Well, I'm not a rocket scientist like Mark here."

"But we still love you." Mark raised his beer in a toast.

Brandy held out her hand in a quiet gesture. Mark smiled. She continued. "Energy doesn't go away. It transfers, right? I remember that much from science class." She paused. Mark nodded for her to go on. "A beam of sunlight comes through the atmosphere and hits the ground. It has photons, energy. It leaves bits of itself as heat as it bounces. It doesn't go away. Its energy is absorbed or bounced until it has been transferred into everything it touched." Brandy held out her coffee cup and drew lines in the air with her finger to demonstrate the bouncing of light. "Same thing, I think, with us. We're energy. When our energy stops being in our body, it goes somewhere else. Maybe it just gets separated from time. So we don't see it anymore."

Susan tilted her head to one side, a puzzled look on her face. "Cool."

Mark interjected with his best professor voice, complete with fake Hungarian accent, "You know, mathematically, time doesn't exist in one direction. It exists, but we are the only ones that experience it linearly. Mathematically it doesn't have to be that way. What if ghosts just get disconnected from the path of time that we experience? Maybe they are free to come and go through time. To them it looks normal. To us, we only see them when they appear synced with our time. Sometimes that would only be for a glimpse."

Blaine added, "Ooooh, how do they keep their clothing with them then?"

It was Mark's turn to raise an eyebrow at Blaine. "I suppose they can bring things with them through time."

Susan giggled. "Naked ghosts. "

Blaine stood up. "All this is making my head hurt. I'll just leave it at there is a ghost in the cave." He looked at Brandy. "Maybe he followed you home like they do at that Disney ride." He searched in the air for a name that wouldn't come to him.

"Haunted Mansion," Brandy supplied.

"That one," he slurred slightly and smiled, then left.

Mark stood with careful attention to his beer. "Well, I gotta go find a tree. Hold this, I'll be back." Susan grasped the bottle with dedication to the task.

Susan and Brandy were alone. Brandy leaned forward, "Man, why did you have to talk about our dive earlier? I don't want people knowing where my grandma's cabin is, Susan. I like Mark and all. He's probably the only other person I'd consider taking there besides you. But, I don't want anyone else knowing."

"Oh, no one would know where it is. I wasn't giving it away." Susan held the bottle away from her as if Mark would return that second and take it. Brandy reached out and took the bottle from her.

"I just like to keep it to myself. You know. It's where I grew up. I don't want people there." She paused. "Except you."

"OK. Sorry. I wasn't thinking like that." Susan pouted slightly then perked up. "I want to go find your ghost. Maybe he did follow you home and you'll find him in your sleeping bag tonight."

"Well, I hope he doesn't snore." Brandy tossed out the last cold remains of her coffee and placed Mark's beer bottle in the cup holder of his lounge chair.

A figure approached; they couldn't see his face. The flames of the bonfire were behind him and kept him in shadow. He lurched and swayed towards the women then nearly fell in Susan's lap.

"Thereyouare." It came out as one word.

"Here I am." Susan's slurred response.

He tried to grasp Susan's hand and help her to her feet, but was so unsteady she ended up being the steadier of the two, both threatening to fall on Brandy. Defying gravity, they managed to stay upright.

Brandy watched the bonfire, not caring to watch where the two wandered off to.

Cavers danced, shadows writhed, camaraderie commenced. After a while Brandy climbed into her tent and tried to shut out the world. The sounds of tent zippers and the rustling of sleeping bags surrounded her. Her last thought before drifting off to sleep was not of mysterious ghosts, but of the large rock at the bottom of the pit. There had still been dust on it from when it had recently fallen and broken in two. They had just missed getting struck by it. She took a deep breath and let it out slowly, with it letting go of what might have been and went to sleep.

4 BLINKING.

The heart in his body raced and pounded. This was not his heart. This was not his body. He inhabited it until he didn't. Pains of hunger gripped him. He hated eating. It slowed him down, wasted his time. He shifted and fidgeted. Pains again. Sometimes he would forget for days until he was so weak he couldn't concentrate. He ignored the pain.

Yindi stood unsteadily. Why couldn't he just run? Go. Go. His body urged him to leave.

"Will that be a day pass or are you staying for the whole event?" someone asked.

He flashed a broad grin. "Just a day." His voice croaked, unused. A nervous catch in his throat. He cleared it. Shifted. Fidgeted. Wanted to leave.

He took his lanyard, tossed money onto the folding table, flashed his grin again. He remembered to blink. It scared them when you didn't blink.

How do they do it so much? He thought to himself: blink, blink, blink.

Yindi shifted from one foot to the other. Consciously he stopped himself and held his breath. He had to fit in. How many times has he failed at that, caught up in trying to find the thing? He had to blend, had to get close, had to be in this crowd. Warmth in his body spread through his diaphragm. The thing, the right thing, the big thing was here.

"Enjoy yourself!" the person called after him. Yindi was already speed-walking away from the registration area and looking for the big thing. He could feel it in his cells. It called him.

Sweat assaulted his eyes. Stars smeared across his vision from it. He tried to walk slowly, to not rush. It caused raw panic to build in him, every nerve and muscle screamed to move faster. He flexed and curled his fists and nervously jangled his car keys.

He drove to the edge of the camping area, looking, scanning. As he regarded the crowd he could feel who could be the next thing or what could be the next thing. The changing colors of possibilities sprang across his vision and overloaded his senses. He couldn't stay too long. He had to move quickly. His heart raced more and he picked up his pace.

He had to find the right thing. He watched a man in a loincloth pass by. The air around him, that only Yindi and his kind could see, was only slightly yellow. Nothing there was the thing. He began to feel ill. He loathed this body, almost wished he could move to another one. But he didn't have time. Though it was easy enough to kill this host, it took too long to inhabit the next and gain full control.

Where was the best thing? Yindi parked his truck and got out. The trees swayed in the breeze over him. Dappled moonlight danced on the ground. The possibilities almost over came him. He needed the best thing; he didn't want to pick anything. Make it count; make it worth it. Fidget. Blink. Sweat.

He smiled. The watcher would fix whatever Yindi broke. The watcher always did. Even changing things back wouldn't fix it, completely. Yindi's smile broadened as he opened the truck's camper. He rummaged and pulled out a duffle bag. The fact that things were once wrong still changed things, moved things, helped push things. Yindi knew that he had to keep finding the things. It felt so good when he did. Everything he adjusted moved a groove in time that even when erased still left a trace. He knew eventually the faded images of what could have been would be enough. When he was able to keep a few large things pushed that the watcher couldn't change, it would all fall apart. That would be utopia. He would be free from the prison of these bodies. At least, that is what he hoped. He didn't know. It was what he had been taught to believe. It is what he felt in the core of his being.

Quickly, getting excited, he laid the instruments out, took inventory. Counting, he liked that. Soothed, he focused on the universe. This tool would do just fine; it felt red. He hefted it, felt its weight, smiled. Now to find the right thing. He sat on his tailgate and surveyed the crowd. Tension rose in him and he nibbled on his lip, already swollen and easy to bleed.

The bonfire was lit and from a distance he could see the flames leap thirty feet into the air. How easy it would have been to push someone in. That didn't feel like the right thing though. No. People sword fighting with marshmallows, no. Lovers making out at the edge of the crowd, no. Dancing bodies, no. Guitar player, no. He scanned anxiously. His heart raced, sweat stained his shirt even though the air was cool. Until…

He saw a woman sitting alone looking into a coffee mug. When his eyes focused on her the universe turned red. This was the thing, the big thing. Yindi stopped breathing. She rose and went into her tent. Yindi's universe promised red, chaos and ecstasy. A yearning burst through his chest with a warmth that flamed his body and face. His heart pounded in his temples. She was the thing. She was a BIG thing. He shuddered in anticipation.

5 BLOOD IN THE WATER.

Darkness.

Cold.

The sound of dripping water in the distance.

Where? Brandy tries to remember how she got here.

"ROCK!" the scream splits the darkness above her. She instinctively recoils out of the fall zone. Brandy crouches under a rock overhang at the bottom of the pit. Cold mud seeps into her boots. A thud. The rope end, visible from Brandy's muddy spot, jumps and jerks erratically.

A loud crash. A medium boulder hits the side of the pit. Chunks of rock and debris rain down. Dust gets in Brandy's eyes. She holds her breath, knowing what comes next. Praying, in that split second, a silent plea that only the rock is falling. The boulder splits in two on the ground in front of Brandy. Nothing else falls.

"SUSAN?" Brandy is on her feet looking up. A rain of sand and pebbles dislodged by the boulder's reckless path falls on her face.

No answer.

The rope sways, a pendulum. Not the steady swaying associated with someone climbing. The rope sways. Steady decaying arcs. Someone hanging.

"Sus…?" Her voice stops, refusing. In the dark, above Brandy, Susan's headlamp shines on the sides of the pit as her body dangles from the rope. The light sways and arcs rhythmically back and forth, spinning slowly.

Brandy hurries to clip into the rope, to climb up to Susan. As her gloved hand reaches for the rope she begins falling.

Why is she falling up? Brandy falls UP past Susan's lifeless body, blood covered face, helmet split, neck twisted. She tries to grab Susan's limp hand, manages to clumsily grasp Susan's chest harness.

Nothing. Brandy is holding nothing, only darkness. She falls up.

Boots replaced with nurses shoes. Warm layers of muddy clothing replaced with a uniform, once white, now smeared with dried red blood.

The blood looks black in the darkness, the same color as what dripped from Susan's shattered face.

In the darkness, she sees light ahead of her. She moves towards it, finds that she is swimming. Panic rises as she realizes she cannot breathe. Dark, cold water causes her skirt to balloon around her. Bloodstains dissipate into black ribbons and trail off into the depths below. Below her, she sees nothing. Susan is no longer there. Only dark water. Breathe. She needs air, must breathe. Panic colder than ice stabs behind her eyes.

She swims towards the light in the distance. A small tunnel—she tries to swim through. Her shoulders scrape the walls. Silt fills the water. She knows there is air on the other side, in the light. Brandy puts one arm in front of her to swim with. Her other arm gets pinned to her side by the tunnel wall. She wiggles and pulls herself through. More silt clouds the water. She twists so that her face is pointed up. Her nose scrapes the top of the tunnel. She can see air pockets. Brandy tries to breathe the air collected there. Lips scrape on rock. Small bits of air filled with sand tease her starved lungs. She searches in the dim light for the next silvery pocket on the tunnel's ceiling, hoping it is air and not CO_2.

Brandy's ankle is caught, yanked backwards. Birthed halfway from the tunnel, away from the light and back into the darkness, Brandy comes face to face with two red eyes. The assailant moves like a snake but has grabbed her and holds her leg tight with what feels like claws, talons. It writhes through the tight tunnel around her body. She tries to free herself, to climb into the tunnel. Brandy tries to get to air. Her movements are thick and slow. Darkness encases her as the creature's body fills the tunnel and blocks the light. Breathe. She has to breathe. The creature wraps around her and squeezes.

***

Brandy jerked in her sleep and gasped. A moment passed. A deep breath. She rolled over in her sleeping bag and curled tightly into a ball, hands clasped between her thighs. Outside Brandy's tent, most partiers had quieted down and turned in.

6 A FOOL.

"Still not there." A thought filled with remorse.

Alexander hated to glance towards the pit. She was gone. He had changed time back as it should be. The cave, his cave, sprawled before him. Alexander did not look towards the place that she once sat, would have sat. He did not shift through time. Alexander walked in the moment, the time that was his and his alone. From this vantage point he could freely move about, the very cells in his body bound to vibrate in sync with this moment. The rest of the world spun, the universe expanded, all else experienced time moving forward. Alexander could feel that it was there, time. Felt it to the core of his being. Felt that it no longer veered towards chaos, unchecked. The absence of the pain that the chaos had caused did not relieve the ache he now felt.

He glanced again. She wasn't there. He moved away from the entrance. He could still see in time where she had crawled and moved through the cave with her friend, the one that would have died. He tried to take solace in that. She no longer visited his cave in mourning. She had still been here. He could still see her. Her path looked blurry to him unless he brought that time into focus. Even then, all he could see were still moments frozen in time. An outsider watching a ghostly world.

He paused at a low crawl, made cramped by stalactites growing from the ceiling to meet their counter part on the ground. Teeth of a gaping monster. Here he did shift through time, moving to eons ago where the stalactites had not grown and the ceiling itself had not settled low. Finding a time in those eons that he had not already walked this path, he slid into time and walked upright through the space.

Once through the passage, he shifted back to his time, his frozen moment. Here he did not worry about colliding with himself in time. It was not a conscious thought, no more than walking is. Children of his kind learned it under the watchful eyes of their parents. He had lost a part of his finger once, in his energetic youth, by recklessly chasing a friend through time. They had darted and slid, drunk with their newly acquired power of slipping through time. They could only move backwards as they were still bound to the global progress of time. Then, the world did not weigh heavy on them. They had not locked into a given time yet, nor had to leave home to become watchers, forever burdened. The object of their tussle could not be remembered. A book? A gem? Food? Something even more trivial? He could not remember. He had made a smart grab for the object from his friend and slipped backwards in time without looking. He ran directly into himself, his fingers overlapping. In a cold, searing flash a small portion of his right pinky finger was gone. Instantly cauterized and smooth. Such was his pain and surprise, he never forgot to watch where he was going again.

Alexander paused again, considered food. How long since he last took nourishment. A week? A month? Years? How long had he stayed near where she had sat? Stayed while the universe had continued forward towards collapse as he ignored the warning signs. In his frozen moment, air stood still. In this still, dark place Alexander wondered what damage had he done to the universe? Why? Why had he sat yearning over a ghost image of a linear? Alexander covered his eyes, the shame of his emotions heavy and loathsome. Yet, he wanted to see her again, even if it was her ghost. Her vision haunted him.

Through a small opening in the limestone ceiling, the full moon streamed in. Dust frozen in the beam. Through time Alexander could see sunlight and moonlight as it streamed through this one room in the cave and would continue in the near future. All others places in this tomb had never seen light, save for this one opening.

Distracted by his own thoughts, he slowed. Dusty leather moccasins scratching against the floor. Soundless in this frozen time. Will her friend die anyway? Is she sitting vigil somewhere else, out in the sun, out of his reach? He had set the course of time back to its rightful place. Yindi would push again, change it again. Alexander would find what and who he could and change it back. He couldn't fix them all. He could feel the universe as it progressed through time. The moon was full there too. It eased his soul. He turned back.

He had never ignored the universe for so long, bringing it to near destruction as Yindi had pushed and pulled, molested events unchecked.

"It barely mattered," Alexander said out loud to no one. He slid through time again to navigate passages, unaware where his feet took him.

Back at the pit. Alexander didn't remember walking here. He sobered, realizing he stood back near her image like a mooning, angst filled adolescent.

Suddenly angry, he faced the blurred image of his love, visible where she would walk through his cave, his home, in the future.

"Why did you come here?"

He turned to her friend, frozen in a smile as she looked at the bats on the ceiling. "You'll die anyway. What does it matter?" His words were harsh whispers.

He kneeled at the place where she would stop and point out the pit to her friend. Gloved hand raised. It seemed accusing to him now.

"I did not want you here. Now I have to see you, I can't rid this place of you."

He looked towards the entrance where she would turn back to look at the cave. The blurry images of the two women walking, crawling, smiling, talking, exploring his dark sanctuary would permeate his vision forever.

"I should have let the world be destroyed."

She would pause. Turn. Her ghostly image there for Alexander to see. She would have a look of curiosity, surprise on her face.

"Why do you haunt me here, my sanctum?" He swept a hand back towards the infinite darkness of his home. There in the darkness, he realized what she would become surprised at. He saw himself, looking at her.

"Fool."

Alexander walked to the blurry ghost of himself. "You slipped into her time."

Translucent, his own face looked at him, through him to

where she stood. "Like a weeping puppy you had to see her so badly, living, that you slipped into her time."

A sound of disgust.

He turned again toward the entrance. Looked from his lost love to himself. "She saw you."

Alexander suddenly thrust his hand out as if to rip the throat out of his own ghost. His hand passed through the specter. Unquenched, his anger boiled. He grabbed the nearest object, a slab of limestone. A grunt. A ton of dark tan rock hurled through the air and time. The behemoth crashed against the wall of the cave and crumbled into large shards.

His anger relieved, Alexander stood still, hands by his side. His body pulling energy from the ground around him in long, deep pulls. Alexander instinctively glanced to see if he had changed anything in time. Unlikely here. A quick flash of alarm. Had he caused harm to her?

The rock shards had caused a slight blockage in the passage. Where she would have walked through the passage, she would now step over large rock shards, covered in dark green growth. Her toe would catch and she would stumble against her friend. They would laugh.

Drained, Alexander spoke to the laughing vision. "I wish you had never come here."

Soundlessly, Alexander turned. He disappeared into the gloom of the cave. Wordlessly, he moved through the darkness, his eyes seeing in the gloom easily. Returning to the dome room, he stood in the frozen moonbeam. A staircase appeared in front of him as he slipped through time. He could see the thousands of times he had climbed this staircase. His ghostly self trapped, ascending and descending. Alexander slipped to a time he had not inhabited and climbed the stairs. The weight of eternity lay heavy upon him. Synced with time he could hear his footfalls echoing in the rock chamber. Water dripped in the distance. His soft shoes scuffed and whispered on the plain wooden staircase. Dust languished in the moonbeam. The blue, dim light crossed Alexander's sharp features with shadows. Dark eyes, pale skin, wide shoulders, narrow hips. His hand grasped the staircase rail, a small portion of his pinkie finger missing. A smooth, round, concave divot.

A heavy wooden door. Alexander leaned his forehead against the carved mahogany. Cold wood on cold skin. With a visible effort he shrugged off concerns and entered his home, back into his frozen time. Behind him, the staircase disappeared; sound ceased; air became dead and cold.

"In a blink she will be gone. That time past." Alexander walked past ornate shelves of deep rich woods and marble. Moonlight, forever frozen, streamed in through the tall narrow windows. Alexander cast no shadow. He spoke to his only company, himself.

"Why bother with such a creature?" Two thousand year old portraits, still fresh and vibrant as if painted yesterday, stared back at him from the high, stone walls. The eyes of ancestors, lovers, enemies followed him as he walked the long corridor.

He stopped in front of a portrait, a young woman dressed in stiff buckskin robes. Thick, straight trees surrounded her. "Nothing can come from such an infatuation but pain." He paused slightly longer regarding a round, bronze face framed by braided hair. Dark hair held in place with leather strips and feathers.

Finally, he left the long corridor and entered a library. Here books, orderly rows, filled shelves from floor to ceiling.

Candles with frozen flicking flames filled every available nook. The room was ablaze with warm light. Alexander sat and gazed through open doors out onto a veranda. Beyond the veranda, a forested valley.

Alexander sat and absently pulled a book from a shelf and sat facing the veranda. The book: heavy jeweled cover, ornately illustrated, long dead language. He did not open it. Instead he gazed across the valley.

Here in his frozen moonlight he could see the valley in its infancy, the water that had covered the mountaintops and forged the valley, the heights that the mountains once reached but had since eroded to. Alexander gazed upon all of time that had passed. It was good; so very few people had been here. When he gazed, he only gazed upon the shifts of the earth. He relaxed and slowly his mind drifted. He thought of grey eyes looking back in surprise, forever trapped in sunlight, staring at his brief existence in that time.

"Fool."

7 COLD, DARK, RED EYES.

Brandy tried to ignore the soft whispers from the other tents. She tried to ignore the unmistakable rhythmic patterns of movement. She was uncomfortable around people, their noises, breathing, living, thinking, fucking. Her feet swooshed across the nylon of the tent as she rolled onto her back and kicked the sleeping bag away. This was the worst part. Being here, alone in the center of a crowd enjoying themselves. She enjoyed the caving, the companionship, at times. At night, though, with nothing else to occupy her mind but dreams...

She opened her eyes and stared at the dappled shadows dancing on the tent's ceiling. A glow stick, sad, pale, green, nearly extinguished, hung in a mesh basket above her socked feet. What had she been dreaming about? She couldn't remember, yet she shivered. She only remembered cold darkness and red eyes. Before she could consider the dream any further she could hear someone walking through the campsite near her tent. The footsteps were uneven and heavy.

Shuffle—scrape—step

scrape—scrape—step—shuffle
pause
step—step
pause
scrape—shuffle—step

Brandy held her breath, unintentionally, and listened to see where the newcomer would go. The steps continued past her tent and on. As the steps moved, she could hear someone shift in the lounge chair outside her tent. Adrenalin pricked her system alive: one person walking, one person sitting. Who was out there?

"Don't be silly," Brandy silently chided herself, forced herself to calm down, to breathe and relax. "It's just Susan with her new friend, maybe. Or Mark." Her mind strained to hear Susan's voice or a noise that would identify the human as friend.

Nearby a tent zipper opened; the sharp, loud noise startled Brandy.

"Hey. Room for one more?" A very inebriated male voice whispered loudly.

"Shhhh," someone hushed the drunk and then giggled. A zipper closed.

Brandy recognized Susan's giggle and smiled. She sat up and started to exit her tent. She'd point the lost fellow in the right direction. She hoped she knew him. With over six hundred tents around her she wasn't sure if she could help him find his bed.

A zipper sounded again.

"Wait a second," the drunk man insisted. "Where's Janet?" he slurred.

Brandy heard a thump and a squeal. He must have fallen

inside the tent. Brandy opened her own tent and exited toward the sound of the drunk just as the unmistakable sound of hurling woke the others nearby.

"Good God."

"What the hell?"

"Damn it! Jake. Get out of my tent!"

"Son of a …"

"Janet?"

"…all in my sleeping bag…"

"Where's Jul….ugggg…..urrp"

Brandy hastily slipped on some flip-flops and ran to the tent nearby to see two pitiful pale legs sticking out of the entrance. Meanwhile the tent bobbed and weaved as if trying to exorcise the demons within. Shouting commenced.

"Jake. Get out!"

"You f…"

"Stop. He's drunk."

Jake rolled backwards out of the tent and landed at Brandy's feet. "Janet?" he slurred.

Susan's male companion came roaring out after Jake, covering himself with a vomit spattered sleeping bag. Brandy reached forward and stopped him with a gentle hand held outstretched.

"Stop. He can't help himself. Look at him." Her hand stayed hovering in front of the man's chest without touching it. She could feel the heat rising from him. He breathed heavily.

Susan poked her head out of the tent entrance, one hand clutching a t-shirt to cover her chest and failing. Her blond hair was matted and stood up on end. "Jake. Damn it."

Brandy helped Jake to his feet, hooking her arm under his shoulder. "OK, Jake. Let's go find your tent."

"I was jus' lookin' for Janet," Jake tried to defend himself.

"Let's see if we can find her." Brandy consoled Jake and half lifted, half drug the thin man with her away from Susan and her evening's companion.

Mark appeared out of the shadows and wrapped Jake's other arm around his shoulders and grabbed Jake's waist.

"OK, Jake. I got Janet right over here and she's waiting for you." Mark looked over Jake's slumped shoulder at Brandy. "Why she's waiting for you, is beyond me."

He winked at Brandy. She smiled back. Together they directed the poor soul to a small camper trailer further from the group. The sought after Janet, braids at either side of her head, stood with open arms.

"Jake, where were you?" Her words were nearly as slurred as Jake's.

"Looking for you." Mark and Brandy handed Jake's limp body to Janet. She shouldered his body on her thick girth easily.

"Let's get you cleaned up. Momma's been waiting for you." The two disappeared into the camper together. The camper squeaked and jostled with their movements.

Mark and Brandy stood outside for a moment then turned and walked back towards their beds.

"If I ever get that stupid over someone, just shoot me, OK?" Brandy leaned her head against Mark's shoulders as she batted her eyes at him.

"If I ever see you act like that, I'll look for the body snatcher attached to the base of your neck." Mark placed a friendly arm around Brandy's shoulders and hugged her briefly.

"I mean, I don't like being alone. But I don't want to be…" Brandy searched for the word. "so pathetic?"

Mark paused. Brandy paused too and looked at him. Before she could ask what was the matter, he asked, "Who's that sitting by your tent?"

They both looked to see someone getting up from a lounge chair and walking away from Brandy's tent. He had a ball cap pulled down over his face, not that it mattered; the dark of the night obscured his features.

"I don't know. I heard him when I was in the tent, but didn't catch a look at him 'cause of all the noise Jake had going on." Brandy tried to catch a glimpse of the person walking away. "I can't tell who it is."

Before they could get back to the tent, the stranger was gone. Mark and Brandy stood for a moment together; the cold night air raised goose bumps on their arms. They looked off into the darkness and couldn't find the stranger.

"He must have gone back to his tent," Brandy guessed.

"Maybe he just got woke up by Jake throwing up all over Susan."

With that thought they turned towards Susan's tent. Apparently the two had been still inebriated enough to bed back down in their stinky tent.

"Oh, that's going to be a rude surprise in the morning," Mark grimaced.

"Never a dull moment," Brandy added. She pecked Mark on the cheek. "See you in the morning when they wake us all up. Hope they wait until daybreak."

"Hope they can wash that out," Mark added and hugged Brandy close in a sideways grip. "Night, darlin'."

Brandy watched Mark walk away towards his tent. She listened to the night wind and the quiet that had settled over the camp. The stars shone bright, the full moon loomed. The zipper sounded loud and alone as she climbed into her tent.

"Night," she whispered to herself.

8 THE CONVERGENCE.

Dawn slowly woke Brandy. She curled tighter into a ball, pulling the sleeping bag back under her chin to ward off the chilled morning air. Her feet rustled against the sleeping bag as she curled and uncurled her toes, unconsciously. Outside her tent the morning stirrings of the early risers could be heard. Birds chirped, crickets buzzed and morning cavers moved quietly. Hushed, almost reverent tones of those gathering gear for the day's journey filled the air. Clinks. Rustles. Zipping. The occasional vehicle engine roared to life and drove slowly away, tires on gravel and mud.

The smell of coffee tempted her to leave the warm cocoon of her tent.

"Mornin'." Mark sat in a lounge chair outside her tent. He held a mug out to her and pointed to a silver pot on a nearby green camp stove. The Sterno smelled metallic. Brandy filled her mug and sat next to Mark.

"Morning," she mumbled. "I'm assuming those garbage bags are filled with vomit covered sleeping bags?" They both looked towards two large garbage bags leaned against Susan's tent.

"The sleeping bags were thrown on the grass. I bagged them. I was expecting more of a ruckus." A disappointed statement. Mark handed a tall metal can to Brandy.

"Me too. I think I would have just burned the sleeping bag."

"And tent," Mark added.

"True. I can't imagine it doesn't smell. Ick. Wait, you bagged them?" She looked at the can. "What's this?"

"Yes. I bagged them. I didn't want the dogs in them. And that is alcohol infused whipped cream. I volunteered at the registration desk this morning. They had some extra from last night."

"How many times did you wash your hands?" Brandy giggled, not waiting for an answer, then added, "What time did registration open?" She sniffed the can's nozzle and held the can up for inspection.

"6 a.m. And I had to take two showers."

"Anyone come in?" Brandy shook the can and debated.

"A group from Colorado and another one from Indiana.

"Raspberry. Did you try it?" Brandy asked.

"Yeah, not too bad." Mark showed Brandy the white remnants of whipped cream in his coffee cup.

She debated a little further. As she pointed the can towards her coffee cup she paused. "This came from registration, right? Not someone's tent?"

"What difference does that make?" He looked at his own coffee cup than back to Brandy.

She stared at him wide eyed.

He stared back and began to reel off facts to her,

mechanically. "Registration. Rick was giving them out. But this was used with the coffee for the evening registration table folk. It closed at 3 a.m. I picked it up at 6 a.m."

She wiped the nozzle on her shirt then squirted raspberry scented whipped cream into her coffee cup.

"I still don't get it. What does it matter?" Mark protested further.

Brandy took a tentative sip at the coffee, then another. She looked at Mark again, wide eyed and pointed the nozzle of the whipped cream towards her chest. She mimed circular motions in front of each breast with the can.

He looked back at his coffee, wide eyed himself. "I didn't think about that."

"You gotta be careful where you get things." She smiled at Mark, a broad grin.

Mark wrinkled his face in disgust. "Damn it, Brandy. Now all I can think about is the germs that could be in my coffee."

"How can you be such a germaphobe and cave?" Susan put more whipped cream in her coffee. "That's surprisingly good." She offered the can back to Mark. He grimaced but took it from her anyway.

"Mud is not germy. It's humans and their germs that I don't like." Mark looked suspiciously at the can then applied more to his coffee. "Besides, I don't let it stop me." He quickly squirted a large dollop of whipped cream into his open mouth. "See?" it came out sounding like "eee" around the whipped cream.

A rustling and squeal from nearby interrupted their antics.

"Susan's up." Brandy topped off her coffee and settled back into her lounge chair for the show.

"What the hell?" was the first high pitched cry.

"Ugggh." A lower growl.

"What was the drama last year?" Mark asked, leaning towards Brandy.

"Left the zipper unzipped whilst drunk and woke up with a raccoon in her sleeping bag." Brandy smiled.

More sounds of erratic movement from the tent nearby could be heard.

Brandy continued. "This year might beat the year I took her keys and she tried to hot-wire her truck at 3 a.m. in the morning. She dismantled the air filter and radiator hose before calling it quits."

"Is she like this all the time?" Mark brushed a ladybug from his arm.

"No. Only when we are out at these events. It's like she saves up the crazy for here."

"That's weird."

From Susan's tent, "Where's my sleeping bag?"

"We cave every weekend together…every weekend."

Brandy shook her head. "She doesn't get sloshed drunk with me. I mean, she has impulse control issues, sure. But she isn't like this all the time."

The two emerged from the tent. Susan peeked into one of the garbage bags then quickly closed it. "I found the sleeping bags. I think you'll need a new one."

"Sorry. I can hit the laundromat today." The male companion showed the contents of the other garbage bag to Susan. She grimaced and held a hand to her mouth. "I don't remember getting sick."

"Me neither. I don't remember putting these out here either." He closed the bag and looked around for more clues.

Mark leaned to Brandy, "Do we tell them?"

"What good would it do?" Brandy got up and rummaged in a faded blue cooler. "Eggs?" She held up a pink carton.

"I have bacon." Mark got up to retrieve items from a cooler near his tent.

Mark and Brandy began to prepare breakfast together on the camp stove. Brandy set a folding table up and placed a plastic bucket of utensils on it.

"She's why I don't drink at these things. I always feel like I should keep an eye on her." She sipped at her coffee and looked down the field for Susan. "We've known each other since the seventh grade."

Mark placed a large pump bottle of Purell at the end of the table. Brandy eyed it, then Mark, and smiled. "We all have our quirks," he said.

Brandy smiled and replied, "And all share a common quirk of loving holes in the ground. So I suppose, it makes everything else OK." She Purell-ed her hands then sat at the folding table.

"Speaking of holes in the ground and caving with Susan every weekend. Sorry she started talking about your Grandma's place last night. I know you are sensitive about that cave getting talked about." Mark placed a plate of scrambled eggs and bacon at the center of the table.

"It's my place. Always has been." she scooped a pile of eggs onto a paper plate. "Been going there since I was a kid. I don't want everyone coming over. Just good friends." She stopped, fork of eggs in mid air. "Does that make me an ass? Most people I know have an open door policy and always have a party of people sleeping on their couch. Me, I'm…" she twirled the fork in the air searching for the word, "Aloof?"

Mark thought for a moment, then answered the question,

"Reserved."

"Hmmmmm." Brandy quietly ate her breakfast, lost in thought.

Susan joined the two. "Gosh, I don't know if I can do breakfast." she grimaced at the eggs, now growing cold. "You didn't hear anything going on last night, did you?"

Mark smiled a broad grin. Brandy kept her eyes fixed on the last bite of bacon on her plate. Susan grimaced again, this time at nothing in general. "Sorry. "

Brandy grabbed Susan's hand, squeezed it and then let go. "Suzie-Q, from what I heard, that mess was there before you got there."

"Seriously?" Susan regretted her loud word the moment it left her lips, another grimace.

"You going to be able to go out today?" Brandy poured a cup of coffee for Susan and handed her a plastic bag full of sugar packets.

"Sure. Maybe we can keep it gentle?" Susan emptied four packets of sugar into her coffee.

"I was thinking about going back to that cave we found. Maybe push the wet crawl at the bottom of the pit." Brandy watched Susan stir the coffee.

Red nails, amazingly un-chipped, clinked on the ceramic mug as Susan drank. "OK. That sounds gentle." No sarcasm was present in her voice. "I don't think I could do a huge vertical pit today." She looked up. "You looking for your ghost?"

Brandy brushed the question off with a wave of her coffee cup. "You want to come, Mark?"

"Nah. Thanks though. I've got plans to drop a few pits." Mark stood. "It's only Friday. We have until Monday."

"Wait, so that was there? Did I clean it up before I went to bed? Who'd do that in someone else's tent?" Susan paused. "I think I need a new tent. I can't sleep in that again." She had perked up and was already up to speed, her coffee cup still half full.

"I'm going to give you decaf." Brandy stood with Mark to clean the table.

Susan looked back to the garbage bags and shook her head.

"Where's prince charming?" Mark inquired.

"Went back to his tent to sleep some more." Susan grabbed a plate of cold eggs before Mark could take them away,

"I just remembered; I had the strangest nightmares last night." Brandy scraped the remaining cold eggs into a trash bag. Somewhere nearby a dog started to bark, a high pitched tune.

She continued, "Something about the pit. You were in it." Brandy pointed to Susan. Paused. Bit her lip. Then continued. "Then I was on a dive and something was chasing me."

"I hate when things chase me in dreams," Susan chimed in.

Brandy became quiet and looked off into the woods. She shivered.

"...truck?"

Brandy turned. "Huh?"

"I said, I'll get my gear and meet you at the truck?" Susan now stood and cleared her plate. "You OK?"

"Yeah, just trying to remember the dream." Brandy shook her head. "Meet you in twenty. See you tonight, Mark."

Brandy slowly walked to her truck and started pawing

through dirt stained clothes. "Red eyes," she murmured to herself.

***

Reluctant to leave his vantage point of the valley, Alexander could feel his strength drain from him. He would have to take nourishment soon. Although his locked time and view of the valley was forever at midnight eons ago, Alexander could feel that the sun was rising in that other time, their time, he often called it. He would have to join their time eventually and eat.

"Not now," he thought. "After a rest."

He climbed back through time and down the wooden staircase to his dark cave. Alexander walked through tunnels and came to a large wall of boulders stacked one on another in a chaotic avalanche. This rock breakdown had fallen from the ceiling long before even he had existed. At the top of the pile Alexander could see the vaulted ceiling that had formed when the rock fell, stabilizing the empty room on the other side of the rock wall. Alexander shifted through time; the sofa sized rocks shifted and rose back to the ceiling. The passage into the small room was unblocked. He entered the room and back into his time. The rocks reappeared as they had been, blocking the room entirely.

Alexander slowly paced the length of the room, twenty feet. Cold flushed through his body as if ice had erupted from his chest. The cold grew and spread to his neck and face. He would need to eat soon. He had waited nearly too long.

"Stupid fool," Alexander whispered, "nothing you can do now." He lay down upon the hard earth and stared up at the rock ceiling. The cold was in his feet now. He would care for his needs come nightfall. Apathetically, he disrobed so that all of his skin could come in contact with the earth. He would need all the nourishment from the earth that he could get to sustain him. Concentrating, he touched calves, back, shoulder blades, palms to the earth and felt his body suck greedily from the energy it found there. The cold spreading through his body abated slightly.

His heart slowed and gradually his mind began to drift. Unconsciously, he reached forward to see where Yindi was. Nothing yet. Odd, Yindi was being still. Alexander relaxed and rolled onto his stomach. Arms splayed out, belly, chest, legs, face pulling energy from the earth. Come the evening, he would go out and feed.

Eventually, his body's pull of energy from the earth became slow and steady. Alexander drifted to sleep in his pitch-black earthen tomb. Then he disappeared.

***

"Goodness, I don't remember the hike being this long," Susan feigned protest.

"It is a little warmer today, I think." Brandy swatted at gnats in her path.

The two women tromped loudly through the thicket of grass. Crickets whined and chirped.

"You too hung-over?"

"Me?" Susan squeaked. "Never."

The grass gave way to sloped, rocky ground. They stopped at the cave entrance.

"No rain today." Brandy briefly looked at the sky.

"You checked?" Susan peered into the cave and turned on

her headlamp. It seemed dim and useless in the daylight.

"Of course." A flat answer. Brandy turned on her headlamp.

"See, there's something cave diving has over dry caving— you don't have to worry about flooding. Kinda."

They stooped slightly and walked into the cave. "It isn't like there aren't other worries at all. Air supply, silted water, air mixture, the bends. But you're right, already flooded, so, no worries." Brandy reached out and squeezed Susan's shoulder. "Goofy blonde."

As they pushed further from the entrance, the light from the sun faded until it was gone. Their headlamps were the only illumination they had. At first the lamps seemed puny, barely cutting through the darkness. Mist hung in the air, swallowing their light. The ceiling slanted up; they were able to walk upright.

"Do you want to push the lead at the bottom of the pit?" Susan asked.

"I thought you said gentle?" Brandy took the coil of rope from her shoulders and untied the knot that held the two loose ends secured.

"Well, no wetsuits today. That's gentle enough. It's hard to breathe in mine. I need to get a bigger size." Susan took one end of the rope and began looking for a natural anchor to tie it to. She considered multiple outcroppings of rock and settled on a literal hole in the wall that had a naturally formed handle of rock. "Did you see this anchor point? I think it is better than the rock we used last time. The rope will angle out of the pit instead of lying right along the floor. That will be way easier to get over the lip."

"Oh good. I'd love to not flail on the pit ledge today. I

don't have the right climbing system for these short drops." Brandy patted her green pack. It rattled with each pat. She tied a foot loop onto the other end of the rope and tested the knot.

Brandy paused and looked around at the edge of the pit. Susan noticed. "Any ghosts today?"

Brandy flushed and did not answer. She smiled and made a funny face at Susan.

Susan looped the rope around the rock anchor point two times and began to tie it off. "Hand me a biner off my pack, would ya?" She pronounced the word bean-er.

Sitting cross legged, Brandy leaned forward on all fours to Susan's pack, loops of rope still cradled in her lap, and removed a carabiner tethered to the handle of Susan's pack. She tested its weight in her hand. "Here, this one looks heavy. You don't want to carry that through the cave."

Susan took the carabiner from Brandy and used it to secure the knot. It clinked closed.

"I almost regret hiking here with my seat harness on. I've got to get those butt straps that keep the leg loops from riding down the thigh when you walk. That's annoying." Brandy checked the D-ring that held her seat harness on. "I'll drop first while you put yours on."

"OK." Susan was already digging in her pack and pulling out a bright pink seat harness.

Brandy secured her clip onto the rope; the teeth bit into the rope and held tight. She mechanically called, "On rope."

Without thought, Susan replied, "OK." Caver catechism.

Standing at the pit's edge, Brandy peered into the darkness then threw the rope down. It slithered and sank. She watched to see it hit bottom. "Thirty feet?" she guessed aloud.

"A nuisance drop," Susan replied in a tone no different

than a congregation saying amen to a preacher's question.

Brandy wove the rope between the horizontal stainless steel bars of her U-shaped rack. Under her breath Brandy uttered, "Beaner, Beaner."

Susan, squatting down to synch up the opposing sides of her seat harness, responded under her breath, reflexively, "Don't be a wiener."

Both women reached to their seat harnesses and checked to see that the "beaners" were tightly closed. Rituals of safety.

Brandy checked the beaner that connected her rack to her black seat harness. "Screw down."

"So you don't screw up," Susan replied.

Brandy double-checked that the locking gate on the rack's beaner was indeed positioned so that the gate was locked in a down position. Even on a small sized pit the two went through safety checks like pilots about to take a plane off into the blue yonder.

"Did you see the video Blake posted on YouTube?" Brandy had turned around and had her heels hanging off the edge of the pit. She sat into her seat harness and watched the rope feed through her rack slightly. She didn't even look down, nor seem to be bothered that she hung out over thirty feet of dark, black air. One gloved hand was on the rack; the other hand held the rope.

"That was crazy wasn't it? He had the beaner's gate on the harness's D-ring. He just sat back in his harness. Not even hard or anything, just a little weight and that gate broke. Popped right off." Susan donned her caving pack, a slim, black, rubber pack.

Brandy checked the security of her rack's beaner again. Confident, she removed the clip from the rope and dangled it at her side. The only thing holding her up from gravity was the friction of the rope through her stainless steel rack, the beaner holding that rack to her harness and the d-ring holding the harness to her body. Her left hand held the horizontal bars tight against the rope, causing more friction. Her right hand held the rope end that trailed behind her down into the depths. She looked down, smiled, then leaned back until her butt came even with her feet. She sat in mid air, the balls of her feet touching the edge of the pit, the rope holding her to the anchor point in the wall.

Brandy's eyes twinkled as she smiled. She descended and disappeared from Susan's view. The whirring sound of the rope sliding through the metal rack marked her descent.

***

Yindi stood behind the same tree that he had the day before. The sun beat down on his face. Buzzing gnats, ignored, crawled at the corners of his unblinking eyes. His muscles were tight and thrummed. How exciting, the thing was her. So, the right time was important now. He was impatient to find the right time. What if he missed it? Missed it. He shifted and watched the two women walk across the field. His breathing stopped.

Both women were the thing. He looked again, unbelieving. Yes. Both. He could feel it, see it, almost taste it. His eyes bulged as he inhaled deeply. A gnat walked across his blue iris, eyes still unblinking. The future universe blazoned red when he focused on either woman. A murmur of delight threatened to escape. Yindi clamped a hand over his mouth like a schoolgirl. He blinked, trapping the gnat in his eyelashes.

Either one. Both. He had never seen that. Alexander had done him a favor by fixing the rock. He would have never seen this had the one died in the pit. Instead the universe was offering him this exquisite choice. He ran a hand nervously through his hair and turned in a circle. Now? Now? No. What if he waited? Oh, it was so hard to wait. He wanted it now.

Not yet. He could feel/see/sense that if he could wait for the right time...

He held his breath again,

If he waited, the damage would be amazing. Orgasmic. Shivers.

Now, now. Wait. Wait.

He had never waited. Could he wait? He would wait. Blood dripped from his lip. Chewing. He turned and disappeared. Waiting: a strange feeling. Anticipation, nervous butterflies in his stomach.

***

"That crawl sucked." Susan sat in the passage. The low ceiling caused her to crook her head to the side. She tried to turn her head from one side then the other, gave up and reclined back on her elbows.

Brandy, shorter, sat with the top of her head brushing the ceiling. "How far do you think?"

"Four hundred feet, easy."

"Wouldn't be so bad if all these huge cobble stones weren't in the way." Brandy removed a water bottle from her pack. The noise was loud in the silence.

"I'd rather be swimming through it than crawling. Another

reason why cave diving is better." Susan lay back and turned off her light.

Brandy sat, drank, turned off her light, drank some more.

They sat in the absolute darkness, silent. The only sound, their breath. Neither one could see the smile on the other's face. In the distance they could hear the occasional water drip. They could hear the air in the space. It felt…like a promise.

"Feel it blow?" one asked the other in the darkness.

"Good air flow," the other responded.

"It goes," both said together.

Without a word, they both turned their lights on, careful to turn their heads and not shine bright light into their companion's eyes.

They crawled on until they could stand. They meandered through passages, tall and narrow. They walked through large rooms where limestone formations dripping water clung to the walls. They crawled some more. All the while, they were silent, lost in the moment of exploring.

Brandy sat on a large boulder at the entrance of a small domed room. "Lunch break?"

Susan stood in the room looking up at the domed ceiling. It stretched beyond the edge of her light's beam. "End of passage, I think. I don't see anything, unless there is something up there." She turned and sat next to Brandy. They sat close together, their warmth a stark contrast to the cold air that surrounded them.

Brandy removed her mud-covered gloves and pulled a smooshed peanut butter and jelly sandwich from her pack. She looked up at the dome above them. "I'm not climbing no dome."

Susan looked up longingly. "I know." She opened her pack,

dug around, cursed, dumped the pack on the ground and triumphantly retrieved a foil package of tuna.

"Lord, that stuff stinks," Brandy complained.

Susan only smiled a reply. Her smile faltered. "What on earth is that?"

"Coffee." Brandy held up a can and smiled her own reply, this smile more devious. She turned the can upside down and pressed a plastic button on the bottom. A click. "It is self heating." She smiled even broader and held the can in front of her in anticipation.

"You'll just have to pee," Susan chided.

Brandy stuck her tongue out.

Silence again as the two ate. Brandy, with a satisfied smile, sipped at her coffee. Water dripped from the formations. A small trickle of water had cut a channel in the floor. It flowed gently past their feet and through a hole in the passage wall. Water traveling even deeper in the cave, slowly carving out passages for cavers thousands of years from now.

They began to pack their lunch remnants away. "Chocolate before I put it away?" Brandy held out a sandwich baggy filled with broken chocolate bar remnants.

Susan reached forward to pluck a piece and knocked Brandy's empty coffee can off the rock between them.

"Oh, sorry."

The can tumbled and rolled into the small stream of water.

"I got it." Brandy bent to retrieve the can. Instead she reached past the can and into the water.

Water dripped from her hand. She clutched something in her palm. "What the hell? Susan you have to see this."

9 DEATH AND LOVE FOR LINEARS.

Alexander shivered. Cold air, cold skin, cold stone floor. The sun had set in their time. He considered. It was her time now. Not theirs.

"Main time," he thought. Not theirs, not hers, just main. He concentrated and willed his body to pull energy from the earth. It felt cold and lifeless. It could sustain him, but not for long.

"What if I just stay here?" Alexander thought. He pictured his naked body flat against the ground. Here where time stood still, no dust would settle on his still form. Slowly he would lose the ability to move but he would live. His body would breathe energy from the earth and continue to keep the cells of his body tuned to this frozen time. Without sustenance, physical food, he would lack the energy to drive his muscles. Alexander pictured himself trapped in a frozen existence with only the company of his thoughts. Perhaps he would lack the ability to even close his eyes. A waking death. With leaden limbs he rolled then drug himself to a seated position and brushed the sand from his chest. The rubble flitted away from him randomly through time and landed on the ground.

A sharp, needy pain gripped him. This pain sharper than the ache he had felt before, the ache caused by a universe moving towards chaos. He dropped his head forward, rubbed a hand over his hair. He should cut it all off, save that nuisance. It would only grown when he was in main time, her time. A grunt. He felt forward for Yindi. Nothing. "Patience is not one of your virtues. What are you up to?"

***

Alexander walked slowly and with effort through time and towards the entrance of his cave. He walked by the vision of himself at the pit, without glancing its way, and came to stand near the ghostly vision where she had turned to look at him. He stared into her transparent grey eyes. Defeated, hungry and weak he walked on.

The full moon hung heavy in the sky when Alexander slipped into main time. A cool breeze brushed delicately on his skin. It felt like silk. Away from his time and the earth of his cave the sharp pangs of hunger hit again. He slipped back to his cold, frozen time to conserve his energy as much as he could. In that future full moon he could see the comings and goings of his love and her friend. She had come back to the cave today. He had been so preoccupied with leaving that he hadn't noticed the new vision of her there. He followed their ghostly trail through the grass and woods. Alexander studied the frozen transparent women for a moment. They had stood by a small truck, talking, examining something in her hands. Eventually they had driven away, east. Alexander stood still and tried to pull energy from the earth. This far from his cave, his dirt, the energy was barely enough to aid him.

Deep inside he could feel a pull on his body. It felt like a heavy ball of tension rolling in his skull until it settled over his left eye. Barely perceptible but heavy as the universe, he could feel there were people nearby to the west. He needed food more than he needed to sate his curiosity about a linear. No good ever came from that. He shook his head. With his back to the road, Alexander walked through the petrified woods in silence. His energy drained with every step away from his cave.

***

"Isn't this the weirdest thing?" Brandy leaned forward and handed an object to Mark. It clinked lightly.

"I don't get it." He held up the necklace and examined it in the dwindling daylight. It dangled from his hands.

"I found this in that cave. We pushed the pit and I found this in a small stream at the end of that passage." Brandy scooted her lounge chair close to Mark's so she could cup her hands around his hands. She turned and guided his hands until a larger part of the necklace was cupped in his palm. She pointed to a large clump of clay embedded into the necklace. "Right there."

"What? Dirt?"

"That's a bat."

"No, it's not."

"Look." Brandy brushed away bits of the dirt with her thumb. A small tip of sterling silver, tarnished and pitted could be seen. It was in the shape of a bat's wing.

"Ok. You found a caver's necklace in a cave." Mark

brushed away more dirt to reveal a second bat, and then a third. "Hold on a sec." He grabbed a red Solo cup from Susan.

"That's my beer," she protested half-heartedly.

Mark dunked the necklace into the cup and swirled it about. Methodically he poked and rubbed, then retrieved a cleaner yet still tarnished and pitted necklace; the three bats frozen in flight were clearly visible now. "Ok. A bat necklace. Why is that weird? You weren't the first one in that cave. Sorry…" He stopped in mid sentence.

Brandy, wordlessly was looking at him. She held up the necklace draped around her own neck for Mark to see. Three silver bats in frozen flight on a chain.

"And they shop at the same store you do?" he finished his sentence.

"No. I made this. There isn't another one like it." Brandy shrugged her shoulders.

"Aw, come on, three bats. That's the NSS symbol," Mark argued.

"National spelio…spelio…sp…Spelunkers Society," Susan tried to interject. She was busy draining the last from the keg. "Damn, nearly empty and it's only Friday."

Blaine had joined them by this time, the eternal smile still upon his face. "Cavers rescue Spelunkers." He grinned wider and began fiddling with the keg. "Don't worry, we got more comin'. I'll see to it personally." He lanked away.

"No, look closer." She took her necklace off and handed it to Mark. "On the back I engraved little swirls. See?" She flipped her necklace over to show dark swirls in the silver. "Kinda like wind, you know. Air blowin'?" She turned over the dark, tarnished necklace. It had darker swirls. "Same swirls. This is my necklace but really, really old."

Mark didn't say anything. He turned the necklaces. Examined them. Reached into his shirt pocket and exchanged his distance glasses for a pair of reading glasses. He examined again.

Blaine had returned, a dolly heavy with a full keg pushed in front of him. "Last keg. I'll be auctioning off my home brew tomorrow night."

"What flavor is it this year?" Susan helped unload the keg, tapped it, sampled the first draw.

"Ooooh, it should be a surprise." Blaine leaned on the empty dolly, then lowered his voice. "Exit Fever Ale. Has some honey in it. Been working on that recipe for six months." He looked around for eavesdroppers. "I've got a reserve stash that isn't going to auction."

"It's for a good cause." Susan poured two cups full from the tap. "Last year they raised enough funds to do four roadside cleanups and donate to a cave preserve."

Around them cavers were returning from their days adventuring and settling into the evening's activities. Old, young, fit, and portly individuals from all walks of life mingled, chatted, befriended, shared food, and drank together. The general sounds were demure and languid.

Susan handed Brandy a beer. Thought better of it and almost withdrew. Brandy stopped her. "I'll take that. You are on your own tonight." She eyed the beer then swigged. They both drank and watched Mark examine the necklaces. Finally he handed the jewelry back to Brandy.

They all sat back in their lounge chairs looking at the necklaces as if they would spring to life as a snake at any moment.

"I agree. That's pretty weird." Mark cleaned his reading

glasses with his shirt.

"Let me see 'em again." Susan grabbed the necklaces.

Silence spanned between them while the rest of the crowd carried on. Bonfires were lit, dancing began, stories were told. Blaine had left the group, unnoticed, presumably to find people more conversationally stimulating than this puzzled group.

"How did you make this?" Susan looked from one necklace to the other. "I mean the real one?"

"It can't be the same necklace," Mark spoke to himself.

"Jewelry class. I took it to get away from work." Brandy pulled another beer from the keg then slouched in her lounge chair. "Still no explanation comes to mind." She put the real necklace back around her neck and held the doppelgänger in her lap.

They drank until the mystery had faded in their minds. Brandy eventually placed the necklace into the console of her truck. When she returned to the campsite, slightly unsteady on her feet, Mark was handing a new bottle of Dickle whiskey to Susan.

"Late start tomorrow?" Susan offered the bottle to Brandy and was surprised when Brandy accepted. "I'm on my own," she added with a wink. "Honestly, I can take care of myself."

"Did you get a new sleeping bag today?" Brandy sipped at the whiskey.

"Oh, hell. I forgot about last night," Susan gasped. She brightened. "I'll sleep in Earl's tent."

"Hope Earl knows that." Mark took the bottle from Brandy.

"His name is Earl?" Brandy blurted.

Later, when she climbed into the opening of the tent she could best focus on, Brandy had forgotten about necklaces, ghosts in caves, dreams of red eyed snakes and the people around her living their lives. The world disconnected and swirled around her in a fuzzy, surreal mist as she struggled to take off her shoes and jeans. Unconscious before her head hit the pillow, she cradled dusty jeans to her chest for warmth.

***

Alexander stood still in a vast open field. Over the centuries, trees would grow and encroach, fires would erase the trees, grass would grow, trees would encroach again and then people would find this field. Under the full moon of main time, Alexander could see the ghost figures of sleeping campers. Over the years they would visit this area repeatedly. He walked among the ghostly images. Bright ghost images of the current inhabitants of time, pale ghostly images of previous visitors cast a fog across the grass and bushes. He focused on current time, ignoring the previous visions that would do him little good.

Here and there isolated individuals were gathered, frozen in their activities, talking, laughing, napping. Alexander moved away from those still awake and focused again on those sleeping. He stopped in front of a large isolated tent. Alexander walked directly into the misty shape of the tent and bent slightly to see the figure there. The man was still awake and reading. The glow from the device in his hands illuminated his face and reflected from his glasses, frozen, cold blue. Alexander walked on.

A little further he came to a cluster of tents. Standing still he searched for Yindi, a mental reach. He could not find him. To be sure, Alexander slipped into main time for a mere second to feel the air and reach again for Yindi. He couldn't remember a time that Yindi had been so still. Hunger gripped him as he synced with time and felt the wind once again on his skin, heard the chirps of the crickets, smelled the cool, crisp night. The evening was quiet and alive at the same time with the sounds of creatures big and small.

Now synced with time, he could see future possibilities, only dimly, very blurry. The tent Alexander had just left, where the man read his illuminated book, had a very fuzzy image of the man coming out of the tent. It shifted and changed as the man inside decided whether he was going to get up and have a snack or go to bed. The image was there, then it wasn't, it went to claim a bag of chips from a cooler, then it didn't.

Finally, the man decided against a snack and the fuzzy images disappeared completely. Alexander watched without reaction. He could slip easily back to his time to avoid detection. The fuzzy possibilities of the near future did not concern him. He could easily move through time, though he was getting weaker by the moment, he needed to eat soon.

Alexander pondered and looked about him. As his eyes roved to the different places he could choose he could see very faint images of himself in these possible futures: himself walking into this tent, crawling into that tent, leaning over someone asleep in a chair in the distance. He shuddered at that image, a bad choice. He decided against the exposed sleeper and the ghostly image of his body leaned over the inebriated soul disappeared. The sound of a dog barking in the distance behind him caused Alexander to turn.

It was then that he noticed one of his blurry possibilities was sitting on an upturned log and gazing intently at a small tent. Curious, Alexander decided that was the choice he would make. Having chosen a path, all other possible versions of him disappeared.

Alexander sat where the faint white ghost of himself sat and he looked upon the tent. One last reach to find Yindi came back with emptiness. Alexander could no longer maintain in main time; his hunger threatened to close down his sight and caused his ears to ring. He would need his last ounces of strength to feed.

He slipped back to his cold, frozen time and walked into the tent, a bare foot visible through the unzipped flap.

***

Shifting and fidgeting and trying to blink, Yindi peered through the scope; crosshairs filled his vision. The world was blobs of green in the night vision scope. When he looked without the scope the universe was still green, not the same, a duller throbbing sickly green. It made him want to puke. His hands shook and his breath was ragged. Sweat beaded on his pale forehead; plastered curls hung limp in his eyes. There. His patience would be rewarded. He could feel the moment coming and it felt bigger than anything he had ever experienced. He watched the two girls. His vision still swam with red as he regarded each one in turn. Both were it. But something else deep inside told him a bigger thing was coming. Wait. Soon. Now. Almost.

A dog growled close by. A small, wiry mongrel. Yindi tried to not look at it. He was watching someone walk through the camp. Now? Now? How good could this be? Was it? No. No. He had to wait. Was this the big thing? The big thing, the right thing was here, and it was…

The watcher!

The dog barked. The watcher turned towards the noise. Yindi held his breath. Sweat beaded. He thought of nothing, searched for nothing, looking at nothing, willing the watcher to not see him. Yindi dared a glimpse through the scope and saw him. His eyes went wide as realization dawned on him. His wait for the big thing was here. This was the universe unfolding. This was the huge thing. Sweat stung his eyes. Yindi needed to breathe. He watched as the watcher disappeared.

The dog growled and came closer, his bark lower and with meaning. The time was almost here; Yindi couldn't miss it. It was big. It was perfect. It promised ecstasy.

With exasperation, Yindi removed a knife from an inner pocket and with a practiced flick ended the mongrel's growling. The lifeless body dropped to the grass. The pleasure Yindi felt was brief, only a mere pale yellow ripple through time. Yindi closed his eyes and savored even that little bit of pleasure. His eyes popped wide, he feared that the watcher would have felt the ripple and known he was here. Back to the scope he looked towards the tent. He could see the watcher's shadow. This would be more than ecstasy. It would be nirvana. This promised to be so much more than the either of the two girls. So much more. The girls led him to the watcher, well, one of the girls. How it had paid to wait. He licked his lips. Yindi raised the scope and peered at the green world, fidgeting, sweating and waiting for the perfect huge thing that was close and soon.

***

In her dream Brandy floats on still, peaceful water, with no shore in sight. Above her, stars twinkle and shine, though they seem odd: fatter, more green, phosphorescent. Brandy squeezes her eyes slightly to cut the glare from the stars. Glow worms. Like she had seen in the caves of Guatemala. Not stars. Glow worms on a ceiling high above her. Funny, the water is so warm, she thinks. It should be cooler. The water caresses and lulls her, rocks her with a gentle hand. She smiles and stretches. Fingers and naked toes wriggle languidly in the warm water. Deep, long breaths. A smooth low moan, not unlike a low growl, in her throat.

A smooth pressure slides around her right ankle and trails upwards. Comforted by the touch she stretches more. Another pressure slides around her left ankle. Brandy looks down and is surprised at how calm she is to find a large black snake wrapped around her left leg and a large white snake with pink eyes wrapped around her right.

The white snake gently curves around her white thigh. The black snake stays wrapped about her ankle and only samples the air with its tongue. Brandy ignores the pitch-dark snake and its red eyes. She reaches out a hand to caress the pale snake. It meets her hand with a solid push then coils gently around her arm. Warmth spreads where it touches skin. The length of the snake, nearly six feet, feels heavy on her thigh and trails across lace panties onto her torso. With a free hand she holds the white snake close between her thighs feeling its warmth. A gasp as the snake's thick weight crosses her breast and encircles her neck. Its tongue tests the flesh there with gentle quivers and flicks. Another low moan. Gently and firmly, the pale snake bites into the soft flesh at the base of her neck and seems to encompass her in total. Warm pressure holding her body close to solid muscle. She arches her back to be closer to the warm strength.

The black snake coils and hisses, ready to strike.

Brandy turns her head and raises her chin, exposing pale skin, lips parted. A quiet cry of pleasure as warmth invades her body.

***

The figure was in front of him, half naked, curled for warmth, hugging clothing to her chest. Pale, bare legs in the dark of the tent. Alexander could only think of the blood the form held for him. For a moment he stood over the form, then slipped into time. Her breath was deep and slow.

A mix of smells filled the air: faint mildew, waterproof chemicals, sweat and alcohol, soap, lavender. The pale ghostly legs and dark lace panties were in stark contrast with one another, but did not compare to the dark warmth he could see coursing through her veins.

Alexander kneeled over the small form and considered for a moment. Hunger threatened to break his control with its ravenous need. She stirred as he leaned closer. An exposed neck, a slow heartbeat, an inaudible sigh, the sound of the sleeping bag as she shifted her weight. Quickly, Alexander pulled the form to him and fed.

He drank deeply, warmth spilling through his body. Energy buzzed through his veins and crackled through his nervous system.

For a moment, nothing else existed but the blood. He ignored the faint memories, feelings, fragments of thoughts that floated through his consciousness like moths. Wispy fluttering, byproducts of life that seeped into him from her as he drank.

The heartbeat beneath him beat steadily. The sound was deafening. Quickly, he unbuttoned his shirt and pulled the form closer. Warm, pink skin soft against pale, cold skin. A moan and the form arched in his arms; a hand softly encircled his back and held him closer with strong, delicate fingers.

Alexander's body pulled energy from her and the thoughts and memories barraged him all the more. So sweet was the warmth he drank. With reluctance he lowered the form back to the sleeping bag. Shudders ran through his body, a spasm of energy as he released his hold on the soft form. He sat a moment on his haunches, eyes closed, savoring the life that coursed through his veins; a faint smile touched his lips.

She whispered something. At first he thought she might have awoke and thought to slip out of time and out of her view. He opened his eyes, ghosts of her memories lingered still and the intoxication of them was euphoric. His body breathed in warm nuzzles of energy from her in gentle pulls from where their skin contacted.

Alexander caressed the marks he had left at the base of her neck. They faded with his touch. Still holding her head, his thumb on her pulsing carotid, he paused when she whispered again. Familiar chin, familiar lips, small, close ears with delicate ear lobes. He expected to see grey eyes, but they were closed. He had never seen those eyes closed. He had stared at the ghost of those familiar grey eyes for a hundred years and never imagined the delicate veins and eyelashes.

Alexander's heartbeat thundered in his chest, drowning out the sound of hers beneath him. At once, a wave of defeat pulled at his ancient bones. He brushed the hair from her forehead. A linear with a temporary life span, useless to love, useless to be close to. Useless to try.

Why would he suffer such a ridiculous infatuation? He did not even question that he had found her. Of course he had. A cynical smile. The universe was cruel in its patterns. The years of emptiness crushed in on him like falling rock. She shifted beneath him, her hand brushed against his thigh. The warmth of the touch, a fire to him. A thumb on her chin, he tilted her face toward him. Useless, he thought, and bent to kiss her goodbye.

***

Red. Red. No longer green, but red. Yindi seized the rifle and peered through the scope. Sweat poured down his face, dripped from the end of his nose and chin. He could only see red. Not just spots of red, the universe was red and complete entropy was inevitable. He couldn't miss it; this was it. The big moment. The end of it all.

In the distance a thunderclap rolled through the valley. The gentle wind, that had been a mere caress for most of the night, strengthened and whipped the sweaty hair from Yindi's pasty forehead.

He could only see faint silhouettes in the tent, so close together they looked like one. The angle could have been better, Yindi thought. If he had but known, he would have chosen a more direct vantage spot. His breath came in wet, ragged draws. Red. So red. It would be magnificent. Finally, death to all. Eternal death to him.

Yindi shuddered, took aim, held his breath, gently squeezed the trigger. A quiet whine of air. Yindi let out his breath with a moan, sinking to his knees as the pleasure of death enveloped him and his vision turned red.

***

Warmth and energy buzzed as his lips met hers. For a moment, Alexander could think of nothing else. Residue of her own thoughts and memories danced with his, tantalizing. His need for her became painful; a desire ignored for a hundred years now yearned for release. Eyes still closed, he laid his cheek against her sleeping face. Life. Short life. How short they live and then he would be alone again. Useless.

He opened his eyes. Alexander did not expect to see fuzzy images of her in front of him. Sleeping linears cast no future fuzzy versions of themselves, as they made no decisions while they slept. She still slept.

Alexander sat back knowing the fuzzy possibility were being decided by someone else. They collapsed quickly to one future possibility. The translucent version of the woman in his arms would open her grey eyes in surprise. Not even a second passed before the future became now. The shot was a thump.

Her eyes opened in surprise and met his. He still held her in his arms, unable to save her, as the back of her head exploded. Red gristle on the sleeping bag and tent.

Grey eyes turned vacant and saw nothing.

***

The red of the universe washed over him. Yindi could feel the unraveling. He gulped; it was not complete. It never was. Never as good as he had hoped. It was good. Good still. Cold shivers.

His breath hitched. Yindi's unblinking eyes stared up at the stars.

***

Her heart had not even beat its last beat. Alexander slipped out of time before he could feel her death. Agony hit him as the universe unraveled somewhere in the future, like a suspension bridge with a snapped cable. That agony paled to the pain of seeing her die in his arms, the warmth of her lips still on his. Incensed, a growl erupted from him as he looked across time for…

"YINDI!"

No longer synced, he could see what had occurred. The distinct transparent images of a bullet as it tore through the air and into the tent, lay in front of him like a thread. He followed it to the edge of the woods.

He continued to yell, rage unheard and unrequited, "YINDI!"

A stream frozen in time, rippled between Alexander and Yindi. Alexander on one side moving in his frozen time. Yindi on the other side of the stream, frozen with the rifle in his hands. A bead of sweat, frozen, dangled from the tip of his nose, reflecting the world around it. Alexander could see the movement Yindi had made, the dead dog, the waiting, the shot, Yindi on his knees in rapture.

Words no longer came from Alexander, only growls of rage. He stopped short as weakness and pain erupted at his feet. He looked down to see the stream still existed in his frozen time and came to his ankles. Leather moccasins barely visible in the frozen current. Alexander searched to find a time before the stream existed, slipped to that time, crossed unhindered, then chose carefully the moment before Yindi had pulled the trigger. He synced with that time, intent on changing it. The brute force of his anger overriding any care or thought, blinding him to anything but the sweating figure in front of him, peering through a rifle scope.

He closed his hand around the throat; a surprised gasp escaped as Alexander hauled Yindi off of the ground. His sneaker tips lightly stirred arcs of dust and leaves.

Their eyes locked as the universe shifted back to where it should be, green, good, living.

"Damn wind," Yindi moaned. "I was aiming for you." He blinked, rubbed his face and seemed unperturbed to be dangling from Alexander's grip. He grumped, "I must have missed if you are here now." Physical pain from this body was a minor annoyance, yet Yindi wilted as the raw need for entropy gnawed at the backs of his eyeballs.

Alexander held Yindi suspended, the anger dissipated from him with each draw of energy his skin pulled from Yindi. The energy began to seep from Yindi, seek Alexander, coolly creep into his veins.

"You would kill me with your own hands?" Yindi taunted quietly, a lover's coo. "Dangerous…" Yindi reached forward to touch Alexander's shoulder. He faltered and dropped his hand as Alexander cast him a withering look of contempt. "for you," Yindi whispered.

Alexander did not release his grip. Effortlessly he held Yindi's body from him.

"Why do you insist on stopping me?" Yindi's voice became a child's whine.

Alexander turned his head slightly to look at her tent, a

85

stolen glance that conveyed more than any spoken word could.

"A linear? You feel for that linear? Your food?" Yindi's laugh was bold and loud, mocking. "You never lear…" He grunted and gasped the last word as Alexander hoisted him higher.

Weakly, Yindi struggled, scrambling to put his feet on Alexander anywhere to transfer the weight from the grip on his throat. A foot found purchase on Alexander's hip and Yindi lifted himself a fraction.

"I'll kill her," he struggled as his foot slipped then found purchase again, "in the day." Yindi smiled, the flesh of his neck and chin bunched and reddening from the tight hold, his smile a grotesque specter. "The universe…" another slip of his foot, "can wait." Yindi croaked a laugh. "This will be fu…"

A dull crack. The smile relaxed slightly. The eyes, still unblinking, dulled.

It was a mistake. Alexander knew it as soon as the bones snapped and that horrible grin went slack. His hand, still about Yindi's neck, grew cold and on fire simultaneously as the energy left the host body and swarmed through Alexander's veins already flooded with warm life. In horror he dropped the lifeless body, too late. The energy that was Yindi sizzled and crackled in blue jagged streaks from the cooling husk and sought refuge in the closest being: Alexander. The dark, thick energy swarmed and curdled in Alexander's veins. Instinctively he tried to return to his frozen moment in time; he could not shift. Pain engulfed his vision and dripped from his teeth. He sank to his knees in the dark dirt.

It wasn't words or images that entered his thoughts from the energy. Instead his brain filled with raw, sweaty needs and desires for death and destruction. Retching a thin line of bile then shivering, Alexander tried to calm his breathing and desperately sought to focus, relax, force the creature from his body.

Through gritted teeth, "Not today, Yindi. You will not have me." His breathing calmed, the cold energy recoiled leaving his fingertips numb.

He struggled to stand; leaves and debris clung to his britches. Focus, relax, breathe. "You will not have her." Numb fingers, numb hands, numb limbs. His chest churned with liquid fire. It hurt to breathe.

Alexander picked up the lifeless body and slung it into the bed of the truck. He concentrated on his breathing and keeping the energy contained inside of him. He struggled. As a second thought he retrieved the dog's body, the knife still buried in the chest, and placed it into the truck bed. Inside him the energy sporadically expanded and jerked, causing Alexander to pause as he climbed into the cab. Another long pause. He closed his eyes, willing the black putrid energy to remain calm; he turned the ignition. Without turning on the headlights he drove the stolen truck containing Yindi's dead host away from the campsite and back towards the sloping hill sides.

Time moved so quickly for him. He disliked being in main time, the seconds moving by and plodding towards daybreak. He longed to move into his frozen time. Alexander concentrated on his breathing. Slow. Steady. Focus. He parked the truck in the woods and carried Yindi the last few miles to his cave. The dog he left in the woods, keeping the knife for himself. Breathing slowly, sweating blood from his pores, Alexander hefted the weight along through main time and wrestled to keep the energy beast contained.

Dawn approached and he could not shift out of its deadly rays while burdened with holding Yindi. He took solace that it would take Yindi time to find another host and take it over, that is if Alexander didn't lose the battle and become the host first. The ball of fire in Alexander's belly, which had drawn in on itself, bucked at the thought of Alexander being the host. Bile rose to his throat and his step faltered. Blood sweat poured into his eyes and stung. He would have to shed himself of Yindi soon.

Alexander looked back over his shoulder. The linears were far behind him now, not completely safe from Yindi, but it would have to do. Dawn was coming. He could feel his strength ebb. He could not risk becoming weak and losing to Yindi. The result would be unspeakable horrors—trapped in his own body to feel an eternity of pain as Yindi tore the universe from its path.

Would Yindi harm her with him trapped inside watching helplessly? Anger rose again and it fueled the energy of Yindi. Alexander took a calming breath. Something stirred on the ground in front of him.

With a mirthful laugh, Alexander stooped momentarily to the ground. The head of the lifeless form lulled on his shoulders. "Here's your host, Yindi."

He picked up a toad and cradled it in his cupped hands. With a spasm, Alexander wretched. Dark tar expelled from him onto the frog. Strings of the goo hung from his lips. A dry heave, a hack.

The toad looked at him, unblinking. Then, it began to convulse. Alexander, not very tenderly, tossed the toad onto the ground. The black goo oozed onto the surrounding grass.

The toad continued to spasm and jerk while Alexander

resettled the dead body about his shoulders, grunted slightly and then disappeared.

Outside the dark had dimmed as dawn approached. Alexander reached the far ends of his cave. A large gypsum-covered room loomed capacious in front of him; white coils of twisted crystal covered the floor in mounds. Alexander dumped the body on a mound. As he walked away his foot dislodged a heap of gypsum. It toppled and rolled, revealing mounds of skulls below. Gypsum-covered hollow eye sockets watched his progress through the room.

With moments until dawn, Alexander plodded back towards the camp. The black of night was streaked with pale promises of dawn. He stood again at her tent. Alexander stole into her time. Peacefulness washed over him as he reached with his soul and found no Yindi, only the steady beat of her heart and the forward expansion of the universe. Peace, if only for a moment, tasted sweet. Yindi would eventually come for her just to spite him.

Alexander pulled the sleeping bag over her pale legs. They had to be cold. What was eternity to her? A distant concept. The sun crept over the horizon; it clawed at him. He couldn't always keep her safe. Shame filled him as he accepted his decision, his weakness. Shame resolved to warm peace and spread through his limbs. Her breath was warmer still on the nape of his neck as he placed a gentle kiss on her forehead then slipped back to his time, forever in darkness.

10 UNEXPECTED RESCUE.

"You going with us today?" Mark handed Brandy a steaming mug of coffee.

The sun was behind Mark, his face cast in shadow. She brought a hand up to shade her eyes. Curled in her lounge chair, bare feet tucked under her, Brandy accepted the mug with a broad smile.

"Nah." She sipped the dark brew. "I think I'll hang out here today. "

"You sure tied one on last night. Hung-over?"

Brandy shook her head no.

"Seriously? How do you do that?"

"Good genes in a bad way." Brandy stretched her arms over her head and uttered a sound of contentment.

Mark continued to gather gear and ready for the day's trip. Susan joined in. "You sure?" Susan hefted her cave pack onto her shoulder then motioned for Brandy to hand a helmet to her.

Brandy passed the helmet then settled back into her chair. "I'll see you when you get back." Brandy twirled the bat necklace around her neck absently.

She waived them bye and waited for them to get out of sight. When she was sure they were gone, Brandy began to gather her cave gear.

***

In their time, her time, the sun was rising. Alexander stood in his dark frozen prison of time. He had fed more during the evening; his skin was warm and flushed. He had not left the field. Alexander stood near the small cluster of tents that he had found her in. The sun in her time barraged his bones with the weight of its rays even as he stood in a moment a millennium ago. He did not give much thought to the chances of him finding her. He had walked the face of this planet too long to believe in pure chance. He smiled slightly; of course it was her that he had chosen to feed upon. Then the universe threw Yindi in the mix.

"Cruel universe," Alexander thought, not for the first time in ten thousand years.

He stood still and watched the faint transparent images of the linears fill the air around him. The forms gradually faded in, glowed slightly, then faded gently away, leaving a ghost trail whitewashing the world in front of him. As the sun rose, however, the images became dimmer and dimmer to Alexander. He struggled to watch her as she rose and exited her tent. He fought sleep; it threatened to close his eyelids as he stood.

A panic gripped his heart tightly. She was seated now, in a future far from him; someone else offered a cup to her. The panic gripped tighter as Alexander realized Yindi would come back and track her just to spite him. In an endless existence a hundred years was a side trip as the two battled one another. One bent to destroy, the other intent on saving the universe.

The sun rose higher; the image of her faded; his eyelids became as heavy as the sun's rays beating down in her time, erasing her vision from him. He wandered from the field towards his beckoning bed of stone.

He stood at the entrance to his cave. Alexander could no longer see where she had stood, the sun too high in her time. He looked anyway, in vain. Disappointment, he could not even see the transparent image of himself when he had slipped into her time so carelessly. As he entered his dark home his body pulled energy from the soil, greedily and he felt mildly restored. Sleep still called for him.

He looked towards the pit. No one was there. Sleep pulled and demanded, Alexander shuffled towards the back of his cave but stopped short. With the sun so high in the sky in main time he could not see through time, could not see himself in the times where the passage was taller, more open and he could walk freely. If he shifted without knowing if he had been there a horrible accident could occur.

Alexander absently rubbed at the missing spot on his finger and considered. Sleep begged. He could not go to his dark room. He would have to make do. He stopped and crawled on hands and knees, hating that he had to do so, chiding himself for being foolish again. Too exhausted to go on, he chose a small domed room that to the best of his memory seemed safe enough. Small rocks littered the floor near where the tall rock walls rose. The ceiling was domed but had not collapsed, heaping piles of stones on the floor. He had fed, so had no need to strip and allow all of his flesh to touch the earth. Alexander chose a clear spot in the center of the room and carefully arranged his body in repose.

His last thought before sleep won and pulled him into oblivion was that he needed to protect her from Yindi. He would have to find her, follow her. Preparations needed to be made.

Sleep won: his eyes shut and his body relaxed, naked skin on cold stone, breathing energy from the soil. Stalactites once long and formidable, shrunk, became nothing, grew again then shrunk once more as Alexander's body moved through time at random. Here beneath the earth where nothing had roamed, nothing had grown, this rock room had existed since water covered the earth, before Alexander's timeline began; he was safe to sleep. Here his body could pull sustaining energy from dark earth unsoiled by the sun and phased through time without harm to him.

Above Alexander's sleeping form a small opening in the domed ceiling would appear, disappear, grow, shrink.

***

Somewhere in the past, a small unfortunate gecko stood in the cold, damp room, unaware that the first indigenous tribe to inhabit the lands above him had just been conquered by another indigenous tribe. He was vaporized to nothing as a pop of air expanded and a large sleeping form encompassed the same space; a second later and the form was gone. Nothing hinted that the gecko once stood there.

***

"I don't remember the walk being this long," Brandy grumbled to herself, slightly out of breath. She looked around at the woods, the grass, the rocks, and wondered if she had lost her way. She had been distracted and thinking about the necklace, the weird dreams, and most of all she was wondering what she was going to do if she ran into her ghost in the cave. Surely she hadn't seen anything; it had to have been her overactive imagination trying to conjure an image from the hazy dimness of the cave entrance. She walked further, hesitating, occasionally looking over her shoulder to see if she had missed a trail in the woods. She had just about given up hope when she came to the grass clearing. Far on the other side she could see the cave entrance.

She stopped and looked at the dark maw in the hillside. No ghosts here, none that she could see. She walked further and stood just inside the opening; cool wind blew from the cave and chilled her skin. She adjusted the rope draped around her shoulder.

"Well, I want a short cut to the back of that cave." A wistful whisper.

Brandy lifted a compass that hung from her neck and took a read of her heading. Correcting for the direction she thought they had traveled in the day before, Brandy walked around the cave entrance and began to climb up the hillside. She knew it was like searching for a needle in a haystack, but this was fun. She walked and measured mentally the direction, and distance and guestimated where she thought she was on the surface over the cave.

Fallen branches and roots caught her boots. Many times the weight of the rope coil, which hung diagonal across her body, shifted as she tried to catch herself, further throwing her balance off.

An exclamation of "Damn" followed each near fall with increasing emotion. The fifth time she did not catch herself and fell face first over a large rock.

"Son of a…" Leaves and dirt filled her mouth, blocking the expletive. She spit them out vehemently and continued to swear.

"God damn it."

Spit.

"Son of a bitch."

Spit. Spit.

"Idiot."

She sat up and laughed at her dirt-covered self. Her laughter caught in her throat.

"What do we have here?"

Three feet from her resting place the roots of a large oak tree looked like bird claws tightly clasping rock. Dry leaves covered the rocks; they stirred and danced in a breeze that came from below. Brandy lay on her stomach and peered into the hole beneath the tree. A strong, cool breeze blew in her face from the 2 foot diameter hole in the rock.

"Found it." Brandy smiled and began to uncoil her rope and tie it to the tree, careful to not stand too close to the opening.

As she went through the pre-check routines she called and answered to herself all the reminders of safety.

"Beaner, Beaner"

"Don't be a wiener."

"Screw down."

"So, you don't screw up."

"On rope!"

"OK."

She only paused for one moment to consider the two rules she was breaking. She was caving alone and no one knew where she was. If she fell or had any trouble, there would be no rescue party looking for her.

"I'll be careful," Brandy told the air. "I won't get hurt," she lied.

Brandy descended the rope for the short drop. Her pack got caught on the rock lip for a moment and she had to negotiate it and herself through the small space. The hole was in the top of a dome room and opened up into a free drop for about thirty feet. She descended slowly and looked at the formations on the ceiling and walls. Her light played across rock curtains, stalactites stretching to meet stalagmites, and ribbons of wavy rock running along the dome sides. An ascender that was tied to her seat harness had come free and dangled. It swayed slightly and clunked against one of the ribbons of rock, called bacon due to the stripes visible in the rock when lit from the side; it made a melodic dong sound.

"Oops."

She paused her descent by pulling the bottom bar of her rack up to pinch the rope. She held the bar tight with her left hand. With her right hand she reached down and grabbed the rope tied to the ascender and tried to reaffix the ascender to a loop on her seat nearness. The ascender fought back and refused to clip in; her gloved hand slipped and the ascender fell from her grip. It returned to its dangling position. She looked towards the ground; her feet were only four feet away from the floor. She dismissed the dangling ascender. It swayed and clinked against the wall.

Her light swept across the rock floor and cast long,

wavering shadows. One shadow jumped out across the floor so quickly it caused her to start. The shadow hadn't been there before, but it was now, and it was of a man lying on the ground.

Conflicting messages raced through her brain. "Scream." "Run." "Move."

She yelped "Whaaaaa!" and tried to jump backwards, an impossible feat when hanging on a rope. Brandy started to spin. Her dangling ascender caught in a crevice in the wall. It clanked and the force of her momentum was caught short by it, yanking her backwards. Brandy's left hand slipped off the braking bar; though her right hand stayed firmly gripped around the rope, it was not enough. She inverted at a 45 degree angle and the spinning caused her head to smack into a rock ribbon. The sound was not nearly as melodic as before. Stars danced in front of her eyes and her right hand lost its grip. She fell the last few feet to the ground. Luckily the ascender bit hard into the rock wall and halted her descent; her shoulders made contact first and not her neck. Not that she noticed; she was out cold.

***

Instinctively Alexander awoke, the loud thump thunderous and extremely close to him in the dark. Upon awaking his body synched automatically with the time and Alexander prepared for a fight, springing to a crouching position. Crouched and still, he fully awoke to survey his surroundings. He had awoken during the day, odd. The weight of the sun outside the cave made it difficult to lift his arms, like swimming through wet wool. He looked up to see the small hole in the dome ceiling that had not been there in his time, but was here in their time. A single shaft of sunlight streamed in, soft and dappled from the tree above. The sun light quickly disappeared in the gloom of the dome but not before it highlighted a single rope hanging from the ceiling.

He followed the rope to the floor of the dome, to the crumpled figure wedged against the wall. Muddy boots, limp gloved hands, broken light, pale face. No blood, he would have smelled it. In a moment he knelt on all fours by the linear's side; muffled sounds in the quiet, damp room marked his movement. She was already starting to come to.

The ascender attached to her waist was lodged in the wall, causing her body to hang from it, hips and torso angled down towards her head, which was wedged between two outcroppings of rock in the wall. The movements of her head, constricted as it was, caused her lower body to bump against the wall of the dome. She moaned a curse.

Alexander studied her for a moment. Legs dangling from the hung harness. No blood. She was moving. He didn't dare shift in time to prevent her fall. It was too dangerous for both of them. He was blind to where things were in time during the day. Instead, he placed the weight of her body on his bent leg, and un-wedged the ascender. With that free, he lowered her body to the ground, gently. Her helmet scraped against the rock wall with the shifting of her weight.

"…uck," she intoned.

Alexander touched her face. Warmth. "You are a surprise." His voice, deep, slow, each syllable molded and articulated from a lifetime of infinite time. The touch of her skin flooded him with wispy memories that had tasted sweet in her blood the night before. He exhaled with disgust and wondered if there was another level of watchers, unseen, moving the universe and the pawns in it. How else could one explain this coincidence? The title of pawn at the whim of something bigger suddenly made Alexander feel unusually small and out of control. He dismissed the thought of another level of watchers, wasted energy to speculate on the unknown.

"Off rope," she whispered and then came awake with a start. She stared at Alexander, blinked for a moment and then blurted, "Where the hell is your helmet?" She tried to look around; hands reached up to free her head. "And your light?" She sat up and winced. "Damn. Wait. Hold on a sec." She tentatively touched the shattered light on her helmet. A click then a small dim light cut the dark and shone bright in Alexander's face. Brown eyes, yellow flecks. "Good enough." She patted the backup light tied to the side of her helmet with plastic electrical ties.

Alexander held her arm as she tried to stand. Her gloved hands left smudges on his pale white skin. "Are you sure you should stand just yet?" He placed a strong hand on her shoulder.

"Weren't you over there?" She pointed to the wall then looked at Alexander's visage. Her light shone across moccasin feet, loose black shirt and odd pants, then back up to his face. Brown eyes, dark eyebrows, sharp nose and a tangle of wavy hair. Recognition, then surprise crossed her face. She flinched with its impact.

"Holy Hell," a breathy exclamation.

"You…you're…yesterday." She paused and looked closely at his eyes. His steady gaze held hers. "I saw you. When I was leaving the cave." A snort of embarrassment. She glanced down, escaping his gaze. "I swear, I thought you were a ghost."

A slight tremor touched Alexander's lips, his eyes softened. "Not a ghost, I can assure you."

She looked around. "Have you been here all night?" Before Alexander could even try to answer. Her mood darkened. "You spelunker. You came in here without anything? And you've been stuck here all night." She stood and began to unhook her gear from the rope. Concern and worry. "You must be freezing. I've got supplies in my pack. Here, sit down." She motioned for Alexander to sit as if he was the patient and not herself.

Bemused, Alexander sat and watched the linear pull the pack from her back and search in its depths. She began pulling things from her rubber pack is if was a bottomless carpetbag. "Here, an energy bar, some water, an emergency blanket to keep you warm. I have an extra pair of gloves and a light. No extra socks though…" She stopped and looked at his feet. "What are those?"

Alexander flexed his crossed feet. "Moccasins?"

"Moccasins." She eyed him.

"They are comfortable." He took the bottle of water she offered then tried not to flinch when she reached forward and placed a hand on his shirt.

"And this? How can this keep you war…" She withdrew her hand quickly. "You are cold. Hold on." She unwrapped the silver emergency blanket and placed it around his shoulders. "This should warm you up." She fussed with the blanket for a moment; it crinkled in the darkness. Alexander reached up and stilled her busy hands.

"Should you not sit down? You are the one who was just unconscious." He held her hands firmly and pulled slightly, directing her where to sit. He did not release them until she had sat down by his side. She looked at the ground, where she had fallen then up at the rope dangling above.

"I was just dazed." She rolled her head from side to side, testing. "Nothing broken." She groaned. "That was pretty bone headed. I didn't see you. It looked like you popped out of thin air and then my ascender got stuck and next thing you know I was upside down." Another groan. "Well, here we are." She held out her hand, paused, took off her glove then held out her pink hand again. "Brandy."

His hand enveloped hers in its grip. "Alexander."

She paused, feeling the strength of his hand around hers.

"Alexander," she repeated then released his hand. Then softly, she asked, "Are you OK? Have you been in here all night?"

He smiled then looked around the room. "I was walking in the woods with my dog." The lie came easily. "He came upon a raccoon and took chase. I followed him into this cave."

"Did you have a light?" Brandy asked.

"A flashlight, yes. I lost it in a crawl. It rolled into a crevasse." He held out his hands, a what could I do gesture.

Brandy took up the story, completing it for him. "You crawled back here and slept for the night with out finding your dog." She hugged her knees close to her chest. "I probably caught sight of you just as you were going in the cave." She put a hand on his shoulder, tentative, soft, then removed it. "I'm so sorry. I caught such a quick glimpse of you, then you were gone."

"I was rushing," said the man who had no need to rush.

"I thought…" she paused, seemed to consider something, then continued. "I thought I was just seeing things, really."

"I ran in so quickly, I must have barely missed you.

Fortunate that you saw me at all." Alexander peered at her closely. "Are you sure that you are well?"

"Yes." Brandy dropped her gaze to avoid his intense eyes. "We need to get you out of here." Brandy drug her pack to rest between her ankles and began returning the contents of her pack with care and dedication to the precise placement of the items. They disappeared one by one.

Alexander watched her movements without commenting.

"Here, use this." She handed Alexander a light. He held it in front of him and eyed it suspiciously. "It goes on your head. I mean, it should go on a helmet, but your head will do." She took it from him, pulled the elastic bands out then motioned for him to lean closer. Alexander lowered his head so she could place the light on his skull, the elastic band whisking across his hair. She leaned in close, her breath warm on his ear as she adjusted the straps. The goal of affixing the light met, Brandy paused and became conscious of how close she was to Alexander. She smiled a quick nervous smile and exhaled, "There." Then sat back from him.

Brandy looked up at the hole in the ceiling above them. "Guess we can't get you out that way."

Alexander did not follow her gaze. He watched her face instead. The sun felt heavier now as it crept higher in the sky. Exhaustion pulled at the backs of his eyeballs. He rubbed a cold hand across his eyes; he exhaled slightly, a human gesture. "I visited this cave when I was younger."

"Oh yeah?" Brandy slung the backpack across her shoulders but made no attempt to start moving.

"We used candles then." His gaze drifted towards the dark beyond them. "There is a very lovely area just back this way." He pointed with his headlamp. "I can take you there." He watched for her reaction. "Seems a shame to waste the trip. We are already back this far."

Brandy considered.

"The formations are so lovely, and frail, your voice could shatter them." He watched her resolve soften.

A sly smile. "You're so full of it." Brandy shifted towards him slightly, her knee close to his. The heat from her body, a mist in the cold air around her.

Alexander reached forward and brushed her knee with his fingertips. "It is on the way out. If you think that you are well enough. You did not hit your head too hard, did you?"

Brandy's smile became a momentary tight line. "Of course, I'm fine. You're the one that was stuck in this cave all night. I'm surprised you aren't shivering." She placed a hand on his chest again, considered something, then started to withdraw her hand.

He stayed her hand with his and held it to his chest, where a heart should have been beating. "I am warm enough."

Their eyes locked in the dimness.

The silver blanket around Alexander's shoulders crinkled and reflected their headlamps as he pulled her to him. A lingering kiss that could barely express the hundred years he had waited to see her living and be with her in her own time. Not the face he had seen as a ghost image and followed from a far. Not the being he had fed from the night before as sweet as it had been. Someone warm and tenderly responsive to his movements. Not someone, her. He had found her. The blanket gave witness to their embrace loudly. She had found him.

A tentative touch, she placed her fingertips to each side of his mouth as if in disbelief, gently pushing him away. He stayed the hands again, this time to kiss each fingertip then to return once again to her lips. Freeing her hands he pulled her closer. The blanket slipped from his shoulders, unheeded.

Brandy leaned back from Alex to catch her breath. "uhhhh," and a nervous laugh was all she could muster. She held up a hand to ward off another advance. He kissed it. "ummmm," she continued shakily. Alexander paused and leaned back as well. A slight smile twinkled. "Umm. Do you? I mean…What…I? …hell." Brandy stopped talking abruptly and leaner forward to continue the embrace. He met her halfway, seeking the warmth of her mouth already seeking his.

It was Alexander's turn to chuckle and hold her face in his hands. "Do you always rescue stranded cavers this way?" A thumb idly traced her bottom lip.

"Only the ones who see me knock myself senseless while upside down." She kissed his thumb, closed her eyes and whispered, "I'm not like this. I must be crazy."

"We'll blame it on the bump to the head, shall we?" Alexander kissed her closed lips gently, lingered slightly, then sat back. "I hope you do not come to your senses."

Brandy smiled. "Let's get you out of here. You must be starving."

Alexander only smiled more.

"Follow me out this way." Brandy stood and held Alexander's hand—coaxing him to his feet.

He looked up towards the sunlight visible through the skylight at the top of the cave. "Oh." He stumbled and caught himself against the wall.

"What's the matter?"

"My knee. I think I did give it a twist. I had not noticed." Alexander sat down and held his leg out for inspection. "It is not swollen," he declared, "but I can not put weight on it."

Brandy considered. "I can go get help." She looked up. "Well, we could get a liter through that skylight, strap you in and haul you out."

"How long do you think that would take?" Alexander asked.

"Just a quick climb out for me. A hour back to camp. Get a team. Hour return. The haul wouldn't be bad. It's a straight shot. We could have you out in four hours. Easy." Brandy bent to inspect his leg. "Does it…?"

"Do not touch it," Alexander exclaimed and pulled his leg back.

Brandy jumped as if shocked with a mild electric jolt. "Gosh. OK."

"I can crawl out of here." He touched her shoulder, wishing he had not made her jump. "It is not bad. I do not want to be hauled out of here on a string." His voice softened in a confession. "I…am afraid of heights." He looked upwards towards the sun.

"Well, I guess if we're careful." She held her black, rubber backpack out. "We can make a makeshift splint out of this. It will keep you from bending your leg."

With a few false starts wherein the splint came unraveled completely, Brandy was finally satisfied with the job. "There. That will keep it steady."

"Where did you learn to do that?" Alexander turned his leg gingerly from side to side examining her work.

"I'm a nurse." A scoff. "Well, I don't fix these types of things very often. I work with the elderly." She placed the items that had been stowed in her pack neatly inside of her shirt. It bulged and swayed as she moved. "Mostly, I dress bandages and deal with the occasional fall." She fussed with a bottle of water that slipped out of her shirttail.

"It feels better already." He stood and tried to keep the weight off it, wincing slightly.

"We'll take it slow," Brandy said, kissing him gently on the lips. She paused, the words' other meaning ringing through.

"Of course." Alexander held her face briefly. "I will follow your lead."

They stooped and began the slow crawl out of the cave. Alexander crawled with one leg and dragged the other behind him. By the time they had reached the exit, the sun had set. They stood together, just inside the cave as the last sunrays fled from the oncoming darkness. Their dim shadows, arm in arm, dissolved into the darkness.

"How's it feel?" Brandy asked.

"Hmmm." Alexander had been looking back towards the cave.

Brandy followed his gaze. "That pit over there, have you been down it? That's where I went yesterday."

"I know," Alexander said distractedly. "I know of the pit." He turned back and kissed her gently on the nose. "I used to wander there years ago."

Brandy touched the necklace at the base of her throat, lost momentarily in thought. A deep breath. She returned to present thoughts. "It's a long walk back. Are you up to it?"

"It really is feeling much better." He glanced behind him again, this time staring into the ghost of his own face when he had slipped into her time just to see her eyes. Grey eyes. He turned to seek those eyes in the moonlight. His headlamp lit her face brightly. The glare of the light caused her to turn away. Quickly, he titled his head to the side to keep the light out of her eyes. "Sorry."

"Do you want to head to your place or you can come to camp with me." Brandy held out a hand as if to stop the words she had just said. "That came out wrong. I mean, do you live close by? Is your truck around here?"

Alexander seemed at a loss for words. Brandy looked startled. "Gosh, you look exhausted. I didn't realize it until now."

"I am fine. A bit in need of rest. That is true." Alexander sat down on a nearby rock. She did not sit. "I had hiked here." He continued. "My home, is not very far away."

"My truck is a little ways that way." Brandy turned and pointed through the woods, her back to Alexander for just enough time that he could slip away undetected, return to his time to sleep and then join her again. She turned back to face a bright eyed Alexander still seated on the rock. "I can drive you home. Actually, we need to get that knee looked at."

"It is better already, see." Alexander said brightly, bending his leg tentatively. "Stiff and sore. But nothing broken." He held the backpack/makeshift splint to her.

Brandy glared, disbelieving. "You took that off awfully fast."

"Do you have dinner plans tonight?" He kissed her hand as if they weren't covered head to toe in mud and dust but sitting in silk finery.

Brandy tilted her head down, a slight blush flared on her throat. Abashed she blurted, "There's a pot luck back at camp. Wanna come?"

Alexander smiled a broad smile, something mischievous in it. "I would be honored."

"You sure your knee is all right?" she asked.

"You sure your head is all right?" he countered.

She bristled slightly and Alexander's grin broadened

"Guess we are both well enough to ignore our hurts. Shall we?"

***

"Man, that was some cave. I thought you said it was an easy cave?" Susan and Mark were unpacking muddy gear in the shade of a tin roofed lean-to. The sign overhead flapped in the breeze. Blue letters declared "Decon Station." A corner had come lose and the string that held it floated on the breeze and tapped against the wood post of the shed.

Tap—Tap—tick tick—Tap.

"I guess I forgot about those crawly bits. Hey, hand me that spray hose, please?" Mark removed his now not so muddy pants from the cleansing chemical bucket and began to spray them. The water threatened to rebound onto everything. He adjusted his claim on the trigger and continued.

"Convenient, your memory." Susan half-heartedly moved her gear around in the bucket then removed them, dripping mud and decon chemicals on the concrete ground.

Mark eyeballed her lackluster attempts to clean her gear. He took a breath as if to say something then reconsidered. She noticed his gaze.

"Oh, I know. The bats." She scrubbed at her gear again and held it up for Mark to inspect and approve.

"It can't hurt," he stated matter-of-factly. He paused and rubbed at his temples.

"How long has it been? WNS keeps spreading and we keep deconning our gear. It isn't making a difference." Susan grabbed the water sprayer from Mark and moved to spray her gear out in a metal drain sink. "You OK? Don't tell me that cave kicked your butt today."

"I'm fine. Just a little off. Got a slight headache." He pointed to a sheet of paper stapled to the wood support pole. It depicted pictures of dead bats covered in white fuzz. Next to the grainy pictures was the warning, "Follow decon procedures to help prevent the spread of White-nose Syndrome." "Besides, I don't want to contribute to this white nose fungus spreading even if it the bats spread it themselves." Mark paid careful attention to his next piece of gear and began the cleaning process, still absently rubbing at his temples from time to time. As he worked, his face became stern; a small pink portion of his tongue poked out his bottom lip as if to aid in his concentration.

"You just like to clean, Mark." Susan hung her gear on the provided clothesline.

"Maybe. I just don't want to be the one that contributed to a catastrophe." He examined his handiwork and the tongue that poked at his bottom lip was satisfied and returned to its rest position. Mark hung his clothes on the next available line. "Did you bring anything for the pot luck dinner tonight? That always stresses me out—bringing something for a dinner that will stay good in the cooler."

When Susan didn't answer he turned around to see if she was listening. Susan stood frozen in place, tattered shirt dripping in one hand and her other hand paused in mid-air outstretched to grab Mark's. Her mouth worked at words for a moment and then finally engaged. "Son of a bitch. We missed something."

Mark turned and froze in place as well. His paralysis was momentary. He turned to Susan quickly. "Don't make a big deal out of it, OK?"

"Do you know how long it has been since she…" Susan protested.

"I know. I know. I was there when she broke up with Mike."

"Who is it? I can't tell." Susan and Mark began to walk forward to greet the couple strolling hand in hand towards them.

Lightning bugs glowed and disappeared in the growing darkness—a thousand temporary glimmering shapes. Footsteps of the approaching couple sounded soft on the loose gravel.

Brandy broke the silence first and answered the obvious unspoken question. "Mark, Susan, this is Alexander." Polite handshakes were exchanged, murmurs of greetings; an awkward silence filled the air between them.

Mark broke the awkwardness first. "Did you find him in a cave?" he mocked, half serious.

"I, uhhhh…" Brandy stammered and squeaked, her voice could not be found. She raised her hands in a helpless gesture.

"Actually, yes, she did," Alexander answered with a mischievous smile. "She rescued me."

Mark and Susan stared hard at Brandy. Susan's mouth gaped for mere moments before her brain engaged and the barrage of questions came pouring from her. "What does that mean? Seriously? What cave? You went alone!" The last an accusation accompanied by fire in her eyes.

Before Brandy could answer, Susan answered her own question. "You're the ghost!"

"Did I tell you she's quick?" Brandy mumbled under her breath.

"The what?" Mark puzzled.

"The ghost. She saw him. We were leaving. He must have been going in." Susan jabbed her finger at Alexander. He bore the pointing patiently and quietly.

"You were there all night?" Mark and Susan asked in almost unison.

"He catches on pretty quickly too." Alexander told Brandy under his breath.

Their reply to Susan and Mark was simple, quiet, resolute. "Yes."

Calamity broke out and the conversation could barely be followed. The four found their way to various chairs as they drew out the story from Brandy and Alexander. Brandy told most of the story, with direction via pointed questions from Susan and Mark.

***

"Why did it take so long to get out of the cave?" Susan eyed Brandy suspiciously, obviously hoping for lurid details.

Brandy blushed slightly but maintained her composure. "He hurt his knee." She explained the wrapping of the knee and the slow crawl out. She did not elaborate on the rappel portion of the cave nor that the reason that they did not seek rescue through the vertical entrance was due to Alexander's fear of heights. Alexander maintained a quiet, bemused observation of the rapid-fire question and answers.

Finally the questions abated and Mark pushed Susan's shoulder gently with an open hand. "What?" Susan whined in mock indignation.

"So much for not making a big deal out of it." Mark

smiled to Brandy and shrugged. "Sorry."

"We just never," Susan started then stopped. "I mean, she just never…" She held her hand out, palm up, indicating Alexander as a being. "We weren't expecting you." Her hand dropped.

Alexander finally spoke, slowly, quietly, though his words carried. "I was not expecting myself to be here either." He squeezed Brandy's hand, which he had held throughout the interrogation.

***

Alexander watched them talk and for a moment forgot to dislike the movement of time and how they experienced every second of it, locked only into that narrow path of existence. He forgot to miss his frozen time, his safety, his loneliness. Alexander forgot the thousands of years and how many times had he fallen for a linear. How many times had he watched them die? He did not think of it. He only listened to the friends discuss their day's adventures and lost himself in their short unaware lives. How amazing it must be to be locked into a forward moving timeline, trapped and finite, unaware, unable to see time, unable to feel the universe. How freeing it must be to live unaware of the forces trying to end time and the forces trying to save it, forces eternally locked in a war.

"…live?" Brandy was looking at Alexander anticipating an answer.

"I apologize. I must have been wool gathering. What did you say?" Alexander met her gaze steadily.

"Where did you say you live?" Brandy repeated. "A ways from the cave. Couple miles?"

"More or less." Alexander hemmed. "To the east side of that mountain."

"I'll drive you home after the auction. OK?" Brandy smiled.

Mark was rubbing a beer bottle to his head. "Over by Chuck's farm?"

"Yes. Past that." Alexander hoped there was a past that. He turned to Brandy. "You do not need to take me home. It has been a long day for you." Alexander squeezed Brandy's hand again; his thumb caressed her thumb. Her warmth felt like hot coals to him. "I'll catch a ride with someone going that way."

"Fun caves on Chuck's farm." Mark told Susan. "Michael's going that way. He doesn't camp. He can take you home." Mark inspected the beer bottle for a colder spot then returned it to his forehead.

"What's up with the head, Mark?" Brandy mimed holding a beer to her head and pointed to Mark.

Mark looked up and acted shocked to find a bottle at his brow, took a sip of the beer then returned it to his forehead again. "Kinda got a headache."

"Cheap beer?" Susan asked.

"Hey, don't pick on Blaine's beer. That's home brewed," Brandy defended Blaine's honor and looked around for him.

The evening was quiet at the campsite. Everyone had eaten their fill from the potluck and had all settled down into separate groups awaiting that evening's auction. Blaine could be seen at a large covered patio area supervising the kegerator which doled out cold draws of the home brew. The keg was housed in an old yellow refrigerator with the appropriate amount of caving bat stickers on the refrigerator door.

"I mean, like PBR or something. Obviously NOT Blaine's

quality brew." Susan wrinkled her nose. "Oh, there's Michael!" She called out to him, "Michael!" Susan ran off.

"Nothing wrong with PBR," Mark countered.

Alexander remained silent on the topic.

"Headache in a can," Brandy commented and then returned to her original question. "But, seriously, you OK?" She pointed again to his head then turned to Alexander for support.

Alexander only smirked, pointed to her head and raised an eyebrow as if to ask, "And how is your head doing?" The gesture was quick and silent. No one noticed but Brandy. She scowled at him briefly and stuck her tongue out as briefly, eyes glittering mischievously.

Mark waived off the question. "It's OK. Maybe the leaky air mattress is getting to me, or something. I'll be better tomorrow."

Susan returned. "Michael is heading out after the auction. He said he'd take you back." Alexander nodded his thanks to Susan. "Did you see the auction items over there?" Susan pointed towards a white trailer surrounded by Christmas lights. "I hope the auction starts soon. I need a new sleeping bag. An air mattress would be great too!" Susan patted Mark's head and pouted. "You feel better. I'm going to go check out what stuff they got." She wandered off again with a skip.

"Man, she's the energizer bunny, ain't she?" Brandy commented.

Brandy, Alexander and Mark pulled their chairs closer to the auction area. Cavers congregated and drank while the auctioneer approached the microphone. The PA system squawked slight feedback causing everyone to wince.

Mark looked like he would vomit. "Oh, I don't think I can

take the noise tonight." With a mumble he excused himself and headed back towards his tent.

Brandy watched him go. "Gosh, I'm worried about him. I hope he's OK."

"Have you been friends with him for very long?" Alexander asked.

"Forever. I mean, not as long as Susan and I have been friends. But Mark and I have been caving together for over a dozen years now." She watched after Mark a little more then turned back to Alexander. "You lived around here long?"

The auction had started and Alexander could not answer over the din of auctioneer. Susan came running back to Brandy. "It's my lucky night!" She nearly tripped and fell into Brandy's lap. Alexander caught her. Brandy hadn't even seen him stand.

"Wow." Susan stood still and blinked for a moment at Alexander. "Thanks." She brushed herself from his grip and then went back to her original excited channel. "My lucky night! They have an air mattress and feather pillow. I'm going to sleep good tonight." She sat and held her auction number out as if preparing for war. The plastic flyswatter boasted a number eleven constructed of florescent duct tape. "It's mine."

Hours later, the items had been auctioned off. T-shirts, cave gear, hunting knives and a few odds and ends had been the focus of heated bidding battles. Wars for jars of moonshine had been waged. The victors drank their spoils and the losers grinned as if they had won anyway. Cavers lined up to pay off their tabs.

"Thanks everyone. Proceeds go to fund the conservation efforts of the grotto." The auctioneer gave thanks, his voice cracked from the evening's effort.

Susan triumphantly held her air mattress out for inspection. "Ha." Was all she could say before walking off to test it out.

Quiet once again stretched across the field as everyone continued drinking, talking and making plans for the next day's cave trips.

"Tomorrow's my last day here." Brandy was looking at Alexander's hand holding hers. She traced a finger around his fingers entwined in hers. "I'll head out Monday morning to go back to civilization." She let out a pent up breath.

Alexander captured her both of her hands in his. "Bring your friends to my cave tomorrow. I'll meet you at the horizontal entrance around sunset." He kissed each fingertip one by one. "I'll show you that delicate section of the cave I tried to get you to see today."

Someone whom Alexander could only assume was Michael called out from nearby, "You want a ride?" and motioned him to "hop on in!"

"I cannot get away until the evening. Meet me there?" He kissed her. Strong. Lasting. A promise of more. "Brandy. Meet me tomorrow?"

"You could sta…" Brandy couldn't finish the sentence. He kissed the words from her lips.

"We can take it slow. I have all of time." Alexander kissed each eyelid. "Tomorrow?"

She nodded and he left.

In the background Michael was drawling in a Mississippi accent, "You ready ta hit the road?" He sounded like Slingblade.

***

The turn was tight. In front of her were Mark's boots. She could hear him grunt as he wiggled on his belly through the tight tunnel. It was tight for him and his massive manly chest, not so much for her. She had plenty of room and thanked heavens he was in front of her. If he couldn't fit, then she could turn around. But Alexander was in front of them and leading them to a new section of the cave. She couldn't wimp. She had to keep up. Mark's grunts and complaints were muffled in the tight rock tunnel.

Finally he stopped for a moment and called, "Resting."

"OK," she returned. Behind her she could hear the sounds of Susan but she could not turn in the confined space to see her. They all rested toe to head to toe to head.

Up ahead Alexander had cleared the crawl. He called back, "In one hundred feet you will be able to sit up right."

"Great." Brandy breathed heavily and turned onto her back. She had six inches of clear space between her nose and the tunnel's ceiling. "You hear that Mark? One hundred feet." She reached forward and tugged on his boot heel, the only part of him she could reach. "You OK up there, buddy?"

"Just a little slow today but OK. Piece of cake." He commented back and then with a grunt he began to belly crawl forward towards Alexander.

They all popped out of the belly crawl into an area just tall enough that all of them could sit and take a break together. Their lights bounced off the rock walls and dimly lit the gloom.

"Up ahead is a slight climb down to the area with all of the formations." Alexander informed them. He reached the toe of his boot forward and touched Brandy's extended boot. She smiled back as they moved their muddy boots together in a dirty game of footsie.

"I would have never seen this passage." Mark pointed back to the belly crawl they had just birthed themselves from. "Could'a walked past that for years and never noticed that itty bitty hole behind that breakdown."

"Yes, I know." Alexander pointed ahead of them. "You are going to love this next place. We have to climb down here." He moved forward and over a drop that the group had not noticed.

Susan pulled herself over to the lip of the drop and peered down. Alexander was already almost to the bottom. "Dude, did he just free climb that drop? That's about 15 feet. Damn."

Brandy appeared beside her and looked after Alexander. "Hmmm. I've got webbing. It's not that bad. Not even that slick." She pulled a 30 foot length of green webbing from her black rubber backpack and tied it onto a rock outcropping. Without so much as another comment she grabbed the webbing and lowered herself down the incline towards Alexander.

"Did you see that?" Susan looked to Mark. "He didn't even have webbing. Free climbed right down. Free climbed."

Mark watched the two lights at the bottom of the climb come together and then disappear under a rock outcropping. "So, he's a rock climber. Big deal."

***

The room was dazzling. White calcite soda straw formations by the hundreds dangled from the ceiling. Each one hollow and dripping a solitary drop of water. Flows of frozen white calcite stone looking for all the world like frozen waterfalls of sparkling milk towered from floor to ceiling. Fluted columns of white and tan limestone rock as big around as an elephant's leg stood erect, tying the ceiling to the floor. Everywhere white calcite gleamed, crystal glittered and trickles of water whispered. The domed ceiling opened high above their heads. At the top of the dome a small steady trickle of water danced out of a very small opening. The water splashed down into a puddle at the center of the floor. Pebbles and smooth rocks littered the floor. Everything gleamed with moisture. Mist hung in the air. Alexander was seated non-nonchalantly atop a 10 foot long 3 foot high boulder, one ankle tucked under the other knee. His boots and clothes had been new clothes when they entered the cave. Now he was covered with mud and dirt, as they all were. His helmet, new and barely scuffed, was bright red. He was smiling from ear to ear as Brandy took in the crystallized room in awed silence.

She whispered, "It's beautiful! I've never seen anything like it." Her scuffed, white helmet tilted back loosely on her head while she gaped and looked at the ceiling. She steadied it with one muddy, gloved hand. "We can't come in here all muddy. We should have a change of clothes or at least boots and gloves." As if to prove her point her helmet sported a fresh muddy handprint from where she had steadied it.

She stood next to Alexander seated on the rock. It was not white calcite and would not be marred by their mud. From their vantage point they could see the formations in the room without entering it completely and without leaving muddy footprints on the pristine formations there; muddy footprints that would never be washed away and would exist for hundreds, maybe thousands of years. Alexander shifted his weight and sat on the rock with his legs open. Brandy fit herself between his knees, her back to him. She was still gaping at the formations when Susan and Mark entered the room from a side passage.

"Wow."

"Damn!"

Alexander wrapped his arms around Brandy's shoulders and whispered in her ear. "I knew you would love it."

"I do. It's amazing. I could sit here all day." She turned her head and looked up at him, beaming. "You've been here before?"

"Yes, a long time ago." Alexander held her chin in his hand briefly. Sadness darkened his eyes then he brightened. "I could look at you sitting here all day." The sadness returned again. He blinked and looked up at the calcite soda straw covered ceiling.

Brandy followed his gaze. "It looks like a birthday cake to me, all dripping with vanilla icing."

The four stood in silence for a long time simply appreciating the amazing beauty that so few people would ever see. Mark began to unpack things from his large backpack. Susan and Brandy, without even speaking, stepped forward to assist Mark. Brandy grabbed a flash and handed another flash to Susan. Alexander stayed on the rock and watched as the two woman carefully removed their shoes and rolled up their pants then fanned out and held the flashes up to illuminate the room as best they could. Mark gave directions and the group adjusted their positions.

"OK, lights off," Mark called. All turned off their headlamps. The darkness was absolute. "OK, ready?" The camera in Mark's hand gave a whining noise and then a series of beeps. "Fire." The camera clicked and the two flashes in Brandy's and Susan's hands illuminated the room in a series of bright bursts. After a few moments Mark could see the results on the camera's digital display. He called for the women to adjust their positions slightly. Each moved carefully so as not to get the white calcite muddy. They repeated the process a couple of times. Mark seemed satisfied, turned his head lamp on again and began to put his equipment away.

"Guess we should head back to camp," Mark ventured. No one moved. They could not tear themselves away from the sight.

"Come on, sport." Susan pulled Mark away leaving Brandy and Alexander alone together.

Brandy could hear them as they moved away back towards the 15 foot climb. Which reminded her of something.

"I thought you were afraid of heights?" Brandy poked a finger in Alexander's chest, which was at nose level. He still sat atop the large rock.

"I am." His answer was quiet.

"You sure free climbed the hell out of that drop for someone afraid of heights."

"I…was…showing off," he searched for an answer.

"Bone head." She pulled on his muddy shirt with both hands. Alexander leaned towards her. Brandy craned her head up to meet his lips with hers. Their helmets bumped in the dimness.

Alexander shifted forward on the rock to better hold her to him. Gravity took hold and pulled him further down the rock than he had anticipated. Their lips crushed together, teeth clinked, Brandy's lip split and began to bleed.

She grunted and stepped back; a nervous laugh escaped her.

"Are you OK?" Alexander tilted her head up to examine the lip. He kissed it, slow, delicate, then withdrew, Brandy still in his arms.

Her lip tingled where he had kissed it. Brandy raised her fingertips to it but came back with no blood. She looked at Alexander with surprise. "Oh, I thought it had split. Must have felt worse than it was."

"That was not my most graceful moment." Alexander smiled. "All better now, though. Right?" He did not wait for an answer but pulled her close to him again; she met him with a fierceness matching his own.

Brandy pressed the length of her body to his, clinking helmets ignored, muddy gloves smearing tracks. Warmth together, so much warmer than the cold around them. Out of breath, she paused. "We're going to have to get out of here, you know."

"Will they wait for us or keep going?"

The warmth between them was electric. Brandy felt like every nerve ending was on fire, sparking with every touch from him. She shivered.

A noise from behind them broke the spell.

"Was that a yell?" Brandy turned her head towards the sound. Then for a moment she was so cold and Alexander was gone, only for a split second. She could not feel him. Then he was there. Later she would think back on the moment and describe it as that feeling one gets when taking that last unexpected stair step, for a moment hanging in space expecting the floor to be there but it isn't. "Wh...?" She gasped and turned back to Alexander.

"Did you hear something?" he quizzed.

"That was weird." She paused briefly and then reconsidered. "Let's go check on them."

***

They found Susan at the bottom of the 15 foot climb about to ascend, green webbing (now much muddier) in hand.

"You OK? Thought I heard a shout." Brandy looked up to see Mark peering over the top of the lip of the climb. He waved.

Susan pointed to a rock on the ground. "I must have a target on my head." She patted her blue helmet. "Mark dislodged that rock as he was climbing up. It started to come down after he had already cleared the lip and I was getting ready to climb. But it just kinda bounced to the side and missed me at the last second." Susan kicked at the rock with the toe of her muddy boot. It left a splotch on the rock's surface. "I sure thought it was going to get me. Damn."

***

Later around the camp fire Susan and Mark exchanged quips while Brandy stared into the fire.

"I tried to drop that rock on your head, but you moved too quick." Mark had a peaked look about him but he was trying valiantly to ignore it.

"Me and my mad ninja skills." Susan was braiding her long blond hair. Strands refused to cooperate and fell out of her hands. She combed them again with her fingers and continued the attempt to tame the locks. "Brandy, you gonna brood all night?"

"I'm not brooding," Brandy said, brooding.

"You're acting all pathetic like," Mark cajoled.

Brandy straightened up, genuinely shocked. "Oh my god, I am not." She looked from Susan to Mark and back again. "Back me up here, Susan. I'm not." No one answered. "Am I?" Still no answer. "Oh my god. That's disgusting. I am not mooning over some guy I met in a cave. Good god." Brandy settled back into her chair; it creaked in protest. She crossed her arms and harrumphed.

***

The hour was late. It was the last night before everyone packed up and went back to their real lives. They would clean off their muddy clothes, fold them and put them away on shelves, don whatever uniform they wore during the work week and go back to the ranks of mortals, working for paychecks and trying not to bore everyone with talk of the things they had seen and no non-caver could even grasp. They all stared at the campfire together in the realization that the fun had to end. At least until they could crawl back into a muddy hole again the following weekend.

Brandy watched the flames flicker and dance. He had said good-bye after they had exited the cave. She didn't want to seem needy. She hadn't wanted to need him. How could she need someone she had just met? Why did she feel so disrupted? Stupid. She crossed her arms tighter around herself and sunk lower into her chair. Pathetic. Mark was right.

"Actually." Mark interrupted the silence. "I have to admit something."

Brandy and Susan looked at him expectantly.

He continued. "I knew that rock was loose. I saw it was loose. My brain said to not touch it." His eyes pleaded with Susan. "But I was confused and things got fuzzy. Next thing I knew I was standing on the damn thing. I looked down and kinda thought—Wow. I forgot this was here."

"You got distracted," Susan tried to make an excuse for him. "You couldn't have known it was loose. You're just trying to persecute yourself. Stop it."

Mark looked miserable, sunken. "No. I know what I was thinking...fuzzy."

Brandy half listened as the two discussed whose fault it was or wasn't. Her mind kept returning to her last moments with Alexander. What a pathetic girly thing. She thought to herself.

She had tried to invite him back to her tent, but didn't know how. She had made a miserable, pathetic attempt to be alluring and failed. Alexander had basically promised he'd call her and then vanished into the woods. What a sap she was. How had she ever even had relationships before? What a pain they are. Such guesswork and awkwardness.

***

A few hours from sunrise they all turned in to get some shuteye. Brandy's dreams were fitful.

***

She is running to the water. It is dark and still. Frantically she is putting on scuba gear and knows that she has to get to the tunnel at the bottom of the watery pit. She has to get there. She can't see what is chasing her. Something is chasing her; she knows it. Darkness. She sinks to the bottom of the pit and pushes towards the small tunnel. Again she is in the small tube of a tunnel. The bubbles from her mouthpiece drift and dance on the close rock ceiling. She is stuck. Trying to move. The water feels like molasses but cold and thick, pins her arms to her. She flails. Panic rises. Suddenly Alexander is there. He moves a rock out of the way so that she can move into the tunnel more easily. She glides in. Peaceful. Safe. Alexander places the rock back on the tunnel entrance trapping them inside. Trapping the thing chasing her outside. Panic fluttered in her chest. Tight. Panic not for herself. She sees that Alexander does not have a mask on. He has no air. She has to save him. She rips the regulator from her mouth and gives it to him, tries to buddy breathe. "Breathe it!" she screams. She is not surprised that she can talk under water. "Breathe it or you'll die!" Alexander refuses. His cold eyes close. She pulls him to her; his skin is ice. He drowns in her arms. She holds him close to her body willing him to take warmth from her. Her mind screams for him to breathe her, as if he could breathe in the warmth directly from her skin. He isn't responsive. Darkness and cold. She is frozen with fear as the first slithering black snake enters the dark tunnel. She can't see it; she knows it is there. It is what was chasing her. Then another. Then another. She can feel them sliding around her ankles, black and hissing. She closes her eyes tightly. She does not want to see their red eyes. "Breathe Alexander!" she tries again. She screams her fear into the black water.

***

Her sleeping mind registered the garbled scream trying to come from her throat. It brought her into awareness as another scream did manage to escape her, strangled and thick. "Noooo." She was trying to yell. The rest of her body woke up with a start. She lay there bathed in sweat.

"Fucking pathetic," she whispered hoarsely to the empty tent around her.

11 DUCKS IN CIVILIZATION. DEADLY DIVES.

Her phone vibrated. Brandy shifted the paperwork from her right hand to her left so she could fish the phone out of the depths of her front pocket.

"Hey! See you tomorrow at 6. K? Me = Starbucks. You = munchies right? Later!" It was Susan.

"How can she be annoyingly chipper even in her text?" Brandy murmured. She smiled and returned the phone. Its cracked surface caught the light before it slipped away into the cavernous pocket, buried with crumpled notes and a forgotten protein bar. She continued down the brightly lit, sterile hallway to file her stack of paperwork.

"Evenin' Bob." Brandy tilted her head towards an elderly man who nodded his head in return. His shadow drug lazily behind him on the tile floor.

"Hello, Mrs. Ingles," Brandy smiled gently, voice raised slightly to be heard.

A bent woman seated in a battered wheelchair lifted her

head at the sound of her name. She raised a hand, a queen's salutation to the masses. As Brandy passed by, the queen began humming contentedly to herself.

Brandy paused in the hallway, looked to her right, down one hall of the ward. Very few patients to be seen. The excitement of 6:15 medication time had passed.

From the hall to the left she could hear the distant whirls and dings indicating that Wheel of Fortune must be on. West Manor's 33 patients had retreated to the solitary of their rooms or the sociable TV room with exception of the queen and Bob it seemed.

She opened the Dutch door to the nurses station, a retrofitted storage closet. A small one at that. Brandy began sorting through the charts one by one, taking care to fill out each patient's activities carefully. She hummed to herself, unaware she had picked up the queen's senseless tune.

Upon each chart a clean label displayed the patient's name and room number. She opened a chart and flipped through it, stopped, wrote a short comment, then stacked the chart on a nearby shelf.

Her mind side tracked while her hand performed the routine of charting bowel movements, eating schedules, no observed problems, visitors or no visitors for her 33 patients. Her second family. Meanwhile her brain produced images from the past six months. The whirlwind of change that seemed surreal. Even now it was still not real. A long distance relationship with a phantom she had met in a cave. Six months and she had not seen him. Texts, phone calls, promises she wondered if he'd keep. She hated being that person who waited by the phone now. Trapped by expectations, still as lonely as ever. Pathetic. She continued to chart. Black pen scratching loudly in the silence.

She had little to write down for each patient. There was very little to ever report. Her thirty-three patients were all capable of taking care of themselves, mostly. Even Mrs. Ingles, who thought herself to be the queen of a long forgotten island. Most needed only supervision and monitoring of their medicines. She opened up the last chart and stopped. She hated this chart most of all.

While most of her patients were old and merely needing supervision, a few were younger than the normal populous of West Manor. These younger patients had psychiatric problems and the subsequent narcotic medications to treat them. She monitored their medicine and any disturbances more closely than the other older patients, who mostly suffered from dementia. Then there was this patient. Sight of the chart caused Brandy's heart to sink. Her head reeled with the impossible-ness of the situation. The chart was only two months old, yet was thicker than any long time patient. "He shouldn't be here," she thought.

She picked up the chart and dared her head to stop spinning and to accept it. He was too young to be here. She had insisted he be here, so that she could watch him. The family had been distraught. They were not ready for this; he was so young. Yet, here he was. His mind slipping and no one able to explain why.

Brandy regarded the name printed on the chart, thinking that at some point this nightmare would end and the name would be different. It wasn't. No matter how many times she looked, it said, "Mark Oliver."

Just two months ago they had been caving together and now…now…he was here, a patient of hers. And the world had stopped making sense to Brandy. How could he be here? She shook her head. The past two months didn't make much sense to her at all anyway, not since the caving trips with Alexander, not since they had said good by and he promised he would see her soon, not since Mark had started complaining of feeling fuzzy and confused, nothing was making much sense any more.

She rededicated her attentions to filling out rows of tight little check marks for medicines given and emotional behavior observed for her patients when the phone rang.

"Hello?"

"It's almost seven o'clock." The curt voice abused her ear.

"Yes." Brandy glanced at her watch. "It almost is."

"You gonna have the patients down here on time for snack time right?"

"I'll make sure Margie rounds everyone up. Jell-O tonight?"

"Hmph." The caller hung up.

Groaning, Brandy hung up the phone and regarded her watch again. At 5 o'clock the patients ate dinner in the dining hall. At 6:15 Brandy would hand out meds. 7 o'clock was the highlight of the evening: patients would return to the dining hall for snacks. Brandy's shift ended during that snack time.

She contemplated finding the nursing assistant, Margie, while she shelved the last two charts. Her fingers lingered, still unbelieving, on Mark's chart. She stared blankly at it wondering again what had gone wrong these past two months to cause this. She remembered the phone call about snack time and considered Margie again. There was no sense in passing on the haranguing that she had just received from the kitchen, Brandy decided. She trusted Margie to get the patients to snack time without being reminded.

A call light blinked on and was accompanied by an annoying buzz. Brandy didn't want to look at the light. She already knew who it was. Her finger traced along the call panel, which hung on the wall: Room 303, Jolanta. The room had two red orange lights that could be lit. Brandy had expected the top one to be lit: the one that was called from the bedside. However, she raised an eyebrow when she saw that the bottom light was lit. The bathroom, rarely lit, usually indicated something of a more urgent nature, a fall perhaps.

A quick press of the blinking button stopped the buzzing. The light would have to be turned off in the room itself.

Margie met Brandy at the door of Room 303. "That lady is a pain in my ass." Margie grumbled, a bit too loudly.

Brandy cringed, mentally calculating how many people were within earshot and if there were any visitors left in the building.

"She fell again." It wasn't a question. "That damned Jolanta. I put her down for a nap today. I did not keep her 300 pound carcass out of bed for more than four hours. Every week she does this. Why?" A rhetorical question.

Brandy did not answer and peeked into the room. She could see Jolanta, a 60ish Venezuelan woman, who was smugly snuggled under the covers of her bed. She snorted. "Jolanta."

Brandy went to the side of the bed. "Jolanta, I need to check your body for bruises or cuts." A detached voice. She lifted the sheet and the woman's nightgown. "You decided to throw yourself to the ground again I see. This is becoming a habit." It had been a habit for months. "Jolanta, you are going to hurt yourself one day. What happens when you break your hip?"

No answer. Only the large, wet eyes of an old woman staring.

"When you break a hip, Jolanta, you will be moved from this home. This is the place for people that need only a little assistance. You will be moved to a nursing home. There they posey people." Brandy poked and prodded the ample flesh; bruises were already beginning to show on Jolanta's hip. "They will tie you around the middle to a wheelchair to keep you from falling." She looked directly into the wet eyes. "Do you want that?"

Wet eyes looked away.

Brandy put the covers back in place and stood up. "Nothing broken today. But we'll have to send you to X-ray just in case."

"We're just going to let her get her way? She throws herself to the ground and gets to stay in bed now?"

Brandy looked at the smug old woman. She couldn't bring herself to be angry with her. Jolanta had found a loophole of sorts. If she fell, due to policy, she was sent to rest in bed.

"Not here Margie. Finish up and meet me at my desk." Brandy reached into the bathroom and with a click turned off the call light. "Jolanta, we will try a lounge chair tomorrow, see if that helps any. Margie, there is a reclining lounger in room 301. If you would, wheel it in here. We'll use it tomorrow."

"OK." Margie continued to grumble under her breath but turned to attend to Jolanta.

Brandy walked back through the hallway. Most of the patients had already gone to the dining hall for snack time. Thank heavens for small favors, perhaps the kitchen orderly would be happy, if only for a moment.

Back at the small nurses station, Brandy filled out the

incident report and added it to a large file. Margie came up to the Dutch door and leaned against its counter. The hinges protested slightly.

"I'll say it again, a pain in my ass."

"We go through this every week. She is loud. She is dramatic. She is behaving like a two year old. We have to be strong parental figures and not throw our own fits." A quiet voice.

Though Margie's 200-pound frame loomed over Brandy's seated, slight, 135-pound body, Margie dropped her eyes and sighed.

In a softer tone, Margie continued, "She just goes limp doll on you when you try to get her out of bed. She refuses to lift a pinky. She's not that old, not a stroke victim, not even that much gone in the head or anything."

Margie started to get agitated again and glanced down the hall towards Jolanta's room.

"The fat cunt," she gestured with a flabby arm in Jolanta's direction, "has diabetes and lost a toe…her pinky toe. So she's in here. None of her family wanted to deal with her so they dumped her on us!"

"Please sign, Margie. You know the drill." Brandy held out the incident report and a pen.

Margie signed while mumbling under her breath, "Ought'a put her back in the wheel chair and not in the bed. We're rewarding her falling down."

"She just becomes more resolved to fall again. The trick is to give her multiple naps in the day to break the monotony of sitting up. Jolanta is depressed. We have made a note for the Dr. to take a look at her med dosage on his next visit." Brandy took the chart and held it to her chest. "If your family did not come to visit you, how would you feel? Can meds help that? Can we?" Brandy's tone had dropped to a whisper.

Margie's bottom lip trembled. "I wouldn't be like that, Brandy—Mrs. Bayents. I mean Miss Bayents," Margie stammered and looked wounded.

"Of course, you wouldn't, Margie. If you were in her shoes you would not make everyone around you miserable. You would smile through any heartache. And you would make everyone around you your family. You wouldn't be like that."

Margie smiled a small smile, a twitch at the corners of her mouth.

A tall, lanky old man eased up behind Margie. He acted as if he had not heard the conversation between the two. However, a faint smile of amusement touched his eyes.

"Honey, I think I need my 7 o'clock meds. Would you care to join me?"

Brandy patted Margie's hand as she retrieved the pen. "Mr. Nashold, I believe you are correct. Time for our 7 o'clock." Turning back to Margie she added, "I will be on the patio if the patients need anything. I'll stick around just a bit for the change of shift."

"OK, Miss Bayents. Sorry 'bout losing my temper."

Brandy smiled and patted Margie's plump hand. "She irritates me too. I would hope that I would be stronger in spirit if I were trapped like she is. But we never know what it is like. Not until we find ourselves in that position." Brandy faltered and slowly let out a deep breath, a wistful, faraway sound. "I'd probably be just as depressed. I'd imagine." Her words barely audible. "I don't think I'd do trapped very well."

They both looked at nothing and then at each other. Brandy came back to the present with a start; she stood.

"Have a good evening, Margie."

"I will. You too."

A small woman who had been slowly walking towards them stopped and touched Margie's sleeve. "Is this the platform for the number 9?"

"Oh, Molly, the train doesn't come by here." Margie took the hands of the frail woman. "We have to go to bed first. This way—I'll show you to your room. Did you like your Jell-O tonight?" Margie and the train traveler held each other's arm and walked slowly down the hall.

Brandy opened the mini fridge under her desk and pulled out a diet cola and an opaque box. The box had the patient's name on it, "Nash" and his room number 304. The box was also labeled in black sharpie "PRN," whenever needed.

Nash watched Brandy's graceful, succinct movements, though his focus was not on her, but on the item she retrieved. She took two Dixie cups off her med cart and filled one with diet coke. From the box she pulled a can of beer, opened it and poured it into the second Dixie cup. She placed these 2 cups on a med tray, grabbed a few packets of chips leftover from that afternoon's lunch and walked towards the back patio. Mr. Nashold held the door for her.

The patio faced a small duck pond. Silently, they sat in worn rocking chairs, the tray placed between them. Mr. Nashold was handed his nightly med of beer and Brandy sat back with her diet coke. Silence, their conversation.

Brandy sipped her drink and enjoyed the silence of her old friend. Nash, 70 something, had been her companion on the porch for the seven years she had worked there. He had always been here, having founded the place. Nash, real name—Mr. Bartholomew Nashold, rarely spoke to anyone.

He was a resident of the home only because of being the founder. He had no need for assisted living. He was still quite independent and only suffered from large growths on his face that protruded as bulbous white tumors. He refused to have them taken off, even though their presence on his face made him embarrassed to be seen. The only exception was when he spoke with Brandy; he never seemed embarrassed with her. When he did speak, his voice rumbled a low, gravely southern drawl.

The April night air was still hot and muggy. An overhead fan tried to cool them but only managed to agitate the thick air and remind them of its wetness. The ducks floated thickly on the water, oppressed by the steaminess of the air.

"There's Bill out there." He pointed to a proud looking duck separate from the group. "He's had his eye on that li'l gal over there on the right. See her tryin' ta ignore 'im?"

Brandy looked without seeing, mentally checking time. Nash was always talking of the ducks. "Mmmm-hmmmm. The white one."

He glanced towards Brandy and wrinkled his nose. "You should watch 'em; you'd learn a lot."

Brandy looked at the ducks for a moment. "Learn from a duck, Nash?" Her voice held a smile. She sipped her coke, leaned back in her chair.

"Oh, you look relaxed enough right now, but inside you're schedules and order. You're on a scheduled relax break. An allow'd relax break. Everythin' is controlled. Lots of people are like that. They don't see life 'less if fits in-ta their schedule." Life was spoken as if it had three syllables. One dedicated to the i.

Brandy turned to him and paused for a moment. It was

obvious to her that this had been on his mind for a while. That was a lot of loaded sentences to burst out of Nash like that. He was not one to normally preach. "Wow, Nash. Is something bothering you?"

He sunk into himself, looking almost sorry that he had spoken. "Usu'lly people are runnin' so fast from one place t'other with so many things on their minds, they can't see it."

"See what?"

"They can't see life happenin' all 'round them."

"I know, Nash. I know." She looked at her diet coke but did not drink, then looked at the ducks again.

Bill the duck had floated by the female and turned his back towards her, but kept drifting to keep her in his sight.

She took a deep breath and spoke into the heavy air. "I go on weekend trips once a month to my grandmother's place as a getaway. But even then I have goals, and things I must do. Caves I have to explore, diving I have to do. I enjoy it yes—but it is all scheduled and goal oriented. Even when I'm relaxing, I'm busy."

Nash nodded his head.

Brandy understood that Nash thought of her as a daughter. She had noticed a softness about him when they spoke, a softness that he did not show to anyone else. She attributed it to the fact that he and his late wife had never had children.

She listened to him and nodded her head. Sipping her diet coke, she wished she had a lemon.

"That duck, Bill, is a desc'dent of one of the first ducks my wife and I put out there. Back 'fore this place was what it's now." The assisted living place had started as their apartment building. When his wife needed help after breaking her hip he brought in a nurse and then to help pay medical expenses he slowly split the apartments into smaller studios and turned the building into a home for those that needed aid. Ever since he had contented himself with taking care of the garden and the ducks.

"I've been noticin' one of your patients is displayin' some disturbin' signs lately." Nash looked longingly at the bottom of his empty Dixie cup, possibly thinking of days long gone when the bottom would never be seen until the wee hours of the morning.

Brandy's interest was piqued. "Oh? What have you noticed?"

Nash had always been adept at watching the patients and knew when they needed more help then what was offered at the home. Brandy regarded his insight with great respect.

"Mark, room 7. When you aren't 'round, he doesn't come out of his room. Kind of a loner type of guy. That's fine—don't bug me none. But, when you are 'round, he's always poppin' out of his room and followin' your every step. I don't like the way he watches you."

Brandy felt sad all over again, that lost feeling crept up behind her eyes and hung heavily. "That's Mark." She pursed her lips. "He was my best friend but he's totally gone…up here." She tapped her temple with a finger. "He started getting confused a couple of months ago and then started getting paranoid and saying he was hearing voices."

Brandy thought of their last caving trip; that made her think of Alexander again and her heart sank into darkness. Pathetic darkness. "Then he became almost non-responsive. He doesn't talk. Doesn't respond, almost like he's concentrating on something deep inside his own head."

"Did they do x-rays? MRIs and stuff?" Nash inquired.

"Yes, every test you could think of. Everything looks normal. He came here and I get to see him when I work. So, I'm not surprised he has an attachment to me. Somewhere he must remember we were best buds." She reached over and held Nash's hand. "It hurts me to see him like this. I don't know what is wrong with him."

Silence stretched between them; they held hands and watched the ducks. Nash absently patted Brandy's hand like a schoolgirl's. "That bothers me even more then. Who knows what is going on in his head and he has some lost memory of being close to you."

Brandy felt guilty that her mind kept sliding to thoughts of Alexander. He had kissed her just as they left the cave. Mark and Susan had been in front of them and heading through the field. He had said he had some traveling to do but would call her soon. He had called. Quick conversations promising to be back soon. He had some unexpected things to take care of. Mostly he'd be out of range. Their conversations sometimes lasted for hours, sometimes were no more than a few words. He was always evasive when she tried to question him. Eventually she gave up and stayed with pleasantries, promises of future embraces, promises of never leaving again. She wondered where he was and if she was just deluding herself. Left to a teenage phone relationship, she began to have doubts. He probably had a wife or a girlfriend somewhere. Wasn't that just her luck? She brought herself to think of Mark. It hurt too much. Perhaps it was more real to her since she faced it every day and that made it harder to think about? She reasoned her guilt to quiet down.

Silence again and then she returned to her conversation

with Nash. "Well, if you want to talk about someone that creeps me out—Billy, room 2. He blatantly flirts with me, if you can call it that. More like…" she struggled for the word and could only think of masher. "It is almost uncomfortable at times. He brings me flowers and constantly asks if I will sit with him at dinner or TV hour."

"That seems innocent enough." Nash was drifting into his own thoughts, his voice distant.

"It's not what he says but how he is. But that isn't everything. I wish that were all. I've had incidents during evening med time. The halls are usually pretty empty as everyone is going to TV or bed. I pass meds out. Before entering any room, I knock and give people time to be decent. Mostly, everyone remembers I'm coming around and waits at their door or outside it. Many times, I have knocked on his door and when I entered found him naked, in the midst of conveniently changing his clothes. Once, he was pleasing himself—obviously wanted to be found."

That caught Nash's attention, he grunted a laugh.

"I'm not embarrassed by it. I am angered by his wanting me to see." She leaned forward and looked at Nash with her cool gaze, "Billy sticks out in my head as something to watch out for. Though, Billy is not a threat—just an annoyance."

"A lot of our residents tend to fit that bill, don't they?"

"Not you, old man."

"Well, then I guess I'll keep me."

"The ducks will keep you."

More silence stretched between them as they both thought about their list of annoying people. Brandy smiled to herself as she catalogued a few random memories.

Leaning over to unlock a wheelchair wheel and getting felt

up by Barstow. "You like that, honey?" he had asked. She had been so shocked she didn't have time to be offended.

The time she sat and listened to two of her patients discuss the local news together—both of them with faulty memories. They kept a running commentary on the possible heritage of the news reporters that to most would have been horribly offensive. But she saw their comments not as something hurtful, more as something out of a time warp.

Her patients. Yes, some annoying, some lovely, but not dangerous. Right?

A commotion with the ducks distracted them both.

The duck, Bill, had been keeping an eye on his little lady from a few feet away. Another male duck, new to the pond had floated up. Bill had turned jealous and launched at the new comer with such a loud noise that nothing could be said until the matter was quieted down. She watched as the new male duck flew to the other side of the small pond and preened his feathers. Nothing hurt but pride.

Just then Margie stuck her head out the back door.

"Sorry to interrupt you all. I'm off in a few minutes. The paperwork is on your desk. Sorry to be so heated earlier."

"No problem, Margie. Have a good evening. I'll see you Monday." Margie disappeared from their sight. Only her voice called back, "Night."

***

"Well old man, I better go do my last rounds and get the next shift rolled in." She leaned over and kissed him on the forehead. "Thanks for the warning. No wild parties tonight, K?"

"Good night, Brandy."

"Night."

Nash didn't follow Brandy in. He would sit and watch his ducks until the sun finally set. Then he would listen to the crickets. Old memories would visit him again and again like comfortable old friends until he was too tired to go on any longer and would wearily go to bed. Tomorrow the day would go just the same as today, the same as they had always gone. Before the month would end, however, he would be horrified to find out just how very right his misgivings about Mark were.

***

Brandy slipped out of the old building and towards her truck. Crickets chirped and chittered. Night's heat melted into her pores. "Silly old man," she thought to herself. But, maybe it wouldn't be a bad idea to be a bit paranoid. Keys in the ignition. Truck rumbled to life. She laughed to herself as a thought crossed her mind. "You aren't paranoid if they are really chasing you. Then you are just being prudent. Or smart." A thump of her thumb on the steering wheel, "Or possibly overreacting to an old man's exaggerations."

She didn't turn the radio on. The drive home was only a mile; her small apartment was just on the other side of the lake with its ducks then up two streets. She could walk home if it weren't for two things. One: she had promised her mom that she would not walk the streets alone. Mom didn't mind her going into caves every weekend, but walk a mile home at night? Out of the question. Two: the heat—ick. You couldn't even get out of the door without wanting to take a shower, let alone walk for a mile in it.

She listened to her thoughts, reviewing what she might have missed in the behavior of her patients.

"Silly old man," she whispered and thumped the steering wheel again.

***

She was still going over the patient's activities in her head when she opened the apartment door. A small, silent, clean studio apartment greeted her. Brandy absently reached down to pet a cat that had died five years earlier. The absence caused her to look up and pause. She missed that cat. Not for the first time she wondered if she should get another. Maybe a dog? Something to bark at intruders. She took her shoes off before stepping off the entryway tile and placed them into the hall closet.

The apartment in front of her was bare and functional: small kitchen table and chairs, futon bed, bookshelf and a battered, second-hand all-in-one exercise machine. Brandy put her small purse and keys on the kitchen table where three chairs seemed to never have been moved and the fourth was not even at the table. It had been moved to a nearby wall and in its place was a much more comfortable chair, an office chair. The kitchen table actually seemed to be used as a desk, where eating might possibly occur.

In the dark, she stripped in the hallway and placed her work whites directly into the washing machine. A soft, cotton robe hung on a hook above the dryer, ready to wrap her in comfort. Whispering noises as it brushed the wall then her bare figure, skin chilled despite the heat outside.

Bare walls, only a few framed pictures broke up the

whiteness. Her mom had hung those. No knickknacks crouched upon the mantle. Only blank silence.

Brandy ate a microwave dinner over the sink. She washed her fork without turning on the kitchen lights.

Her phone buzzed.

Susan texted, "Can't wait till tomorrow! Night."

Brandy smiled and texted back, "Night. :)"

***

The sun was up and it was already hot outside. Brandy looked at the door and was rewarded by the doorbell ringing.

"Hey lady!" Susan, already moving as fast as the sun.

"You've already walked three miles haven't you?" Brandy mumbled, still unintelligible and un-caffeinated.

Holding a latte under Brandy's nose like a bouquet of flowers, Susan hummed, "Mmmm…..the java goddess calls."

"Lovely," Brandy crooned. They hugged. Brandy dropped her head on Susan's shoulder for a moment. "Always my savior."

"If it was me in dire need I know you'd be there for me, sweetie."

"Well, if you ever need to stay up past ten o'clock at night to save the world I'll be right there being perkily annoying for you."

"Yup." Susan nodded her head in agreement.

Brandy took a deep breath then quipped, "OK. I'm set to go." Brandy grabbed a brown bag from the kitchen and tossed it to Susan. "Breakfast."

They turned in unison and walked out of the apartment towards Susan's truck. No baggage between them. No snacks.

No coolers. No clothes, toothbrushes, toothpaste. Other than the brown bag that smelled deliciously of hot egg and cheese bagel sandwiches, there was no visible indication that these two were heading on a three-day weekend excursion.

Brandy would think about it from time to time, the duality of her life. She loved the luxury of just getting up and leaving without the stress of packing, or the inevitable forgetting of something. To make life easier and fit more into her routine, she had everything she needed at her Grandmother's shack, as did Susan. In fact, there was probably more there at the shack than there was at her apartment. Under her grandmother's roof resided more things that told about who Brandy was. At the shack there was just enough clothes and necessities to get by for a few days, not a lot though. A toothbrush, toothpaste and a hairbrush were there. Maybe one or two pony tail holders, not a large selection. Just enough underwear and changes of clothes to span a three-day weekend filled the dresser. One dressy outfit, one set of jeans and three sets of shoes hung in the closet. Tennis shows, flip-flops, and black pumps to go with the one little black dress (for emergencies.)

But for every white wall and non-adorned corner in Brandy's apartment, her shack was just the opposite. There, knick-knacks, pictures, odd mementos, bookshelves, bizarre mismatched furniture and conversation pieces filled the small home.

Many things were her grandparent's memories, and her parent's memories. The "shack," they had called it, a very small two-story A-frame that her grandfather built in the late 50s, had been left to her when her grandmother had died. Now she escaped to it every chance she had. It was where she was herself.

No words were spoken as they languished in the lusciousness of their lattes and cheesy egg sandwiches. Susan pressed play on her ancient IPOD. Nora Jones breathily singing of waking up under a tin roof resonated from the car stereo.

They had a three-hour drive ahead of them before arriving at the shack, in northern Florida. Susan began, "You know, if you just wanted to get away to a swamp, there's one in any direction. Just go thirty minutes. But no, we have to drive three hours every month." Her voice was singsong, robotic like.

With the air of a regal queen Brandy retorted, "Yes, but it's not my swamp."

"Well, your majesty, I want to thank you for sharing your swamp with me all of these years."

"Let them eat cake, and visit my swamp." A quiver appeared in the elderly, now French, regal queen's voice. Brandy waved to the passing cows and fields, much like Mrs. Humms had the night before. Unable to keep the pose long, she giggled a little girl's embarrassed giggle, and melted into her seat.

The trees and flat grassy fields zipped by.

"I think we still have pizza stuff in the pantry and freezer. We'll need to stop in town before we head in. Get some eggs, milk, soy and bread." Brandy spoke to the passenger side window of Susan's Honda Ridgeline. It was quiet and cushy. Brandy wiggled lower into her seat.

"Before you nod off there, queeney…" Susan looked over her Rayban sunglasses.

Brandy cringed internally.

"So, have you heard from him? I'm assuming not, since you haven't spoken a word about him in…" she counted on her manicured fingers, "six months."

"I'm already asleep—can't talk—dreaming of cold, colorful, dark places with fish."

"Cammmon"

"Snouchkk scnooouchk," was the snoring reply.

Susan sulked, changed lanes, passing an overly packed van of tourists returning north from their Disney vacation trip. Luggage filled every available crevice. Plastic shopping bags adorned with Mickey stuck to the windows hinting at where their vacation had been spent.

"Bitch."

"Ignorant Slut."

No answer.

"Maybe he got trapped in a cave again?" Susan wondered.

Brandy turned and stared out the window, resolving to not think about him, resolving to forget. He probably had a wife and she was not going to pine anymore.

When they arrived, the sun was just starting to climb higher in the sky. They stopped in town, if you could call it that, for the few necessities they would need.

"Hey Rick!" Brandy waved to the owner of Big Pop's, which served as a grocery store, hardware store and bait shop. If you were in a pinch, you could get married there too. Rick was the local notary and fire chief.

"Hey there Brandy, Susan," Rick nodded his head towards each of them. He squinted towards one side of his face when he spoke, which always made Brandy think of him as Popeye.

They made idle chitchat while Rick rang up their purchases.

"How's your son doing?" Brandy asked.

That Popeye grin broke out on Rick's face. "He's doin' so

well. Yup. He went and got another research grant and is out in waders right now catchin' his frogs."

"Any luck?"

"Nah, he won't get them until the fall. He's just lookin' to see if there is anthin' else to be seen. I'm tellin' ya, you should go out with him again, give 'im a chance."

Brandy cringed again internally; externally she seemed pleasant, if not slightly intrigued. "I could never take him away from his waders. He needs a wader research gal to go with him, find his mutant frogs and help him dissect 'em."

The curse of being single, everyone wanting to change that fact about you, like it was a disease needing to be cured.

Brandy took the paper bags from Rick and paid her bill. "Thanks, Rick. See you next month."

"Bye ladies. You stay safe. I always worry about you two. So many accidents you hear about."

"Thanks Rick. We will," they called back. As they left, the screen door banged loudly behind them.

"You didn't tell me about him?" Susan asked as they got in the truck.

"I dated him once in seventh grade. We went to a dance together. I don't think it counts."

"Oh." Susan paused thinking, "OK, you didn't tell me about him in seventh grade either." She started the truck.

"Remember the Sadie Hawkins dance?"

"No."

"It was the when you were off on a vacation with your Dad."

"Oh."

"So, I went with someone and didn't tell you about it."

Susan stopped the truck in the center of the parking lot.

"Why?"

"It wasn't a big deal or anything. He was kinda geeky, you know. He was really nice though. Good heart."

"I wouldn't have made fun of you, if that's what you thought."

Brandy leaned her head back on the headrest waiting for Susan to put a few more thoughts together. Susan had let off the brake and the truck started slowly out of the parking lot.

One.

Two.

Three.

The truck stopped again.

"Oh my goodness, Sadie Hawkins dance. That means YOU asked him to the dance, not the other way around."

"Bingo," Brandy thought, then said, "Don't be pissed I didn't tell you. It was just no big deal."

"I can't believe I never heard about that, but I'm not pissed."

"No?"

"Silly bean, why would I be. It just makes sense. You never went with anyone—always told them no when they asked you out to those events. It would make sense that you asked a guy out. Don't look now but you have this little control issue thing."

"I do not."

"Do too."

"If I had a control issue, why would I let you drive, or call you my savior when you bring me lattes in the morning? I should bristle and be awkward, etc. etc. Don't stereotype."

Susan rolled her eyes. "Yeah, and how many years have I known you to finally get past that control slash trust thing of yours?"

"Am I that awful?" Brandy's tone had a touch of vulnerability that usually didn't creep into her voice.

"No. It took until tenth grade, probably, for you to be yourself with me. So, I'm not surprised I didn't hear about Scotty Banks the frog boy."

Silence stretched between them while Brandy categorized her emotions. She accepted the fact that she had a control issue and was comfortable with that. Still, your best friend didn't have to bring it up. But the truth was the truth. She settled back into the seat once again at peace with herself.

"Was that your first kiss?" Susan ventured

"Snnooooorrrrre," was the reply.

***

They headed towards the shack. The winding road took them through the swamp. Small dirt roads led off of the main road here and there. Mostly to higher marshy land where hunters had hung tree stands. It wasn't hunting season, except maybe open season on humans for anything that stung or bit. Most things did.

They hadn't seen any sign of life for ten miles. Just as the road took what seemed to be a U turn, a small gravel driveway appeared off to the right. It disappeared quickly into a thick wooded swamp that seemed to have only enough solid dirt to hold a single road, the rest of the area was soft looking ground, dotted with knees of Cyprus trees poking through the green scum covered water.

They had to stop so Brandy could unlock and open the battered gate. She locked it behind them.

The narrow gravel driveway twisted and turned for another half of a mile until the trees and swamp receded to show a two acre opening of dirt, grass and her grandma's shack. Behind the shack was more swamp and a few trails that headed off into the woods. Down one trail was the place that they would spend most of their time this weekend. The pit. A spring fed pond that had been a place to swim, float, fish and lounge for all of Brandy's childhood. Only in the past five years had Brandy found out that secrets were to be found in that pool of water. These secrets called her back month after month.

"Do you want to go to Devil's Eye this weekend? Or stay here?" Susan asked as she put the groceries away in the small kitchen. From the kitchen window you could see the path that led to their pond. Though Susan had no ownership to it, whatsoever, she still thought of it as partly hers. She had found the cave there and showed it to Brandy.

"I guess we could. We could go to Devil's Eye, take the scooters and go to the Junction Room and get a good long trip out of it."

Devil's Eye was a large underwater cave system, open to the public. The Junction Room could be found about a mile from the entrance, a long haul underwater in tight twisty passageways. Underwater scooters were used to help divers get there faster and save that ever so precious air mixture in their tanks. The Junction Room was a beautiful room that begged for divers to pause and look. But no one really could, that ticking clock always pushing them ahead, with an eye on their cylinder pressure. How much gas was there left in the tank? All too often cave divers would arrive at the mystery filled room only to hurry on through one of its many passageways, giving it the name of Junction Room. One room that offered so many choices. So many passageways branched off from the room. Brandy and Susan were determined to do each and every one. There were many parts of the system that they had not explored yet.

"Well, let's do our watery pit today and do Junction Room tomorrow? Sunday is a whatever day?"

Brandy smiled to herself. Scheduled even when I'm relaxing. Goal driven. That whatever day will end up having goals and deadlines too, she thought. "Sounds like a plan."

***

In just two hours the two ladies were hiking down the wooded path, so clearly seen from the kitchen window, towards their spring. Brandy had rigged a small wagon to carry their tanks and gear to the spring's edge. It even had a small compartment that held her coffee thermos and two cups. When she came out of the water the first thing she wanted was something warm.

The pond was technically called a sink. Brandy's grandmother had never called it that, not knowing that it was a sink. It was merely the pond—and would always be called that. To the average observer, it was just a small pond that didn't even look big enough to put a boat into. The edges of the pond were scummed up with algae, but the center always stayed clear. A small dock with steps led down to the edge of the pond.

Brandy parked the wagon at the dock's edge and they silently went through their rituals of preparing to dive. Finishing dressing, zipping up dry suits. Changing flip-flops for booties. Checking hoses and connections on their tanks, placing those checked tanks on their backs, checking their packs on their hips. All rituals were done silently while mental checklists reeled in their heads. It seemed an unspoken rule that no one should speak during the suiting up. Both were checking and double-checking their gear. They were even subconsciously checking each other's progress of checking their gear. Always making sure everything was working; any mistake made now would cost them their life down in the cold water.

Brandy looked to Susan who was just finishing her final checks. Masks on foreheads and regulators hanging in front of their necks, they nodded to each other.

"3600?" Brandy pointed to Susan's air pressure gauge, indicating the psi number.

"3600," Susan nodded.

"Me too." They both had identical sized tanks so no further math was needed to make sure that they each had the same amount of air. Not a coincidence, a choice. Susan and Brandy had caved together so long they had worked out any stressors and had their dives down to a science. "OK. Turn back at 2400?"

Susan nodded her head again. "Wanna try it today?"

Brandy looked at the small pond and bit her bottom lip. "Yeah, I'm game. Let's see where it goes."

The it in question was a small lead at the bottom of the cave that had gone unnoticed for many years. It was behind a larger rock and covered in mounds of silt and sand. Brandy thought for a moment just how small it was. If it narrowed too much once they got in there—she shook her head. Swimming backwards out of a tight squeeze was not something she wanted to think about. Though Brandy had found it a year ago, they had not explored it to its fullest. Susan had gone part way through, but Brandy had not followed her. Today she would try to follow.

They walked down the dock and stood above the water, placing their masks over their faces and mouthpieces in their mouths. Susan first, then Brandy, raised one leg and stepped off into the pond; each one sank in turn into the cold blue water.

Cool silence. Sounds of their exhales floating away from them towards the surface. Enveloping stillness. Coolness. Weightlessness. Peace.

Brandy closed her eyes to feel all around her—the peaceful emptiness. She floated for a moment, hearing, feeling her breaths. Feeling her heart beat. Susan waited patiently. She herself enjoyed the peace under the surface, but realized that her best friend not only enjoyed it, she lived for it. She watched as Brandy floated, relaxed and seemed to unfold in the water. Brandy's eyes opened and met Susan's. They both smiled around their mouthpieces. Bubbles escaped happily and rushed to the surface.

Susan led the dive and Brandy followed. They dove towards the bottom in unison. Brandy looked at the depth gauge dangling from her hip: thirty feet. She turned to watch her exhales bubble to the surface. Breathing would use up twice the amount of air at this depth. They kept moving towards the bottom, somewhat more hastily. The deeper they went the more air they would use. After ninety feet they would be using four times the amount of air than what was needed on the surface.

They reached the bottom, still in unison. Here they floated for a moment, their buoyancy on point so that they floated level and needed to expel the least amount of energy to progress forward.

At the bottom there were many passages that led off in different directions much like the Junction room at Devil's Eye, but on a smaller scale. Guidelines wrapped around a large rock at the center and led off in different directions towards each passage Brandy and Susan had explored. Off of one particular passage that was very wide and curved left, was a large room they called The Cathedral. The room itself was one hundred feet wide and had a sloped ceiling that angled upwards. The ceiling formed an arch, and the breakdown that had fallen from the ceiling, many eons ago, littered the floor. One extremely large piece, however, stood 80 feet high in the very back of the room. The arched ceiling domed around its large presence. The room struck a diver with a sense of awe and stillness.

It was one of Brandy's favorite rooms. She and Susan often came down here. Truth be told, Brandy came by herself sometimes, breaking the cardinal rule about never caving or diving or cave diving alone. She dared not think of the last time she had gone into a cave alone and came out with a would-be lover, who probably had five kids. She brushed the thought away.

Their dive so far only reaching 100 feet. To dive any deeper, past 130 feet, was considered dangerous diving. At those depths, gas mixture becomes a very tricky equation. Too much nitrogen in the system or too much oxygen could lead a diver to become confused. Down deep where there is not very much room for error, confusion quickly leads to death. Even at a hundred feet, they were pushing their luck.

Brandy believed that her little pond did not go beyond the

"safe" depth of 130 feet. She would find, eventually, that any depth was not safe depending on who you dived with.

Brandy reached for the guidelines wrapped about the rock. She clipped a small, purple plastic marker onto the guideline that led towards the Cathedral Room. Its triangular shape pointed towards the exit. Susan moved close to the line behind Brandy and they began to swim. Though visibility was good, it would be too easy to lose the line and become disoriented, wasting precious air.

They went past the path that led to the Cathedral Room and down to an area at the bottom of the pit that was filled with breakdown rocks which had long ago parted ways from the ceiling and now lay littering the silt floor. Some were the size of TVs, some the size of coffins. Behind a particularly large boulder, though not as large as the boulder in The Cathedral, they found the hole they were looking for.

Susan turned to look at Brandy and moved her handheld light in a circle, meaning OK. Brandy gave the OK sign back with her light. They both glanced at their gauges. Susan pulled a reel of white line from her belt and tied it into the existing yellow main line. The bright white of the new line shone brilliantly in the silted water against the dimmer, older gold line. Brandy placed another purple triangle marker that pointed away from the new passage and towards the exit. She marked it with a waterproof maker, "SB5." This was the fifth passage they had explored, "Susan, Brandy, 5." They didn't know where this lead went. It looked tight—very tight. Sometimes tight passages opened up. Sometimes they opened up into large rooms. Sometimes they continually narrowed until a fish couldn't even get through.

The last time they had dived, Susan had wiggled into the

tight space and went about fifty feet back. There she found that the tunnel widened enough that she could pull her head up into a small hole and almost be in a sitting position if she rolled on her back and kept her legs in the tunnel she had just swum through. With enough wiggling and moving of her legs she could curl up into a tight egg, a fetal position, roll around and place her legs in the tunnel that had been ahead of her, scoot in, roll back over on her belly and swim back the way she came. The tanks and hoses that she held in her hands quadrupled the difficulty of the gymnastics. The tunnel was much too tight to accommodate the swimmer with the tanks on her side or back. They had to be pushed carefully in front of the diver, slowing down the progress.

If nothing else they could make it 50 feet. This much she knew. But was there another turn around place past that? If not, they would just wiggle butt backwards. Not a favorite sport of hers but very possible. Now, the issue was to get Brandy into the tube. She had not been in yet. First up—the entrance.

Susan took her tanks off and carefully placed them inside the tube. She put the reel of line inside the tube, careful to not tangle the line with her hoses. She could only fit in with one arm in front of her and one arm behind, minimizing the width that her shoulders would take. Even with that space saving technique she still had to get past the boulder that jutted up right into the center of the entrance. She placed the highest point of the offending boulder at her belly and curled around it until she was wedged. The widest part of her body was her hips, even wider then her ribcage. She just had to get it in there. Fat at this point didn't matter. Fat would smoosh and shift. Bone would not; it would only break. She poured herself as much into the tunnel as she could, willing herself to be smaller, to contract, to get past the sticking point. She only needed to offset her hips just a fraction of an inch and the pressure was released; she was through. She could not turn back to watch Brandy come through. She went forward to the tight turn around spot, which seemed tighter today, and pulled the guideline behind her.

The line settled on the ground, unnatural white against brown rock. Susan tied the line off to a small rock jutting from the side of the tube and put the reel on the floor. She did her small gymnastics: roll, curl, unfold, roll, then looked back towards the way she just came. She could see Brandy's light. She couldn't tell if Brandy was through yet or not. By the way the light faced the side of the tunnel, Susan guessed that Brandy wasn't through yet.

***

Brandy had watched Susan go through the tunnel. It was hard to see. As Susan had wiggled through, silt and debris had been kicked up. She waited for a few moments after her pal had stopped resembling Winnie the Pooh with flippers. She wanted things to settle down a bit more so she could see where things were before pouring herself through. Brandy followed the same positioning that Susan had. She tried to place the high point of the boulder in her belly so that she could bend around it. However when she poured herself into the tightest spot she found that her rib cage stuck firmly. Unlike Susan's womanly proportions, Brandy's largest bone structure was her rib cage. With the tanks, one arm and its shoulder ahead of her, one arm, shoulder and her legs behind her, and her chest stuck firmly on a rock, Brandy tried to relax. She turned slightly one way then the other to see if anything would give. She tried leaning forward, placing her forehead near the side of the tunnel, hoping to get her rib cage to concave just enough. Her spine yelled from the abuse on the opposite side of the tunnel.

"Well, that's a fucker," Brandy thought to herself.

By this time, Susan had swum back through the tunnel and was facing Brandy, giving moral support. She tried not to get too close, to allow room for Brandy to come through. Brandy was trying hard to bend her forward arm back to touch her rib cage and to feel for anything that might move. The other arm was behind her trying to do the same. She looked at Susan. The tilt of her head said everything. Susan pointed to Brandy then held up one hand, the thumb clenched tightly between her first two fingers: "You stuck?"

Brandy raised one finger in reply: "F.U."

Susan mimed pushing Brandy, then reached out and grabbed her hand and gave it a squeeze and a tug.

Brandy momentarily thought about trying again. She could squeeze through if she really tried. She could gain maybe another ½ inch if she let out all of her air, and pushed through. She knew she could do it. She could fit through anything Susan could, just with a little more effort on her part. She motioned for Susan to back swim and give her some room. She reached up with her free hand and grabbed ahold of a small outcropping of rock in the tunnel. She took a good breath, relaxed, let out every bit of her air and concentrated on squeezing her rib cage as much as she possibly could. At the same moment she pulled with the one hand, pushed with the other and kicked as much as she could. She could feel herself going through; she had to get through or she would be unable to take a breath. Now was not the time for panicking. Just then, her hand slipped off of the rock and her elbow crashed into her tanks. Although things move slowly in water, the force of the impact broke a seal on one of the two regulators. The gas inside the tanks began escaping as fast as it could. Brandy nearly panicked as she saw the rush of bubbles coming from her tank. All of that air and she was stuck in a place that she could not even take a breath. In a split second she calculated how long it would take for her air to escape if she did not get to the valve and shut it off. She tried to take a breath, but doing so would pin her more in the position she was in. Panic began to take hold and her body flooded with one thought, "I will die here and Susan will be stuck in the tunnel because of me. Could she push me out of the way or would she die too?"

It wasn't the thought of her own cold death that got her moving, it was the thought of Susan, in a panic, trying to move Brandy's body out of its pinned position. She could see Susan trying to get around each of the extra tanks and possibly being unable to and….

Seeing in her mind's eyes Susan's wide terror filled eyes, Brandy instantly put all of the right priorities in place. She pushed with all of her might backwards so that her chest became unpinned. Then she was able to take the breath that she so needed and reached forward, pulling the tanks towards her and turned the valve so that the rush of bubbles would stop.

She floated against the roof of the tunnel, still curled around the boulder and waited for the adrenalin to rush through, shaking everything in its path.

Susan's hand reached through and patted Brandy on the head. Brandy pushed her arm back through and gave the OK signal. They held hands for a moment, unable to see much of each other. The sound of their expelled gas floating to the tunnel and flowing along its surface back behind Susan was drowned out by their beating hearts.

***

Later on the surface they sat on the dock, feet dangling in the water.

"Santa-Monica-Beach, that's not a good way to start out the weekend," Susan whistled.

They talked about what happened, if maybe they should leave that passage alone.

Just like a horse rider getting back on the horse, Brandy perked up. "Devil's Eye tomorrow then? I've got another tank in the garage. It's a little bigger than yours—we'll have to do some math to see when our turnaround point is."

"I've been wanting a diving computer. They are kinda neat," Susan said.

"Expensive gadget that shouldn't cost that much."

"Supply and demand. Not many of us crazy enough to do this and need one."

"Crazy all right."

"Nuts."

Brandy looked at her tank. The regulator was busted but could be repaired. "One tank still full, we could at least just go back in this little pit here and lounge around, look at the little fishy. Can't go too deep to get in trouble."

Susan looked at her friend who could have so easily seen death just minutes before. "Confident," she thought, "and just plain stubborn."

As if Brandy could read her friend's thoughts she beamed to Susan and said one of her grandmother's favorite sayings, "You can kill me, but you can't eat me."

***

"Why doesn't the pizza guy deliver here, Brandy?"

"Used ta" Brandy, who tried to hide her central Florida twang, easily slipped into the accent of her youth.

"What did you do? Piss him off with your girlish charms?"

"'Gater got 'im. That pepperoni will drive 'em wild." She picked a few pepperonis off the top of the lonely last piece. It was nearly naked.

"Was that before or after the mosquitoes ate him alive?"

"Prob'bly after. They were just tenderizin' him for old Fred, don't ya see. He's gettin' a bit old."

Susan broke character first. "Have you really seen that gator or are you just fooling?"

"Oh yeah. You don't want to go off that way in the swamp." Brandy motioned towards the north of the shack. "They've been dumping alligators and snakes and everything that was getting in the way in suburbia out here. It's like something out of a horror film. Daddy tried to go boating up that way one day, 'bout ten years ago—just to see. Said the gators he saw out there made his legs turn to water. He turned back and no one else goes out there." She poked at the naked piece of pizza and settled for a bite of the crust. "The bigger animals don't come this way, except for Fred. Guess he likes being alone. He stays out here." Brandy pointed to the south of the house. They were facing west—behind the house. To the east was the driveway out.

"You don't feed him or anything do you?"

"Golly no! Don't want him to confuse the two topics—me and food."

"Surprised we don't see more alligators when we are diving in the pits. Did you see any yesterday at Devil's Eye?"

"Only some littler ones further out along the river."

"I never see any big ones. What happens when the little ones grow up?"

Brandy pointed back to the north of the shack. "Out here—or Gatorland, unless they are killed. They eat good."

Susan wrinkled her perfect nose and made a face.

They finished picking at their non-delivery pizza and languished on the back screened in porch. A bottle of wine sat between them. The night crickets sung in the thick air. Frogs croaked. Friends talked.

Brandy sunk into her chair dreading going back to work, back to civilization where there were real schedules and goals and things that had to be done. At least out here it was her schedule, her goals and if she wanted to change them she could and would. If she decided to throw the whole day's plan right out the window just so she could watch a thunderstorm come through, no problem. But there, back there—that was the real world. She didn't want to go back. Especially now that she had to face Mark every day. The thought of not wanting to see him flushed her full of guilt. She pushed the thoughts aside, not wanting to ruin a perfect evening. She tried to replace the guilt with the excitement of Alexander returning soon. She frowned instead. Not only five kids, but three ex-wives. She was sure of it.

Susan came out of the kitchen door with bowls of ice cream and interrupted the thought.

"Mmmm, lovely," Brandy crooned.

The evening was perfect and peaceful. Unknown to them, the next time they would be at the shack it would not be so perfect and not so peaceful. In fact it will be the most terror filled day of their lives.

12 I AM NOW.
SNAKES, INTESTINES. STAND OFF.

"I still have time." Alexander smiled to himself. He reached out, willing himself to not find Yindi. Hoping Yindi was still in his transformation stage. Where would he take hold? Surely that toad had not held the energy sucking bastard long.

The sleeping form in his arms stirred and threatened to wake. Alexander drew what he needed from the body without even heeding it. Touched the wound, healed it, continued to stoop there momentarily lost in thought. The body shifted slightly again and murmured. Alexander did not hear, he was too busy trying to find Yindi; knowing that once Yindi took a new host, he would need to act fast to protect Brandy. A gasp from the linear as he awoke and tried to climb out of the buzzing numbness of sleep—electric cobwebs. Alexander shifted out of sync with time and was out of sight. The linear jumped in his sleep, startled, wrote it off as a bad dream, rolled over and went back to sleep.

In his cold, detached time, Alexander went over the

preparations he had made. How could he prepare for an attack that would hit in an unknown spot? That wasn't true. He knew who the attack would be on: Brandy. So he had to only prepare in places that she went. The attack would more than likely be in one of these places. Luckily, she was extremely predictable so far. Alexander paused to add, and unlucky. He slipped into main time. The dust settling around him in main time echoed loudly in his ears as he considered the choices. He could wait until the attack came then go back and change it as he did with the shooting. She could be attacked in the day; he could not go back in time and fix that. The sun, the weight of all of that light through time would be agonizing. Could he survive it? He had never tried. He was patient and had all of time—what were forty or sixty years to him? He would not fear an attack in the day until it came to that. Alexander doubted Yindi would not do it; it would ruin the fun of tormenting him.

The old shed, where Alexander stood and pondered his dilemma, felt abandoned. From the lack of ghost images, it had been abandoned for more than a few years. Alexander took his shoes off to better feel the dirt earth. He drew energy from it. It tickled at his toes. The dirt had been taken from his cave and placed here, where this shed would be built. It had taken considerable effort and care to make sure that he took from a far unused portion of the cave, so as not to open areas that would allow light in and ruin a safe haven for himself for the rest of eternity. He had done it himself, not wanting to involve Sherpas or bring attention to his cave and thus change the current running timeline. Painstakingly pulling load after load of dirt away from the cave, making mounds, shifting into time to get a vehicle to pull the moss covered mounds out of the forest and to the undeveloped areas around where Brandy's routines took her. He still had five more mounds to distribute. His body ached from the work that had taken months in main time to complete.

Yet, he was thankful for his earth at the moment, it fed him as he stood in this forgotten shed. From his vantage point, he could look through the ghost images of time to see her in main time, rocking on a back porch. An old man sat next to her. Ghost images from the past showed that they had sat here many, many times. Further in the past, Alexander recognized the old man from the last ghost image that had visited this shed. A solemn look had been on his face as he had locked it and walked away. The shed now only had spiders and other crawling animals as inhabitants. This place would be a safe haven for him in a pinch. He couldn't sleep here, but he could draw energy from here. He considered digging a place to rest in a sunless place, hating momentarily the horrid weakness of uncontrollable time shifting as he slept. In his time, he could stay awake for months, even in a place that would have sun in main time, the trick was to feed regularly and pull energy from his earth. He hadn't fed regularly in centuries, since he had stayed in his cave mooning over the visage of Brandy at the edge of the pit and let the universe nearly destroy it and himself. Now he was regaining his strength and feeding again. But still mooning over her visage.

"Fool," he thought to himself, but did not move from his place and looked again to make sure that she was safe. Brandy's ghostly image stared out across the water unaware.

Alexander moved on, cold and silence around him as he went back towards his cave to move the last of the mounds out to Brandy's weekend shack. He could speed up the process and enlist help, hire teams in any time period but he didn't want to affect the timelines. Forever doomed to move things alone. Not for the first time he thought of how moving through time was a punishment.

He reached again for Yindi, did not find him. The energy he perceived felt like gloomy clouds growing, an approaching storm. It weighed heavy in his joints and dark upon his skin. Yindi would emerge soon and all hell was going to break loose.

***

He stares at the bowl of Jell-O in front of him. How did that get there? Mark looks up at the TV. Wheel of Fortune is on. The spinning wheel is mesmerizing. Trying to concentrate makes sweat break out on his forehead. Where is he?

Buzzing in the back of his head, like an argument he cannot hear but feels. Wooly, sweaty. Hair stands up on the back of his neck. Dangerous.

Sweat beads and trickles. Mark chews at his bottom lip. Where is the danger? How to escape? Perhaps someone can help. He looks around him. His neck turns like it is on ball bearings, not affecting any other part of his body, disjointed, disconnected. Old people all around him. Drool spilling from their bottom lips, some humming to themselves; that one definitely is sitting in a pile of poo, the brown stain creeping up the back of his orange polyester pants.

The poo man turns to Mark and offers a wide, wet grin. "U," he says and points to the screen.

Mark is standing now. Doesn't remember standing. Gurgling in front of him. Looks down. Hands around the poo man's neck. Gasping, he steps back, releasing his hold. The old man's orange pants are reeking now. Mark backs up another step. The old man's grin has turned down into a slow motion jeer. "Uayaaaah," he grunts then returns to watching the TV. Someone on the screen is trying to fill in the blanks for "Let Sleeping Dogs Lie." No U to be seen.

Mark's vision swims, it was red, physically red while he had his hands around the poo man's neck. It caused his heart to race, excitement. A stroke? Mark shakes his head to clear it. Now the world is normal again. Mark tries to speak, cannot. Realizes he hasn't been able to in a while. Crazy?

Where is…Brandy.

He remembers. She's here. Everyday, standing by him and smiling. She wears white, not her normal dirty, used caving clothes. She is sad and looks at him with pity. He hates that look. The buzzing gets louder and now he can hear it in his ears, an incessant buzzing like a swarm of locusts. Looking around, no one else seems to hear it. Mark stumbles to the nurses station where Margie is picking up her purse and leaving.

A need builds in him, a desire to move. Mark's vision swims, colors that shouldn't be there become visible. Greens, yellows, oranges, reds—some colors felt but not actually seen. How can you feel a color? But it's there—the red. He longs after it, skin goose fleshed, an incantation screaming in his ears now.

The thing.

The thing is here.

Mark looks again at the orange pants man to see if the voice is coming from him. The man is obliviously drooling at the TV.

Now.

Now.

NOW!

Panic floods Mark's senses with clear understanding. Brandy. Somehow she is the thing. Whatever that is. More importantly, she is in trouble. He has to warn her.

Margie pauses at the nurses station and looks at Mark. "Good night, Mark." She turns and walks towards the front door.

Trying to run towards Margie. Feet slow to respond, held in place, like not his own anymore. Mark stumbles, hands outstretched. Sweat pours down his pale, drawn face. Pupils dilate. Gaping mouth trying to scream, yell, plead.

"Br.......aaaaaaaannnnn, Braaaannnnnnn, ghhhhhhhh, aaaaaannnnn." A whisper. He holds his hands to his face to hopefully help his mouth make the right shapes. The effect is comical. He is alone in the hallway with no one to see.

Breathing fast, pulse racing, sweat pouring, unable to move. Panic. Vision smeared with yellows and reds. Pulsing with his racing heart.

Now.

Now.

Mark tries to run one more time.

Now.

He knows where the danger is.

Now.

Inside. He has to warn Bran…

I am…now.

***

"Have a good three day weekend, did ya?" Nash rocked and sipped his bear. The back porch was empty except for Brandy,

Nash and buzzing mosquitoes.

"Yup. It was good." Brandy added nothing else. The absence of details caused Nash to raise an eyebrow, but he did not comment further. Brandy patted Nash's arm and added, "I need to go in and close out the shift."

"Yup." Nash nodded in agreement. Crickets in the distant serenaded their approval.

***

The floor was quiet. From the TV room, murmurs of a live studio audience cheering answers to a half watched game show haunted the air. Patients not present in the TV room were tucked away in their rooms preparing for bed. Brandy gave a wave to the night nurse who was busying herself with paperwork. The nurse gave a nod of response. Brandy looked forward to getting home and taking a hot bath, getting the stink of bleach and alcohol off her skin.

The door to Billy's room stood halfway open. Brandy barely gave it a thought until a strange moan came from inside. She paused. Was that pain or something she should ignore? She stood still, listening for movement inside. Brandy has been caught by this trick more than once. Nash's conversation from Friday still lingered in her ear. He had warned about Mark being dangerous; she had countered with stories of Billy and his annoying habits.

With these thoughts and warnings running through her head, she stood at the door and knocked. "Billy—are you OK?"

No response from inside.

"Billy, I'm not coming in there so just put your pants back

on and come out here."

Still nothing.

She was just about to turn around when she heard a moan from the bathroom.

"…need help…"

She thought that maybe he had fallen or was having a heart attack. Whatever the reason, she could hear a small voice requesting help. Against her initial reaction and better judgment, she entered the room.

She hesitated, thinking that she should call someone. She poked her head out into the hallway looking for Margie. Of course, Margie had already left. She could call back to the night nurse. A glance told her the nurse was no longer at the station. No one was around.

She went into the dark room. Inside she looked fervently at the dark bedroom—no Billy. She scanned the bed, which was made. She scanned the room, a small table and chairs, a reading chair. All empty.

She heard a noise in the bathroom and walked towards the door. The bathroom was a tight space, barely enough room for one person to exist. She walked in and paused. The shower was running, steam filled the air, mist fogged the mirror. The shower stall bottom was square, white, dingy plastic. It had no door or lip; older patients could easily step into it. The old, tan shower curtain hung just inside the edge of the shower bottom. Water dripped from it.

She rattled the curtain and lifted it up to peek for feet. "Billy, I need to hear you tell me that you are OK."

Billy wasn't in the shower. The bathroom door closed behind Brandy, cutting off any exit. From his cramped hiding place behind the door, Billy advanced towards her, pushing her into the shower. He was nude, his intent obvious. She back peddled to put distance between them. The shower curtain rustled as she passed it. Hot water plastered her hair to her neck. Her back pressed to the corner of the shower stall.

Billy advanced into the shower, the curtain ripped from its hangers as he moved it aside. He stood half in and half out of the shower. Brandy, cool under fire, knew she could not overpower Billy. She also knew that he was a push over and would easily back down.

"William." She'd bet he was called William when he got in trouble. She continued, "William Anthony Drummen. Are you misbehaving again? We'll have to take away your dessert privileges."

With that, he stopped and looked ashamed. He sunk into himself, hot water steaming the air between them.

"I'm sorry…I didn't mean to. I mean. I wouldn't want to do anything…I thought you might want…might be interested." He gained just a little bit of strength and moved towards her again, stepping fully into the shower, groping.

She reached forward, grabbed the shower handle and flipped it to pure cold water. The change in temperature startled him. She jumped out of the shower and hit the call button on the wall; the sound was sure to bring the night nurse.

She turned around and reprimanded Billy again, "Now William, I don't want to see this behavior again. You'll have to behave yourself or you will be kicked out of the Manor and sent to a larger mental hospital. You do like your home here, don't you?"

"Yes, Ma'am."

"Then I need you to stop these antics. Please clean yourself up."

Brandy held her hands on her hips. Her uniform plastered to her body.

The night nurse came in at that moment. "Is this guy giving you problems, Miss Bayents?"

"I think he just needs some assistance getting dressed." Brandy stood up, seemingly un-phased that her pressed white uniform was dripping wet.

"Oh, he'll get assistance, honey." The nurse, a stout woman whose angular, German face lit up in a frighteningly way, looked at Billy sharply. "I'll assist his ass into a posey." She eyed him up and down sharply, "Sedated too." She smiled.

Brandy turned the water off and stepped away from the night nurse not commenting on the vigor with which the nurse planned Billy's evening. "Good then."

Brandy turned, heading back to the nurses station to fill out an incident report, trailing a path of water behind her.

**

It hit him like a thunderclap of pain that struck somewhere between the back of his eyeballs and where his stomach had lurched into his throat. Alexander stumbled and fell to one knee. The shovel in his hands dropped to the cave floor. The time had arrived; Yindi had arrived. Brandy was no longer safe. He let out a pent up breath he didn't even know he had held. Alexander placed the shovel against the wall, leaned against a mound of crates all filled with dirt, ready and waiting. For not the first time he considered why he was doing this at all. Why care about a human so intently? She would die in a blink anyway. He was playing into Yindi's mischievous hands by caring for this mortal. The thought of turning his back on

Brandy, no matter how short her life span, filled him with shame that caused his cold heart to sink to his toes. He had done that once before. Turned his back, tried to pretend that he did not care. If only he could harden his heart, remove his weak emotions and truly not be phased. A rueful smile touched his lips as he slipped out of sync with main time and moved towards Brandy. "Always a fool," he whispered and was gone.

***

Nash leaned on the nurses station counter. Brandy was finishing up her report, a towel wrapped around her shoulders, hair still dripping wet. She pulled the towel tighter trying to will away the shivers that shook her body.

Quietly, Nash ventured, "I just heard. You OK?"

Brandy closed the folder with a thump. "Yeah. All in a day's work."

"You're shaking; want to go outside and enjoy some hot humidity? It should cure you of those chills." Nash's gnarled hand opened the door.

"That feels much better." Brandy sank into her normal rocking chair. She could feel the dampness on her clothes begin to steam in the oppressive humidity. "I think I'll turn into a dim sum dumpling now. Nicely steamed."

"Boy, I could sure go for some Szechuan right about now." Nash patted his thin belly.

Silence.

Nash's voice graveled, "Guess you told me, huh? Billy is more trouble than Mark."

"Oh, it's nothing." Brandy shrugged it off and laid her head back on the rocker. She closed her eyes and took in a deep breath. "Men make advances all the time on me, they just pop out of the woodwork. You get used to it. " She opened her eyes and smiled at Nash.

"Don't belittle the event," Nash warned. "You did very well in there. That could have been a bad situation."

"It's over. I don't want to dwell on it." She closed her eyes again. The subject closed.

They heard a terrible crashing commotion from inside the building. Brandy was half out of her chair in a sprint towards the door when the night nurse came running out. Her pressed white shirt was dark with large wet stains. Brandy stared at the dark, red splotches for a moment before looking for a sign of injury on the nurse.

"Not my blood." the night nurse managed between gasps for air. "Billy." Another gasp. "You gotta get in here. Oh, Jesus wept, Billy."

The door closed behind them. Nash could see the large red handprint the nurse had left on the glass when she opened the door. It dripped in the moisture collected there.

Her eyes at once registered the unnaturalness of Billy's position; her body froze in the doorway. Next to Brandy the night nurse sat, stunned, in a chair outside Billy's room. She did not look at Brandy, nor the doorway, nor the horror within the room.

"Did you call the police, Jen?" Brandy said robotically to the nurse.

"…yeah…" Jen whispered through a mouth that gaped open in astonishment.

"Oh, Jesus in heaven." Nash peered in over Brandy's shoulder. The war veteran who served two tours of duty as an engineer in the Korean War stepped back from the doorway.

"I'll keep everyone in their rooms." He wandered down the hallway telling Bob and Mrs. Humms and other patients that they needed to wait in their rooms for a bit. Give the emergency crews room to work. Everyone responded to that. They did not want to be in the way if someone was having a heart attack or stroke.

Brandy could tell from where she stood that the man inside of the room was not living. The smell that rolled through the air was that of blood and excrement. She did not want to enter the room but could not keep herself from doing just that.

"Jen, did you go in there?"

"Yeah, I went to check for a pulse. Almost tripped, tried not to step in the stuff on the floor. Then ran and got you." Jen kept her eyes away from the door and would not turn her head, to keep from possibly seeing the specter again.

"You didn't posy him?" Brandy asked more questions to stall going in.

"No. That would have been cruel. I did sedate him." Jen grunted. "Maybe it helped ease the…the…" She raised a hand to her mouth and looked as if she might vomit.

Brandy stepped into the room gingerly. Billy sat in his reading chair. The only light in the room, his reading lamp, cast a dim yellow glow eerily on Billy's slack, pasty face; long shadows fell from his nose and eyebrows. Brandy couldn't see his eyes. They were hidden in shadow. It was the unnaturally large gaping mouth, the arms that went in the wrong directions that told her he was dead. Billy's arms were bent at the elbows behind his head, as if he had been leaning back, arms behind his head contemplating something. She looked closer to see why his arms seemed wrong and noticed that the elbows were too close and on the wrong sides of his head. It looked as if someone had grabbed his elbows and pulled them together like a pair of scissors. But pulled them too hard and they had crossed, like a cheap pair of scissors might if you yank the handle too tightly together. Billy had a robe on; it was loosely tied at the waist. Brandy followed the contour of the arms, apparently ripped from their sockets, but could not confirm her suspicions by seeing the flesh around the shoulders; it was covered by the robe. Her eyes kept returning to the gaping mouth. It gaped open in a scream. Her eyes kept returning to it because it wasn't quite right either. Something about it made her think of a comic book. One of those horror comic books that she had seen as a kid where a skeleton only half covered in flesh opened its mouth to scream and roaches came out of it. His mouth opened unnaturally wide. It had no muscles and barely any skin to hold it in its normal range of motion. That's when she realized that his jaw was unhinged as well. The killer must have reached in and pulled his mouth down, springing the jaw from its hinges. She could see something white in his mouth. She looked down at the waist of Billy's robe, realizing that it was loose around him because it wasn't tied at all. The belt from his robe was in his mouth.

"Won't hear the scream," she whispered to herself.

At Brandy's side, Jen looked more convinced that she would throw up.

Brandy had only looked at the top half of Billy. She could hear the sirens approaching, turning up from the main road.

"He won't need those sirens," she thought as she looked at where the stench was coming from. After having his arms ripped from their sockets, he couldn't fight back. He couldn't be heard as he screamed. He could have only watched as someone disemboweled him. His innards lay about his lap and around him on the floor. The muck and gore barely illuminated by the reading lamp. Portions of his intestines were clenched between his toes. They must have fallen there during the struggle. Brandy thought. She looked at the large puddles of blood on the floor.

"He must be covered in blood," she whispered.

The sirens were getting closer. Only ten seconds had passed. Fifteen more and they would be here.

She looked at the floor and saw a half moon of blood every few feet. The bloody footprints crossed the room and went in to the bathroom. The same bathroom Billy had accosted her in not even an hour ago, but a century ago. The light was not on.

The sirens were closer now. "Must be five of them." She counted unconsciously.

She took a step in and looked at the bathroom door, noted the door swayed and a shadow fell across the door knob from the inside, inky dark shadow in a dark room.

Brandy tapped Jen on the shoulder and pointed to the bathroom. Jen's eyes flew wide. "Shhhh," Brandy mouthed. She was rooted to the floor, unable to move as the door swung open. She could barely make out a man's outline. He swayed back and forth, shifting his weight from one foot to the other, quickly. He rubbed his hands on his arms as if he was cold. Brandy was reminded of the skinny guy in the movie The Sixth Sense, who stood in the bathroom accusing Bruce Willis of failing him, just before he shot himself. Her mind thought, most absurdly, "The camera should be panning from right to left now as he talks to me. He should go out of frame just as he raises the gun." She began to shake.

"Have you seen your lover lately?" Mark whispered. His voice sounded unholy and flat. "I bet he'll be here soon."

Words failed Brandy. She could only stare. Inside her skull, Brandy yelled at herself to speak, talk, scream, run, lock the door, get out of there. She was unable to do anything.

The sirens stopped outside the door.

"I'm going to have fun with you," Mark purred. He came forward one step towards Brandy.

A message of disbelief reached her body "that can't be Mark" and she turned on the bedroom light. It bathed the scene in a dead blue glow. Mark did not step any closer. She tried not to look at Billy, not wanting to see. Looking at Mark was no better. She could see the gore dripping from him, arms to elbows, spattering his shirt and face, slicking his hair down, the gore from Billy's body.

Police doors opened and closed. She could hear distant talking. Nash's voice. "In here. This way."

"What have you done?" Brandy's voice returned. Her voice sounded disbelieving, a frightened lost child.

Mark's lips stretched into a wicked grin.

Then the screaming began.

***

The policemen looked everywhere at once as they rushed through the small entryway. They passed the nurses station, the door still partly open, charts scattered on the desktop. Nash led them towards where Brandy stood frozen in a doorway, her body stiff and shivering. Jen turned to face Brandy and erupted into a fit of screaming then crumpled to the floor.

The older police officer, with cold, blue eyes, turned to the younger thirty something officer. He nodded. The officers drew their guns and motioned for Nash to stay back.

Brandy turned her head, almost imperceptibly, and met the policeman's eyes. She pleaded with wide eyes for him to not advance. Just a gentle shake of her head and a twitch of one finger. She returned her gaze to inside the room.

***

Inside, Mark had taken another step closer. He reached forward and placed a bloody hand around her throat. Brandy was frozen in place, her breath hitching in a staccato rhythm. She could only think of the blood and gore on his hands now touching her skin; the coppery smell was pungent. She stammered, "Mmmmark. Muuuu. Muuuu. Mmmmm," her voice pinched into a whimper.

"About time you got here," Mark sneered.

"Why are you doing this, Yindi?" Alexander stood in the shadows next to the doorway. He placed a hand on Brandy's shoulder protectively. At his touch, her eyes became glazed and unfocused.

"You are so weak, this thing you have for linears." Mark squeezed Brandy's neck slightly. "It's going to be the end of us all." He paused and looked at Alexander. "I do love that about you."

"It gets tiresome," Alexander whispered. "I can keep killing you to slow you down."

"You won't, not this one." Mark leaned close, his voice a harsh whisper. His body looked poised to jump. For his bravado, he was clearly leery of Alexander's reach. "This one, her and her other friend from the cave too—they all are…things. Oh, they feel so good to kill." Mark rubbed a hand up and down his arm, scratching sounds. "You can't kill this one." He bobbed up and down on his toes, becoming excited. "When I do kill them, it is going to be amaz…" In a quick dart, Mark reached forward and in one swift gesture, snapped Brandy's neck. She crumpled to the floor. "I have so much more fun when my host is new and strong."

Alexander caught Brandy and eased her fall to the ground. Sounds of the policeman reacting in the hallway caused him to quicken his pace.

"You can't keep saving her either," Mark taunted. "You'll do as much damage to time as I do." He shivered and bit his lip. "It's delicious."

Alexander locked eyes with Yindi/Mark, grimaced slowly as if biting back words, then disappeared with an audible pop of air rushing into take the place of where he had knelt.

The policeman burst into the room with guns aimed to kill…

***

Brandy turned her head, almost imperceptibly, and met the policeman's eyes. She pleaded with wide eyes for him to not advance. Just a gentle shake of her head and a twitch of one finger. She returned her gaze to inside the room.

Mark stood in front of her covered in blood. Her brain played tricks and sought out odd details to avoid facing the horror in front of her. She wondered at the different way Mark held himself, fidgeted, nibbled at his lip. That was unlike him, as if being covered in someone's intestines was absolutely normal. He reached forward and wrapped his fingers around her neck. Blood seeped from Mark's hand and dripped onto her shirt. His hand squeezed.

Brandy's voice became a whine. "Mmmmark. Muuuu. Muuuu. Mmmmm." She hated the sound of it, wanted it to stop, but couldn't. She shook her head. Had she tried to pass out? Her vision had become tunneled and her ears rang. Someone was screaming. Jen was screaming. Mark was screaming, holding his arm to his chest; the hand bent at an unnatural angle. Policeman behind her were shouting. Mark pushed her to the ground and ran past her.

"Freeze!"

A door slammed.

Thuds of a door being banged with knight sticks.

Glass broke.

"Outside, he's outside."

Nash stooped next to Brandy and put a consoling arm around her not even heeding the bloody handprints around her neck and on her shirt. Officers rushed past him, heading towards the front door, to follow Mark on his flight.

"You OK?" Nash brought a chair over for Brandy to sit down in.

"He tried to choke me. This is Billy's blood. His too—he has a large cut on his hand from where he…" The facts poured from her in a cold, emotionless staccato. She pointed at the room; the door was shut, thankfully. She couldn't see Billy in the room's light. "…Billy's teeth." She envisioned the hand pulling on Billy's jaw, teeth cutting the killer's flesh in the brutality of the moment.

Still trying to give statistics and facts, Brandy allowed Nash to sit her in the chair. She faced Jen. Tears streamed down Jen's face.

"I had left him there in his chair. Said he was gonna read and be good." In-between hiccups and snorts Jen wiped her tears with the sleeve of her scrubs. "I was getting patients back to their rooms—telling them everything was OK, just a little excitement by Billy when I heard this…gargle." Jen looked at nothing as her mind replayed the sound. Something it would do many times over for years to come. "You know, like somebody throwing up. I've heard it a hundred times on this floor. We always got someone pukin' or shittin' around here. Well, maybe not that bad. But it sure seems like it, at least once a month." Her eyes were wide as she looked at Brandy. "I heard someone throwing up. So I went to the door to see if it was Billy. The stench hit me. I thought I was right, but knew that stench was all wrong. Too strong. Too heavy."

Brandy reached forward and patted Jen's boney knee. Jen was unaware of the comforting. "That sound—that wasn't vomit. That was his guts hitting the floor. That's what I heard." She shuddered. Her mouth opened and closed a few times and then she leapt to her feet and headed for the nearest bathroom, retching into the porcelain she found there.

"Nash, was there anyone else in that room besides Mark and me just now?" Brandy looked confused.

"No. Just you two. And…" he nodded towards the door, "and Billy." His voice became a whisper.

"I phased out in there," Brandy explained. "It was weird. A feeling I had for a brief moment. Kinda out of body feeling, you know? I guess I almost passed out." She barked a small laugh. "Pathetic. All weak kneed when faced with a raging lunatic who was once your best friend."

Nash patted her hand and looked worryingly at the closed

door. Bloody smears lay across its stark white surface.

***

It is cool in the pond. His wrist screams with agony. Yindi is floating; ducks move about him, eyeing this intruder. His new host body is strong, even with the months it had taken him to gain control. The body is still strong. Now, with a broken wrist. He focuses on the pain for a moment, not liking it. Just as he had grabbed the neck of the short linear, Brandy, he had been surprised by the screeching pain that had erupted in his arm. The watcher had broken his wrist. Not his neck, like their last meeting. He had run. His hand flopping unnaturally and causing jolts of pain and nausea. He'd have to get it fixed somehow. And the body was brand new too. He is relaxing anyway, the water safe. The watcher, like a mighty lion, doesn't like the water. Can't come in. Can't? Never seen the watcher come into water. Around him, in the darkness, he sees the flashlights, the activity, everyone searching for him. It was a mistake to kill the linear from the shower. That linear did not make him feel better, he did not feel the universe hiccup—no time nudge—it was something the watcher could have reset, should have reset. Why didn't he? Yindi floats and ponders; not normal to think of past things, he thinks. For a brief moment anger flares in his body, adrenalin, hot flush, rapid breath. He holds his wrist tightly to his body so that it cannot cause him more pain. He is floating. Holding his arm. Planning. Now. Best to think and plan now while the body is fresh and working well. Never learned how to keep his host running well and stay in peak performance. He waits for the linears to stop looking for him here. The flashlights are moving on. No dogs. Silly linears. He wonders where the watcher is now. In the night he feels vulnerable. He will wait for the sun. Yindi listens for the things; they whisper to him, tickling at his spine. Things that need to be changed, broken, moved, touched. The need in him builds to a yearning until it drowns out thought and planning. Yindi fights to think beyond the need, to plan beyond now.

***

"If you think of anything else. If he tries to contact you. Here's my card. Call us immediately."

Brandy stood in stunned silence as the officer held a business card out to her. She wanted to rail, to scream, to beat something with her fists as the reality hit her. She would have to go home now. To a silent, empty apartment and her once best friend, now brutal killer was out there. Would he come after her?

"Are you going to have someone watch my place?" she ventured, voice tentative.

"We're going to have a patrol car drive by your apartment during their shift." The officer stood still and awaited her response.

She nodded and looked at the card, unsure of what to do next. The officer returned the nod, turned, left. Brandy stood at the nurses station and watched the officers walk down the hallway, shiny black shoes clicking loudly. They turned the corner and were gone. She absently slid the card into the pocket of her fresh scrubs. They had taken her uniform as evidence.

With a visible shake she set her jaw and turned to the new

night nurse; Jen had been sedated and sent home. "Thanks for covering Jen's shift. Lucy will cover my shift tonight." She looked at her watch. "I mean, today. In a few hours. Gosh, the sun is almost up." Brandy shrugged and stretched. "I'm going to go catch up on my sleep."

***

Brandy stood in the hallway of her apartment, stripped, put the clothes in the wash. As she put on her bath robe, she double checked that the front door locks were secure. After a moment's hesitation she reached into the coat closet and removed a metal bar, a house warming gift from her mom. Brandy butted the metal reinforcement bar under the doorknob. It wedged there, one end under the doorknob, the other end securely on the floor. She checked the locks again.

"Lot of good that is going to do. He can just come in through any of the nine damn huge windows." Brandy looked towards the bank of floor to ceiling windows. The sun was just beginning to cast shadows across her stark apartment floor.

"Why did I get an apartment on the first floor?" She regarded the windows again, once beautiful and now a perfect place for crazed intruders to crash in. Brandy hugged her robe tightly to herself. She muttered to herself, making her way to the shower. "I would not survive the zombie apocalypse in this place."

The shower was scalding. Brandy tried to lose herself in the steam and ignore all the crowded, buzzing, chaotic thoughts in her head. Images of a loop of intestine caught in Billy's toes. Gore dripping from Mark's arms. His hand around her throat. The menacing snarl on his face. "I'm going to have fun with you," he had said. She tried to not think about it. Obviously, he was delusional. His eyes were aware, not delusional at all. They had purpose. She turned the cold tap off, letting the hot water scald her skin. It did no good to push away the shakes that rattled her teeth.

A noise caused her breath to hitch. Had she heard something? She turned the water off and pulled back the curtain, instantly upset at the opaqueness of the curtain. Why didn't she have a glass door she could see through? The bathroom door was perpetually open, a useless piece of wood for a single woman. No sounds but the draining of the water in the tub. The AC kicked on. The vent whistled above her. Nothing.

She could not see the shadow that passed across the windows in the living room. It passed slowly, came closer, loomed in the window, then slid away.

The phone buzzed on the kitchen table. Brandy jumped. Dripping. Naked. She picked up the phone by the third ring. The name displayed by caller ID made her pause.

"Hello?" She reached for a towel and cradled the phone to her ear with a wet shoulder.

"Brandy. Are you OK?" Alexander's deep voice.

The phone tried to slip; she caught it, switched ears. "How did you know…?" She left the question unfinished. It must be on the news already. Something that horrific had to have made the local news.

He paused. "It was your friend, Mark." A statement, not a question.

Brandy sank into the chair. "It was horrible." She shuddered and dried her hair. "I don't know where he is. He tried to strangle me then ran off. I don't…"

"I can not come be with you right now. You are not working tonight, are you?" Alexander's voice was full of concern and warmth.

Brandy unleashed anger on him, being the only available recipient. "So, are you married?" she accused, then instantly wished she could take back the words.

"No," his patient response.

"I'm sorry," she whispered. "I haven't seen you in months and I'm beginning to think you're married with three kids and just stringing me on." Brandy went to the bedroom and pulled on a large t-shirt. It came to her knees. "I'm so high strung right now, I'm lashing out. It's not your fault. Sorry."

No answer from the other end of the phone for a moment. Then, "Does Mark know where you live?"

"Yes." Brandy's voice sunk. "Of course he does. He was my closest caving buddy."

"You need to go somewhere he does not know."

"I can come to your place," Brandy joked.

Silence followed by more silence.

Brandy quickly added, "I'm kidding. Sorry. Bad joke."

"I wish I could. It would be…" Alexander trailed off. "…complicated." He ended.

Brandy sighed.

More silence.

"I suppose that does not help you believe that I do not have a wife and three children." A smile in his voice.

"Four kids?" she asked then smiled herself. "Anyway, yes, I need to get away. He knows about my grandma's shack too. That's my normal get away."

"I have been traveling so much lately, time slips away from me when I am focused on…work." He added, "No kids, not even four." Then in a serious tone, "If I could be there right now with you, I would."

"Where are you at today? Some place exotic?" Brandy pulled on fuzzy socks and wiggled her toes.

"The good news is that I am done with the construction job and am back. I know we have not seen each other since we parted at the cave that day. I have not taken you out for a formal night on the town..." Brandy's laughter interrupted Alexander.

"Well, crawling in a cave is the best date I can imagine. I mean that place was beautiful. And I don't have to be treated to anything." Brandy's voice bristled momentarily for the word treated. "You've been away for six months. It's OK." She paused. "I'm off tonight. Do you want to get together and go out? I've gotta catch up on some sleep first."

"Me too." Alexander agreed. "I always work nights and have become accustomed to sleeping in the day. I'll pick you up at 8 p.m. tonight?"

"Sounds like a plan. I turned my alarm on and am going to catch some shuteye. Patrol cars are going to do drive-bys. I'll be fine." Brandy checked that the locks were still engaged and turned on her alarm. It beeped cheerily.

"I do wish you could go some where else just for today at least." Alexander ventured.

Brandy stood staring at the large windows, her back against the laundry closet folding door. "You know what? Susan. He's never been to Susan's place. Why didn't I think about that before?"

"Sleep deprivation and shock." Deadpan voice, he continued, "I'll pick you up tonight. Text me her address, please?"

***

Thirty minutes later she walked out the door and turned on her alarm. Calls to both her mother and Susan had taken place. Her phone vibrated.

"Park in the front visitor parking. I'll meet you at the corner." Susan

"OK. Be there in 5." Brandy

***

Brandy parked in the visitor parking area and stood at the sidewalk waiting for Susan to come out and meet her. The town house that Susan lived in was in a gated community and not for the first time Brandy thought of how much she liked the gated community thing. Now, more than ever. She wanted to be behind a locked gate and somewhere you needed to be let in. Her phone buzzed.

"On my way." A text from Susan.

"K." Brandy replied.

Brandy saw Susan walking towards the locked gate and waved. She hadn't told her very much and suddenly she wanted to talk to her best friend about everything, no matter how tired she was. She started to walk towards Susan. She wanted to start talking right away, even from this distance, but the noise from an approaching bus was loud and squealed in her ear. Already she could imagine the cinnamon rolls and coffee they would have in Susan's breakfast nook. She could vomit out this horrid memory and then tuck it away. Even as she thought that, she knew it was a lie.

Susan was getting closer now. 50 feet away. The bus brakes squealed behind Brandy, she couldn't think for the loudness of the bus. Brandy thought briefly that she wouldn't feel safe until Mark was found. Would he come after her? Of course he would. The look in his eyes. They had burned with hate.

Susan had stopped walking towards Brandy. Her hands had raised, her eyes wide with terror.

The shadow of the bus loomed on the sidewalk, engulfing Brandy's small shadow. She could feel the slight temperature change it afforded her, the sun brutal with its heat even at this time of the morning.

The push felt like a large solid gust of wind had come at her from the side. The bus did not have time to hit the brakes. Susan screamed. Brandy had barely enough time to let out a surprised exhalation of breath.

Brandy heard her own body thud and crunch before her world went dark. Her cell phone fell into a puddle of blood. The cracked screen displayed a screen saver image of her grandmother's shack. The morning sun reflected in the growing puddle of blood.

13 STANDOFF REVISITED.

"Alexander!"

"Susan." He joined Susan at the glass window.

"She's sedated right now." Susan pointed to the supine figure in the room; beeping equipment and hoses adorned her like alien creatures.

"How long does it take for these types of wounds to heal?" Alexander placed a hand on the glass. The orchids in his other hand sagged, unheeded.

"A while. Broke leg, fractured pelvis, couple cracked ribs, fractured face for heaven's sake." She broke off into a sob. "What happened to him? How could Mark do this? We were his best friends."

Alexander put an arm around Susan. Her strong, lean frame shook with stifled sobs. "He was not himself. You cannot blame him," he soothed.

He stood near her and counted her breaths. How fragile these linears, he thought. Short lives, easily hurt. Nothing near what his species was: nearly immortal, stronger, able to time shift from the moment of their adolescence on. Yet, saddled with the responsibility of keeping the universe from unraveling at the hands of the chaos creating manipulators like the one he called Yindi.

Brandy drew a deep breath and moaned slightly, her eyebrows furrowed as a dream unsettled her rest. He touched her brow, gently. At once her eyebrows relaxed and she settled again into deep sleep. How amazing that the linears and his kind had once been from the same gene pool.

"Alexander?" Brandy's voice was slurred and slow.

He answered her with a soft kiss. "I am here." His breath warm on her cool lips.

"Won't make our date tonight." She tried to smile, but it waned.

"Do not worry. You will." Alexander smoothed her hair and kissed her nose softly. He wished that he could give energy instead of taking it, give her energy to help her heal inside. The most he could do was heal small wounds, nothing more than a bite. It did not matter that she would be gone in forty, sixty years. It did not matter that his life would continue forever forward until the end of time. It only mattered that he change this event, to remove this pain from her. Anger rippled through him, visceral. He would keep killing Yindi over and over again, hang the consequences to the universe and its precious time line. What did it matter? Perhaps it would be better if it all burned with him in it. "I will pick you up at Susan's place for dinner. Just you and me. I have been gone too long. Time is too precious to you. I forget that."

He adjusted the orchids so that she could see them should she awake in the next moments before this time line ended.

He held her face, his thumb brushed against her lips. She

faded into deep slumber once again. With a soft pop of air, Brandy was alone in her room. The machines beeped and buzzed, registering her vitals for a nurse somewhere to monitor.

Susan opened the door to the room. "Alexander?" a stage whisper. Perplexed, she looked around to see no one there but Brandy's sleeping form and the persistently beeping machines.

Alexander stood for a moment in his frozen time watching the ghosts of time fold out in front of him in slow, translucent paths. Brandy lay in the bed, glimmering in main time, a ghastly apparition. Susan walked to the bed and adjusted the orchids. The room was filled with images of comings and goings of hundreds if not thousands of linears all to the same place in various degrees of pain and mourning. They clouded the air and obscured his view of Brandy. For an instance he could believe that they all stood visage over her, all felt the anguish that speared his cold heart. Yet, unlike them, he was not powerless to help. He had to focus on main time and her for the hordes of linears past to dim and disappear.

He moved quickly, not wanting this timeline to continue any longer. Even though he knew it would end, he could change her suffering; the thought of it continuing any longer than it needed was unbearable. Soon Alexander was back at the mound of dirt that in main time would become the shed behind the nursing home. He took a frozen moment to soak the energy up from the earth there. He had fed recently, so at least that nuisance was taken care of. The energy from the ground seeped into his bones and fortified him with a resilience. He turned towards the grounds where the nursing home would be built and focused on time as it spread out in front of him.

***

His frozen time lay over ten thousand years in the past from Brandy. He stood on his precious energy-giving earth and watched the ghosts of hills eroding, a stream that once ran through then sunk into the ground, a forest that grew tall, burned, regrew. People on foot, living in huts made of hides, battles, horses, huts burned to the ground, a cabin and a family, the cabin burned to the ground, a small town. A war, the town decimated, a field of grass and a small stream struggling to survive, deer, a building, a couple hand in hand at the pond, the building of the shed around him. The old man who visited the shed, the couple, old and bent, at the pond; the old man alone at the pond; the old man visiting the shed, sad, alone, closing and locking the door; Brandy on the back porch with the old man the last night he had seen her. Her smile melted his heart from where he stood. He stood still as the story of ghosts played out before him. A nurse came out of the door and spoke hastily to Brandy. He could feel the ache creep into his bones, a feeling that tasted bitter in the back of his throat, the moment when Yindi had fully taken over his host. Slowly, Alexander walked towards the building and focused on the moment where Yindi had confronted Brandy.

***

Alexander stayed in his time as he walked across the hill. Silent. Cold. Eternal. He slipped through time slightly to avoid the energy-draining stream. The ghost images in front of him shimmered and became the only image he wanted to see. A smear of yellow tinged the ghostly, translucent image seated in the room. Alexander wasn't interested in that dead linear. It was a small change, an acceptable change for his purposes. Instead he focused on the Brandy standing at the door, Mark/Yindi in front of her. Alexander could see himself standing to the side of the duo, where he had once broke Mark's wrist to keep him from breaking Brandy's neck. Careful to not collide with himself he slipped slowly into sync with the other Alexander in a standoff at the door. Thousands of years of practice allowed Alexander to slip silently into the time with barely more than a whisper. The stench hit him first, the excrement and blood emanating from the still seated figure. Alexander's nose wrinkled slightly in disgust.

He could hear his other self saying, "It gets tiresome," barely a whisper. "I can keep killing you to slow you down."

They had not noticed Alexander yet. He considered his options, while Mark taunted the other Alexander.

"You won't, not this one." Mark took a step back from Brandy, who stood dazed with eyes unfocused. "This one, her and her other friend from the cave too—they all are…things. Oh, they feel so good to kill." Scratching sounds as Mark rubbed a hand up and down his arm. "You can't kill this one."

Alexander watched his other self from across the room. The scratching sound irritated him. The whole scene irritated him, like an itch he could not scratch deep in the center of his back. His other self looked up and noticed him standing in the room. He put a protective hand on Brandy and both Alexanders turned to Mark. Mark took another step away from them.

"This human is a thing. You can't kill him." His breath hitched and manic. "You'll be doing my work for me." His words became a plea. "You'll ruin the game," he whined.

Alexander's other self asked, "Kill him?"

Alexander considered the suggestion. Mark judged the doorway, ready to bolt.

Alexander grabbed Mark by his collar, yanking up. "Not safe. He would probably jump to Brandy." He nodded back to the dead linear. "Let the police catch him and deal with him. They will keep him locked away."

His other self smiled, "That will make for a small peaceful break."

From the hallway they could hear the police advancing down the hallway.

"Grab his arm." The other Alexander complied. Brandy still stood stunned in the doorway while the Alexanders each grabbed Mark by an arm.

The police were almost to the doorway.

After finishing their task, the other Alexander slipped out of sight. Alexander went to Brandy and brushed her lips with his then slipped out of time as well. She stumbled backwards a step as the policeman pulled her away and the other rushed in with his gun raised.

"Freeze," he yelled.

Mark could only sit in the pool of congealed blood with his head hung. His eyes burned with hatred until consciousness left him.

***

Brandy turned on the alarm and stood still in the hallway. She stood motionless in front of the washing machine. The phone in her hand rang; she jumped.

"Shit." The caller ID read ALEXANDER. Brandy paused, hating how her heart raced. "Alexander." She hoped she didn't sound needy and pathetic.

"Brandy?" His voice low and full of concern. "I heard about Mark. Are you all right?"

She sunk to the floor and held the phone to her ear; her keys fell from her hand and clinked on the floor. "Oh gosh, I don't even know how to describe it. I've never seen anything like that. And he was right there." A sob hitched in her throat and she grimaced with impatience. "I must have blacked out a little. I really don't know what happened. One minute he was looking at me and squeezing my neck. The next he was sitting on the ground knocked unconscious. I don't know how that happened."

"You are so strong," Alexander said. "You must have done that. "

Brandy answered with a squeak, "Maybe he slipped? I can't remember."

"Adrenalin will do odd things. The important thing is that you are unharmed." His voice was soothing and calm. She nodded in agreement.

"Must have erased my memory of the thing. It will come back later, maybe." She hugged herself and tilted her head back to look at the ceiling.

"You need to get some sleep, Brandy. Very quickly, I wanted to tell you that my construction job has concluded. It has been too long that I have neglected you. Will you forgive me?" His voice held a hint of a smile.

"You know." Brandy stood up and began to disrobe in front of the washing machine. The scrubs were brand new and did not need washing; she had changed at the nursing home.

She dropped the scrubs into the washing machine. Habits. She moved the phone to her other ear. "I was beginning to imagine you had a wife and three children somewhere."

"Only three?" he chuckled.

"Four then. You admit it." Brandy closed the washing machine lid and put on her robe.

"No. I am guilty of losing track of time. I will not let that happen again." His voice was stern, then softened. "Would you like to meet me for dinner tonight? Eight?"

"Are your kids coming?" Brandy chided, then felt bad for broadcasting her insecurity. "Sorry. I would love to see you again." She paused then took a chance, "I've missed you."

Alexander's voice was quick to respond, "I promise to make it up to you. I will find a perfect place. Pick you up at your place"

Brandy nodded first then said, "You've never seen my place. Do you know how to find it?"

He chuckled. "Yes. I can find it. I will pick you up at eight. Do not stand me up."

"You know…" Brandy laughed lightly, "crawling around in a cave is a fine date to me too, you know. I'm easy that way." Brandy stopped and looked at herself in the mirror and rolled her eyes. She mouthed the words, "I'm easy," then mimed shooting herself in the head with her pointer finger. She almost missed his response.

"…I have enjoyed being in the cave with the vision of you," he had said. She thought that was what he had said.

"Until tonight?" She wanted to end the conversation before her tired brain said something more stupid.

"Tonight," he answered.

Brandy hung up the phone and turned on the shower.

Within minutes she was sound asleep with the covers around her ears. The phone, unheeded, vibrated on the dining room table while haunting dreams plagued her sleep.

***

She is walking on a narrow road that twists and turns. Her feet make no sound, though leaves litter the ground. A screeching noise fills the air and tears at her senses. She tries to run from it. It is louder and impending, a feeling that it will overtake her. Brandy is running, flailing, grasping to pull herself out of the narrow road, which has filled with water. It pulls at her ankles with its current. The water runs red in rivulets around her feet. She is barefoot. The leaves give way to pebbles that hurt her feet. She is hobbled and cannot run. Screeching behind her. She cannot turn, is unable to turn around to see what is barreling down behind her. The warm air from it pushes at her back. She is overtaken and all goes white. She is surrounded by light and her only thought is relief that the screeching is gone. In the whiteness, dark shapes are slithering towards her bare feet. She lifts her feet, tries to avoid them. She is overrun by the smooth moving serpents. Falling. Grasping. Unable to breathe. The white light is blotted out by cold, heavy, writhing forms. She tries to break free one last time.

Deep sleep carried her away from the clutches of her dreams.

14 LOCKED TIME.
WEDNESDAY, AGAIN AND FOREVER.

Brandy woke slowly. The blankets and sheet bound her feet and clumped under her uncomfortably. She tried to slither a foot out from underneath the lightweight blanket and escape to the coolness of the air. Stretching, her hand came across her neck and she realized she was sweating. The light outside was waning. Had she slept all day?

"Uggh." Kicking a little more franticly she was able to dislodge both feet and a knee. The cool air was refreshing. Wondering what time it was she sought out the phone on the dresser. The screen showed seven missed text messages and three phone calls from Susan. "What on earth? I told her I was sleeping."

"Something happened. Call me!" 10:20 AM

"Wake up." 11:32 AM

"OMG." 12:15 PM

"…" 1:45 PM

"It's Mark. I went to see hm." 2:15 PM

"i don knw what to do. plees calll m." 3:00 PM

Brandy scrolled to the last text from an hour ago. "Hs dead." It was five o'clock and Brandy felt her world tip sideways. Bolt upright in bed, she dialed Susan. It rang. Unanswered. Went to voice mail. "Susan. I'm on my way over. Stay right there. Call me."

While she dressed hurriedly she called Alexander. Voicemail. "Damn it." Without leaving a message, she hung up. He never answered his phone when she called anyway. She pushed out the nagging thoughts that he had another life she was not privy to. Now was not the time. Did Susan mean Mark was dead? She looked at the text again trying to wish the letters to make more sense. "Hs dead" Did that mean "He's dead"? Or something less ominous? She looked at the text keyboard and tried to find letters that were close to H and s to spell out something else, something that made sense, something that would make this horrible sinking sensation in the pit of her stomach go away. It couldn't mean that. Obviously, Susan was maybe ill. Or on a bender.

The doorknob slipped in her hand; she fumbled her keys; the doormat curled up and lodged under the door keeping it from closing. "God Damn It!" Brandy yelled, and kicked at the doormat. Had Susan ever been on a drunken binge at home? Not that Brandy ever knew. Susan saved the shenanigans for the camping trips. This wasn't like her at all. What was going on?

With a deep breath, Brandy focused and tried to clear her head. She would drive over to Susan's house and figure out what had happened and what all this meant. Right now, she had to focus and get there. Running thoughts around in circles in her head was not going to fix anything. She turned the radio on. Listened. Turned it off, annoyed with the sound of it, and drove in silence.

Meanwhile her mind raced and chanted the mantra, "Hs dead. Hs dead. Hs dead. Hs dead. Hs dead." in time to the wheels on the road.

***

No answer at the door. Brandy tried the phone. It rang. Metallic chimes echoed in the stillness. The sound resonated, stilled, silenced: unanswered.

"Susan!"

Knock, Knock

"SUSAN!" Still no answer. Brandy paused, considered, then used her key. The alarm was not armed; it beeped a gentle hello, no obnoxious bleating, begging to be turned off. "Susan?" Brandy began her search of the house.

Purse on the floor, overturned, contents strewn. Lipstick uncapped and smeared on the white marble tile. Brandy couldn't help but notice it was in the grout.

Shoes. Socks. An empty wine bottle.

That was the clue Brandy needed to hasten her search. "Suzie-Q?" The living room was only a few feet away. A foot with red painted toenails was slung over the arm of the couch. "Found you." Brandy peered over to find her friend, lipstick smeared across her face, hair sticking up on end, snoring. A half empty bottle of wine sat on the coffee table, the glass next to it stained with red lipstick and lying on its side.

Brandy grimaced. She'd never seen Susan like this during the workweek. Quietly, she set to cleaning and straightening up the mess.

Her phone rang just as she was wiping up the counter in the kitchen where apparently a sandwich had been made with much gusto. Mustard and crumbs littered the countertop.

"Hi Alexander," she whispered.

"Is everything all right?" he answered in a whisper. "Why are we whispering?"

"It's Susan." She found the half eaten sandwich on the floor on the opposite side of the kitchen counter. "She's blacked out. Drinking." Brandy threw away the sandwich and closed the garbage can lid. "She sent me some weird texts. Something upset her today. I…" Brandy broke up unable to speak the words aloud yet until Susan had confirmed them. "…I think something happened with Mark."

Alexander didn't answer right away. When he did, his voice was careful and slow. "Are you sure?"

"No. I'm not sure about anything. I came right over when I saw her weird texts and found her. She's a slobbering, snoring mess. I'm going to stay here and be here when she wakes up."

"Do you want me to come over and keep you company?" Alexander's voice was quiet.

"Oh my gosh, our date. I'm sorry." She leaned against the fridge. "Do you mind?"

"I will bring Chinese and wait with you. I do not have to go to…work…tonight." Alexander paused, waiting for a reply.

Brandy absently rearranged the magnets on the fridge. "I'll make it up to you someday." Relief in her voice. "Actually sounds like a great first date. You know, minus the passed out drunk friend on the couch."

***

Susan sat up in the dark room and screamed, "…oooo…nooOOOOOOOOooooooo!"

"What the hell?" Brandy handed her Chinese take out container to Alexander and stood from the couch. "I'll go check on her." She walked to the bedroom.

Susan was still sitting bolt upright in the bed. The light from the bathroom cast her shadow on the wall. It wavered and danced like a writhing demon. Her eyes were wide open, unseeing.

"Susan, lay back down," Brandy cajoled as she approached the bed.

Susan's head swiveled towards Brandy's voice; eerily, no other muscles twitched. She sat unseeing, unblinking.

Brandy paused, looking into those wide eyes. "That's creepy as hell, Susan," she whispered. "Lay back down. Let's sleep this one off. K?"

Wide eyes. Unblinking. No response.

Brandy pushed on Susan's shoulders. At first there was no movement. Then, with a sudden collapse, Susan lay back on the bed and closed her eyes.

"Jesus. Linda Blair much?" Brandy whispered to herself, watching to make sure Susan stayed lying down and did not pop back up.

When Brandy entered the living room, Alexander returned her container of chicken fried rice. "Have you ever seen her like this?" He poked at his own container of Egg Fu Young with chopsticks.

"Never." Brandy snuggled closer to him on the couch and resumed eating. She nodded towards his container. "Not too hungry? "

He muffled a grin by tilting his head away. "I had a late lunch."

They shifted together to find a comfortable position, legs and arms entwined to accommodate their meals "Oops." Brandy tried to catch her fork as it summersaulted out of her fried rice. Alexander caught it with extraordinary speed then dropped it as if it were a hot poker. "Oh, gosh. Are you OK?" Brandy reached for his hand. Alexander had already bent to retrieve the fork with a napkin.

"It stabbed me." Alexander stood with the fork clutched firmly in a napkin. "I'll wash it off."

"No idea yet what happened?" he called from the kitchen.

Brandy tried to use the chopsticks, failing miserably. "No. Nothing yet from her." She stabbed a piece of chicken with one chopstick triumphantly and held it out for inspection. "Maybe she'll sleep through the night. We'll find out in the morning." The piece of chicken fell back into the container. Alexander speared it with the fork and handed it to her. She noticed the paper towel still wrapped around the fork. He used it to hold the fork to her. She paused to look at the paper towel then him. Raised an eyebrow.

He returned her look with a "what" expression, free hand raised palm up.

"Germ-a-phobe?" she asked. "You can touch my fork. Really." She bit the chicken off the end of the fork then took the utensil from him.

"I did not yet know how to tell you my secret." He smiled softly, eyes lowered.

The scream that came next brought both of them to their feet. Susan was at full volume calling out for Mark to stop.

"It's like having a baby," Brandy chuckled. She looked at Alexander. "You're changing the diapers."

She left him in the living room, a perplexed look on his face. After a moment he followed her.

***

Susan's eyes burned from white hot sockets and sweat glued long hair in disarray around her pinched face. Susan looked desperately from Brandy to Alexander as they stood around her full of concern.

"Brandy! Oh mygdd, Brandy," her voice slurred but strong. "I went to see 'im at the nursing home. Take him a breakfast croissant sometimes, you know. He used to like them." She accepted the mug of hot steaming tea Alexander offered. Gulped, not heeding the obvious heat then continued. "Nash told me what…what happened. There was tape and police and guys in jumpsuits. I mean…" Susan trailed off and gulped more hot tea. The words poured from her as fast as her thick tongue could allow. "…couldn't believe…so I went to see 'm. Had to look at him. Thought maybe they were wrong. That maybe it was a trick." Susan's eyes went wide. "How could he do that? Nash didn't tell me how. The day nurse told me." She paused.

Brandy tried to interject, "It's OK. They have him put away. He had a psychotic episode, that's all. He's not himself…it isn't his fau…"

Susan's sudden burst of crying interrupted Brandy. "You don't know. Don't…know…" Her sobs came in hitches with each word. "He's…dead…he…"

A large bubble of snot had formed at the end of her nose.

Momentarily Brandy was mesmerized by it as it grew and shrunk with her breaths.

"…killed…"

Brandy grabbed a tissue and held it to Susan's nose, more to try and stop the words than to stop the growing and shrinking bubble. Susan grabbed Brandy's hand.

"…he killed himself…"

sob

"right…there…"

sob, bubble grow, shrink,

"…in…front…"

sob, breathe, bubble grow, shrink, grow

"of…me…" Brandy pushed through and held the tissue to her nose again.

"…right in front of me."

Alexander went still next to Brandy. His hand on her shoulder squeezed a little too harshly.

She looked up at him, comprehending the reason behind the binge. "Oh my god," she whispered. "Susan, I'm so sorry." What could she say? What could she ask? Unable to stop the words, she asked, "How?" The word hung harsh and sharp in the air between them.

Susan's sobs hitched and silenced. Her face went slack and for a moment her eyes became vacant, pupils dilated, breath even and slow.

Alexander pulled Brandy back away from Susan. Brandy did not fight him, not quite wanting to be next to Susan either. "Susan?" The cup of tea fell from Susan's hand and spilled boiling hot water on her legs. She did not react. "Jesus Christ, Susan?" Brandy grabbed the tumbled mug and pulled at the soaking blanket in Susan's lap.

Susan did not blink, only sat there staring straight ahead. Slowly, the corner of her mouth twitched into a smile that hitched and faltered like a marionette under an inexperienced puppeteer's guidance.

Twitch.

Twitch.

Staring forward.

"What the fuck?" Brandy reached out and slapped Susan across the face.

Alexander stood still, watched the exchange, staring at the specter on the bed.

Susan's head tilted to the side, blond hair fell over her face not quite covering the jerking failure of a sneer. Unblinking, staring eyes gazed hazily. Her voice took on a different quality, tighter and faster, no longer sobbing. "He waited until I stood in front of his holding cell. He whispered my name. Like he had to tell me something, a secret, a confession. I leaned to the bars wanting to hear him. My fingers were on the bars. He touched them. Softly. Took my hands and put them on either side of his face. The guard yelled. He ignored them. Put his hands over mine. Then he twisted his head. His own head. He twisted his head with my hands on his face. I could feel the bones in his neck snap. He dropped dead against the bars with me still holding his head. I screamed so loudly no noise came out."

She fell back on the bed, smirk still on her face, asleep.

"Fuck." The only response Brandy could give.

Alexander responded, "Indeed."

***

Friday. She looked everywhere she could but at what was in front of her. Any other detail to occupy her mind but the one she should be regarding. The wind blew gently through the trees. The sun was warm on her face and clouds floated gently. Birds chirped. Frogs croaked. Wildlife fluttered about. Brandy watched as a red ladybug walked across the silver plated railing around the casket. It ambled steadfastly across the hills and valleys caused by the velvet curtains. She watched as the ladybug walked, stopped, walked further, and kept steady progress guided by some unseen force. How long did she watch its path along the curtains until it curved around out of sight? She continued to watch for its return based on its trajectory. Eventually it reappeared, walked straight again for a while then curved around out of sight. She continued to watch as the ladybug appeared, disappeared, curved, straight, dipped, paused then disappeared for the last time. It did not reappear. Her heart sank when it did not come into her view where she expected it to. Did the ladybug back track? She did not see it and finally, sniffing, resigned her eyes to look at the open casket where Mark lay. He looked wrong. That couldn't be him. He looked not like Mark. Too dark. The make-up was wrong. She continued to look everywhere else while the silence of everyone sitting awkwardly in their private grief screamed in her ears. She was more than happy when the ladybug appeared again back where it had first started. She wondered, did the ladybug even know it was starting over in the same place, that it would re-walk the same terrain? She felt sad for the ladybug, not understanding the bigger picture.

Susan interrupted Brandy's thoughts; dark sunglasses obscured her eyes. "Can we go to your cabin and get away from," she tilted her chin towards the casket, "thisss?" Her whisper was distant, like she was speaking from far away.

The ladybug had disappeared again. Brandy patted Susan's hand. "I have to. I have to disappear from all of this or my head is going to explode."

"I don't know if I can dive." Susan grabbed Brandy's hand and squeezed. "I'd be too distracted, I think."

"I think I have to." Brandy leaned her head against Susan's shoulder. "Wish Alexander was here."

"Where's he at?" Susan leaned her head against Brandy's.

"He works third shift, you know, night construction or something. So he's off sleeping right now. Said he'd meet us at the cabin tonight if we went. Want to..." Brandy quieted as the funeral director approached the podium indicating that silence would now be filled by hollow words she still could not hear.

"OK," Susan said and then quieted for the ceremony.

They nodded, prayed, stood, smiled and shook hands at the appropriate times in the blur of the funeral, holding on to one other so that the world did not tear them apart. Susan grasped Brandy's arm tightly, a lifeline.

***

The world felt wrong to him. He knew he had to put it back. How could he? How could he allow her to be under that bus again? Yet, here, he could see, feel, taste as he walked through the streets at night, that things were wrong. If the yellow smear across his vision of time didn't convince him that this was not the correct time stream, the ache in his bones hammered the point home.

***

Alexander walked the streets in the early morning, the sun threatening to come up. It ebbed and pushed at him; an impending threat. He stayed in main time, stayed in her time. How could he allow her to befall harm? He could stay in this stream and live through the ache and pain in his bones for forty, fifty years, what was that? Sixty years at the most. Or he could allow the original time stream to reoccur; throw her back under the bus and he would not ache, time would not pull at him. He would not feel pain. She would, however, be in agony. Mark would not be dead and Yindi would not be…he did not want to think what Yindi was in this time line. Whose body Yindi was inhabiting. Surely he should have known that Yindi would not have stayed in Mark's body rotting in a jail cell. He would not find respite, no escape from this eternal curse of keeping time in check from Yindi's antics.

***

Alexander found himself in a foul mood, angry at all creation and the time streams that he was a prisoner to watch and protect. He walked amongst the linears not heeding where they went or where he walked. Twisting and turning amongst the modern street, his footsteps resounded against the tall steel buildings and echoed amongst the concrete sidewalks.

***

"I thought you were a rock star." Someone called from his elbow. The fellow was dressed in brightly colored shorts and an even louder colored shirt. The linear held a plastic bag from the local Hard Rock Cafe. Alexander looked up and realized he was standing in front of the Hard Rock Cafe in Nashville. He paused. How long had he been walking? Apparently between his time and main time for hours, days?

To his right side was a back up of limos, busses and Penske trucks full of luggage. Obviously, some group of famous people was in town. This unsuspecting linear had witnessed Alexander appear in main time as he walked contemplating the end of this time line.

"I am no rock star." Alexander walked straight toward the linear. The hunger inside him grew like a warm entity in his chest. It expanded and filled his body with a thrumming.

"Oh, I mean. I thought you were with…" He pointed to the limos. "Hey, where are they hiding Paul McCartney?" The linear clutched the plastic bag to his chest like a talisman. He was slow witted, innocent, and only looking for famous people to take pictures of. Alexander noted that his socks did not match. He dismissed the thought.

"Come with me. I'll show you." Alexander put a bold arm around the linear's shoulders.

He stammered in response, "…there are all the limos. I thought you were a rock star…" He flustered and held his bag tighter. Too late, his eyes darted around looking for a possible escape.

Alexander turned the corner with the prey in his arm and then together they disappeared from main time. The air flowed into the space they once inhabited; shrubs near by swayed in the sudden turbulence. Their shadows disappeared.

"What's this?" the linear asked, already breaking out into a cold sweat. His body swayed against the sudden absence of sound and movement. His ears rang with the nothingness and his stomach lolled against the nowhere-ness.

"Nowhere." Alexander looked into the linear's eye. Very rarely had he brought an awake being here. Usually it caused complications tearing their brain from time while conscious. The eyes that looked back at Alexander were wet and moved erratically. This linear was slow, and had no decision trees in front of him. His mind was as unattached here as it was in main time. Unusual. Alexander was feeling exceedingly evil and angry. Make them hurt, writhe in pain. Make them twist in agony to pay for what he was going to have to do to Brandy. He did not care. "Here," He held up his hand to indicate the cold place where time did not move. Sound did not vibrate. Shadows did not flicker. "Here, is where you die."

He leaned forward, suddenly flush with hunger, ripped the throat from the linear, drank from the well within. The body kicked and bucked feebly in his arms, then dropped to the ground. Useless. Broken. A red tennis shoe lay devoid of foot, covered in blood, dirt, leaves.

The anger drained from Alexander leaving him as cold as the frozen sunlight that fell soulless on the ground. Forever trapped in this timeless hell. Alexander walked slowly away from the husk.

***

The current main time continued forward while Alexander plodded in his frozen time, angry at the universe. Brandy and Susan stood arm in arm as they watched Mark's casket lowered into the ground. Pulleys creaked and clinked against metal. The slight whirring sound of weight on webbing as it descended.

Brandy stood on tiptoe to whisper into Susan's ear, "On rope."

Susan did not respond. She looked straight ahead, dark sunglasses obscuring any emotions or reactions.

Brandy nudged her with an elbow. "Sorry. Bad joke."

Still no response from Susan. Then suddenly, "I don't think I feel well, Brandy."

She hugged herself tightly, goose bumps on her arms." I swear it is like another voice in my head. I need a drink." Her words tumbled in turmoil, a hissed whisper.

Friends and family stepped forward, tossing flowers in after the lowered casket.

Brandy whispered, pleaded. "Come on, let's go to the cabin and dive the pit. No little leads though. I don't think I can do that. Especially after last time." It was Brandy's turn to shudder and rub arms covered in goose bumps. The memory of her regulator leaking air and being pinned behind a rock still shook her awake at night; was still fresh. She needed to get away, now more than ever.

"OK. I guess a gentle dive would feel bett…" Susan's voice trailed. "You can't hear that?"

Brandy absently twirled her bat necklace while she frowned at her friend. "Are you drunk?" A query, not an accusation in her voice.

"I have to be altered to get through this." Susan tossed a white rose onto the casket. It barely made a sound as it landed amongst the others. "Don't judge."

The crowd dispersed and gathered into clumps as the mourners walked through the green grass to their cars. The cars were a mismatch of vehicles. Jeeps with bat stickers, muddy four by four trucks and utility vehicles intermixed with sleek sedans and town cars. Cavers and non-cavers.

Hugging Susan tightly, Brandy assured her, "Never. Let's get through this."

***

It was nightfall by the time they pulled into they cabin's winding driveway.

"I can't believe it has only been a week since we were last here. It feels like a month." Brandy turned off the headlights. The only light was a utility pole lamp that hummed. Moths circled it, endlessly.

"A year, at least," Susan answered, her voice flat and distant.

"That breeze feels nice." Brandy turned towards the wind, eyes closed, a tight smile.

"Want to dive now? Just to the bottom of the pit? Look up at the stars?" Susan slipped off her heels and stood barefoot in the grass.

"Yeah. I could do with some mindless floating. I'll put some beer on ice for when we get out." Brandy eyeballed her friend.

Susan caught the glance and snorted. "I'm sober now. Swear. No flask anywhere on me."

Brandy smiled. A noise on the porch stopped her short; a quiet creak that pierced through them.

"Hello ladies." A slow deep voice echoed to them.

"Holy shit, Alexander. You scared the hell out of me." Susan threatened to throw a shoe in his general direction.

His feet were perched on the porch railing, one ankle over the other. The light from the utility pole in the yard cast long shadows along the dark wood slats.

Brandy paused, uncertain of how pathetic she would be if she ran to him. She hated how much she needed to be held at that very point in time. Just once to have someone hold her and make it all go away. Wouldn't that be nice? Tears sprung to her eyes, which annoyed her even more.

She shook it off and put an arm around Susan. "We're going for a therapy dive."

Susan returned an arm around Brandy's waist. "Gonna look up at the stars."

"Well." Alexander took his feet down. His loafers made a soft thud, on the porch. "I have to tell you a secret then." He eyed them both, walking towards them. "I cannot swim." Hands held out at his side, a helpless gesture.

"Guess you get to wait on the shore for us and be camp dog." Brandy and Susan approached Alexander and stopped. Their toes pointed towards one another in the patchy grass. Alexander's thick soled loafers, slightly scuffed and worn, Brandy's black pumps, worn patches on the backs of the heels from driving, Susan's bare feet. Black worn pumps shifted in the dirt then approached the loafers where they stood apart and still. "Have a fire waiting for us?"

"I would be happy to oblige," Alexander replied. He eyed Susan wearily, taking in all of her from the bare feet to the perfectly applied red lipstick. "Glad to see that you look better than the other night."

Susan smiled and glanced away. "Looks can be deceiving," she mumbled, then brightened. "I gotta get out of this and into something rubbery." She bounded past the embracing couple and into the cabin.

"She's much better than the other night." Brandy watched

to make sure Susan was out of earshot. "But still in a dark place. We'll get through this." She paused, momentarily taking in the nearness of Alexander. "I'm glad you could make it tonight."

"I apologize that I could not be with you at the funeral today." He brushed a wayward hair from her forehead.

"It's OK. I mean, you didn't know him more than a little and it would have been weird for you." Brandy led them towards the screen door.

"It will be OK." Alexander kissed her gently. The screen door shut behind them with a clunk.

***

Alexander stayed in the linear timeline. He did not have to. He could have slipped out and completed a million other things then returned when the main timeline had moved far enough forward and Brandy and Susan had returned from their dive. Yet he sat, like a linear with nothing to do but to wait with time. The night air was still. Insects buzzed and whirred in the dark. Alexander let his mind drift as he watched the surface of the water for any indication of their return. This time line would end. He could not deny the fact that Yindi had jumped to Susan. It would only be a matter of time before Yindi would have full control. He needed to go back and restore the timelines. He poked at the small fire before him and coaxed it into life. The sparks jumped and spattered. Pops hissed from the pine wood. He should end this now. Pick any moment to go back to and divert this timeline back to an original stream.

He pondered his choices. The first choice had all three live: Mark, Susan and Brandy. He could go back and reroute Yindi from taking over Mark to begin with. Easy enough, Alexander thought to himself. He threw another log chunk on the fire. Sparks flew towards the sky, fading embers sent upwards. He could watch where Mark had gone and keep him from encountering the toad that had been Yindi's temporary host. He paused to wish, uselessly, if only there was a way to contain the energy being or destroy it once and for all. Alexander brushed the thought away. A millennia of trial and error had proven ineffective.

His second choice was to allow the timeline to occur where Brandy was thrown under the bus. It meant Yindi would inhabit Mark, but Brandy and Susan would live. That time line had felt slightly off track, but if he was truthful, not exquisitely off course.

The third option, presently, was this course where Mark died, Yindi inhabited Susan and eventually Brandy would die too. Obviously this one had to end. Not only did it feel wrong, it pulled at his soul as time slipped and bumped from its course. This timeline had to be fixed.

Alexander stoked the fire again and slowly mulled over his options. He stood and stretched, an almost human gesture, and looked at the still water. He decided it was time to leave and perhaps he could redirect Mark to not encounter the toad. That would at least slow Yindi down a little bit. Alexander watched the water, hoping to see movement. Hoping Susan and Brandy would return. He would like to say goodbye to her one more time in this timeline, even if it was useless. He gave a snort, as he regarded the uselessness of watching this timeline any further.

Soft puff of cold breath as he dipped his toe in the water. The ripples radiated gently from the shore. A leaf, set a float by the slight movement, gently edged from the shoreline and floated towards the center of the pond. Bubbles floated up from below dissuading the leaf from continuing any further along its trajectory. It spun and toppled, moving off at an angle, dipping into the water. Capsized and sunk into the deep.

It was then that he felt the change. He felt it before he could feel the shifting of time and see the color change in his vision. The sick feeling was like falling in a dream and waking just before hitting the rocky ground below. In front of him the world took on a shockingly white glow, eerie and overblown. A searing screech filled his ears, high and sharp. The bubbles broke on the water and with each burst Alexander could feel time slide and fall. An inevitable realization crept closer to his consciousness yet he fought it off in disbelief.

The diver broke the surface, alone, and swam towards Alexander. Blonde hair plastered to her face. The scuba regulator hid her cunning grin.

Alexander was unaware of the steps he had taken into the water. The water lapped around his darkening jeans, sapping the energy from him slowly. He did not care.

She removed the regulator from her mouth. Scratches bled from the side of her face. Susan/Yindi walked towards Alexander then turned back towards the water.

They stood in silence. Staring at the water, the universe glowed white to both of them.

Susan/Yindi peeled the wetsuit from her/his frame. "That was the easiest one yet." He dropped the scuba tanks to the ground. They splashed in the shallow water. "Helps when they are drunks." He/she stretched out her hands to regard them. Broken and chipped nails, the red polish looked black in the dim light. He leaned towards Alexander and hissed, "Look at that white light. Entangled time. No matter what you do, THIS moment will happen. You cannot change it. She will die in that water."

He patted Alexander on the shoulder bravely, a wet smacking sound. "Feel that? Time pooling into this moment, rutting in." Susan shivered and a hand flew to her chest. "God, that's delicious. This moment cannot be escaped. You can change parts of it and try your best to keep her from coming here and going down there—but time will make it happen. Maybe you can drain the water? Somehow this moment will play out." Susan turned and looked back towards the forest. "And look back in the past, can you see? I can't—but I know it is there. Other moments, all glowing white and locked. YOU can't change them. They are all bundled up and entangled in this new rut we have made in time together." She held out her hand to indicate a past she could not see as if it stretched out behind them.

Alexander did not turn, did not look at Susan. He continued to stare at the water. It rippled and lapped around his legs. He was still standing there staring at the water when Susan stripped from the wetsuit and walked back towards the cabin, her laugh echoing as she left.

∗∗

"This human is a thing. You can't kill him." His breath was hitched and manic. "You'll be doing my work for me." Mark's words became a plea. "You'll ruin the game," he whined.

Alexander stood near Brandy while the newest Alexander stood on the other side. Both Alexanders looked at each other. His other self asked, "Kill him?"

Mark judged the doorway, ready to bolt. Then a sudden change came across the world, unseen by the linears. A grin spread across Mark's face as the room took on a white glow, sudden and hot.

A third Alexander appeared behind Mark, paused to take in the change in the room. All three Alexanders looked deflated. The first Alexander, closest to Brandy, looked at her dazed eyes. "This moment has locked."

The second Alexander shifted closer to Mark. Mark took a step back and bumped into the third Alexander. Mark's grin never faltered. "I told you that you'd make a rut in time."

The third Alexander, his pants legs still dripping wet from where he had stood in the pond helpless as Yindi/Susan had killed Brandy under the water far below, grabbed Mark by the wrists. The sound of bones breaking was hollow and thin. The sound of Mark's screaming was high and shrill. The Alexanders stepped back and disappeared with a collapse of air.

Pop.

Pop.

Pop.

Someone yelled, "Freeze!"

Mark held both arms to his chest, hands jutted out at crazy angles. He shoved Brandy towards the policeman.

Brandy caught herself before she fell backwards. The policeman moved around her, quickly making way towards Mark as he fled.

Their nightsticks banged on the swinging doors, still pivoting on their hinges.

Somewhere a glass window was broken.

The policeman yelled, "Outside, he's outside." And then so were they.

***

Brandy stood at the front door, phone pinned to her ear by her shoulder, keys in hand. Her voice was desperate and tired as she spoke. "Thanks for letting me come over. I can't stay here. It is all just too creepy."

The key refused to insert into the knob. Brandy stabbed it at the lock. Her over night bag slipped off her shoulder and yanked her arm down. The phone slipped from her shoulder and clattered on the ground.

"Damn it." Brandy kicked the phone out of the doorway, bent over and yelled to the phone. "Hold on, Susan. I'm dropping everything."

She took a deep breath and completed the complex task of shutting and locking her door. The sun was coming out and long shadows danced across the floor. Once she confirmed the door was locked, she retrieved the phone from one of the shadows. "Ok. I'm back. I feel so bad that I snapped at Alexander on the phone. I'm just so freaked out. Mark…" Her voice hitched and the bag slipped from her shoulder again. This time it yanked the phone from her face, rebounded and hit her in the face. "Fuck."

"Text me when you get here, OK? I'll meet you at the gate." Susan's voice was quiet, almost a whisper on the other end of the line.

"OK. I'm supposed to meet him for a date tonight." Brandy peered around the parking lot looking for anything unusual before she walked towards her car. "I don't know if I'll feel up to it. I just want to crawl into bed and not come out for a week." She checked the back seat of her car, twice. "Maybe ten."

***

Yindi/Mark held a broomstick against the laundry room door. It speared a roll of duck tape. Sweat rolled down his white, clammy face. He tried not to pass out. The duck tape stuck to his lip. He grunted and exhaled as he pulled it free, using his cheek to keep the roll in place as he maneuvered his hand.

He couldn't help but grin even as the pains of nausea hit again. The pain from his hands was tremendous, throbbing, white hot pain that screamed the wrongness in his extremities. He had seen the white light engulf the moment at the nursing home. Three Alexanders, all looking defeated. Could it be such a victory? Yindi could not see the other timelines, could not know what other things could have happened. Trapped to depend on linears and their timeline inhabitation he could only see the timeline the linear could see. He could feel though. Oh yes, he could feel the pull of the universe, the rip tide of time as it listed and pooled into this timeline. He worked at the duct tape and bound his broken wrists to be straight. The sound of the tape pulling from the roll could barely be heard over the oversized dryer his back rested against. Something heavy thumped and bumped in the dryer. He pushed his bent hand against the laundry room door, straightening it. He chewed on his lip and focused on pulling the duct tape around the swollen wrist. Wrap by wrap he grunted and grimaced. He tested his fingers, still working. No bone poking through the skin. He grinned even wider. Yindi/Mark looked down at his blood spattered pajamas and bare feet. Perhaps the thumping in the dryer was a pair of shoes. Yindi/Mark was happy that things seem to finally be going his way. He worked at removing his pajamas, his hands painful and clumsy. Finally, going his way. He had to move now. Had to go. Had to go find her. Needed to take the next move in this game. He stood and peered from the apartment complex laundry room. This would be fun.

***

No one noticed the man in baggy jeans, duct tape wrapped around both wrists and shoes a size too big, slink from the end of the complex and disappear into the wooded area.

***

She had already had two cups of coffee and an egg-white omelet when Brandy had called. Brandy hadn't given many details, only the basics and it was obvious her friend needed some company. Who could survive seeing their best friend go crazy like that? Susan locked her condo door behind her and descended the five steps to the pavement. Her complex was gated and visitors had to park outside the gate then register at the clubhouse with security. She pulled her phone from her pocket and with perfectly painted red fingernails texted, "On my way."

The response from Brandy was immediate. "K."

The sidewalk wound towards the front of the complex. Wrought iron gates and brick walled fences kept her from the world. The main street was ahead. She could see Brandy, bag over her shoulder, phone in hand, walking from the visitor parking lot. Susan waved. Brandy waved back.

Movement from the side caught Susan's eye. It was someone walking fast, and directly towards Brandy. Susan tried to raise her voice and held her hands out in a universal gesture of stop. Time seemed to slow as nothing else mattered but what was in front of her. She was powerless to stop it, unable to reach her friend in time. Mark was running towards Brandy, his arms raised, a wild grin on his face. He pushed her. The impact of her and the bus was a sound that would echo forever in Susan's dreams. Brandy hit the side of the bus, just at the bumper. Her face impacted, a crunching, smacking sound. She bounced back, her right leg buckled and she reached out with her arm. The bus, already in mid stop, screeched to an abrupt stop but not before Brandy was caught and pinned in the wheel well, arm twisted incorrectly behind her head.

Brandy's cell phone bounced and skidded across the pavement. By the time Susan was able to reach Brandy a rivulet of blood led from the carnage at the bus to the phone. Their texts were still visible on the cracked screen.

"On my way."

"K."

15 PAIN EVERYWHERE IN NOWHERE.

There was a beep somewhere. It ebbed into Brandy's dreams.

Steady.

Rhythmic.

Peaceful.

Brandy is running. Trying to move her feet. She looks down and expects to see snakes tangled around her feet: moving, writhing, clinging. Instead she finds intestines. They are moving like snakes, bloody gore dripping and viscous. Headless intestines move against one another in a blind attempt to keep her feet from moving. Brandy tries to stomp, to jump, to escape. They become heavier and bind her legs.

"You should not fight them." A voice is talking from behind her.

She turns her head, unable to turn her feet. She cannot find the person that spoke.

Billy is approaching her. His jaw hangs from its hinges absurdly. His voice is unhampered by the mangled mechanism. "Answer the beep. I pressed the nurse call button in the bathroom. That means it is urgent."

Brandy couldn't help but look to his abdomen. Just as she expected, snakes of intestines ooze out as if sentient. Their writhing is mesmerizing.

"Answer the beep." Billy keeps talking through his nonworking jaw.

She reaches forward to try to fix the jaw. Maybe she can make it re-hinge, she thinks. Billy is not where she reaches.

"Stay still," she is whispering.

Beep.

Billy is sitting on the floor in front of her desperately trying to put the intestine snakes back into his torn abdomen. They are slipping from his grasp. Sliding between his toes.

Beep.

He is looking at her now. Blood tears run down his face. "Answer the beep. I need you."

Beep.

"I can't move." Brandy points to her body now covered in intestine snakes. They are so heavy, she feels smothered.

Beep.

Beep.

There is nothing. Brandy floats. Is floating somewhere, nothing above her. Only white blankness.

Beep.

"Can you hear me?" Alexander's slow voice is calling out to her.

She tries to answer but is silent.

Beep.

She feels cold, nothing, nowhere, empty. Lost. Fear.

Beep.

Beep.

Beep.

***

Beep.

Beep.

Beep.

The sun on Brandy's face is a welcomed warmth. She turns her face towards it and regrets the movement instantly. Pain explodes in her face, neck, arm. She is dimly aware of pain in her leg, back, pelvis. The right side of her body feels stiff, too swollen to exist. She envisions images of the Stay Puft Marshmallow Man. Her body feels held down, unable to move. She would panic except that she wants no more pain and moving seemed to cause it. Her eyes wouldn't operate and open. She concentrated on sounds. Tried to ignore the pain, which now once acknowledged seemed to grow and expand and become all encompassing.

Beep: a heart monitor. She knew that sound. She listened to the steady rhythm of it.

A very quiet whirl and clunk. An IV pump had just administered another dose. She knew that s....

Numbness.

Nothing.

***

Her tongue was stuck to the roof of her mouth. It felt huge and pasty. Her lips were cracked and painful. She tried to open her eyes again. They refused. Or perhaps they couldn't. She moved her eyes from side to side under her eyelids. She could feel a weight on her eyelids, could hear a slight sound. Bandaged? She tried in vain to lick her lips.

A cold cloth was held to her lips. So much relief, she tried to turn her head towards it.

"Relax. Let me do the work." Alexander's voice.

Jumbled thoughts fell into her brain and twisted. Why was she hurt? What had happened? She did not remember anything. She croaked a nonsensical sound.

"It would be useless for me to tell you to not speak, I suppose." His voice, slow, steady, a rhythm with the heart monitor as backup bass. "You should not try."

She pursed her lips in response. They stung. She could imagine them cracking and bleeding. She could taste the bad breath on her teeth. How long had she been like this? Why?

"We are going to keep you sedated for a while longer. Let you skip a bulk of the pain." Alexander explained and reapplied the cold cloth. "Here are some ice chips."

The ice was pleasure extraordinaire. She could concentrate on that and ignore the creeping pain that was starting to worm its way through her body—a whisper at first, becoming more urgent and loud.

He kissed her cracked lips. She wanted to recoil, to tell him how bad her breath might be. She could not muster the energy to do so. Her lips tingled where his kiss had been. She had a fleeting memory of a kiss in a cave. How long ago?

"I will be close by." Alexander's voice seemed further away.

A mechanical whir and clunk.

Beep.

Nothingness.

***

The sun again, touching her face. She could feel it at the tip of her nose. The bandages must be off her face. Before she could confirm, the nothingness took her.

She awoke. Must still be the same day, she surmised. The sun was on her right cheek now. It was difficult to put thoughts together. Maybe she would nap a little more.

Brandy awoke again. Fuzzy thoughts swam and collided. She could feel the sun on her right ear. Her head must be facing north. She took comfort in this understanding of her surroundings and slid away into the darkness.

***

Nothing. Floating. She is trying to move, is held down. Susan is beside her. Brandy turns her head to see.

"Right in front of me," Susan is saying. Her red lipstick is smeared across her face. She is crying.

Brandy tries to reach and comfort her. Her hands are stuck or held down. She can only whisper. "It's OK. It's going to be OK." Her voice is a dry croak. She hears her voice somewhere else, in the distance as if playing on a TV.

Susan grabs her arm. Her grip is harsh and strong. Brandy opens her mouth to object. Instead in the distance, she can hear her voice say, "Stop. You're hurting me, Susan." It sounds like a TV underwater. She distractedly wonders if a TV could be heard underwater. The grip will not let up. The pain sears up her arm and into her shoulder. Brandy wishes Susan would stop grabbing her. She will not let go.

She opens her mouth to scream at Susan; water rushes in.

She feels the blackness coming. Maybe it will take the pain away? She welcomes it, hoping that it might.

***

The world became more to her, slowly. At first she could only hear the absence of the heart monitor. "I'm not dead," she thought. She could feel her heart beat in her throbbing extremities. Though they seemed distant, like they belonged to someone else. Ignorable. She could not hear anything else. Or could she? A wind blew outside. A curtain clicked on a windowsill, an insistent staccato. She could feel the gentle breeze in the room, slight air movement. A foot shifted on the floor, barely audible. The curtain stopped its clicking as it was pulled across its rod. Brandy tried to open her eyes and found they were already open looking up at a dark ceiling. Now she registered the dim moonlight interrupted by a shadow as someone came towards her.

"Welcome back," Alexander whispered.

She took a deep breath. "How long?" A croak.

"Three weeks." He stood at the bedside but did not sit.

"Wow," Brandy mouthed. The effort hurt her face.

"It is going to be a very long recovery." He circled the bed and took her left hand.

Brandy realized her right one was bandaged. She glanced down, trying to see all she could without moving her head. She raised an eyebrow, which hurt, and looked back towards Alexander, the question unspoken but unmistakable. "Status?"

"The right side of your body has suffered damage. Broke femur. Compound. Rod. Plate. Pins." He stroked her thumb with his. "Fractured pelvis. Healing. No complications."

She winced and smiled sardonically. "No sex for you," Brandy whispered.

"Not for a while, this is true." He squeezed her hand. "There is more. Broken right arm, at the elbow. Pinned. Reattached tendons. Broken fingers. Pinky and ring."

"Fu…" Brandy could barely croak.

Alexander continued, "Fractured eye socket, nose and cheek bone."

"Oh." Brandy understood why eyebrow wiggles could hurt so much.

Alexander smiled, a wrinkled expression of disbelief. "You lost a canine tooth."

"I'll make a bad vampire now," she tried to joke. Her words were muffled as she explored the gap in her dental line up.

Alexander froze, unsure what to say for a moment. His face relaxed and he smiled again. "Indeed."

He held a water glass and straw forward. She accepted and tried to drink while lying down. He stopped her and held out his hand. "Hold on. This will work better." He held his finger over the end of the straw, moved the straw to her open mouth and released his finger. The water dripped in.

She accepted it then her expression changed, darkened. "Sit me up. No internal bleeding on the fractured pelvis?"

"No."

"Then I can sit up. My ego won't survive bird feeding." Brandy could feel the pain kick up a notch as the bed was adjusted to a slightly seated position.

"I can see how this is going to go." Alexander smiled and held the water glass close for her to drink.

"Do you remember anything yet?"

Brandy drank slowly, licked her lips and closed her eyes. "Was it Mark?"

"Yes."

"Is Susan OK?"

"Yes."

"Was Mark…caught?"

"No."

She paused. "Are we safe?"

"Yes." Alexander put the water glass on the table. A pool of condensation reflected the full moon that shone in through the open window. "I promise. You are safe. He can not find you here."

"Where am I?" Brandy started to slip back into sleep as the whirring machine administered the next round of morphine.

"With me." Alexander lowered the head of her bed and watched her fade back to unconsciousness.

***

The sun was back again. Sliding from her nose to her ear. A new noise seemed to come from all around her, a gentle hum. She held her good hand to the bed. It vibrated slightly. I'm definitely not in a normal rehabilitation home, she thought. She had seen a bed like this once before. Pretty expensive, alternating air mattress with static float, prevents bed soars and sleeps like a dream. The gentle hum lulled her, enhanced the sense of floating.

Brandy listened for other noises, activities in the hallway, call bells, nurses talking at the station, squeaks of white nursing shoes, the unmistakable sound of sick people: retching, coughing, questions, tense, low whispering. She heard nothing.

"That's enough of this," she thought and opened her eyes. The sun was brighter than she had hoped. It made her eyes water. Brandy patted the bed with her left hand and found a remote control clipped to her blanket. She brought it to her face and flinched when it swung on its electric cord and nearly hit her nose. "Dipshit," she hissed. After some study she raised the head of her bed up via the correct button and took stock of her situation.

She found the IV cord that led from her arm to the machine. She tugged on it gently to bring the machine closer. Upon inspection she realized it was no longer auto distributing the narcotics. It was set to patient distribution. No wonder she was awake. She could hold off on a dose for a while. Though she would have to still dose and wean off the numbing drugs. How long had she been on them? How long since Alexander had said she had been out three weeks?

Inspection of her body, a delicate process of removing blankets with her left hand then replacing them, showed a cast from toe to hip on her right leg. Her toes stuck out like pale, white aliens. So far away, she could not imagine reaching them. They had to be gross and need a wash. Someone had painted the toenails red. Closer inspection showed the left foot had been equally assaulted.

"Susan." Brandy smiled and wiggled her alien toes.

Groping inspection found a catheter and to her horror, a colostomy bag. "Holy hell, that has to go." She wondered what type of internal damage had been done that Alexander had not mentioned. She took a deep breath testing for broken ribs. Found two suspect ribs that shot pain through her side as her chest expanded with air. The pain was short lived. Healing.

Brandy poked gently at her pelvis. Mild pain there. Healing.

She regarded her fingers, which were unbound. Her arm was still in a cast. Healing.

She looked towards the window where she had last seen Alexander. How long ago was that? Her brain felt foggy and unresponsive. She let go of the question.

"OK. Leg and arm are the biggest issues now. Manageable," she whispered to herself. She reached up and touched her face. A ragged raw two-inch scar accented her right eyebrow. "Oh." Alexander had not mentioned that either. Unconsciously, she had been tensing her feet and legs during her exploration. The pain began to intensify and sweat broke out on her upper lip.

A table was close by, she reached for the water glass and took a sip. Lowered the bed. Pressed the red button to self administer a dose of morphine. She looked around to find a clock, but found none. She marked where the sun was in the window, one third down the length. I need a clock to measure time. She thought. Get this down to three a day. Then she was out.

***

She missed the night. It was day again when she awoke. This time someone was in the room. She thought it was Alexander but found a small woman busying herself at the foot of her bed. Brandy watched as the nurse, round and short, dressed in all white, finished her task and straightened. Gloved hands held a pitcher of urine. The nurse disappeared behind a door, which Brandy had not noticed. Flushing. Washing. Water being poured out. More washing. The nurse reappeared. Silent.

238

"Hi," Brandy greeted the nurse.

The nurse paused, looked at her, cocked her head to one side and smiled. She did not speak.

"Where am I?" Brandy asked. The nurse wore no nametag, nor hospital insignia. Brandy looked around the room. This was not a stark hospital room. Warm wood crown molding, carpeted floor, deep window sills with billowing satin curtains. Was this a private health center?

The nurse paused, smiled again, an apology with a gentle twitch of her head. The understood signal for inability of speech.

"Oh." Brandy understood.

The nurse curtsied and left the room.

"Well that was weird as hell," Brandy whispered to herself.

The nurse returned with a dainty tray of food. Or Brandy suspected it was food. It all resembled different colors and textures of applesauce. Mashed potatoes with gravy, indeed, applesauce, meatloaf-ish mush that did smell good though. Brandy could not deny that. The tray had a steaming cup of something, milk, and a vase containing a delicate rose and fern leaf. Brandy hoped for coffee and was not disappointed. She drank gingerly and was content. The nurse left again and did not return for another hour to remove the empty tray, which sat in front of a sleeping Brandy. The nurse lowered the head of the bed.

A routine ensued. Brandy would wake, fight off taking the morphine and concentrate on moving the parts of her body that could move. Someone had placed a metal triangle over her bed. She could use that to pull herself up and gently reposition her body. The nurse would silently bring food. Brandy would silently eat. She would give in, self dose and sleep. Some evenings Brandy would wake to find Alexander in her room. She was usually too groggy to ask him questions. Others nights she woke to a dark, empty room.

A week passed. Brandy thought it was a week. When she woke she found that the IV was gone. So was the colonoscopy bag and catheter. She had to pee. A portable potty chair was set up next to the bed.

"Oh F me. You have got to be kidding." Brandy glared at the chair, then at her unused leg, the broken leg and broken arm. There would be no long walks today.

The nurse appeared at the doorway. She smiled and clapped her hands together. A gesture of "Let's get this done. Shall we?" She did something with her feet under the bed and the whole bed lowered towards the ground.

Brandy sat up and tried to swing her legs off the side of the bed. The leg with the cast to her hip stuck out stiffly and almost a moment too late Brandy realized that gravity was going to pull it to the ground with a thump, and that was going to hurt like a son-of-a-bitch. She grabbed the leg with her good left hand and lowered it to the ground almost gently. The nurse assisted. It still hurt like a son-of-a-bitch. She breathed out of her mouth in slow measured puffs.

"Can I put weight on it?" Brandy asked.

The nurse nodded.

Careful to avoid the injured arm, the nurse put her hands under Brandy's armpits and braced her knee against Brandy's good knee. With the nurse as her brace, Brandy stood and pivoted towards the blessedly close potty chair. Brandy felt humiliated and relieved at the same time to be moving.

"Well. It's a start," Brandy stated resolutely.

The nurse nodded again.

***

The moon was just a sliver. Brandy watched as it slipped across the open window. It took hours. She drifted in and out of a dream state, unable to focus on the paperback facedown on her lap. A stack of unread paperbacks littered the bedside table. A clock ticked off the time. In bold red numbers it glared 9:42 p.m.

"I can hear you over there." She smiled and lifted her drooping eyelids.

Alexander, leaning against the doorway, uncrossed his arms and smiled in return. "There is no fooling you, I suppose."

He came closer and continued, "How are you feeling today?"

"Sick of sitting still." Brandy took a deep breath and let it out. "I gotta get moving."

"Agreed." Alexander stepped out into the hallway and wheeled in a wheelchair. "It is even electric, since you cannot push with your bad arm."

"Well." Brandy sighed again. Release from one prison to another. "I'm loosing track of days."

"That happens here." Alexander locked the wheels and waited for Brandy.

"What's going on Alexander?" She pointed to the bed, the chair, the room. "I know I've been out of it a good long while. But there's something odd here."

"Yes. I owe you an explanation." Alexander held her left hand. "You have to trust me."

Brandy looked at the chair with trepidation. "This isn't a

hospital. I've only ever seen the one nurse." Brandy pointed towards the end of the bed. "There isn't a chart at the end of this bed or outside that door from what I can see. I need to see the doctor and see what he's been prescribing."

Alexander smiled. "There is a lot of explaining that I have to do." He tugged on her hand. "Some of it you are not going to believe."

"You'd be surprised. I'm pretty open-minded." Brandy squeezed his hand.

"I do hope so," was Alexander's response.

Brandy stood on her good leg and leaned forward to hold onto his neck with her good arm. "You are taller than the nurse." She leaned in closer, her head and neck against his cool chest, allowing him to assist her with situating the broken leg.

He flinched just slightly and pulled back.

"Oh, did my necklace catch on your chest hair?" Brandy giggled. "Sorry!"

Alexander bent forward and helped Brandy sit into the chair. He straightened and pulled the collar of his shirt gently. "Inevitable." He smiled.

She raised the leg extension and felt immediate relief as her right leg became more horizontal. "Ah, better."

"Time for me to show you around and explain some things." He started to push the wheelchair.

"Hey." Brandy stopped him. "Let me take her out for a spin."

He smiled and stood back.

It took some muttering and well placed curses before Brandy could maneuver the chair through the doorway without banging her bad foot against the doorjamb.

***

Whatever Brandy had expected to see outside her room was not at all what she found. Wide, wood paneled, brightly lit hallways. Oversized, gilded framed paintings adorned the halls, which seemed to stretch on forever in both directions.

"OK, you better drive. I'll get lost." Brandy gave up control and looked up at Alexander. "Is this your house?"

"I can not fool you." He kissed her gently. "Yes."

Brandy shivered. "Mark doesn't know how to get here?"

Alexander squeezed her shoulder, reassuringly. "I can promise you there is no way he can get here. It is the safest place away from him in the whole universe."

She reached up and held his hand on her shoulder. "Thank you." She remembered when he held her hand to him when the first met in the cave. "Just pathetic." She thought but said, "Susan hasn't visited."

"That would be one of the drawbacks as well. No one can find you here." Alexander pushed her through the hallway and to a large open dining room.

"What, no huge library like in Beauty and the Beast?" Brandy laughed.

"Well." Alexander pointed through double doors to the left. Beyond was a sitting room with floor to ceiling hardbound books. A wing-backed chair faced the wall, which encompassed a floor to ceiling window and fireplace.

"With windows like that the view must be stunning." Brandy took control of the chair again and navigated the room to get a better view through the large window.

The view was barely visible with the slim moon low in the sky. Alexander turned off the lights in the room so she could better see the stars. They exploded in the sky. No city lights could be seen in the distance to block out the view of the night sky with their ambient glow. The Milky Way seemed so vibrant she felt as if she could reach out and stir it with her hands.

"Wow. I'll have to check this out in the daytime," Brandy said.

"I have a wonderful dinner prepared for you." Alexander motioned towards the dining room.

"Talking dishes and tea pots?" Brandy smiled.

Alexander looked at her questioningly.

"Never watched a Disney film before? You know, 'Be our Guest'?" She put her hands in her lap so that he could push the wheelchair.

"No. I do not watch films. I prefer to read." His voice was quiet and distant.

***

They situated themselves at the dining room table. Gleaming mahogany set with bone white dishes and red linens. Brandy held up the utensils for inspection. The gold gleamed in the candlelight. "Very nice."

"I am glad you approve." Alexander rang a bell and three wait staff entered the room with steaming trays of food.

"Seriously?" Brandy looked at Alexander.

"It is not usual. I … hired them while you are here." He accepted a glass of red wine from the porter. "I must admit, I do not cook. You need food." He raised his glass.

Brandy raised hers. "I should only have one of these, considering the amount of pain pills I'm still downing. One won't hurt."

Alexander seemed at a loss for what to say as a toast. He opened his mouth to speak, but before he could, Brandy interjected.

"To now. Nothing else matters." Brandy clinked her glass to his.

"Indeed."

***

"What do you mean you are taking her?" Susan stood at the coffee vending machine in the hospital. The machine spit and spurted into a small paper cup. She checked its progress.

"She needs to be away from here until Mark is found. It is not safe." Alexander handed a coffee stir to Susan.

The cafeteria around them was filled with orderlies in scrubs chewing without seeming to taste their food. Clusters of worried people filled various tables and picked at food, their conversations lulled.

Susan and Alexander stood at the end of the cafeteria. They stood close together, their conversation low, a reverent respect for all of those in pain.

"To some place you won't tell us about? That pisses me off." Susan stirred sweetener into her coffee and sniffed at it suspiciously. Her nose wrinkled. "It feels like you're kidnapping her. I mean…" She took a sip and found it not too objectionable. "What about her mom? She's gotta have something to say about this."

"It was her idea basically." He leaned against the vending machine and regarded the room. "I know a specialist. I suggested it. Her mom agreed. Brandy will get the best of care. Mark will not reach her there. She will be safe."

"That's insane," Susan pouted. "Who ever heard of just letting your best friend disappear? You must be cracked. And Mrs. B. trusted you? She's never even met you before. Hell. I've only met you a few times." A few people turned to regard Susan's outburst.

"I…" Alexander started.

"Let me guess. Mrs. B said if Brandy trusted you she would trust you too. She has got to be the most gullible lady. To this day she still thinks Brandy and I went to summer camp when we were 17. We caught a ride and went to Bonnaroo. Had a blast. She believes anything Brandy tells her."

"Something tells me Brandy never misled her." Alexander slipped two quarters into the machine.

Susan eyed him. "I did trick her into the ride and Bonnaroo. She had no idea till we got there. I told her we were going to ride with Jimmy to camp. Said he was a counselor. She didn't talk to me for days. Once you get in there, you can't get out. Cell phones weren't invented then."

"You kidnapped your own friend?" he joked.

"For her own good." Susan softened. Her eyes pleaded with Alexander. "You promise me she's going to get better?"

Alexander put an arm around Susan's shoulder and they walked back towards Brandy's room, each with a coffee in hand. "I promise she will return in excellent health. She will be better before you can imagine it and she will be safe."

They stood at the doorway and looked in at Brandy's still form. Her swollen face could barely be seen under the bandages. Just her chin and bottom lip were exposed. Heart monitors beeped steadily.

"I feel guilty even thinking this." Susan emptied the coffee cup, grimaced. "Is he going to come after me?"

"Not this time," Alexander thought. He said, "He has no reason to. Maybe you should go on a vacation just in case?"

"Wait a 'sec. what do you mean "not this time"? Was there a time he was coming after me that I don't know about?" Susan gripped Alexander's arm.

Alexander smiled briefly then his face became serious. He leveled a gaze at her. "It is the best thing for her. I promise to keep you updated on her progress."

Susan relented. "OK. I'm not going on vacation though. That's absurd. He has no reason to come after me. It was just a psychotic break. "

Alexander and Susan walked arm in arm into Brandy's room. Her heart monitor beeped steadily. He reiterated, "I promise to keep her safe."

***

Brandy was mopping up gravy with a biscuit and smiling contentedly. "You barely touched your dinner." She indicated Alexander's plate still littered with picked apart remains of a turkey dinner, mashed potatoes, carrots.

"Did you like it?" He placed his napkin over top of his dinner plate. A porter stepped in and whisked it out of sight.

"First solid food I've had in…" Brandy looked at Alexander expectedly.

"Six weeks," he filled in the gap.

"It was excellent." She leaned back in her wheelchair and adjusted her leg, wincing with the effort. "So, I guess this was our first date, officially."

"Well then, could you suffer through some dessert?" Alexander motioned to the three wait staff that surrounded the table. They nodded and disappeared through the far swinging door. "How is your pain level?"

"Tolerable. I'll need to lie down soon. But first…" Brandy was interrupted by one of the wait staff entering the dining room with a white dish in his hand, a golden dome on tope. He placed it in front of Brandy and with great flourish, removed the gold dome, revealing a chocolate mousse. "Nice." Brandy picked up a small gold spoon and took a sample. "Would you like a bite?" She held out a spoon of mousse to Alexander.

He smiled and leaned closer, never moving his eyes from hers, and took a nibble of the mousse offered. She leaned forward and kissed him.

"This was a nice date." Brandy motioned to the door through which the wait staff had once again disappeared. "That's kinda weird. But I appreciate the thoughtfulness of everything."

Alexander gently pulled her to him and returned the kiss, mindful of her broken arm, which was perched between them.

Brandy still held the dessert spoon in her hand and brought it up to eye level. The gold gleamed in the candlelight. "Hound dog chased a raccoon into a cave, huh?"

"There are probably a few things I need to explain. I do not know if you will believe me," Alexander smiled.

***

Mark/Yindi donned a hospital gown. It flopped open behind him, bare skin exposed. Is she still here? He grabbed a lonely IV stand and rolled it along with him. It clinked loudly. A saline drip hung unused. His hands ached and throbbed where Alexander had broken his wrists. He had managed to bind them better and they were more stable than before. He held the loose end of the IV tubing in his hand and walked slowly down the hall. His gate uneven with anticipation that he struggled to conceal, just another ambulating patient, nothing more to see here.

His heart pounded.

Here.

Now.

He had held off for so long. The call to maim time wheedled at his bones.

Mark worried at his lip. Is she here? He stood in the shadows of a long hallway listening to the people come and go. So many possible things here called out to him, so much mayhem that could be done. Nervously his head twitched and spasmed from side to side as each room he walked by held another potential thing that could be disturbed.

Here?

No.

There?

No.

He ignored the distractions. Yindi fought to keep control of his raging desires. Brandy. He needed her. They had brought her here.

Twitch.

Turn.

Peek.

Hope.

No.

A room full of a hopeful family around a middle-aged man. Mark paused at the door listening to their joy. Snatches of conversation tempted him to pause.

"…can't believe you'll make it to the ribbon cutting…"

"I told you it was a false alar…"

"…can't be too careful…"

"We'll make a difference in this…"

Someone inside the room paused and looked Mark's way. He hurried on before they could suspect him of anything. He could not call attention to himself. Had to stay hidden. Had to find her. She was here. Had to be. He could feel it in his bones.

Mark/Yindi recalled the crunch of her skull as it hit the bus. A crack. He had run back into the alley and away from the incident before she had even hit the ground. Could not be caught. Could not be changed. It was good, he thought. It was very good.

Now to find her and play some more. Even though it was night, and Alexander might be around, Mark/Yindi did not care. He knew he could not be killed now. He did not know for certain what the moment was going to be. Yindi did know that in the nursing home the universe had turned white. That meant time had locked into a series of events that could not change. He was as trapped as a linear and could not see what the future event would be. Alexander could. From the look of defeat on Alexander's face, it was something amazing. Yindi could not wait. He stepped his pace up a little more. The saline bag swung on the pole. Oh, it was going to be the end of everything. Freedom. Chaos. Joy.

Where was she? He could feel the draw of her now. The big thing, as she was to him, a humming energy beacon. Brandy was up ahead. Was Alexander there too? "He won't kill me. He can't kill me. This isn't the moment," Yindi kept singing in his mind. Over and over. "Can't kill me. Won't kill me."

Just as he couldn't kill her. Yet.

He rounded the nurses station. The nurses studied charts, spoke on phones and busied themselves with more paperwork.

A phone rang near Yindi's elbow. He jumped. The nurse eyeballed him blandly and answered the phone. After a pause she said, "You'll have to give me more information than that. I have six patients with heart pain."

Yindi moved away from her voice and towards an open door. She was there. He knew. Right there. The chart on the door confirmed it. "Brandy Bayents." Yindi gently opened the door and stepped inside as if it was his room. Nothing to see. Just a patient strolling into his room.

The room was dark, the monitors quiet. Brandy lay sleeping on the bed, a figure loomed over her. For a brief second the figure raised his head and met Yindi's eyes. Alexander smiled. He gently lifted Brandy's body to him. They disappeared.

The air collapsed inward to fill the void.

For a moment Yindi could only stand and sway to and fro. He twisted the IV tubing in his hand.

Twisted, un-twisted.

Twisted.

Un-twisted.

"Aaaaaaaahhhhhhhhhhhhhrrrrrrr!" An outburst full of spit and rage erupted from him. He wanted to hit the wall, pound the whiteboard on the wall but thought of his broken wrists. Insult to injury, it angered him more. He kicked at the bed and it jolted across the room. The oblong table capsized and spilled the water pitcher onto the floor. Orchids bounced on the linoleum.

He then turned, abandoned the IV pole and ran down the hallway and out into the night. The nurses sat at their station stunned at the noise. They blinked wordlessly at each other; the door at the stairwell banged closed.

***

The sun was high in the sky but it must have been early morning yet; the sun wasn't peeking into Brandy's window directly. She blinked and stretched gently, mindful of the painful limbs. Nothing screamed at her loudly. She enjoyed the ability to be awake and not overcome with pain. She wiggled her toes against the soft, warm blanket, not as painful as yesterday. Solace where she could find it. Time passed. She wasn't sure how much. Twenty minutes? An hour? Did it matter? Brandy breathed in deeply and listened for anyone near by.

Silence.

Eventually the necessity to visit the bathroom and the want for coffee caused her to stir. She raised the head of her bed and began to compose her thoughts for the day. Goals: get to the bathroom on her own in the wheelchair, eat, drink coffee, maybe roam the hallways today and get out of her room, nap, repeat, then end the day. Funny. It didn't seem like much, but every single goal took concentration of movement, orientation of wheelchairs and unresponsive, no, painful and unresponsive limbs in casts. Each accomplishment would take time to recover from and eventually she would need to succumb to a pain pill at least once, if not twice. Brandy snorted.

She reached for a cup of water from the pitcher on her

nightstand. A small postcard was placed next to it. Brandy picked it up.

Dear Brandy,

You won't believe what I won. A cruise to Alaska!! It was only valid this month. I am taking oodles of pictures for you. You HAVE to do this cruise—you would love it. No email here. I'll get them to you when I get back.

Love,
Susan

The front of the postcard showed an image of a ship's prow overlooking an iceberg. Brandy looked at the back again and then the front. The back was addressed to Brandy's apartment.

"I'll be damned," she whispered, somewhat disbelieving.

The wheelchair was parked, with its wheels locked, next to the bed. She maneuvered herself into the chair with only minimal bumping of her broken leg and arm. Sliding down into the chair was one thing. She looked back at the bed, which was four inches higher than the wheelchair. Getting back up was going to be another thing all together. She fumbled with the feet peddles at the bottom of the bed. It was already lowered as far as it would go. Well. She looked again from the wheelchair back up to the bed. She would figure something out. Too bad she didn't have her climbing gear. She'd rig a harness. Brandy tilted her head and smiled. That would be a good use of her gear, she thought.

She listened again. No one around. No nurse. No

Alexander. No one. Just her. Had she slept through breakfast? How quickly she had gotten used to someone bringing her food. Brandy shuddered and frowned. She'd go find breakfast. She did not need to have food brought to her, that was silly. A box of cereal and some boxed milk would set her up for a week's worth of breakfasts. Time to get this back under control, or better put, in her control.

Brandy unlocked the wheelchair and wheeled towards the bathroom.

The house was eerily quiet as Brandy wheeled down the hallway. The electric motor hummed quietly and the wheels squeaked on the wood floor. This was a large house. She roamed through the first floor and found a staircase that spiraled up grandly towards a floor out of her reach. On the first floor she found oil portraits in all manner of styles depicting a wide range of individuals in period clothing. Brandy wondered if these were portraits of movie actors? Perhaps people portraying famous individuals. Brandy look again trying to understand if she should recognize the people. She could not. She did not have enough knowledge of historical figures to recognize these people, she thought. She recognized periods of clothing. A woman of Native American origins, her face broad and strong. A man in plain linen clothing, he looked like a farmer dusty from the fields. A man in elaborate, embroidered coat tails and stiff white collar. Another young woman in early colonial American dress stood with a dog, pre-civil war era maybe. Image after image in gilded frame lined the large hallway. Doorways opened off the hallway to reveal empty rooms with large windows and well oiled wooden floors. The walls seemed to be hand-hewn beams with chinking between them. Brandy ran her fingers along the white plaster between the beams expecting it to be flaked and pitted. It was smooth as if finished yesterday. In fact the whole place had a distinct feel of being brand new, hand made but with years of collections of artifacts careful placed about. It also felt empty. Brandy did begin to wonder what would happen if she did need help? She banished the thought. She could get by alone today.

At the end of the hall she found the dining room to the right and the library to the left. She also found a breakfast laid out in the dining room. Cereal in crystal canisters. Biscuits wrapped in linen cloth in a small basket. The smell of the warm biscuits reminded Brandy of her hunger and she was suddenly thankful someone was assisting her. She would have to learn to be OK with being helped. She looked at the table again for signs of a beverage. Nothing there.

Brandy peeked through the swinging door into the large kitchen beyond.

"Hello?"

Carefully, she motored her wheelchair to the swinging door until her extended right leg hit the door. She looked at the wheelchair footrest, hoping it would not scratch the deep mahogany door. With careful movement of her left thumb on the lever she pushed the wheelchair forward using her footrest to open the door in front of her. There was no one in the kitchen. She maneuvered around the large wooden island in the center of the kitchen and found a silver percolator sitting on the stovetop. The stove was on low heat, the flames turned down low. She considered what to do and how best to make her movements through the kitchen as succinct as possible. She took a coffee cup and saucer from the counter top. It had been set out waiting for the coffee to be ready. Brandy placed the coffee cup in her lap between one thigh and the wheelchair side and the saucer on top of her casted thigh. She turned the burner off and with her left hand placed the hot coffee pot on the saucer and held it in place with her barely functioning right hand. Brandy then carefully began to back out of the kitchen.

She watched the coffee pot with an eagle eye. If it tipped over and poured down her cast she would be in a heck of a mess. As she passed the counter she grabbed a hand towel off a hook and wrapped it around the coffee pot. Luckily, it seemed to be stable.

She looked mournfully at the ancient stainless steel ice-box. She wished she could have some cream for the coffee, but she did not have the hands or lap for it. She would have had to pack that first. Brandy sighed and resigned herself to cream-less coffee. After a tense second at the door she was able to roll to the table without spilling the coffee. Once she was situated, she had to rest from all the effort, which silly enough to her, had been extraordinary.

With deep satisfaction, she unpacked the coffee percolator and poured herself a cup of coffee. It smelled wonderful.

As she began to eat biscuits and drink coffee her mind drifted back to her dinner at this very table and the conversation she and Alexander had the evening before.

***

"There are probably a few things I need to explain. I do not know if you will believe me." Alexander had smiled gently and paused as if he didn't know how to go on.

"Go on," Brandy urged.

"There are many things about me that you do not know."

256

He paused again and took the spoon from her hand. "And I want to tell you everything about me. I do." Alexander dipped the spoon into the chocolate mousse and held it up for Brandy to bite.

She eyed him for a moment, unsure. "Are you an international drug trafficker?"

"No." A smile in his voice.

She took the bite offered. "Sex ring trafficker?"

"No."

Brandy took the spoon from him before he could try to feed her another bite. She continued her inquisition, "Movie producer?"

"No."

"Did you come by all of this honestly?" She spooned another spoonful and offered it to Alexander.

He nibbled, smiled, dabbed his finger into the mousse and then dolloped it onto the tip of her nose. "All completely honestly. I built this." Alexander looked around; his eyes sparkled. "However, there is much of my life that is very secret. That is true."

"Bi-sexual?" Brandy raised an eyebrow then thought better. "I didn't say that in a judgey manner," she added quickly.

Alexander laughed gently. "I do not know where to start."

"Oh, porn?" Brandy raised both eyebrows. "OK, now I would get a little judgey."

"I do not even know what that is." Alexander looked quizzical.

"Now, I know you're lying." Brandy tried to cross her arms, remembered the cast, and settled with resting her left hand over her right cast. She winced at the pain that slight movement caused.

Alexander took her hand in his. "It is too much to explain and we are nearing the end of your tolerance to be out and about. "He kissed her hand. She frowned at him slightly, lips turned down at the corners.

He continued, "I brought you here to keep you safe and let you have a chance to heal. You are under the best medical care I can offer you."

"Who's my doctor?"

"I have a friend who has done me the favor of overseeing your case. I meet with him every night." Alexander looked out the dark windows.

"Why hasn't he visited." Brandy stared at him, the mouse dollop still on the end of her nose.

"If you were in any trouble, it would be arranged. However, you are healing well and time is the real thing you need. Time and rest. It is your best medicine in this case." He took a napkin and removed the dollop. "We are very … remote. No one can visit you here. You are safe. That is all that matters."

He stared at her. His gaze was steady and firm. Brandy broke the gaze first.

"I guess I should thank you. I must seem ungrateful. I am grateful, really. Just, don't understand everything." Brandy leaned back in her chair. She leaned a little to the side as her leg reminded her why she was here. Her breath caught as the pain stabbed through her.

Without another word, Alexander kissed her on the forehead and wheeled her back to her room. Once there, the nurse appeared out of nowhere and assisted Brandy with getting back into bed. The nurse was silent and efficient. Once back in bed, the nurse disappeared out into the hallway leaving

Brandy and Alexander alone again.

"Does she have a name?" Brandy whispered.

"Janice," Alexander whispered back.

"She doesn't talk?" A slightly louder whisper.

"She cannot." He offered a pain pill to Brandy. She took it without comment. He continued, "I usually do not bring other people here. It is unusual." Alexander pulled the covers up to Brandy's chin, carefully. "But you were a reason to do things in an unusual manner."

Brandy's eyes drooped. Alexander whispered, "I promise to tell you everything in due time."

"OK," Was all she could say before falling to sleep.

***

He had expected it to hurt more. Alexander walked in main time, slowly, looking for his next meal. He wondered why this adjustment in time that he had made did not hurt him as it should. He had removed a living being from the timeline and that should hurt. It should cause a hole in the timeline where all interactions that should have taken place would not and that should cause a small upset in the time stream that ultimately should ache in his bones like drippy, inflamed arthritis. Yet, it did not hurt as much as he was expecting. Ahead of him on the street a gaggle of young linears had spilled out of a bar and were smoking on the street, half empty beer bottles in their hands. Their laughter floated across the night air to him.

Alexander passed them by and they did not even raise their heads to understand how closely potential death had walked by them. His thoughts turned dark, to time long passed when he had walked amongst the linears and hated them; hated their brevity, their blissful ignorance, their inability to feel the pull of time and the universe, their inability to feel the wrongs and an ignorance to not feel compelled to set it right else suffer an unquenchable, gnawing pain for eternity. He had let his hate consume him and for a small amount of time, a few hundred years perhaps, he and Yindi had terrorized the world together. Alexander shuttered to think of the devastation he had wrought, and that he had enjoyed it. Shame caused him to drop his eyes and step up his pace, pushing further on through humanity. The young linears continued to smoke and drink, their laughter tinkling, diminishing, then gone. Alexander turned the corner and walked up a long, dark alley.

Why did removing Brandy from the timeline not cause it to shift?

He paused in front of an apartment building and looked up. 2 AM. Most of the lights were out. He could eat well here. He slipped in and out of time to navigate through to the bedrooms of the sleeping individuals. Stand in main time, climb the stairs like a normal linear. Approach a locked door, slip to a time during construction when the door did not exist. Slip back to main time to find the sleeping linear. Alexander walked amongst the sleeping apartment building drinking his fill without ever disturbing a single soul. They would not remember him except for a fleeting dream. No gaping wounds, nothing more than a fading mark easily attributed to an insect bite would indicate his passing presence.

Of course, there wasn't much interaction she would have been having while here. Alexander thought. She would have been an ignorable patient, needing care but not interacting with nurses. She would have been inconsequential. Not causing much disturbance to the time stream. It was the only explanation he could come up with. While she was here with him, main time moved on. He made appearances there and kept Susan updated. Sent her away on a vacation, all useless things to do. That timeline would be changed when he brought Brandy back. However, keeping things even made things easier for him. Minimized the ache and distraction he would feel if time started devolving. He would know. He would feel time change. When he began to feel that ache that he knew so well, it would be past the time to bring her back. He hoped she was well enough by then. When she re-entered this timeline, she would need to be ready for…

His thought was interrupted by a sound up ahead.

A bottle tipped and rolled, glass clinking, then slowing rolled to a stop.

A boot scraped on gravel grit, weight shifted as someone pushed off from leaning against the wall.

Another shuffle of feet on gravel as the weight distributed to two feet then walked out of the shadows to face Alexander.

They stood there, facing each other in the dark alley. The air was damp with rain. Summer had not rolled in yet, but the thick air promised it would arrive soon.

***

Main time slowly crept forward. Alexander could see brief glimpses of the possible futures as ghosts. The possibilities of where his adversary might go and do played out in front of Alexander, ghostly translucent images blurred, changing, ebbing, changing again. The second it took for his opponent to decide what to do played out all of his choices in the air for Alexander like a projected slide show. Alexander waited patiently for the second to pass. The ghostly possibilities collapsed and one glimmer of a ghost image appeared in front of Alexander as the man in front of him decided. Before the adversary could take action and, with his knife raised, step towards Alexander, Alexander stepped in and met him there, bent the knife away. The knife clattered to the littered pavement. Their chests touched. Alexander's was still and cold. The opposing man took deep shuddering breaths. Alexander could feel the heart hammer away in his opponent's chest. Could feel the blood flowing through the man's veins, raw noise to his ears. They stood that way, poised, one still, one breathing hard.

"Where is she?" Yindi all but screamed.

"Removed from here, from your reaches," a quiet whisper. Alexander took a step forward pushing Mark/Yindi's back to the cinder block wall.

Yindi wrinkled his nose. "That's not playing fair." A whine in his voice. "You'll have to bring her back. Eventually." He tried to push Alexander away. His hands were useless and stiff, wrapped in soiled braces.

"Eventually." Alexander whispered. He could already see the fleeting ghost images of Yindi wanting to run away. Left or right, which way would he run? Alexander indulgently stepped back.

Yindi turned to the left and ran. He paused momentarily at the end of the alley as if to hurl an insult Alexander's way, thought better of it and continued to run on.

Alexander watched him go. He knew what the future entangled moment of time was. Alexander had stood there and seen Brandy go into the water and not return. The water had burned at his ankles as it lapped and moved, sapping the energy from him. She had not returned. She had died there. Time had turned white and entangled with now. He was holding off the inevitable. She would die in the water and he could not change it. Yindi would emerge from the water the victor. Perhaps he had to inhabit Susan, perhaps he could be inhabiting someone else like Mark. Either way, Brandy and Yindi were going into that water and Brandy was going to die. Time had turned white. There were factors now that could not change. Alexander could not keep that time from happening. Deflated, he turned, disappeared.

***

The sun streamed in through the large windows in the library. Brandy had wheeled herself to them and sat transfixed in the sun. She tried to enjoy the warmth of it. The valley lay out before her, green, lush, surrounded by a mountain plateau. Hawks lazed in the sky above. Clouds drifted below her. North, on the far ridge, a thundercloud had formed; a dark sprawl crept slowly across the bluffs. She watched; minutes passed, a half-hour. The thundercloud had spread and was creeping up on where she sat. The wind kicked up as the darkness descended upon her small view of the big world beyond. Leaves flew and hit the window pains. The hawks could no longer be seen. Lighting struck in the distance. Clouds and mist obscured the valley from her view. Soon, the clouds engulfed the window and flashes of light indicated the lighting was around her. The hair on the back of her neck stood on end with the static charge in the air. Briefly, Brandy considered that she was sitting in a metal chair. Perhaps the only metal thing in view. She smiled. "Well, that would be something wouldn't it? To be struck by lighting in this…whatever the heck this place is," Brandy thought.

She sat there daring the lighting to strike her and watched the rain beat against the window. Nothing struck its deathblow and the rain only fell loudly. The pain in her body steadily thrummed and eventually became all encompassing.

"Fine." She muttered and wheeled herself towards her bed. Evening would be upon her soon and she wanted to nap before Alexander appeared. He never visited in the day. She knew, his construction job. He was a night owl.

Brandy wheeled her chair to face the bed. Using her good arm, the metal triangle suspended over the bed and a small wooden board she was able to hoist herself into bed and use the board to help her scootch up the 4 inch height difference between the chair and her bed. The effort left her winded, nauseous and ready for a nap. She reached for her pain pills and a glass of water.

Rain pelted loudly against her small bedroom windows while she drifted into a sleep that took her far but not completely away from the pain. Brandy woke briefly and took another pain pill and a glass of water, forgetting that she had already taken her dosage. Sleep or something resembling it pushed Brandy into oblivion for the next three hours.

***

The storm had passed. Fat, wet raindrops still clung to the window. The moon was high and shone brightly, framing Alexander's visage in the window.

Brandy could barely raise her head, struggled to open her eyes, the narcotics pulling at her will to stay awake. Her tongue felt thick and useless in her mouth.

"Where am I, Alexander?" she tried to ask. The words were slurred and barley recognizable. "Something is weird. I know it." Her tone was accusing. "Tell me."

Alexander approached her bed and held her hand to his chest. She looked at her hand, not recognizing it as her own for a moment. Then seeing that it was hers, tried to pull it back.

"Tell me. This is not right. I feel lost here." Her slurred words broke with unfathomable sadness.

Alexander slumped as he heard the ache in them. "I had to bring you here," he whispered. "It was not right." He kissed her hand. "It could have killed you. But…" Alexander trailed off. His eyes glistened; to Brandy his tears looked red. She blinked her own eyes as if she could clear away his tears.

"You had to heal. I had to get you away from…the danger." He affected a deep breath. "I do not exist in your timeline." His words became a tumble, rushing to escape him. "I exist outside your timeline and brought you here." Alexander looked up then kissed her hand again. "Here, to my home ten thousand years before your time. To keep you safe for as long as I can."

Brandy tried to raise her head, tried to question. Her eyes drifted and became unfocused; with effort she steadied her gaze upon him even as her voice became more slurred.

"…oouuu a time lord or somethin'?" she managed.

Alexander shook his head, not getting her question.

She tried again, "'ime 'ord." She winced with the effort. "F'k." Brandy pulled his hand to her mouth and returned the kiss, gave a halfhearted shrug. With extraordinary effort she whispered, "I trust 'ou."

The last image she saw was of Alexander smiling. It touched her heart. Then she drifted into a fog of sleep where nothing existed, not her, not Alexander, not Mark, no screeching busses, no red eyed snakes, just blackness, a perfect nothingness. She welcomed it.

16 10,000 YEARS &
10 WEEKS. CONFESSION.

The coffee was getting cold. Brandy continued to drink it anyway. She stared off at nothing, brain in neutral. Silence surrounded her. Not even a ticking of a clock, she suddenly thought. In fact, she had not seen one clock in this massive house except for the one in her room. That one had appeared six or more weeks into her stay. Was that the only one? She glanced around the library to confirm her suspicion. Bookshelves lined with stacks of ancient books encompassed the room. From her wheelchair she could only reach a few shelves and had been afraid to touch the tomes; they ranged from scrolls that she dared not touch, illuminated manuscripts she dare not breathe on, to pristine first editions she had re-shelved the moment she realized their age. She stayed contented with the paperbacks that had been left in her room. Brandy scanned the shelves. Yet, nowhere in all the stacks of books nor on the ornate tables did she find a clock.

She took a sip of coffee and grimaced at the lack of heat.

The kitchen was too far away, she decided, to wheel in and reheat her coffee. Besides, the stove was a retro throw back, a wood-burning stove. Complete with smoke stack disappearing through the ceiling. Slowly, she took another sip of coffee and listened to the silence. She could use the crutches, Brandy considered. They were back in the bedroom; she had not used them for trips longer than bed to bathroom. After another moment's consideration she sipped at her cold coffee and dismissed the thought as too much effort for today.

"Wonder where Janice hides now?" Brandy muttered to herself and nibbled on the breakfast that had been left on the table for her. In fact, she had not seen Janice, the mute nurse, in a long time now. Evidence of her existing abounded: prepared meals showing up on schedule, made beds after Brandy left the room, clean stacked laundry waiting to be put away when Brandy returned. Everything left in such a way that was convenient yet left some work to be done by Brandy. "Just how I'd do it for a patient that needed to feel independent," she told the air around her.

Brandy wondered how Nash was. He would be worried and would want to know how she was doing. How was he doing with the aftermath of Billy's murder by Mark's hand and the attempt on her own life? Nash, the nursing home, nurses, patients and the mayhem felt a million miles away.

Silence engulfed her. The clink of her coffee cup on the saucer rang too loudly in her ears. Brandy put the cup down and looked towards the sun-drenched window. "I'm officially bored. Time to move. Let's see what is outside, shall we?"

It took an hour and a half to get from thought to execution. Cleaning her plates from the table and getting them hand washed took thirty minutes of sweat-wringing effort to reach the sink, let alone carry everything on her lap. At least it was an electric wheelchair, she had thought. The effort of wheeling, now that she had some use of both arms, would have made the balancing of dirty plates near impossible, she imagined. She eyeballed the knives in their block. It wouldn't take long; she could take off the arm cast. Though arm and leg did not itch, she ached to move her arm. The swelling had reduced so that the cast wiggled on her wing, which she imagined to be shriveled and pasty white. It was getting close to time to free the arm, she was sure. The leg was another story all together. It screamed with pain if she twitched her foot. Any effort caused the leg to sear from knee to toe. The cleaning of the dishes left her winded with a cold sweat on her upper lip. Fifteen minute rest and then she retrieved the crutches. Finally she had wheeled back through the house and sat eyeballing the step up to the front door; a wide marble landing stood between her and her goal.

Would it be unlocked? Brandy had found many rooms locked on the first floor as she had explored. Ten to be precise. Who needed that many rooms? The front door was massive, large oak and hand hewed. As she wheeled closer, crutches held across her lap, she could see her fear was unfounded. There was no lock. Not a single one. "Odd. Are we really that far away from everything? No fear of someone breaking in, and with all of this finery?" Brandy thought back to the gold utensils and fine bone china. That was real gold, wasn't it? Yet, no locks.

Carefully, she locked the wheelchair and used both arms to push off and stood on her one good leg. Her right arm felt good, she realized. She leaned on the crutch deeply so her right arm, still bent in its cast, could hold on to the shoulder and handgrip. To counter, she leaned more on her good arm and leg. The pressure under her armpits was an incorrect posture and would pinch a nerve if she stayed in this position long. Her arm had to come out of that cast soon so she could crutch for further distances and explore past stairs. Paused there with her left leg on the marble landing, about to shift her weight onto the good leg and pull the rest of her body forward, she realized this might be a mistake. Why would she want to risk going up and down stairs? What if something happened? Seriously, she had good balance. Brandy snorted. This is no different than climbing in the cave. three points of contact and vigilance. With that boost of self-confidence she used her thigh to raise her body up onto the landing and then shifted the crutches to also rest on the landing. Her right arm did not protest and her right leg stayed suspended in the air with no weight on it. It also stayed quiet. She pulled on the heavy door and stepped out onto the porch. There she paused, with her breath caught in her throat.

The porch wrapped around the house. Its wide expanse housed rocking chairs, obviously hand made. The thick, rough wood gleamed as if still green with sap. The woods around the house were thick, mature and seemingly never ending. She could see nothing more than trees. Brandy navigated her way to the porch where no trees were visible; this would be where the windows of the library looked out. Here, the valley stretched out for miles of forest-covered lushness. Despite the summer month a cool breeze pushed at her. She sat in a nearby rocking chair, careful to assemble her limbs without causing pain. Brandy placed her crutch between the chair and railing to create a makeshift leg rest and elevated her be-cast leg.

She let out the pent up breath she had held captive and

with its release she relaxed. The open expanse of beauty relieved any trapped feeling she had harbored. Brandy sank into the chair and rocked slightly, as much as her elevated leg would allow. Nothing but nature. Cicadas chirruped. A nearby squirrel chittered. The air had the promise of rain by evening. Despite herself, Brandy grinned widely and promptly took a nap.

***

It was a soft nudge at first, pushing her drooping hand. Brandy shifted in the rocking chair, her hand swayed, fingertips brushing the porch. The nudge insisted again at her fingers, pushing her hand so that it continued to sway. Again, it pushed and a wet something pressed against her hand. She startled and woke and startled again as a weight landed in her lap. The startle was merely an intake of breath and her eyes opening wide. That small amount of reflex caused pain to sear through her leg. Brandy hissed.

"Son of a bitch." The weight in her lap accompanied another nudge of something warm against Brandy's other hand draped protectively over her leg, bent there by the cast that bound it.

The cat stretched and looked Brandy in the eye, defiantly. "Meow." Then the scraggly tabby head butted her face.

After careful inspection Brandy decided the cat was a stray. No tags, torn ear, broken tail that curled back sharply along the cat's body. However, the orange coat seemed to be mostly free of fleas and such. The cat curled into a ball on her lap whether she approved or not. Seemingly content, the cat purred, nestled and fell to sleep. Brandy absently stroked the cat and fell back to sleep her self.

***

A new ritual. Brandy enjoyed the company and looked forward to her nap on the porch with the cat. Day after day with no one else to talk to, Brandy took a bit of food from her plate and traversed to the porch to feed the cat and nap in the warm late morning sun. Lately she had begun to also come back out to watch the sun set, now that she was growing stronger. Brandy had lost track of what day it might be, but today felt clearer. She had spent the last two weeks weaning off the pain medicine and only taking one at the end of the day. She felt stronger for it. More in charge of things. She rocked slightly in the chair and looked at her withered, but free right arm. That cat nestled against it and purred. Slowly, Brandy wiggled her fingers and rotated her stiff wrist and elbow. The cat protested by eyeing her with one sleepy eyeball. Brandy winced at the tightness in her joints, but relished the freed limb.

Janice had come into the room the week prior and brandished a small electric "saw" which vibrated and cut away limb imprisoning casts. The nurse had held it in front of her triumphantly with a raised eyebrow as if to say, "It is time to set you free."

She had set about her work silently, and Brandy barraged her with questions which were answered with nods, smirks, raised eyebrows, cynical smiles and heart wrenching empty stares and stony silence.

"It's been weeks since Alexander has been here, I think." Brandy wondered what day it was anyway.

An empty stare in response.

"Where are you during the day when I'm twiddling about? What if something happens to me? If I fall or something. There are no phones, no way to call for help. I feel like a prisoner." Brandy's words tumbled and she was happy to have anyone to talk to. Even if she did not speak in return.

A smirk. The nurse held up a finger, a "hold on" gesture.

The saw whirred and dust marked its path along the cast's length. They both watched the progress. After two lines were cut on each side of the cast the nurse grabbed each side and pulled the pieces apart like a clam shell. With blunt scissors she cut away the gauze. The smell of the rancid skin hit them both. Janice made a smirking frown and looked at Brandy.

"I can't wait to soak that in hot water and scrub off the dead skin." Brandy picked at the yellowing flaky skin scaled on the length of her withered arm. "Ick."

In unison, both turned to look at Brandy's leg. Janice put her hands on either side of the cast and held it firmly. She gave a grim look, tight lips. She waited for Brandy to get the message. Janice shook her head for emphasis, her lips a white, thin line.

Brandy knew. "Don't move it, I know. It can't be mended yet." Brandy gently poked a finger between her thigh and the cast, now dingy and soiled from weeks of sponge baths. "Swelling is down though. Starting to itch. There must have been dissolvable stiches."

Janice nodded.

"How many pins?" Brandy ventured.

Janice held up six fingers then began to apply the loud, buzzing saw to the leg cast. Dust filled the air as they both waited in anticipation to see the long-lost leg.

"Ten weeks since the incident?" Brandy thought, "Twelve, maybe?"

"Do you live here?" Brandy asked still wondering how alone and far away she was from civilization. She felt isolated, trapped and slightly kidnapped from the rest of the world. No sound of planes, trains, phones, anything to indicate life beyond her own and occasionally Janice. Brandy began to feel flushed with anger. Sweat beaded on her forehead. Where was her family? Where was anyone? Why did no one come to see her?

She knew though. She was safe. Mark could not find her here. Wherever here was. She thought of the bloody intestines looped between Billy's toes. Safe here. Her sweat turned cold.

The whirring of the saw stopped. Janice paused to look at Brandy. She patted her good leg, a comforting gesture, mistaking Brandy's unease as concern for the saw. Brandy had cut off many casts during nursing school. They had taken turns putting casts on each of their classmates and in turn taking them off with saws much like this one. It sounded loud, but could be held directly against the skin and not cause any harm. Brandy gave a weak smile of reassurance. With a ripping sound of gauze, the cast was taken off and the shriveled, scaly leg was unearthed.

"Well, there's a good sight to see!" Brandy exclaimed, and she felt hope. Just a glimmer. Hope all the same.

***

On the porch, relaxing and enjoying her newly freed arm and her somewhat freed leg, Brandy twisted her leg slightly to examine the new cast, this one with a Velcro walking shoe at the bottom. Her first few steps had been tiring and liberating at the same time. The black Velcro strap flapped in the slight breeze. Brandy considered her plight. Something was weird about this place and it ate at her brain like buzzing bees. An image came to her as she tried to understand the feeling. When she had studied piano as a child there had been the metronome that she had used to keep time. Black. Evil. Hated. Day after day as she practiced her scales she kept time with the relentless tick-tocking of the metronome. One day she must have over tightened it; the internal spring had sprung and the once steady beating paused and slipped. Sometimes it wouldn't even tick tock back and forth at all, the weighted spindle would hang to one side and refuse to move. She would flick it with her finger, causing it to begin with a start and then it would pause and list over to the side, dead weight, refusing to budge. Somehow that had made it even more evil to her, as if it sat there menacingly pulled back on its spring, coiled and ready to strike at any moment, specifically when she was not ready to play the scales in time. An evil jack in the box ready to judge her inability to hit the notes correctly. Its silence louder than the menacing tick and tock. Brandy brooded at the thought. It felt like that. Something coiled and waiting. And wrong. Tick-tocking like a clock. A memory floated to the surface of her mind. Something Alexander had said. She had been drifting off into a narcotic sleep. His words were unreal. Something about his time or her time, ten thousand years ago. What had he said? Maybe talking about this place, this mountain? That didn't seem right. The dark, menacing, sprung metronome ticked in her mind as if it might spring into action, causing her thoughts to untangle. Yet, it stayed still.

The cat nudged at her as if sensing her dark thoughts and

she absently scratched its orange ears.

"I'm just going stir crazy," she said to herself, thinking about this secluded place, nice as it was, with no phone lines and no cell service. "A little stir crazy."

***

The sunset was brilliant as she opened the door, down to one crutch and walking with her cast. The Velcro shoe protested with each step as the fastener received the stress of her forward movement.

Clunk of the heavy casted heel, roll the leg forward, Velcro protests, lift, click of the crutch repeat.

She stood there, coffee clutched in one hand, crutch held under the other arm and waited for her tabby friend to appear. Soon a meow followed by a dash of orange and a slinking shadow ran smoothly across the porch and towards her cast. The cat purred and rubbed against her legs. She gently nudged the cat away with the crutch so she could walk forward unencumbered.

Once seated, the cat jumped into her lap and head bumped her chin.

"I brought you a treat," Brandy greeted the cat, then produced a bit of bacon, wrapped in a linen napkin, from her pocket. The cat pawed at it and snatched it with one deft claw. "Be nice now." The cat took the bacon and jumped away to gnaw on its newly found dinner.

Brandy watched absently. The air was warm and a gentle cool breeze touched her skin. Had to be near August, she surmised. Lightning bugs began to light up the air around her.

A gentle cough behind her caused Brandy to turn.

Alexander leaned in the doorway, a bouquet of wildflowers in his hand. He smiled gently.

She wanted to be upset and to yell at him for her loneliness, but surely he had good reason to have been away. She was too happy to see him and any bitterness melted.

His gentle smile and sappy flowers warmed her and she couldn't muster any cross words to say. She smiled in return and embarrassingly felt a glow of red touch her cheeks, a school girl blush. She breathed out a small laugh that sounded nervous and mortified her even more. A grown woman, blushing and almost giggling at flowers, for heavens sakes. A sarcastic voice whispered inside that she was so starved for attention Jack the Ripper could have shone up with black roses and she probably would have been happy. Well, maybe that was going a bit too far.

He interrupted her internal dialogue of girly shame, "I was detained away much longer than I had intended. I hope you will forgive me." He took her hand from the arm of the rocking chair and kissed it gallantly. His lips were cold and felt like fire.

Brandy cleared her throat, an uncomfortable tickle having taken residence there. "I…" she stammered and hated herself for it. Heat pricked her face and she blurted, more angrily than she had intended. "I feel kidnapped here and out in the middle of fucking nowhere."

He knelt beside her, her hand clasped to the side of his face. Cold face, hot hand. "I want to tell you everything and let you hate me or love me as you would." He paused, deep brown eyes burning into hers. Brandy returned the gaze, refusing to shy away. "You are healing and soon will be ready to go home. A few more weeks now, perhaps. I had to keep you…"

Alexander stroked her hair, fingers entwined in her wild curls, "safe. Away from him."

The intensity of his gaze and voice caused Brandy to look away. Tears suddenly stung her eyes. She blinked to clear her vision. It did no good. A deep sob shook her. "I can't stop seeing his eyes." She meant Billy's dead eyes, but then Mark's dark, hate filled eyes also clouded her memory. He had wished her dead. She couldn't remember the bus, only the last time she had looked into his face. He had been screaming maniacally and pushing her into the hallway. As he ran past her, his arms cradled protectively against his body, he had sneered at her. It was only a second, but it was bone chilling and she imagined was the same sneer he had worn when he had pushed her into the bus.

Sobs shook her again and she tried to control herself with a deep breath. It shuddered from her. "I hate feeling helpless. It pisses me off." She tried to smile. Alexander kissed the top of her head and held her to his chest. He held her tight as her sobs diminished and became slight hiccupping hitches in her breath.

He did not say meaningless, consoling words. Only held her silently waiting for the storm of emotions to abate. She relaxed her head against him and loved him for his silence.

Alexander absently stroked her hair, as he still knelt on one bended knee. The flowers had been dropped onto the porch. He seemed to remember them and placed them in her lap. She sniffed and plucked at them. "Thank you. They're very pretty," she whispered.

She looked at him then, her eyes puffy and red rimmed.

"I do not want you to be so full of sorrow. I should have not been away so long. You have so little time now with me and I would not waste another moment." Alexander bent down and kissed her. He gently encircled her with his arms and held her as tight as he could, hand tangled in her hair. His ice cold lips melted against her warmness. Brandy gasped from the surprise of the embrace then reached with her good arm to pull him closer.

***

"Excuse me, sir?" The pimpled boy's voice breaks and squeaks. "Sir?" He holds out a dollar bill, shaking it to get the man's attention. "Your change."

Mark, distracted and muttering, takes the bill without looking at the teenager. Hair falls in his eyes, it reminds him to blink. Blink. Blink.

"You OK?" the kid continues; his voice hitches an irritating octave higher. "You're sweating bullets." The last a whisper as if the kid might have thought of one or many reasons, very unhealthy reasons, that cause bullets to be sweat. Hastily, the kid retreats from the counter and sits on a stool. With a dismissive wave he calls, "Have a nice night."

Mark takes the dollar, stuffs it in his pocket and begins to unwrap a candy bar. A tired, electric buzzer chimes as he leaves the convenience store. He stands on the sidewalk, chewing mindlessly. His mind is blank and waiting for a need to overtake him. He feels empty and soulless, time has changed so many times and now a moment has been locked. But what moment? Where? Yindi tires of this Mark body already. It is hungry and needs to replenish itself often. He finds it tiring. Where did Alexander take her? Where does he go when he is not here? Oddly, Mark/Yindi becomes dark and loathsome of his own existence. He drops the candy wrapper to the ground and walks away into the darkness. His hands are stiff and the fingers mostly work. Two fingers on his left hand bend at odd angles and do not respond as well as the others. A claw. They cast distorted shadows on the ground behind him in the buzzing light of the utility pole.

He will wait. She will return. Alexander will return. Yindi will be waiting for them. They have a date in the present somewhere and from the look of defeat the Alexanders had at the nursing home the future was going to be awfully wonderful. Someone was going to die. A slight spark came back to Yindi/Mark and his pace quickened as he stepped out of the light of the parking lot and slid down the back alley.

***

Their kisses became urgent and insistent. Carefully, with false starts ending with Brandy whispering, "arm," "leg," or "wait," and peppered with, "ouch," and "OK," the two entangled in a half-disrobed, gasping entity.

They lay on the porch together, her shirt under her leg's cast, stabilizing it. His arm still under the small of her back where he had guided her weight towards him. Alexander's skin felt warm and Brandy literally tingled where they touched. She traced a finger along his muscular back and imagined she could feel static electricity trail in blue sparks. He nibbled gently at her neck, sending shivers down her spine. She arched closer to him. Brandy had to be conscientious not to curl the toes of her bad leg, and to keep it relaxed so as not to cause too much pain. Despite their efforts to protect it, the constant motion had caused it to ache.

"We should go inside," his voice a hoarse whisper in her ear, "Let you rest."

With that he stood, offered her his shirt, which hung loosely on her and covered most of her modesty, then lifted her in his arms from the porch.

She pulled his face towards her and kissed him deeply. The moonless night was dark, the fireflies the only source of light. Her lips lingered on his. "OK," she mouthed.

Neither gave much notice to the cat nearby as it licked its paw, oblivious of any carnal activity. Blue starlight glinted on the orange fur as he cleaned himself.

Brandy heard the tabby cat let out a shriek of dismay when Alexander took a step backwards, starting to turn on his heel and carry her towards the door. In an instant she and he began to fall. Alexander's eyes had grown comically wide, a look of shock she had never seen on his calm features. The shock dissolved quickly, the corners of his lips pulled down in dismay. She gasped and before she could let out a noise, Alexander had vanished. For a terrifying split second she was falling through mid air, nearly naked, and Alexander was not there. The air around her seemed to rush to where he was not; it was cold on her skin. The hair stood up on end. She could feel the absence of his skin against hers where he had held her weight and his skin had warmed against hers.

"Ahh…" was all she managed to squeak before Alexander returned. He held her again, though not the same way. His hand had been higher into the bend of her knee. Now it was lower on her thigh, awkwardly so, in fact. The other hand was higher on her shoulders to compensate as if he had moved in that moment he was gone. And he had been gone. She had seen him vanish. He had not been there. Alexander slowed her descent and took her weight into his body gently until she settled against his steady chest which gave no evidence of having been in a falling state. He stood solidly.

"Oof," Brandy exhaled with the sudden stop, though Alexander had cushioned it as much as possible. It had still been a shock when mere split seconds ago she had been on a crashing trajectory with the floor.

With a stony face, Brandy calmly but insistently asked, "What. The. Fuck. Was. That?"

Alexander sighed, then smirked. "One would think I could have better timing at these things. Yet, oddly, time is quite the issue with me."

Brandy lashed out, "Like disappearing for weeks at a time?"

"Yes. It is difficult to distinguish seconds from weeks when the moon is not out." Alexander carried Brandy into the house. The cat was no where to be seen as the door closed behind them.

"And flat out disappearing." She hit his chest with a gentle fist. "I ask again, what the fuck?" She pushed on his chest. "And, put me down. I can walk."

Alexander paused at the two double doors. He rocked her weight mostly to one arm and opened the doors, effortlessly as if she weighed no more than a towel. "I had a surprise made for you." He ignored her request to be put down.

The doors opened into what she assumed was his master bedroom. She stiffened in his arms. "Not this." Alexander nodded to the grand bed. Dark carved wood spindles held the tall bed from the floor. Its boxy shape was slightly irregular, the mattress thicker. "I do not sleep there." Alexander walked through an open sliding door. "This." They entered a large marble tiled bathroom where an oversized claw foot tub sat in the center. Steam rose from the bubbled surface. "Do you think your plastic air bag for your cast will survive being submerged?" He looked at her leg, smiling. "Even if it does not, Janice is not too far away; we can put another cast on."

"This doesn't change anything." Brandy was cross as he placed her on her feet and held her hand to steady her. She regarded the tub, then Alexander. "How is this steaming hot? You couldn't have drawn it before you came out to the porch. Did Janice draw this bath?"

"No. I drew it." Alexander motioned for Brandy to sit on a bench next to the tub. "Before I caught you." He continued.

"When you disappeared?" Brandy refused to sit.

"I built the bathroom and bedroom and then drew the bath for you when I disappeared." Alexander motioned again for Brandy to sit on the bench. He held a robe out for her this time.

Numbly she accepted the robe, held it to her chest and sat on the bench. Her cast stuck out in front of her. She looked up at him. "I..." She paused. Rethought. Turned her head to the side and looked up at him, her mouth pursed questioningly. "You disappeared in the cave too. Right after we heard Susan yell."

From the end of the bench, Alexander picked up the plastic air bag for her cast and held it with a silent gesture, offering to put it on her leg. Brandy smirked. It made her think of a twisted fairy tale; instead of a glass slipper she was given a crazy dude with a plastic bag for her leg and a delusional state.

Brandy looked at the tub, then looked back at Alexander. "I'm not wasting this tub water. Even if I am having a delusional moment."

She held her leg out for him to pull the air bag over her cast as far as dignity would allow. Brandy took it from him at mid thigh and pulled it the rest of the way, nearly to her groin and fastened it there. She had never tried to submerge with the thing and suspected this would end badly.

Alexander turned his back to offer her privacy. She continued while disrobing and eyeing the steaming water, "This felt the same way. Like the feeling you get when you take a step at the end of the stairs, except it isn't the end of the stairs, it's an unexpected stair step. And for a moment you hang in space expecting the floor to be there but it isn't." She put her left foot into the tub. The warmth was exquisite. The noise of the tiny bubbles sounded like crinkling Christmas wrapping paper to her. She grabbed both sides of the tub and gently lowered herself in, with her right leg held up in the air. She placed the cast on the wooden brace and slunk into the water until the liquid covered her shoulders and the bubbles came near to her nose. "OK," she proclaimed.

Alexander turned around and sat on the bench beside her. He handed her a large sponge and lavender smelling soap. She accepted the offer, still feeling like she must be in a drug-induced hallucination.

"So, you time traveled to build a tub for me because you knew the gig was up and what better way to soften the blow that you are a time lord, or something, than bubble baths." She sunk a little lower until the water lapped at her chin. Alexander scooped a small bit of bubbles away from her face, to un-obscure it, and placed the bubbles on her head.

"Is it working?" he said coyly, smiling.

"This is good for a hallucination. I must still be asleep on the porch with the cat." She stretched her good leg and enjoyed how much warmer the water felt on her healing right arm than it did on the rest of the body, almost as good as the hallucinated sex, but maybe not quite as good. She smiled. "I'm not hallucinating this, am I?"

"No. You are here. Let me explain." Alexander took her hand in his and began his improbable tale.

***

The water was beginning to cool, bubbles nearly fizzled, when Brandy finally held up a hand. "You have to stop now. My head is going to explode." She took a washcloth and carefully tried to wash her broken foot's toes, exposed at the end of her cast. The chipped toe nail polish Susan had painted on her toes had nearly grown out. Red half moons at the end of her toes, it looked obscene to Brandy, like blood tipped nails. She shivered. "So, Mark isn't Mark. He pushed me under the bus because he is Yindi messing with you because basically he is bored and I'm a dalliance. You can travel through time and he can't. You brought me here so I could heal up. And I am ten thousand years in the past from my friends, my family and where I should be."

Alexander had given her the simplest version of the story he could muster. He only spoke of this timeline and what she would be able to remember. He left out the other timelines where Mark had killed himself and Yindi had taken over Susan. He left out Susan killing Brandy in the water. He also left out that time had frozen there, that the time stream had locked and she would die in the water eventually and there was nothing he could do to stop it. All time streams would lead to a death in that water. It had been so cold when he had stepped into it. He had not even broached the subject of how he had let the timeline play out where Susan had died at the bottom of the pit, just so that he could see Brandy come and go to his cave in mourning and how he fell in love with her then.

Brandy started to stand up out of the tub, she raised an eyebrow to Alexander. He held the robe up for her and averted his gaze, demurely.

"You are taking this pretty well," Alexander spoke into the thick, oatmeal colored cotton robe that he held in front of his face.

Brandy had scooted from the lip of the tub to the bench, holding her leg out in front of her. She took the robe and wrapped herself in it, repositioning so that it covered her completely. The slightly big robe engulfed her and she nestled into it. "Seriously, I'm pretty sure this is all a delusional state caused by over medicating and I'm going to wake up soon in a crappy hospital with a cracked skull." She touched the mending fracture on her cheek.

She inspected the cast, it was only mildly damaged. She shrugged it off, few weeks left to go anyway and a nurse at the ready to replace it. Didn't really matter.

"Ok. Let me replay this again." Brandy watched as Alexander bent to her foot and affixed her Velcro walking shoe onto her cast. Again she was reminded of glass slippers and scoffed. "I did see you in the cave that day when Susan and I were leaving. You were watching us walk across the field."

Alexander handed her crutch to her. She stood. "The next day I rappelled into a pit entrance and a shadow had appeared which startled me. I slipped and hit my head." Brandy rubbed her naked foot on the bath mat to assure dry skin. Marble floor was going to be tricky with wet feet.

Alexander made a hold on gesture and from a shelf nearby produced her house slipper.

Brandy continued, "And the reason that shadow appeared is because you had, due to a set of circumstances that you have not really explained, fallen asleep in your cave in a different area than usual."

Alexander nodded and moved slowly by her side as she walked into the bedroom.

"And when you sleep, you randomly move through time." She paused, staring off into space, remembering coming to in the dark pit, her head hurting from being conked against the wall and finding Alexander holding her, trying to unhook her from the rope and gently lower her to the ground. She had mistook him for a spelunker lost in the cave and had instantly set about to take care of him and rescue him. "You had appeared in that moment, in that area of the cave and then I startled you awake."

He nodded again and did not elaborate further.

Brandy remembered the connection she had felt with him, instantly. It was the way he had looked at her as if he had known her forever and she had finally turned around to see him.

On the large bed, her nightclothes had been laid out. She paused and looked at them, then at Alexander.

He finally spoke. "I thought you would like this bedroom better." He pointed towards the drapes. "It has a much better view." He opened the heavy drapes to reveal a large window seat that afforded the same spectacular view as the library.

"And you haven't seen Beauty and the Beast?" Brandy whispered, more to herself, as she was drawn to sit in the window seat. Satin embroidered pillows cushioned her. Brandy

287

smiled slightly as she noticed the small clock hanging on the wall. She pointed at it and turned to Alexander. "Thank you?" she ventured. "This is all a bit too weird."

He sat opposite her and helped her position her leg, sitting carefully and resting her feet in his lap.

"You didn't explain. Why do you sleep in the cave? Which is below us, I take it." Brandy smirked at the look of surprise that appeared on Alexander's face. She pointed out the dark window. "That ridge line, I know it. Mountains don't change, really. Well, not in ten thousand years. This is the same mountain range that I walk and cave in. The trees are different. I've been staring at it for about six conscious weeks."

"You have known that something was…unusual?" Alexander's voice was nearly a whisper.

"Don't dodge the question. Why do you sleep in caves?" Brandy poked her good foot into his stomach.

Alexander held her toes from inflecting further bullying and gently kissed them. "I can see all of time in a fashion." He kissed her toe again and held it in his lap. "Energy is partly what sustains me. I am very sensitive to it." Absently, he stroked her foot with his hand. "If I stood in the daylight, I would experience all of daylight that has ever existed. All of that energy would destroy me in an instant."

Brandy urged gently, "Go on."

"When I sleep, I can not help that my body travels through time, randomly. A cruel trick of nature." He laughed sardonically, a short chuckle. "Caves are areas that have never seen the sun. Therefore that is where I sleep. I choose places carefully that are open and have been open for millennium so that I do not wake up embedded into a wall."

"And that day you were in a different area that did have an

288

opening at the top, where I came into the cave." Brandy held her hands up to indicate the small size of the opening. "The opening was pretty small and it was a pretty tall pit. The sun would have never reached the bottom."

"True. That opening is new. I had not noticed it before." He smiled and looked down. "I fell asleep there, which is an unusual place for me, and you fell into my life. I happened to appear when you were there. Your yell woke me up and I...synced with your time." He shrugged his shoulders. "It is the only word I can use to describe it."

Both became quiet and looked through the window at the moon which was now visible. White silver suspended in ink.

Time passed without another word. She was the first to break the silence. "So that next night when we visited your cave with you, you disappeared for a moment, like tonight. Susan had yelled. Tell me what happened. How does it work?"

"You mean, how do I work?" He chuckled.

"I guess so." She pulled the robe up to her ears and held it tight. "I mean, I can't even tell you how I work as a huma..." Brandy paused realizing the implications of her words. Her face dropped, her hand gently covered her mouth.

Careful to not jar her cast, he slipped closer to her on the cushions. He pulled her left leg around him and held her close. She allowed it and did not stiffen at his touch. He looked relieved. Their faces close, eyes seeking, he ventured a tentative kiss. Soft. Gentle. Lingering.

"You are real. And this is real. And I am here?" Her breath was warm on his face.

He kissed her more deeply then dropped his head to her shoulder. She cradled it there. His answer, barely audible, "Yes."

Brandy inhaled a long breath, held it and exhaled shakily. "Well, of course it is. I wouldn't be able to do anything easily or normal." She laughed. "So tell me what happened when Susan yelled in the cave. I can take it."

"I believe…" Alexander began. "I believe, that Yindi had begun to take control of your Mark by that time. Yindi, you must understand, only wants destruction. He destroys and causes chaos to see the universe collapse." She could feel him look up at her, his head tilted on her shoulder. "Time, the universe as you experience it is held together by events. It is like a river and time runs through the river bed. If Yindi disrupts enough events eventually time can be moved from the course it should take and then chaos begins to reign, eventually, one would surmise collapsing time and the universe. An unwinding."

"Entropy," Brandy whispered.

"Yes. Of course, he and I are not the only beings trapped in this dance. Hundreds of thousands of us throughout the worlds and times. The energy beings, the manipulators, relentlessly changing what should be, propelled only by their base needs, gaining an elation with each small and large chaos caused." Alexander raised a hand and touched it to his cold chest. "Watchers, such as myself, locked to an area and timeline, coupled with this chaotic energy beast. Forever trapped to undo the wrong that they have done, to keep the universe and timeline we are bound to unharmed as best we can."

"What happens when you don't. You can't undo all he does. He can adjust things in the daytime. You can't go there?" Brandy stroked his hair. He relaxed further into her embrace.

"True. Not all things need to be corrected. There are many

things that have no consequence to the river of time."

"How do you know the difference? What should be and shouldn't be?"

"When I look at time, I see things in colors. Things that have been manipulated take on a tinged coloring: yellows and reds, like bruises and wounds." Alexander absently stroked her fingers. "It also hurts me, a weary ache. If I were to let things be molested and not fix the bigger things eventually I would be in crippling agony."

"You speak from experience, it sounds like," Brandy said

Alexander continued, ignoring the implication. "That day when we heard Susan yell, I left you and searched through time to see what had caused her yell. Mark had stood on a large rock that came loose and tumbled down towards Susan. In the altered time the rock had hit her. It weighed over a hundred pounds. I see time like watching ghosts dance transparently in front of me. I pick the moment I want to enter and do so." Alexander sat up and looked at Brandy. "I slipped back to the point where the rock would have hit her and instead pushed it aside. It bounced harmlessly away. Then I slipped back out of the time so Susan would not see me. It took a fraction of an instant."

"Then you came back to me in…m…my time," Brandy finished for him.

"Main time, I think of it as. The now moment the linears in the universe experience."

"Linears?"

"Those that experience time linearly. You can not see anything but your one stream."

"Yuck. Linear."

"It does sound one dimensional, does it not?" He held her

hand. "Brandy…" he questioned.

She tilted her head, questioningly.

"I have to confess…" he started.

Brandy stopped him with a gesture. "Hang on for a sec. I need to process this first before you have a further confession." She urged him to stand so she could move out of the window seat and also stand. "Would you have any wine? I think I could take a drink just about now. I need to rest and put this leg up; it's a throbbing mess. Join me?" Brandy pointed to the large bed. "It looks big enough for both of us." She raised a finger. "No monkey business. Be close to me though, so I know I'm not hallucinating."

Alexander supervised her until she was reclined with her leg propped on a pillow.

"I will return to you within the moment." Alexander left the room.

Brandy stared out the dark window into the night.

***

The sun rose the next morning and Brandy found herself alone in the bed. He had held her and they had remained silent for hours until she had fallen asleep. A note on the bed-stand, written in elegant heavy-handed script read: "Until tonight. Love, Alexander."

"Just my luck. How am I going to explain this to Mom. Or Susan?"

Brandy spent the day bringing her small belongings from the old bedroom, which resembled a hospital room of sorts, to this bedroom. It marked a moment, she understood, a turning point. She was healing now and no longer a patient. The last item, a small wooden box, contained her silver bat necklace. She took it out and held it up to the sunlight. It shone and twirled at the end of her fingertips. Brandy put it around her neck, feeling slightly more like herself with it in place. She pulled it over her chin and let the bat dangle there. A smile of understanding crossed her face. "Of course." She flicked at the necklace again and let it drop to her chest. "I was always here."

That evening, he met her at the dinner table. They ate silently for a while. Alexander seemed to be waiting for Brandy to initiate the conversation. Eventually the dam of questions she had built up all day burst.

"Have you ever changed my timeline?" It was a quiet question. She did not raise her eyes from her dinner plate. "Has Yindi succeeded in killing me in other timelines?" She met his eyes then. Grey, cold, pleading eyes.

"Yes," a whisper of an answer.

"How many times?" Brandy waited patiently for the answer.

Alexander hesitated.

"You have to count?" Her voice raised a slight bit. "Really?"

"I saved you once from the bus." Alexander poked at his dinner plate, barely eaten. "It ended even worse and I had to put the timeline back to this one. The manipulated one is the least affected timeline for the stream. Though it is manipulated, it is the correct timeline."

"How was it worse?"

He looked at her, eyes wide. "It does not matter. It no longer exists. There are millions of ways things can occur. This one is the one that flows the best. Even if it felt like ragged agony to see you go back under that bus for a second time."

"That had to have been awful. How horrible to see something like that twice. Thank heavens I only had to experience it once. Hurrah for linears." She reached out and held his hand.

***

She lay on the pillow, her hair spilled out in dark ringlets. Alexander lay next to her. They faced each other, nose to nose. The clock ticked on through the evening as they spoke throughout the night. Brandy spoke of her childhood and tried to ask of Alexander's. He avoided many questions deftly by asking more about her past.

He pulled the blanket softly up to her chin when her eyes began to droop. With a slight grimace he recoiled when his hand brushed against her necklace. The movement startled her back to alertness. She grabbed his hand and examined the small red mark. Brandy touched her necklace gently.

"Gold utensils, not silver." A quiet statement.

"An allergy of sorts. Silver burns my skin," Alexander offered.

Brandy bent and kissed his inner wrist where the burn mark was already starting to heal.

"Then, I'll get rid of this." She took the necklace off and placed it in the wooden box by the bed. The silver glinted one last time as she closed the lid.

She pulled herself closer to him and together they lost themselves until the dark hours of the morning. In their activity, the wooden box was knocked from the bedside table and it lay forgotten under the bed.

***

A thousand years crumbled the house into disrepair, alone in a young forest. Rains, fires, ice, sleet degraded the house, roof, porch, dusty floors, until the box was buried in the ground. Rain pushed the box further until it too slowly disintegrated, releasing the necklace. Limestone rock opened small cracks due to the insistence of the rain. Small inlets of water crept lower and lower taking with it the necklace until it fell to the bottom of a dome room into a small stream bed eventually to be found by Brandy and Susan when pushing a grim stream crawl.

17 ALONE AND DOOMED
IN THE DAYLIGHT.

The sun had set and stars gently winked into view. Brandy bent her stiff knee and rolled her ankle. She ran a thumb across the side of her thigh where the bright pink, ugly scar rubbed against her jeans. Brandy walked gingerly on the dirt path near the house. Tall, flaming torches lit the way. Her crutches steadied her step. It felt weird to wear two of the same shoes again. Finally she caught up with Alexander.

He turned from away from the valley when she approached.

"Rain will be coming in from the north soon." He pointed. The stars disappeared along the opposite mountain range where large clouds hung low.

"I know," she smiled, "I can feel that in my bones like an old lady."

He put his arm around her and held her close. They stood silently and watched the night.

"Will you show me where you sleep?" Brandy said at last.

"You would not be able to reach it. Even if you could crawl." He hugged her tighter, a solid grip on her shoulder. "When I go there, I must slip through time to before the ceiling collapsed and when areas are not choked with formations. This way I can walk unencumbered to my sleeping chamber."

Brandy thought for a moment. "Wait, that means you can go back in time as well? Before you were born?"

"Of course. I do not experience time as you do. It is all here, every moment, for me." He sighed slowly, though it was an affectation and not a symptom of actual breath.

He motioned to a bench made of stone. They sat together and looked off into the darkness. Brandy shivered at the cold stone. Her voice was a soft plea. "Tell me about your childhood, please. How do your people live?"

"I have parents like you. Grew from a baby to a young man." He turned to look into her grey eyes. "We really are the same species. My kind are linears, in the beginning." He smiled and dropped his eyes. "We are raised in caverns below for the safety of our parents, who have already changed." Alexander pointed at the sky. "As children we would sneak up during the day and see the sunlight, green grass, blue skies."

"You couldn't see time then?" Brandy asked.

"As children we could see an extremely limited amount of time, just the amount of time we had been alive. He placed a hand to his chest. "When we mature we are sent away from our families, our time, our home and we become locked to a place and time. When we lock, that is when all of time becomes visible to us and we can no longer venture out in the day."

"So, a bunch of naked kids running around in the fields without supervision didn't cause problems or raise any suspicion?" Brandy cocked her head to the side and raised her eyebrows.

"Certainly, there were those that met an ill fate and did not return. Snake bites. Bears. Occasionally someone would be spotted by a nearby tribe and be taken. During the night our elders would find the child and bring it back." Alexander touched his hand to his chest. "We were not naked." He glared at her.

"How do you pick where you lock to?" Brandy leaned against him more and avoided his glare.

"There is a ritual. By then we have learned to slip through the small amount of time we can see effortlessly." He touched the missing part of his pinky finger. "We have to be careful to never collide with things as we slip into a time, else we erase it. If it is ourselves then we erase parts of ourselves." He showed the finger to her. "Childhood game of chase. I learned well the lesson to be careful."

"What's the ritual?" She touched the smooth pocket of missing flesh. She brought his hands to her lips and gently kissed the divot.

"It is a going away celebration, generally." He paused then continued quietly, "A ritual as old as our ancestors meant to prepare us for the eternity and responsibilities to come." Alexander's mouth pursed into a tight grim frown. "Afterwards, one's parents will go back to their locked time, as they had to synch linearly to have children and it is a strain to stay in main time. All will separate and rarely see each other again. So it is a good bye of sorts." Alexander looked up at the stars and was silent a moment.

Brandy laced her hands in his and waited silently.

After a while he continued, "That was ever so long ago

from this time. Thirty thousand years." He turned his gaze towards her and smiled. "Let alone your time."

They sat in silence and listened to nature around them chirp, croak and whistle. Brandy ventured a question, "And you never see them again?"

"You see, I had to travel for years to get to this land before I synced. I had to find a suitable place where light had not been. Then when I found the right place I began to change, to sync and fall away from the time I was born and move to my own time. This time where we are now is thirty thousand years from my birth time and ten thousand years before yours." Alexander paused as a coyote's howling echoed in the valley. "They are quite loud tonight," he commented.

"So, while you were a…linear…kinda…you hitchhiked to here. From where?" Brandy urged him on.

"It was a treacherous journey across the mountains, though not as treacherous as my ancestors took to get to the place that I was born. I must have walked for years, or so it felt. It was an intuition that led me, an instinct, I would suppose." He patted the stone bench. "Then I found here. I built a small hut at first when I could walk during the day and explored this cave. It pulled me deeper and deeper in. Eventually, I was unable to go out into the day; I had fully synced and had decoupled from time."

"How long ago was that when you were still a day person?" Brandy pushed for more information.

"Before I synced, your species was just evolving, from ours. The ones that could not sync with time." He looked away from Brandy. "I grew up with a friend who could not sync. She was sent out to be taken in by a local tribe and stayed in the daylight."

"What was her name?" With a gentle finger, Brandy pulled his chin towards her face. "How old were you?"

"Adolescent? That is so long ago, I have long forgotten," he answered, then kissed her forehead.

Alexander took his hand in hers. "I have kept you out too late. You should rest now." He urged her to stand.

"I'm trying to sleep in the day more and…" Brandy paused then continued in a whisper, "I wish that I didn't sleep alone. Is there no way to…be with you?"

They walked back towards the house and Alexander did not answer for the longest time. Arm and arm they walked slowly, Brandy negotiating her crutch.

"I will stay in your bed while you sleep some of the night and then leave when I must," he whispered.

"I hate waking a…" An unexpected hitch broke her voice. Brandy caught herself. "…alone. Gosh, what a pathetic wimp I am." She brushed at her eyes and tried to smirk away the emotional outburst. Her brow darkened with embarrassment.

"Let us enjoy the times we have and not bemoan the moments we do not." He kissed her gently and they continued down the path towards the candlelit house.

***

The nurse had stopped visiting. Brandy had last seen her one morning standing just outside the large bedroom. While heading towards the kitchen to make a morning pot of coffee (on the wood burning stove) Brandy had almost tripped over the silent nurse.

"Oh good golly—we need to put a bell on you." Brandy exclaimed, stopping short by placing her crutch tip against the wall for support. The shaft nudged Janice's shoulder. She smiled an apology.

There were tears in her eyes when she leaned forward and embraced Brandy in a matronly hug that knocked the breath out of her. With a thwump Brandy patted Janice on the back reassuringly. "You must be leaving?"

Janice held Brandy at arm's length and nodded quickly then dabbed tears from her eyes with the edges of her long white sleeves.

The sun was just setting and long shadows filled the hallway. Janice squeezed Brandy's arms gently then held a finger up while she dove into her apron pockets with the other hand. Shortly she produced a small tissue-wrapped bundle tied with a small emerald green ribbon. She cupped it in two hands and held it out for Brandy urging her to take it with a small squeak. Brandy had never heard Janice be vocal. The sound was quiet and fragile.

Brandy balanced her crutch under her arm and took the package. Silently, Janice watched as Susan unwrapped the package to reveal its contents.

"Thank you," a whisper was all Brandy could manage, then tears crowded her own eyes. She blinked them away and hugged Janice tightly. "I love it."

Brandy held the gold pocket watch in her hand and opened the inside to read the engravings.

"This must be very old!" Brandy exclaimed, then tried to put it back into Janice's hands. "I can't take this—this is yours."

Brandy looked at the engraving. "Your father's?"

She paused and looked at Janice's shaking head. "Husband?"

Janice held up an empty ring finger and shook her head

again then held her hand to her chest.

"Brother?" Brandy guessed and Janice nodded and smiled. "I really can't."

Brandy tried to put the pocket watch back into Janice's hands, but she shoved them in her pocket and turned her body away, shaking her head. Janice smiled coyly.

"You are quite the conundrum." Brandy relented, and softly added, "I will always think of how you helped me heal. Thank you."

Janice hugged her again then headed towards the front doors where a leather satchel and jacket were leaned against the wall. The mute nurse hoisted the bundles and with a nod walked out into the night. The door closed softly behind her.

By the time Brandy had crutched to the door the nurse was gone. She stood looking into the newly fallen darkness as if Janice might appear again.

A voice from behind her crooned, "She left already?" Alexander placed a hand on Brandy's shoulder, softly.

"Where did she go?" Brandy looked at the gold watch in her hand and held it out for Alexander. "Where did she come from?" She turned to him. "And what is this? Why does being with you give me so many questions?" She turned and shut the door, frowning as she did.

"That," Alexander indicated the pocket watch, "is a gift her brother gave her before he went into the Army and was killed in battle."

Brandy held the inscription to the candle light and read the words aloud. "The only reason for time is so that everything doesn't happen at once.—R.C."

"Why would she give it to me? Shouldn't she want to remember her brother?" Brandy's voice broke with emotion. "I mean, damn. I'm just a patient." Her voice dropped to a whisper, "Why?"

Alexander held her hand and led her to the kitchen. Together they made coffee, the clinking of their cups loud as Alexander briefly told Janice's story.

"Janice enlisted after her brother was captured by German soldiers in WWII and was presumed dead. She was a nurse, much like yourself, in New York." He pointed to the watch. "Her brother, Jonathan, gave that watch to her before he shipped out. It was something he had found at a second hand store with Janice. He bought it for her."

"How is she here?" Brandy sipped tentatively at her steaming cup of coffee. Alexander held a cup but did not drink it.

"She was stationed at a small hospital that was taken during an occupation of the town. They killed the patients and she tried to cry out and put herself in front of the patients to save them. With ammunition being in short supply she was rendered mute by her captors, tortured and thrown into a well to die. I found her there and brought her here to take care of you." He turned and cracked an egg into a pan, checked the flames underneath it, adjusted the flue and then continued. "I can move things with me through time." He raised an eyebrow towards Brandy. "Inanimate things. Unconscious things."

The ice-box, complete with a melting block of ice, stood in the corner. Brandy opened the door to find a glass bottle of milk and dashed a cap full into the eggs Alexander was scrambling with great concentration. "There," she said to the eggs. "Why unconscious?"

Alexander was distracted checking the heat on the eggs, lifting the copper pan away from the flame and stirring.

"Hmmm? Yes. I can see the alternate timelines when conscious beings are awake. Myself included. The timeline is constantly shifting and not in focus as each being is making decisions and moving about. I cannot move someone through time that is shifting underneath them. Colliding with myself is one thing." Alexander held up his truncated digit to make his point. "Tearing apart in multiple time streams would be very painful and instant death to myself and whoever I was carrying." He placed the pan back on the heat and watched the steaming egg intently. "I try to avoid that, really."

"So, you brought her here. Did you take her back?" Brandy pulled plates down from the cupboard. They clinked loudly in the still evening.

"No. When she went missing it started a revolution of sorts in the town where she had been a nurse. The small group banded together and overthrew the gorilla group that had been holding their township hostage. Her death was meant to be in the timeline. As was her brother's. I cannot adjust that." Alexander piled the scrambled eggs onto one plate and ignored the additional empty plate. He set the plate down at the table and motioned for Brandy to sit and eat.

"Where did she go?" She stopped to fan her mouth. "hot hot hot hot."

"To be with her brother. They have a small home they will keep together not all together too far from here. There is no one around this land in this time. They will live in peace, undisturbed, for the rest of their linear days." He handed a linen napkin to her and Brandy tried to demurely cover her mouth as she tried to both chew and suck in cool air at the same time.

"You took the brother before he died too?" Her voice was

muffled from the napkin.

"Yes. He had been tortured senseless and left to burn in a building." Alexander paused and looked away. "I promised her that if she helped…" he paused until Brandy had conquered the hot eggs and stopped fanning her mouth. "…helped you, I would save him as repayment."

Brandy eyed him.

"She agreed to be here. I was not holding her here against her will. Please, do not think I could do such a thing." He returned her gaze with wounded eyes.

"That must have been a hard conversation to have with her. One minute she was in a well, the next she was—here." With determination she scraped the last bite of scrambled eggs onto her fork.

"It was not an easy task, this is true." Alexander smiled and looked towards the kitchen window as if remembering something. "Both were challenging." He took the plate from her and went to the sink. "I am more patient than most challenges, however." Alexander pumped the handle on the faucet until water trickled out.

"Is my old room the only one with electricity?" Brandy took the cleaned plate from him and dried it. They moved together easily as an understanding unit. "I like the rustic charm of everything. I guess this is as off grid as it gets."

"Generator. Just for that room." Alexander opened the small icebox door and peered in. "There is still chocolate cake. You must want that."

"You don't eat with me. I mean sometimes you do. But not all the time." Brandy asked, in an overdramatic stage whisper, "What doooo you eat?" She drug out the "oooo" smiling widely.

Alexander held the cake tin in his hand and froze mid turn. He dropped his gaze and hefted the lid from the tin, peered in. "I do not bake. You will miss Janice's cakes and bread." Alexander busied himself with slicing a piece of cake off for Brandy and with a purposeful motion cut a slice of cake for himself. He placed the plates on the kitchenette table, dug a fork into the cake, ate the bite with relish and smiled mischievously at Brandy. After I moment he continued, "I will miss her cakes too."

"You are a very bad liar," Brandy said around a mouthful of chocolate cake.

Alexander's voice lowered, "Yes." He paused and put the fork down. "There is where we differ the most." He pointed towards the cake. "I can eat and process food like any animal. Yet, it is not the main source of my sustenance. It is useless to me, really."

"Are you telling me this cake is not going to make you fat?" Brandy eyed him suspiciously, her lip curled in mock contempt.

"Indeed, I am." He took another bite and smiled, chocolate at the corners of his mouth. "In actuality, the food you eat does not even taste pleasant to me. Except for sweet things."

"That's not even fair. Sweet tooth and crazy metabolism." She exclaimed, "What then?"

"Hmmm?" Alexander muttered.

"What do you eat then?" She snuck a bite of his cake with her fork and he stabbed at her fork but missed.

"I do not know how to explain it—it is so different from most things you know." He feigned taking a fork full of her cake; their forks clinked in a fencing duel until he relented.

"When I sync to a time I also sync to the place. I don't understand what it is, but the soil, rocks, area—it sustains me. My body draws energy from it when I come in contact with it." Alexander reached out and touched her face. "I also draw energy from you as well, when in contact." He paused as if to say more, but did not continue. He dropped his hand.

Brandy grabbed his hand and brought it to her lips. "You can travel away from this area, though, right?"

"I take soil with me for an energy source. Even an amulet around my neck, against my skin, will keep me from…starvation. It takes planning but it is possible." Alexander turned towards the window and tilted his head. "Did you hear that?"

The tabby cat jumped up onto the window ledge and meowed to them through the glass. The moonlight backlit his fur—a ghostly silhouette.

"Well there's the troublemaker." Brandy went to the window and tapped. The cat pawed at her hand. "Of course, he outed you, so I can't hold a grudge for him tripping us."

"Indeed." Alexander stood behind her and wrapped his arms around her. They rocked gently. The cat turned his tabby coat to them and began washing his face.

***

Dark curtains muffled the sun. Silence. Alone. Brandy started from her sleep and sat bolt right up in bed with a yelp. She was surprised to find herself holding out a hand, as if to ward off a blow. Bad dream, she thought to herself and lay back upon the bed. Her heart hammered so loudly in her ears she could not think about rest. She listened to the house creak around her and wished for company. She missed her grandmother's cabin, her things, her sheets, the comfortable way the mattress knew her and yielded to her tossing and turning, even her coffee cup, the one with the slight chip in it from when she had dropped it against the sink one early morning after an insomnia night.

Silence.

Emptiness.

Brandy kicked the sheets from her body and was reminded by searing pain that she should not move her leg and arm quickly.

"Fuck."

Sweat broke out across her body, instant clamminess. She lay back again and concentrated on catching her breath and calming down the shooting pain. It passed after some time.

Gently, this time, with concentration on movement and shifting of weight, Brandy got out of bed and turned to smooth the sheets into place. Old habits. She pulled at the luxurious, dark cotton sheets and heavy quilted down comforter until they obeyed and pulled taut against the tall mattress.

She looked at the extra height under the mattress and nudged at the box with her toe. A strong wooden box sat under the mattress and bedsprings. The box itself was constructed of deep mahogany, its surface polished darkly. Alexander had explained it the night before while they lay together wrapped in each other's arms. The sun was soon to rise and Brandy was nearly asleep, her eyes drooped as his soft voice carried her thoughts to dreams.

"The box below the mattress is filled with soil from the cave where I sleep. I find that it replenishes my energy to have it where I am when separated from the earth." He had explained.

"Do you walk barefoot 'lot?" Brandy's voice was slow and quiet with inevitable sleep.

"I'll sleep naked in the dirt to keep my energy up if I have gone too long without eating." He laughed under his breath. "The cold does not bother me as it does you." He shifted his weight to pull her closer.

"…get dirty?" she mumbled.

"Do I get dirty?" he repeated. She nodded her head imperceptibly. "No. Where I sleep things do not interact as they do when time is…happening. Time and gravity hold still there. Dirt does not interact with me. Things do not weigh what they would in your time. Frozen time."

Brandy absently pulled a stray hair from her face and let her hand rest upon his chest.

"Heart beat." She put her fingers to his neck, a loving nurse. "Warm." She assessed his vitals. Brandy let her hand drop and caressed Alexander, a loving temptress. He responded to her touch. "Hard," she insinuated and suppressed a throaty laugh.

Alexander enfolded her into his arms and murmured a response.

"Hmmm?" Brandy murmured into his shoulder.

"Not always warm. Only when I am…" He pulled her to him causing her to gasp in surprise. "…with you." Alexander bit at her shoulder, his curls brushed at her face.

Brandy arched towards him; the sheets pulled by gravity eventually drifted to the ground.

***

"Is this a strain?" Brandy did not open her eyes. She seemed asleep.

"What is that?" Alexander looked down, his chin against her hair.

"Being in main time with me? You said that after your bar-mitzvah your parents return to their time since being in main time is a strain." She tilted her head up to try and see his face. "Are you harming yourself to keep me safe from Yindi? Although sweet, that pisses me off." Brandy gently smacked his chest with the back of her hand. She became more alert. "Seriously. Wait a sec." She sat up in bed, holding the sheet to herself for modesty.

"I can't stay here forever. What are we doing here? I can't passively go along and let you keep me locked away." She instantly regretted her words and slumped. "That came out wrong. I mean…" She touched his shoulder and searched his eyes for understanding. "I am so very thankful you brought me here, kept me safe and let me heal." A deep breath. "Helped me heal. But I can't be here forever. I don't belong here."

Alexander regarded her for a few moments then softly answered. "I can take you back to whenever. It will be as if you never left. This is a…" he searched for a phrase, "…stolen moment in time for you." Then he added, "for us." Alexander pulled her to him. At first she resisted with pursed lips. A gentle tug and she folded against his chest, her head upon his breast.

"I'm not used to this," she whispered at last. "Your heart beat is very strong." She mumbled to herself, then continued to Alexander. "I've spent my whole life being independent and I don't want that taken away. It is hard to be helpless and out of control of the situation." She shrugged slightly. "Cabin fever. I suppose."

Absently, Alexander smoothed her hair, pushing at a wayward clump that had stuck to his mouth. "Such a short stolen moment." His voice was filled with deep sadness, it pulled at Brandy.

"My lifetime must be such a blink of time to you." she spoke quietly.

After a moment she patted his chest. "How many—what did you call me—linears, have you brought back to your time?" She held her hand up over her head in a stop gesture. "Wait, maybe I don't want to know that answer. How old are you?"

Alexander covered her hand with his and returned them to his chest. He breathed deeply, their hands rising and falling with the expansion of his lungs. "You ask a lot of questions, my dear." He finally answered. "I do not count years, since I do not experience time. I only judge against your time, main time." He whispered softly and as he whispered, Brandy's eyes drooped again. "Yes. I have had loves before. Not many. There have been those who were linears and one of my...kind." Protectively, he enveloped his leg over hers.

She snuggled closer, her breathing becoming more regular. Eventually she drifted off to sleep and Alexander lay still holding her warmth close to him. Brandy had tried to wake herself when he had risen from her bed. Sleep pulled at her deeply and she could not rouse herself from it more than a whispered grunt. Dreams swirled and mixed so that she could not tell whether she dreamed he had been there holding her or if it had been real.

Brandy pulled at the covers again to make them straight. Her silent catechisms, which had been absent while she was healing, now returned as commentary to her everyday movements, "Make your bed. So if you totally fuck up today at least you have done one thing right." She languished, lucidly thinking, "Even if it isn't your bed."

***

As she slipped into slumber, Alexander watched as the sun threatened to burst through the darkness. It pulled at his strength and made his deep hunger a cold pit in his stomach. He would need to feed and could not, would not, compromise Brandy while she was healing. Even if she was whole, with such intimacy he could not ask that of her, share with her that part of his existence. She had been so accepting of everything; however, this need for linear blood as food might not be so palatable. What had Yindi chided? "You fell for a linear?" The statement, "You fell in love with your food," implied in his sarcasm. A familiar embarrassment filled Alexander with brief sorrow for Brandy. It felt like a lie. How could he be who he truly was with her? She would not understand. How could she?

Alexander slipped away into his frozen time. The cold, still air instantly chilled his skin. He walked south to where he could slip into main time and feed easily without notice before the sun in main time rose.

***

A movement at the edge of her vision caught her eye. Brandy put down the book and looked up expecting to see Alexander walking into the library.

Nothing was there.

"Hmph." She looked again and listened for movement.

Nothing.

"Odd." Brandy went back to her reading.

Again in her peripheral a movement caught her attention. A whiteness—maybe? She kept her head straight and mentally checked her body's functions.

Migraine?

No.

Vision issues?

Not really.

Mental functions?

I am sitting in a library, reading a book that was brought back in time, probably, and will be crumbled into ashes ten thousand years before I will be born. I've had three cups of coffee and I am still tired.

Smart ass.

The disturbance in her vision was gone and Brandy chalked it up to vision migraines, until a thought occurred to her, a bolt of lighting to the heart.

Jesus, god, I can't be pregnant can I?

He said you couldn't.

Didn't my momma warn me against what guys will say?

He had sound science.

Dumb ass.

Seriously, he said it was impossible.

Let's hope so.

Brandy realized the internal voice was in fact that of her mother. With a pang, she missed home and the internet.

***

"There you are." Alexander leaned against the doorway and regarded Brandy.

Brandy paused mid sip of wine. "Here I am." A guilty smile spread on her face. "I'm having a bad day...errrr...night." She held up the wine glass. "I found your wine cellar. I chose something that didn't look too expensive." She sipped again. "Hope you don't mind."

He looked at her and she continued on, her words slightly slurred, "Damn vision migraine all day. Been having them more and more. Like fuzzy things at the sides of my viss...." Brandy faltered and tried again to meticulously work out the syllables, "...vish-----onn."

He regarded her in silence. She continued, "Pissin' me off. Like I'm seeing things." She drank deeply.

Alexander poured himself a glass of wine and held it aloft for a moment while looking Brandy up and down with gentle eyes, sipped, exhaled. "You are going to have to return to your time."

"Damn. I'll replace the wine," she said half mockingly.

"Silly. That is not what I meant. Please, drink the wine. It is here for you." He kissed her, lingering for a moment before explaining, "The longer you stay here, the more fractured your brain will become since it is out of sync with your time now."

"What?" Brandy took another sip and motioned with the nearly empty glass to Alexander. He obliged and filled the glass.

"Linears," he stopped then continued again, "you, sync with time as it moves just as I sync with my own frozen time. It is entangled with how your brain is wired and fires through its neuron circuits."

"I never read that in nursing school," Brandy giggled. "And

I took extra neurology classes." Brandy looked into her glass questioningly for a moment and began to try and fish out a particle of cork with her finger. She missed, grimaced, fished again, missed. "Hold on." She looked up from her glass, finger still knuckle deep in the wine. "What about Janice?" She looked down and tried to fish out the piece of cork one more time. "How can she stay here and not have her brain disinti…" She frowned at the floating particle then gave up her struggles.

Alexander held out a dishrag to her. She ignored him and continued to speak while sucking at the wine on her dripping finger, "Dee-sin-ti-great," she annunciated.

He peered into her glass at the floating particle and dabbed at it with the dishrag then answered her, "Janice and her brother do not have timelines in main time. They would have died, you see." He showed her the particle on the white fabric and smiled.

"Congratulations," she grumped then continued her inquisition, "So, if you take someone that would have died. They are OK here and don't start having these…" Brandy raised her hands up in the air, the wine sloshed about in her glass, "visual disturbances that kinda suck."

"This is true. I have to make sure they will make no disturbances in the time line here. It is a rarity that I would bring someone back and let them stay." He leaned forward and touched her hair, with his thumb touched the scar on her forehead gently. "How long have you had these vision disturbances and not told me?" His question was gentle but concerned.

"Coupl' weeks," she answered meekly. "S'at bad?"

"We have limited time now." Alexander took her hand. "Come, let us do something fun tonight. If you are strong

315

enough to venture into the wine cellar, you are strong enough for a stroll." He paused to regard the glass then looked at the bottle. "Unless you are not going to be steady on your feet."

Her glare was answer enough. The raised single finger, a punctuation mark.

"You are going to love this. I have a special night planned for you. Perhaps you should drink some coffee first."

***

Stars, so clear and so crystal they felt inches away, hung above Brandy and Alexander as they walked through the woods. Brandy walked slowly, using a cane to steady her gate. Each rock or root that caused her foot to bend slightly to the side was agony. She tried her best to hide her discomfort knowing that the movement would only cause the muscles to return to normal, no matter their complaint. The pain was a healing pain, ignorable, though persistently annoying.

"Am I steady on my feet," she harrumphed. "Jerk." She smiled. "Alcohol doesn't affect you either, does it?"

Alexander stood near by not offering to assist and walking slowly enough to not cause her to rush. "Actually, Yes. But differently, I believe." He added, "A different rate."

"So, you can drink people under the table? That comes in handy." Brandy sucked in breath as a particularly annoying rock cantered her gate, bending her ankle and putting stress on her calves and knee to counter balance.

"Indeed. It has come in useful at times." Alexander said no more and held a hand out for Brandy.

She rolled her eyes and took it, then smiled and softened towards him. "OK."

They continued, arm in arm, to walk through the night. Alexander lit their way with a flashlight.

Brandy pointed to it. "I kinda expected a lantern."

"I am not a Neanderthal," Alexander smirked.

Brandy thought for a moment. "I dunno. Who knows where your family tree goes back. It makes my head hurt."

"Here we are," Alexander interrupted Brandy's commentary on his ancestry. "This area will collapse in a couple thousand years. So, you will never see this one in your time."

Alexander pointed to a rocky karst area with a large gaping hole in the center of it. Trees perched around the hole grasped the rocks with their gnarly roots, silent sentinels waiting for their demise with the eventual collapse. Above the pit entrance, a large wooden structure had been erected. It contained a pulley system to hoist a wooden elevator, of sorts.

Admiring the scrollwork in the wood, Brandy commented on the artistry. "This is amazing! Did you make this?" She ran a finger along the oak. Delicate curves and flowers adorned its surface.

"I have many hobbies. One has to, through the eons." Alexander was oddly demure.

"You have many hidden talents I don't know about, I take it." She opened the gate to the elevator. The gate came to her waist and was fastened with an exquisite gold handle, also adorned with scrollwork.

Alexander did not comment as he helped her into the elevator. It bounced slightly as it adjusted to their weight. He pulled down hinged benches so that Brandy and he could sit.

"Nice touch," she complimented.

After closing the gate, Alexander took a heavy rope in

hand, untied it and began to lower the elevator by hand. Brandy looked above them to see the pulley system then peered over the side of the elevator into the darkness below.

"How deep?" Her questions were shotgun quick.

"300 feet," Alexander answered in quick retort, his voice not showing the slightest effort as he effected their descent, feeding the rope hand over hand through the pulley.

"Do you have lights?" She looked around them, but could not see in the dark.

"Yes. But not yet."

"Do you see in the dark?" She paused. "Wait, I think that was a stupid question."

"Of course."

"What? That was harsh." She pushed at his shoulder, or where she hoped his shoulder was.

"I mean, of course I see in the dark. Though I do enjoy candlelight."

Around and below was total darkness. Brandy sat patiently, accustomed to the dark.

"Look up, my love." Alexander whispered.

Brandy turned her eyes skyward. As they were slowly lowered, the sky above retreated from them until it became a distant, dark circle filled with stars. Outside of that circle, dark walls sloped up over top of them and the bottom of the pit belled out. On the sloped, dark ceiling thousands of glowing dots lit the cave. As they lowered, the points of light on the ceiling and the circle of stars became a unified sea filled with points of light.

"Wow," was all Brandy could whisper.

Seeming to hover from the darkness, glowworms clung to the ceiling everywhere. The retreating circle of celestial stars could not outshine the glowworms and for a moment Brandy was put off balance, unable to ascertain what was near and what was far for the points of light floating disembodied across her vision.

"Wow," she said again.

She turned to Alexander; now, in the dimmest of glows, she could see the reflection in his eyes. A brief glimmer of light dancing in the darkness, he was looking at her and not the glowworms.

"This is beautiful," she gasped, then looked back to the glowing ceiling.

She could feel Alexander moving next to her. He bent forward as if reaching to the floor of the elevator.

There was a pop and the sound of pouring. After a moment he said, "Hold your hand out."

She complied and felt a small glass placed in her hand.

"Champagne," he explained. "Wait…" he whispered in a jovial voice.

She heard another pour and then his voice next to her, "This is your cave. Only you and I have ever been in here. No one else ever will." His voice faded slightly as he turned his head from her and looked around. "To me, it is the most beautiful sight. For all eternity, here I will only see us."

He clinked her glass gently and they drank the champagne in silence, watching the sea of glowworms and stars above them.

"And now…" his voice broke the silence with a low croon.

"There's more?" Brandy felt herself being set up from where she had leaned on him. Then the warmth of him was gone. She could feel the air next to her collapse away in a small pop. She held very still.

***

From in front of her his voice intoned, "Your dinner." In an instant candles blazed around the cave and lit up the entirety of it. In front of the elevator, in a flat part of the pit, sat a small table with two chairs. Upon it a dinner had been set. The candles flickered on the white tablecloth.

"You watched Beauty and the Beast," she chided.

"I did." He opened the elevator gate and held out a hand for her. "You quote it so very often, I had to."

Brandy walked with his help on the uneven floor to the table and sat. She took in the dance of the candlelight with the awe of a child. The candlelight threw warm, flickering light onto the flowstone and rock formations. The shadows danced delightfully. "You make it hard for me to say I hate romantic gestures and all that mushy stuff. This is a lovely and very thoughtful gesture. What you went through to make all of this possible…" she held his hand to her chest, "for me. It's just too much."

"I cannot explain how little time I have with you. I want every moment to count so much to you." Alexander leaned forward across the table and held her hands.

Brandy paused, "You mean compared to your…life…or existence."

"Of course." Alexander glanced down at her hands and squeezed them delicately. "It is how we met, at the bottom of a pit." He glanced up at the ceiling. "The actual pit that we met in has not opened to the stars yet, so I can not take you there."

"Seriously, Alexander, this is the sweetest thing anyone has ever done for me." She leaned forward. "I'll cherish this moment for the rest of my life. As corny as that sounds, it really is true. Thank you."

Brandy leaned forward further and he met her lips with his. Awkwardly bent across the table, candles at either side, they kissed deeply. Hands clasped, his free hand holding her face to his.

They parted and Brandy stood, walked clumsily around the table and took both of his hands in hers. She beckoned him to stand and led him from the table.

"The dinner will get cold," he protested without sincerity.

"I got a clue you can go back in time and tell yourself to delay bringing that dinner down here and when you lit the candles, please bring a blanket." Brandy worked at untying his britches. She muttered to yourself, "You stopped paying attention to fashion in the 1700s, but I like it. Actually, 1800s, those are cotton." She tugged at the rawhide string.

"You catch on very quickly to the concept." He paused her from her untying and held up a finger. "I'll show you this time."

***

She stood, shirt half unbuttoned, and watched as he disappeared. First he was there, then he seemed to fade sidewise in almost a slight wave. She was sure the silhouette of him moved like a wave, rippled. The air around where he had stood rushed into the empty void. In the stillness of the cave the air movement made her skin tingle with the cold breeze.

She waited for a moment, holding very still for fear of getting in his way when he returned. To her right she heard a sound and turned. Five more candles blazed to life in an instant, as if on their own accord. The candles surrounded a blanket strewn with a dozen or more pillows that had not been there a moment before.

Brandy stood still, barely daring to breathe.

Alexander did not appear. She began to worry momentarily.

A thought flashed across her mind, "Am I strong enough to pull that elevator up the shaft with the rope?"

Even with the pulley she didn't think so. Another second passed and Brandy took a deep breath and cleansed the panic from her mind. She trusted Alexander. He was waiting. A mischievous smile brightened her features and she stepped carefully towards the blanket. Upon closer inspection, she realized it was a pile of thick blankets and silk sheets. She pulled a sheet over herself in a shroud and stooped to one knee. Her right leg protested bending, so she kept it straight in front of her. Under the shroud she unbuttoned and removed her shirt, then slipped off the stretchy pants she had come to favor. She gave up reaching the socks and left them on. The angry scars on her leg felt like neon in the dark. Before she dropped the shroud, Brandy grabbed two large pillows. She held one in front and one behind to maintain her modesty. Standing, she struck a pose and let the sheet fall from around her. It pooled at her feet.

Delicately, and most gracefully, despite her stiff leg, she proceeded to perform a burlesque in which she turned (slowly) and switched hands so that pillows always covered and almost exposed delicate flesh. Her hair had grown longer and brushed her shoulders as she turned her head from side to side. Brandy giggled to herself as she tried her best to be seductive.

Turn, turn, cover,

move, almost show,

cover, turn…

ever so slowly.

Brandy turned once more and came to a stop, steadied herself with one leg extended gracefully, toes pointed and her weight on her back leg. A moment passed and then she saw him gently glide into view in front of her less clothed than herself—lacking pillows. As he appeared the air pushed at her gently where he occupied the space. The cold draft caused goose-bumps to rise on her flesh. Alexander gently took one pillow from her then the other; they dropped to the pile of blankets at their feet.

He held her hands and lowered her to the ground so that she need not bend her healing leg. "I will remember this moment forever." His voice was heavy and deep. "I love you, my sweet."

She kissed him in return and when they parted whispered, "I love you too."

***

The water drips and drips around the candle, and finally onto the candle. The flames gutter and go out. Smoke floats up from the wick. One by one the candles are going out around Brandy and she gasps at the darkness that envelops her. The water becomes a steady pour. She hears it gushing in far away passages. The cave walls begin to weep with foam and precipitation as the water pushes calcite through the cracks. She hears lapping water somewhere, hitting a wall and receding, hitting and slurping against the surfaces, filling. The rushing water in the distance sounds like a jet engine. Every fiber in her being screams that she needs to leave; she has to get out of this place. She claws at the ground around her, unable to see.

The first lick of cold water touches her fingertips and she recoils. Franticly she is trying to remember where she is, how did she get here, where can she go to be safe? She is feeling around in the darkness trying to find higher ground. The echoes in her ears are familiar. She is in a cave. She doesn't know which one. The water laps at her naked toes; it is cold.

Further in the distance she can hear the sound of the jet engine of water; it surges in a far away borehole and then changes pitch. She envisions the passage between where she stands and the borehole is filling. She knows it is. It is a small passage and it is filling with cold water. The sound of the jet engine diminishes, as the passage between her and it is submerged, sumped, in cold, dark water.

A voice calls to her, "Brandy. This way!" It urges her further away from the filling passage. She moves towards it.

"You have to go lower," the voice urged.

Brandy froze. Lower? Lower than the rushing water? That's suicide. Lower.

The voice urged. It is Susan's voice. "Lower, Brandy. This way."

Brandy follows the voice, going lower in the darkness. She feels the air around her move. She is in a pit, high above her is an entrance. The air blows past her, up and out. Behind her the water fills the passage extending from the bottom of the pit. She hears the gulp of air escape as the side passage completely fills. It sounds like a burp of air as the last bubble of air escapes, then she can hear the jet engine of water in the further passage no more. Brandy only hears the rising water lapping against the walls. She yearns for the voice to call to her again in the darkness.

The water rises to her ankles and chills the skin as it goes. The current pushes from behind her and pushes her forward and lower, with the water as it seeks to follow gravity.

"Brandy, you have to follow me this way." This time the voice is Alexander's. He sounds so despondent, as if he has given up hope. "Yindi is coming. We have to get you away from him."

She reaches out a hand to find Alexander. The water rises to her thighs and it is harder to walk. The surge pushes her forward; she is resisting, trying to stand her ground. It is useless. She is pushed forward.

The dark will not relent, the water will not relent. Adrenaline surges through her veins even as she becomes cold and unable to move, her limbs sluggish. "Alexander?" she tries to cry out. The water reaches her chest and with it cold fingers grip her heart. Her feet become leaden blocks. Her hands tingle as sensation leaves them, blood drawn back to raise her core temperature. She can feel the beat of her heart thump in her temple. It is a scared beat that pounds and thumps its protest.

Red eyes open before her in the darkness; dark hands grab her and hold her steadfast as the water rises to her chin.

Brandy tries to scream, but draws in cold water. Sputtering, she jerks and shouts to Alexander.

She cannot see in the darkness, but knows he sits above her in the wooden elevator. He holds the rope carelessly in his hand. She fears he will let go and the elevator will drop into the water. He does not move to help her. A sadness resonates from him. He looks across the rising water, not seeing her.

"Alexander!" she tries again in vain to call out to him. The water gushes in and when she tries to draw breath to scream again, she sucks in ice cold water. It fills her lungs with its sharpness; spasms spread through her limbs. She chokes and seeks air only to find more icy water.

Alexander. She can't see him. The water covers her eyes and he disappears from view as he starts to hoist the elevator and himself via the thick rope.

Her vision is filled with glowing red eyes that are embodied by a darkness that engulfs her.

Darkness. Absolute.

***

Brandy woke up screaming. The pillows and blankest were strewn about in the darkness and the candles had burned down, almost guttering. Alexander at once held her.

"A bad dream," he soothed.

She explained what she had seen and experienced. He held her as she tried to dispel the shivers and emotions the dream had wrapped around her.

"Let us go home," he finally said. "I want this place to stay a happy place."

It was near dawn by the time she had bathed and was ready to crawl into bed. He lay with her for a moment. Eventually he spoke. "When time changes from its normal stream and veers you feel it in your dreams. I experience it as pain."

She started to ask a question. He stayed her with a raised finger.

"While you are here, main time has a slight alter without you in it. You feel that alteration, a ripple. That is you not there. Add to that, Yindi alters and changes the course unchecked without me there to fix the trouble that he makes. Yes. It does cause me pain, but bearable, for the moment." Alexander pulled the covers up to her chin and smoothed them down.

He continued without her even asking. "Yindi is an energy being, older than my species. He can only inhabit hosts and sees time in a linear fashion." Alexander grievously whispered, "He has inhabited your friend Mark."

Brandy stayed silent so that Alexander would continue.

"He, Yindi, seeks to destroy the universe by constantly moving time from its natural course, by altering events, things. He seeks the destruction of everything and the release from the hosts he is forced to inhabit."

"What do you seek?" Brandy ventured a question, her voice tentative.

"To keep time running as it should and the universe moving forward as it is meant to." Defeated, he continued, "Right now it is not quite on track in main time. I have to go back soon. You do too."

"And when I go back?" A quiet stillness entered her voice.

"He will work to destroy you, if for nothing more than to spite me," Alexander answered.

"I can't stay." Brandy spoke quietly to herself, "I can't outlast an eternal energy being." She held up her hands. "You can only keep me safe at night and I'll be on my own during the day."

"You are a very good at guessing. Yes, that is entirely true." He threw himself on the bed next to her; the bed bounced slightly. "He can be slowed. He is in a mortal form, I have to contain him somehow."

"Can you destroy him?" Brandy wondered aloud. "I guess you can't try to move him through time while he's deciding about things, and shifting his own timelines and disintegrate him?"

"Very good idea. Yes, it is entirely possible. However..." He plucked at her fingers one by one and let them drop back to her chest. "When he is killed his energy leaves the host and takes over the next closest thing. I can not be holding him, lest I be overtaken by him."

"That sucks."

"Indeed."

"Also, it serves no purpose to destroy him. There are a thousand others across the world that would take his place." He flopped onto his back and held his arm up over his brows while regarding the ceiling.

"How do you contain him then?" Brandy asked.

Alexander turned to her and thought a moment. "I am not sure." He paused. "There is something else. There have been timelines that I have played through, when I tried to keep you from being hurt."

"You mentioned earlier. What else?" Brandy goaded.

"One of those moments became permanent." Alexander looked away and would not meet her grey questioning eyes.

"What do you mean, permanent?" She pulled at him.

"When events get changed too often they form a rut, if you will. When that happens an event...rolls into this concave portion of time and can not be changed." His voice become a whisper.

"...and that event was...is....will be?" Brandy matched his whispering tone.

"I could not see. You and he were under the water out of

my view."

Brandy squeezed her eyes shut for a moment, blocking out her imagination, failing.

Alexander continued, "At your grandmother's cabin."

"I see." Tears slid from her closed eyes. "When?"

"That is a mystery to me. I cannot see it yet. I can feel it there like a beacon. There are other moments between now and then that are permanent. I call them white, since that is the color I see them in." Alexander kissed at her tears.

"Good things?" Her words were barely audible.

"Our cave this evening." His voice hitched with emotion. "I meant it, I will see it forever since it is linked in these permanent moments. It is a white moment. Locked."

"Does permanent mean that they happen exactly that same way should the timeline be revisited?" Hope registered in her voice.

"They are malleable on fine details. However, usually there is something in it that is permanent. Ours tonight—us in that lovely cave. Time turned white in my vision the moment we descended. We will always descend happily into that cave." Alexander did not notice the tear that had slid from his own eye.

Brandy noticed the blood red tear. "Is there one more secret that you haven't told me?" She kissed it away and added, "I'm extremely good at guessing, you have said so yourself."

For a moment Alexander was unable to answer, a look of fear on his face. He searched for words, found none.

"You are warmer at some times than others. Your coloring is more flushed then. You breathe more and seem more…" here Brandy paused and gently added, "…human." She brushed a thumb across his lips. "Other times, you barely have a heart beat and do not seem to breathe." She smiled, her voice barely audible. "I'm assuming this has to do with when you eat. And not the energy from the earth stuff."

Alexander's face fell slightly. "How long have you known?"

"It took the longest to realize that a dream I once had wasn't a dream at all." Brandy crossed the room and sat near the window, looking out into the darkness. No moon lit the sky. "I don't think it was a dream anyway. Was it?" She turned to Alexander.

He did not answer. Tentatively, he crossed to her and stood near, not daring to touch her. Finally he answered. "In your tent."

"You were there." It wasn't a question.

"Yes." He did not move and stood stiffly at her side, an eternity of space between them.

"I had bad dreams that night and some very good ones." Brandy took his hand and pulled his arms around her.

Alexander relaxed and let out a pent up breath. He buried his head in her hair and breathed the scent.

"Before the sun comes up, tell me what I don't know, Alexander. How long have you known me? How many times have you changed time for me? Why do you cry tears of blood?" She leaned her head against his chest.

"You do ask so many questions, my Brandy." Alexander then began to explain the hundred years that he spent ignoring the universe while he pined over her ghostly vision in his cave until he could stand her sadness no more. He told of how she had been shot by Yindi, how she had been thrown under the bus twice and avoided the part of time where she had died at the bottom of a water hole.

"And the tent?" Brandy questioned. By this time they were

seated side by side in the window seat. The sky was beginning to lighten.

"I did not know that was you," he replied.

"Have you…done that to me since then?" A gentle question.

"No. I could not." His eyes were wide and he held a hand to his throat. Long fingers lingered at the divot at the base of his throat.

"You can." Brandy squeezed his hand.

He squeezed her hand in return and said nothing. They watched the sky lighten holding onto the last moment he could stay with her before leaving to his dark sanctum.

18 WATERY DEATHS.

Susan paced back and forth as she spoke on the phone.

"I have no idea. They have no idea. She was checked in. I saw her. " Passers by glance nervously at the agitated woman, bright red fingernails motioning wildly. "I stepped outside for a moment to get an orange juice and when I came back she was gone."

She paused a moment, listening.

"I mean, gone. As in, not here. The bed is empty. The place is a wreck too like someone threw a temper tantrum in here. She couldn't have…"

Susan stopped her pacing and held a hand aloft in a what the hell gesture. "Of course she couldn't get up and walk away. She was thrown under a bus last night."

A nurse excused herself at Susan's elbow. Susan jumped with a start, looked at her position in the center of the hallway and moved to the side. "Yes, they could have lost her. She could have been put in a different room and they won't admit it."

Susan collapsed onto a bench. Defeated she added, "I can't believe this. They lost Brandy."

The phone buzzed against her ear. "Hang on, getting a text. She pulled the phone from her ear to read the message.

The incoming text was from Brandy's phone.

"What the hell?" Susan exclaimed.

"I was brought to grandma's cabin. Come visit me here?—B"

Susan texted back, "How are you conscious?"

"Long story. S'OK. Bring coffee? :)"

She blinked at the phone for a long time and reread the text. How could Brandy even be conscious? She had seen her go under that bus, had heard the smack, seen the blood. She wrote, "On my way."

The response was immediate, "K."

***

Alexander stood by her as she explained the dosage.

"This will knock me out." Brandy handed a capped syringe to him. The syringe was painted red.

"This will wake me up." The second syringe was painted green. She put it in his breast pocket and patted it gently.

Brandy continued, "I'm going to have a hell of a headache from that."

There was a moment of hesitation; they looked at the red syringe without moving.

"I would change all of the universe to keep you from harm," Alexander gallantly declared. "You can stay here with me a little longer. Away from…"

Brandy arranged herself on the bed. "The migraines and

nightmares are getting worse. You yourself said it could cause irreparable damage if I stay."

She sighed and leaned her head against him. He touched her face and returned the sigh.

"You gave me time to heal. I'm stronger now." Brandy closed his hand around the syringe, red paint on it glinting in the dim light. "I have to go back. He has to be dealt with."

"He will wait until day to avoid me." Alexander looked at the clear liquid in the syringe. It reflected the dim light. "I have told you the locked moment in time is in the water. It will happen no matter what we do."

"You can't swim without water wings so I guess we'll never know what happened in the wat…" Brandy stopped and eyed Alexander. "Wait—who came out of the water? Did you see that?"

Alexander dropped his eyes. "It was a different time line than this one. In that timeline Susan was taken over by Yindi and was in the water with you, so there is no telling what is actually locked." He kissed her softly and smoothed her hair. "Let us chose when our battlefield is then." He held the syringe to her arm.

"I hope he takes the bait," she murmured. Brandy held his hand tightly and when the barbiturate overtook her system, her grip relaxed.

Alexander picked her up in his arms, paused and then they disappeared.

***

Susan stepped onto the porch. It was near two am and she shook with exhaustion. "Brandy?" She paused on the first step, hoping for a reply. The phone buzzed in her pocket.

Bedroom. Can't walk, silly. Door open. The text from Brandy read.

"How can you be typing and awake after this morning?" A quiet comment, more to herself. Susan skipped the next step and opened the screen door. Only briefly did she register that the bedroom light was not on, in fact no lights were on.

"Did you bring a nurse with you?" Susan whispered a little bit louder as she closed the door behind her. "Margie?"

Susan dropped her purse on the table with a loud plunk. Whatever had been on the table was jostled by Susan's purse. It slid along the table. She moved her purse to the side to see what had been disturbed. It was the smear of blood on the cell phone's cracked screen that caught her attention first: Brandy's phone. She had last seen it on the pavement in a puddle of Brandy's blood this morning, eons ago. Susan blinked a few times as the thoughts formed in her mind. How did Brandy text from the bedroom if the phone is here?

Then the world went dark.

***

"I wasn't kidding about the headache." Brandy sat up in the bed. She felt around with her hands until she found the bedside lamp, turning it on with a click. Warm light filled her small apartment bedroom.

Alexander held a cold cloth to her head. "You can rest here for a while until the affects wear off. He will not come to you at night while I am here."

Brandy's eyes flew wide and she pushed past Alexander to head towards the bathroom. She reached the toilet in time to be sick.

He held the cold cloth out to her again. She took it to wipe her mouth and grunted, "Uggh. I don't think time traveling agrees with me." She turned towards the toilet to retch again.

Alexander sat on the edge of the tub, patiently waiting.

Brandy looked up at him from her slumped position on the floor, arm draped around the toilet rim for balance. "It's customary for the guy to hold the girl's hair back out of the puke."

Alexander regarded her, slightly amused. "I have no experience with this. I do not know the customs." He then reached to hold her hair.

She slapped his hand away gently. "Not now. I'm done." She paused. "No. Yes. Yes, done." She wiped her mouth again and leaned back against the sink cabinet. "You mean, you don't puke?"

Alexander shrugged, his mouth pulled to one side. "Not usually," he grinned.

"Don't get drunk, don't puke, don't gain weight. Man, sign me up." She patted his hand.

He tried to protest. "I have explained, this is impossible…" The misery in his eyes stopped Brandy's joking.

"I know. I'm sorry, Alexander. I shouldn't joke." She put her head in his lap and held him. The tub was cold against her stiff leg. "It's hard to deal with and…"

The phone rang, a shrill sound. "Why do I have a land line?" Brandy mumbled as she stood up, slightly unsteady on her feet, and limped towards the kitchen to silence the insistent ringing.

"Hello?" she questioned the handset irritably.

"Brandy?" the voice at the other end of the line squeaked.

"Susan? What's the matter?" Brandy looked at Alexander, her eyes wide with surprise.

"Brandy? How? I don't…" Susan's crying voice pierced her ear.

A growling voice spoke sharply in the background. Brandy strained to hear the words. She did not have to hear what the voice said; the tone was informative enough.

Susan continued, her voice quick and near hysteria, "It's Mark."

Ragged rasping breathing.

"He's here."

Sobs.

"He's hurt me," Susan sucked in deep ragged breaths, rattling her words.

"Where are you at?" Brandy asked.

"Your grandma's cabi…" Susan screamed in panic.

The sound of the phone being dropped caused the handset to crackle loudly in Brandy's ear. She pulled the receiver from her head and winced. Her grip tightened on the ancient phone, "Susan? Susan?" Brandy leaned heavily against the wall.

The line had gone dead.

"That was fast. We haven't been back long enough for him to know and react, have we?" Brandy spoke to herself mostly, then turned to Alexander. "He has Susan at the cabin. Was that in any of your other timelines?" Brandy tried to keep the accusation out of her tone.

"No." Alexander regarded her gaze evenly. "I was trying to keep you away from the cabin. I can go and stop him from taking…"

Brandy held her hand up to stop him from going any

further. "He'll take her in the day," she hissed, a breath of dissatisfaction, "No matter, we'll always end back there." Brandy shrugged her shoulders. "Maybe her being there is a good thing? Maybe, that's the difference between this time and the other timeline." Brandy started to gather her keys and purse and she spoke quickly. "In the other timeline Mark died and that thing took over Susan. So she was there, really. This time it will be all of us. The three amigos." By now Brandy stood at the door; Alexander followed her. "Maybe we'll win this time?" she said hopefully and waited for Alexander to respond.

He smiled, "Or we can keep trying again until we do." He walked ahead of her through the door, she could not see that the smile did not touch his eyes.

"That's the spirit." Brandy closed the door behind him.

***

Yindi nearly skipped from one side of the living room to the other while Susan spoke on the phone. He could feel it coming together now—a destruction. Somewhere it begged for him.

The wood floor creaked under his feet as he paced, skipped, turned, paced more. His bare feet left traces of sweat to mark his path. He nibbled on the ends of his swollen fingers absently, fingers splayed from taped broken wrists.

She would come to save her friend; Brandy would. His eyes stared into the dark, unblinking. Brandy and Susan—both of them. He would have both of them, both the things. Scrumptious. Yindi anxiously picked at a hangnail and worried over how long Brandy would be. She needed to come as fast as she could.

How healed was she? How long had he hid her away somewhere. Unfair. Not playing the game by the rules. He stamped his foot impatiently. Susan's crying interrupted him and angered him more.

"Tell her NOW!" he yelled at Susan from across the room.

He wanted both of them. Each one alone was a thing to be manipulated and adjust time, both of them together would push the timeline further out, delectably off track. Yindi bounced on the balls of his toes. He could imagine the crash of time as it changed. The look of pain on Alexander's face when he lost his linear, his food, his love. The ecstasy of ruining this moment filled his senses.

Now. He needed this NOW.

She needed to be here NOW.

He couldn't wait much longer.

Now.

Now.

Now.

Now.

She was talking into the phone. Yindi could see her lips moving but the pounding of his heartbeat in his ears drowned out her words.

Yindi/Mark jumped forward and yanked the phone from Susan's hand to yell into it himself. In his exuberance, he over exerted his grab smashing the handset into Susan's face. She screamed then collapsed on the floor.

Ignoring the collapsed figure Yindi held the phone to his face and yelled, "NOOOOWWWW!!!" The dead line hummed its dial tone in response.

Yindi dropped the phone onto the floor and began pacing the room again.

Outside, the moonless night ebbed away into dawn.

***

Alexander pondered as Brandy drove, frantically.

"We can not make it there before dawn. I will have to stay in my time and watch…wait until your time becomes night again." He watched the passing scrub brush give way to palmettos in the shadows, ghastly shapes, scratching the ink sky.

"Well, I can try at least." She drummed her fingers on the steering wheel. "I could call the police. They can get there before I can." She pumped the brakes slightly as they rounded a long sweeping bend in the road. Brandy held the steering wheel with one hand and reached for her front pocket.

She stopped and frowned. "Oh yeah, that was probably left at the hospital or under a bus. Funny, hadn't thought about it in…months?"

Alexander did not respond. He stared out the window, lost in thought. He felt the silence between them. "My apologies, what?"

"I was trying to remember how long I was back there with you—in your time." Brandy provided.

Alexander shrugged. "I do not measure time. It is difficult for me to tell you."

The tires hummed along the pavement for a long duration of silence that strung out between them.

Brandy broke the silence, "Tell me more about the moment in the water. The frozen moment. What is going to happen?"

Alexander did not tear his eyes from the landscape; he spoke to the darkness, "There is no way to tell. This timeline is different. I fear I will lose you and am helpless to stop it. Helpless in the day. For all my strengths I cannot stop this moment. It will always come back to here." He turned to her. "I cannot go with you during the day. I can watch from my time and adjust things to help you, put things close to your path."

"What do you mean?" Brandy slowed the car as they turned took the off ramp and left the highway.

"I can watch this timeline from my time. It will unfold. I can go to the last evening and adjust some things without severely altering this timeline." He leaned against the car window, the inky sky enveloped him, the glowing dashboard lit his face with an eerie green glow.

"I'm still not following. I mean you can't...oh, I see. You can see how this plays out then go back and adjust things in the evening, the night before. Like leave a gun or something. "Brandy's eyes shone bright as she tried to contemplate the best strategy.

Alexander, slowly answered, "I can not change too much, only minor adjustments to help you. You cannot kill him. He would take over you." Alexander glanced at the road in front of them. "That would be undesirable."

"If you are taking orders, for one, can you keep him from hurting her?" Her voice quivered. She pointed out the window. "We should have taken me there, darn it. Saved time." Brandy's voice was harsh, accusatory. "You couldn't have known," she softened.

"I thought we would have time to prepare and be at the

cabin first." He paused. "Stop the car."

"Why?" Brandy slowed the car and pulled to the side.

"Moving at significant speeds alters my ability to slip through time. I will go back and tell us to go straight away to the cabin." Alexander straightened in his seat and tugged unconsciously at the seatbelt.

"I would normally say yes, but we're forgetting that major hangover headache. I need a little bit of time to get through that." Brandy rubbed her forehead.

"I can not put you back into the time stream before I took you out. Being out of sync like that would cause you harm, ultimately." He explained, "Otherwise I could take you to the cabin before he gets there."

Brandy quipped, "The earth is moving at a significant speed; how can that not bother you, but a car does?"

Alexander smiled. "I am not sure. The best way to describe it is if you were to swing a bucket full of water on a string the water would stay in the bucket. Time must be like that around the earth. "

"I saw a pilot pour and drink a glass of water while doing a barrel roll in a jet." She blinked at the road ahead, looking for something and turned the radio volume down, not noticing the radio was not on. "OK, we're about twenty miles away. This is the last glimpse of civilization before we get there."

She stopped the car in the parking lot of Pop's, the general store/bait shop. The windows were mostly dark. One window towards the back of the store glowed dimly.

"Mr. Banks is probably getting ready to open the store." Brandy pointed. "I suppose you need to slip away here pretty soon. The sun is getting close to rising." She grabbed his hand and held it.

Alexander leaned forward and kissed her deeply. "I will adjust what I can to assist you. It can only be where he cannot see it. Else he will see the yellow of time having been adjusted. He will know that I was there and may get suspicious. Yindi does not know about the frozen time in the water. It will pull him there all the same like it will you."

"I guess, get the scuba gear ready by the side of the pond. Me, Susan and…him" She shuddered. "If we have to go in that water, I'll pick the time we do it. Yindi doesn't know how to scuba, I'm assuming." She raised her eyebrow as a question.

Alexander shrugged. "He only inhabits the hosts but does not learn from them."

"Mark didn't dive anyway." A shadow moving across the back window caused Brandy to jump. "I need to get out of here . Go get this done. Maybe I can drown him."

"Get him in the water with you and Susan. That is the locked part of time." Alexander pulled her to him and held her close. The embrace was awkward in the cramped quarters; neither seemed to mind.

She looked up at him. "There's a tight tunnel at the bottom of the pit. I can lead him in there. There's a rock in front that makes it a tight fit. "

"Can he get past the rock?" Alexander smoothed her hair absently.

"If he doesn't care about Mark's body and is motivated he could. It is tight." Brandy shuddered remembering getting stuck on that rock and watching air leak from her busted regulator hose and float towards the ceiling. "I died in the water, didn't I?" Brandy whispered, her breath puffed the fabric of his shirt collar.

"It was a different timeline." His answer was barely

audible. "That was night and I was still helpless."

"Why?"

"Water. I cannot easily go in water, it drains all energy from me. I cannot shift time in it. It renders me nearly useless." He held her even tighter. "Yindi has similar issues in that he can not easily leave a host that is in water. At least there is that. Not unless he is in direct contact with the new host."

"There are some serious disadvantages to being immortal," Brandy bemoaned.

"Indeed," he whispered back. He kissed her again and before he disappeared he sat her away from him, smiled and added, "Watch for the thing I will leave for you to help. I do not know yet what it is."

The air around them shook slightly and then stopped. Alexander looked towards the back seat, smiled slightly, then disappeared.

Brandy turned when she felt the push of air against her face. A second Alexander sat in the back seat of the car. She turned towards the empty front seat then back again to the back seat. Water dripped from Alexander's hair and soaked shirt. He looked weary and drained.

"I will tell you what has been adjusted that will help us trap him." His sunken eyes blazed. He touched Brandy's face and smiled. His eyes twinkled with mischief. "Quickly, before the sun rises."

***

Yindi stood in the kitchen, Brandy's broken cell phone in hand. Concentration and pain caused sweat to break out on his face.

With fingers that splayed from broken, mangled wrists he

texted, "Bedroom. Can't walk, silly. Door open."

The phone slipped from his hands, he tried to catch it but hissed with the pain that shot through his wrists, swollen and purple. Yellowish tinged flesh crept out from under the duct tape bandages. The phone clattered onto the kitchen table. He reached for it, but the sound of the opening front door stopped him.

Yindi shrank back into the shadows and hid behind the refrigerator, waiting.

"Did you bring a nurse with you?" Susan called out as she walked into the kitchen. "Margie?"

The tension rose in him as he coiled to jump and strike Susan. She picked up the phone from the table and understanding registered on her face as she recognized the phone.

Yindi lunged forward, hand outstretched to grab the long, blonde hair. Sweat gave his face a sheen in the stark kitchen light. Outside the sun had not risen yet.

An outstretched hand pulled him off his feet by the throat, stopping his forward momentum.

Susan turned and gasped. "Alexander? Mark?" She held the phone out. "This is Brandy's?" Susan looked around. "Is she here?"

"Not yet." Alexander plunked Yindi into a kitchen chair and motioned towards the ancient Bakelite kitchen phone. "Let us call her, shall we?"

Susan faltered for a moment, staring at Mark then Alexander in disbelief, "OK?" She lifted the receiver and began to dial.

"Brandy?" she spoke into the receiver. When she heard the voice at the end of the line she sighed in relief and began to shake. Tears sprang to her eyes. "Brandy? How? I don't…."

Yindi shifted in his chair and kicked out at Alexander, trying to dislodge himself from the iron grip. He shouted in the effort and yelled in agony as his broken wrists thumped against the chair.

Susan continued, her voice pinched and frightened, "It's Mark. He's here. And A…." Yindi kicked again at the table, which pitched forward knocking Susan back a step. She rubbed at her hip where the table had made contact as she listened to the voice at the other end of the line. "Your grandma's cabin…" Susan jumped back and dropped the receiver as Yindi kicked with both feet and managed to dislodge himself from Alexander's grip for a moment.

Alexander grabbed the dropped phone receiver and clunked Mark/Yindi on the head. The sound was a dead thunk. Yindi's eyes rolled into the back of his head and he pitched forward.

Planting a foot on either side of Mark/Yindi's unconscious body, Alexander effortlessly heaved the husk back into the kitchen chair; metal feet screeched on the tile floor.

"Hand me that apron." Alexander held his hand out. Susan handed the red apron to him. He began to tie Yindi to the chair. The out of context text on the apron blazed in neon rhinestones "What happens at the cabin, stays at the cabin."

As Alexander tied the apron tightly he explained to Susan what was about to happen. She did not ask questions throughout his explanation, though her legs buckled and she sat ungracefully into a kitchen chair. Her eyes grew wider as the moments ticked on.

The darkness in the kitchen window began to fade. Alexander looked at the growing light and stood still for a moment, looking into the past for a moment he could slip to and be safe from the sun's rays. "Brandy will be here shortly. Remember what I told you. I'll go get the scuba gear ready." Alexander walked through the back door. Susan did not follow and did not see him disappear.

She sat staring at Mark, unconscious, tied to the kitchen chair, blood dripping from his forehead. Finally she whispered, "Exactly, why do we have to get him into the water?" She stood and crossed the kitchen. "I think I need a drink."

***

The sun painted the sky purple and orange as it rose. Brandy turned onto the dirt rode that led to her grandmother's cabin. The air was already still and close with heat even this early in the day. She pulled to the front porch and killed the engine. Nothing could be heard except for crickets and frogs in the woods around her. She turned the radio off; it had not been on and she caught herself, hand still on the knob. Her hand was shaking. A loud banging startled her. The back porch screen door had been kicked open and banged loudly against the cabin. She heard a scream.

***

Yindi stumbled from the back porch and rolled in the dirt. Leaves and sticks stuck to his shirt. He rolled and stood clumsily. The world swam in colors in front of his eyes. He could feel that Brandy was near. And Susan. He could taste the red of the possibilities. Killing them both would be pure ecstasy, time would slant, Alexander would writhe in agony. But where? When? He could feel the moment building like a thunderstorm on the horizon. Soon and near.

***

Susan burst through the front door and ran towards Brandy. They met at the front of her car.

"You're walking?" Susan held Brandy at arms length. "I don't under…"

"We don't have time right now for me to explain. " Brandy pulled at Susan's hand and they ran towards the left of the cabin—the opposite side of Yindi/Mark.

Susan followed afterwards. "We're out of wine. I want you to know. He must have drank it all."

"What are you talking about?" Brandy pulled Susan behind the shed. The door stood open. She peaked inside—the gear was gone.

"After seeing Alexander this morning and him tying Mark up to the chair and Mark trying to come after me—I went to get a drink, but the wine fridge was completely empty."

"Alexander had to get ahead of you I see. You must have gotten blitzed and ruined the whole thing. Wonder which one of us died that time through?" Brandy leaned against the shed. It creaked slightly. "Remind me, the next time we see Alexander, to ask how many times we've gone through this." Brandy listened in the direction of the cabin. "Come on, if we're lucky, Mark will chase us."

Susan stared after her for a moment. "If we're lucky."

Yindi/Mark yelled from behind the cabin, "You!" A maniacal laughter issued from his throat and made the hair on Susan's arm stand on end. Susan jumped and backed into the

348

shed. An old shelf that had been precariously perched against the shed lost its purchase and slammed into Susan, gashing her head. She gasped, held her hand to her head; her eyes fluttered and she slid along the shed wall threatening to lose her grip on consciousness.

"Shit," Brandy hissed and caught Susan with her arm. "No matter what she's going to get clunked in the head?" She whispered to the air not knowing if Alexander could hear her.

"I'm OK." Susan straightened and looked towards the cabin. "He's going to kill us. We gotta get moving."

Brandy helped Susan to her feet and leaning on each other for support they ran towards the pond.

***

Alexander stood at the water's edge. The time was the night before and all was still. He watched main time expand in front of him leaving ghostly white images of what would be. He wiggled his naked toes in the dirt, drawing energy from the cave dirt he had transplanted there.

Ghost images of Brandy and Susan came up the path at a fast run. He stood still as Brandy's white ghost ran right through him and aimed towards the scuba gear he had placed at the pond's bank. She stopped and smiled at the message he had written in the dirt then she looked around. He could see her mouth something, but he could not hear what she said. A pang of regret hit him, his mouth pulled at the corners in a frown. The images of Brandy and Susan began to fade as the sun rose higher in main time. She erased the message with her foot and said something to Susan. Susan stumbled ungracefully as she entered the water. Brandy reached for her, examined her head. They nodded to each other. With a final check of their air gauges they disappeared into the water.

Alexander shivered remembering the last time he saw the both of them descend into the water together. Susan had been the only one to return. Susan inhabited by Yindi stripping naked and laughing at the destruction he/she had caused.

He could see the ghostly visage of Yindi/Mark running down the path towards the pond. Alexander considered moving something into his path to slow him down. A moved log this evening may cause a stumble in main time. Even as he moved a rock into the path of Yindi/Mark he knew it was useless. The fading ghostly image moved to the right of the rock and missed it. Yindi/Mark would have seen the yellow tint on the rock as being something adjusted. As it was, Yindi looked down at the place where Alexander stood/had stood the night before. The sand must have appeared yellow to him, having been adjusted. A quick grin crossed Yindi's face. The visage of Yindi dodged to Alexander's left. Alexander held out his hands to choke the specter, uselessly. Yindi ran past him in main time, unaffected by Alexander's throttling of the air the night before.

The sun rose higher and Alexander's ability to see was fading fast. He could see the dimmest of outlines as Yindi/Mark grabbed the last scuba tank and regulator, donned it and entered into the water. Alexander waited for time to turn white, for the locked moment to happen. It did not. What had he miscalculated? What was different? Why had time not locked to that moment where Susan/Yindi and Brandy had entered the water and only one had come out? What was the locked variable? Alexander's mind raced as he tried in vain to consider the possibilities.

***

Brandy smiled as she put the scuba mask onto her face. "I know," she said before nestling the regulator in her mouth, covering her smile. She erased the words, "I'm here," written in the dirt next to the wagon full of gear.

Susan paused with her mask on her forehead. "Why do we have to trap Mark in the water, again? Am I hallucinating?" She touched her forehead and her hand came away bloody. "I'm on a bender and imagined Alexander and the directions he gave me. They make no sense."

Brandy removed the regulator from her mouth. "Well, Mark is possessed by an energy being that can't transfer to a new host if trapped in the water. Mark is gone. He's not there. It's just this energy…" Brandy stepped into the water. It lapped at her ankles.

"Demon?" Susan supplied.

Brandy nodded and looked at the water, then back up at the trail leading to the cabin. "He'll be here soon. We have to set this up."

"And I have to be there too?" Susan stepped into the water and looked down at the inky depths.

"Yes. It's inevitable. If we make it out of this, I swear, I'll tell you everything. A lot of wine will have to be poured for you to believe me." Brandy put the regulator in her mouth and gave an OK sign.

Susan tilted her head to the side. "So it's a joint hallucination. OK." She placed her regulator in her mouth and returned the OK sign, red thumbnail, dripping red blood.

They descended. One remaining scuba tank and regulator

hung from the red wagon on the dirt. Black tape was wound around the tube to the regulator, a loose end flapped slightly in the breeze.

***

The darkness of the water enveloped Brandy as she descended. She breathed slowly and the exhaled bubbles rose to the surface. For a moment she watched them float away from herself and welcomed the weightlessness. Movement to her left brought her back to the moment. Susan rolled and looked at the surface of the water next to Brandy. They held hands for a moment, then in unison turned, flipped on their hip mounted canister lights and swam towards the large rock at the bottom of the pond where the dive line would start.

Brandy and Susan located the line in the depth. The visibility was pristine. They each located the line and began to swim towards the small tunnel, moving their fins ungracefully to stir the silt behind them—marking a trail. They neared the small opening to the tunnel and paused. Brandy rubbed her arms, the coolness already getting to her bare arms. Susan unclipped a light from her belt and tried to throw it into the tunnel. It floated and landed in the opening, just beyond the large rock. The light shined up at the ceiling haphazardly. Brandy reached into the tunnel, around the rock, and with the barest scrape of her fingertips was able to hook the light's strap and tried to push it further into the tunnel. The light landed face down and remained visible from the tunnel's opening.

Susan tried to push past Brandy and go into the tunnel. Brandy stopped her and pointed to her head; shook her own head no. Susan was in no shape to go in. Blood continued to drip from the gash on her forehead and stream out behind her.

Brandy took her tank off and pushed it through the opening. It moved sluggishly, slowed down by water. Unable to move at any speed, nightmarishly slowed by the water, Brandy pushed herself around the rock and into the tunnel. She struggled to bend around the rock, the high point of it digging into her sternum. She kicked with her fins and then stilled as she felt Susan place herself against Brandy's feet, offering herself as a support. Brandy placed her finned feet against Susan's back, unable to turn and look at Susan due to the confined space, and pushed. The ceiling scraped along her back and a small jutting rock jammed into her shoulder. With a silent grunt she birthed into the small tunnel and was able to reach the light. The tunnel was too small for her to turn and see Susan. Brandy could only look forward. She grabbed the light and her tank. Without the tank attached she floated to the ceiling and had to expend energy keeping herself righted. She relaxed and let herself float against the ceiling. Her exhalation bubbles trickled behind her and towards the opening of the tunnel since the path she faced trended lower and lower as it became smaller and smaller. She floated forward about two body lengths, pulling her tank with her. The tunnel widened slightly and turned to the left. Brandy pushed the light around the bend so that it was not visible from the tunnel's opening. She could only guess it wasn't visible, the tight quarters kept her from turning her head to see behind her. She pushed her tank in front of her and bent forward, placing her head into the turn. By balling her body up as tightly as she could she was able to float against the ceiling and placed her head and torso in the bend of the tunnel. With a twist, she rolled her knees to the ceiling and pulled her head back, upside-down, towards the opening of the tunnel. Her head scraped along the rock and she was thankful for the helmet. Once about-faced in the tunnel she spun to be facing right side up.

Ahead of her she could see Susan peeking around the rock. The silt was considerable, yet she could make out an OK sign, a flashlight moved in a circle. Brandy returned the OK, then grabbed her tank and began to swim towards the tunnel opening.

Brandy carefully placed her tank on the other side of the rock. The tube hung on a rock for a moment and Brandy felt the adrenaline pulse through her, remembering the last time her hoses had caught and she had been stuck. She did not have time to be stuck, to lose air, to die. She had to get away from this tunnel and away from him. He would be here soon. The adrenaline surged and her heartbeat pounded in her ears. Her breath became more ragged and she wasted air. Susan reached through the tunnel opening and grabbed Brandy's hand, instinctively. Brandy closed her eyes and willed herself to calm down, to push through. She pushed her head out of the tunnel and wrapped herself around the rock. Oddly, coming head first out she was able to find a groove in the ceiling to place her shoulder. It was much easier and she came out with barely any friction. She floated outside the tunnel staring back at it stupidly for a moment then regained her senses.

Brandy grinned around her regulator at Susan and Susan grinned back, both a spectacle with bleeding foreheads. They held onto the dive line and made for the other side of the pond. Susan untied the dive line as they progressed. They kicked madly as they went, stirring up as much silt as possible until they had reached the halfway point, after which they floated gently towards the other side of the pond.

***

Yindi stumbled across rocks and roots as he made his way to the pit. The path in front of him was littered with things tinged yellow, altered. Alexander had moved things into his path to slow Yindi's travel. His eyes stung as sweat rolled into the unblinking orbs. How odd for Alexander to adjust time. Yindi smiled. He could feel the pull of the thing—the things—the elation of destruction that would be his, in the water. It called and beckoned, itched behind his eyeballs. They would both die. Both women. He regarded the red wagon, empty save for the one tank, mask and regulator hanging over the side, decorated by a coffee cup holder hanging at a diagonal off the edge.

He wondered how deep they were. Did he need the air tank? Now. He thought.

Now. It was here.

Now. He had to go.

Now in the depths.

There.

Here.

Now.

He grabbed the mask and clumsily

Now

put it on his face…

Here

Yindi did not know how to turn the air on, what a safe pressure was. He…

355

There

turned the knob slightly and watched the gauge

Now

needle rise. It couldn't be that deep, he surmised. He could

NOW

float to the top if he ran out of a…

NOW NOW NOW

Yindi stopped all thought except for following the thing. The imminent thing that was in front of him. He walked into the water and disappeared. Ripples from his descent danced and pushed floating leaves in pirouetting spins. The leaves spun away from where Yindi had descended. Bubbles rising from the depth interrupted their path sending the leaves spinning wildly in different directions.

***

Brandy watched her air bubbles rise to the surface of the pond. She pushed Susan back against the rock wall, under an overhang and watched their bubbles begin to collect on the rock ceiling. The water was murky at their depth and it was hard to see. They waited in the darkness, their lights extinguished. The only visible light was dim and far from them. Without her light she could not see the air gauge. She looked anyway at her tank. How much time did they have left?

***

Alexander stood transfixed. Main time continued to move forward. Yet it did not turn white. It did not lock. What was missing? Something was wrong. He had misjudged,

356

misremembered. He stepped towards the waters edge and frowned. Minutes in main time passed. He dared not let this timeline play out only to have something else locked. Perhaps it was only her death that had locked time. He sat in the dirt and felt the weight of reality hit him. It had been in vain. It was her death that had locked time. There was no avoiding it. That must have been what he had been doing revisiting Brandy in the car. Saying goodbye. Alexander stood and turned. He would go say goodbye to Brandy in the car.

***

Brandy imagined she could see a shape descending in the darkness in front of her. She imagined the light winked out as something passed between her and the light hidden in the tight tunnel. She imagined and hoped she had enough air. Susan reached for her hand and they held on to each other in the darkness trying to fight dark images that would raise their heart rates, quicken their breathing and sap their air even further.

***

Yindi swam and could only hear the continuous warble in his head. There. Now. Here. NOW. The Thing. He swam towards the dim light and felt it beckon him closer.

***

Susan tapped Brandy on the shoulder. She held out a flat hand and rotated it side to side. "Not OK." Then pointed to her regulator. There were no bubbles coming from it—out of air.

Brandy handed Susan her regulator and they began buddy breathing. Each time the regulator was passed precious air escaped to collect at the top of the rock ceiling. They clung tighter to one another.

***

Alexander stood at the water still, shoulders slumped, defeated. Slowly, mechanically he turned to slip back into time and say goodbye to Brandy. The sand beneath his foot gave way under his weight and his foot slipped into the water...

***

Yindi heaved himself around the rock, oblivious to the protests from the flesh and bone he inhibited. Just as he pushed with his last effort and flowed into the tunnel, flesh ripped and bleeding, the time around him turned white. A locked moment. Was he always in this tunnel? Had he been here before? It did not matter. He could feel the thing in front of him, pulling him in.

***

...and time turned white. Alexander's eyes went wide with realization. HE had been standing in the water when time had locked. The water had been seeping into his bones and pulling energy from him when Susan/Yindi had emerged triumphant from the water. It turned white when HE had stepped into the water. It wasn't the death. It was him. Alexander had appeared in the car, not to say goodbye to Brandy but to give a message—and wasn't he sopping wet? Drained? Alexander turned back towards the pond and began to look through time to find a moment when this pond did not exist. It had once been capped with a limestone rock, with very little water. A river ran nearby and only a small stream flowed into this pit that one day would be a river, which would disappear leaving a pond with a submerged pit.

Alexander synched with that time and began to climb down into the pit. The stream splashed and doused him. Carefully, Alexander lowered himself to where the small tunnel would be.

***

Yindi pushed forward trying to find them. They would be in front of him. He could see their light. A nagging in the back of his brain made him hesitate. Were they in here? He could see their light. The tunnel was snug and scraped his shoulders. He had to keep one arm forward and one arm behind himself to wriggle through. The tank pressed into his soft belly and scrapped eerily along the rock floor of the tunnel.

He paused as time around him turned white. Locked. He had done nothing to lock time. What had locked? His breathing became ragged as adrenaline hit his system. He continued on. The thing had to be in front of him.

Here.

Now.

Here.

Yindi came to the bend and was thankful for the extra room. He could pull both arms in front of him. Then he saw the light on the tunnel floor. This wasn't the thing. With a growl he pushed his body as far into the bend as he could so that he could try to turn around. His hoses tangled and ripped the regulator from his mouth. His knee became lodged between his chest and the tunnel wall. Yindi wriggled and screamed. Bubbles shot from his mouth and filled his ears. He paused, eyed the wall and banged his head hard against the wall to experience the pain. It seared through him and caused his panic to stop. Carefully he reached a hand between his chest and ankle to retrieve the regulator and place it in his mouth. He relaxed and floated as best he could and with that free hand pulled at his foot. Centimeter by centimeter the knee dislodged and he could turn. He banged his patella on a rock, sending more shooting pain through his mortal body.

The hoses had wrapped around Yindi's leg and threatened to pull the regulator from his mouth once again. He could not untangle the hoses and ignored them, pulling himself once again with one arm in front and one arm behind back through the tunnel. Then he saw the bright yellow eyes in the darkness peering back at him from the tunnel's opening.

***

Brandy felt it; the air stopped flowing. She pulled the regulator from her mouth and looked at it then turned to Susan. They had no choice but to leave now. Already the need to breathe was creeping in like a cold panic. As they kicked off to push for the surface an implosion of movement met their ears—a shock wave of something in the water. They continued to swim towards the surface. Brandy looked back once to see the light below them wink out. The pit below was hidden in total darkness.

***

Alexander stood and watched time as the rock, which had once been part of the limestone cap, fell and wedged itself in front of the small tunnel's opening. He steeled himself for the energy draining of the water to hit him then realized he had one last thing to do. He disappeared to tell Brandy what he would do.

***

On the surface, Brandy and Susan sat on the bank, feet in the water, breathing heavily.

"Is that it?" Susan sobbed. "Do we call…"

Brandy patted her hand. "We can't. He's trapped as long as he is in the water."

She placed the scuba tank in the wagon and tapped at the empty air gauge.

***

He had been dripping wet in the car, he explained that it was from climbing through a stream in the past. They had sat in the car not an hour ago; it felt like years. He had explained that he would seal the tunnel shut. The pit itself was a cave and had not received sunlight in the deeper areas; he could slip through time and appear in it during main time. He'd push the rock over and close the tunnel.

She had jumped into the back seat as gracefully as she could with mending limbs to kiss him. His eyes were sunken, just from the limited exposure to water. How would he deal with appearing in a pond full of water—that's what the implosion noise must have been, Alexander appearing in the water.

The light from the tunnel had winked out.

"Yes, but you can't slip through time when you are in water, right?" She had asked.

"No. I can not." His answer had been low and quiet as he smoothed her hair behind her ears.

"How will you….?" She had pleaded with him, searching for a different way.

"I can not place rocks or dirt from my cave there around the tunnel, Yindi would see it, though that would help me sustain." He had shifted his weight to pull closer to her. "I have a pendant and literally rocks in my pockets. It will hold me for a while. I only have to wait until the evening to surface."

"This will help, right?" She offered her wrist.

***

On the bank, Brandy touched the wrist she had offered to Alexander. The wound was already healed. She hoped it was enough to keep him whole until the sun went down.

***

Alexander stood again at the bottom of the pit thousands of years before main time. The limestone cap had broken and pieces of it had fallen to the pit's ground. Alexander was careful to stand in the dark shadows where light had never been. He placed his hand upon the large rock and enjoyed watching time unfold. Brandy and Susan finding this tunnel. Brandy nearly getting stuck. He ached to move the rock and erase that moment of struggle but could not. It might change events, he could not live through this timeline again and see her under the bus again, chased by Yindi again. He would rather float at the bottom of the pit in oblivion without her than see her pain again.

The thought of her pain stoked his anger. He watched through time as Brandy went into the tunnel, moved the light and then came back out again. Her ghostly image swam through him. He stepped to the side so that the vision of Yindi would not swim through him. His anger renewed. He slipped into main time and steeled himself for the excruciating weight and pain of the water that would separate him from the earth and drain his energy. Alexander buried his feet in the floor for leverage and placed a hand upon the large rock. In the tunnel Yindi had turned and was looking back at him. With minor effort Alexander heaved on the rock so that it fell blocking the tunnel. The barest slivers of light, dim and fading, glowed from around the edges. Yindi battered against the rock from inside the tunnel, futile, weak.

Alexander curled into a ball and floated against the rock overhang, conserving his energy. He hoped he could make it to night. He tried to sync into a different time but could not see time. He realized he could see no ghostly images around him. That was strangely peaceful. He stared off into the darkness, at peace.

***

Yindi clawed and battered at the rock. He felt his lungs struggling, this host's lungs, not his. Struggling. Gasping. Feeling darkness creep in at the edges of his vision. A burning sensation spread through his limbs, a cold voice filled with reason demanding that breathing in, even of the water, would be fine. Breathe. Draw breath. Gasp. Cold water would feel good. Yindi struggled and succumbed. Gasping in cold, dark water. It filled his lungs, burning. His last vision was of green time, a universe that was right, a timeline that was whole. He tried to leave the host, knowing it was useless. Instead he stayed as the host's vision went dark and the body stopped functioning. Yindi floated and stayed, trapped in the darkness.

***

In main time, Susan and Brandy sat by the water's edge watching the sun climb higher in the sky. Ripples cast out from their dangling feet in concentric diminishing waves.

Brandy finally broke the silence. "Let's go get your head looked at. He's not going to be able to come out until the sun goes down."

Susan looked at her bewildered, blood trickled down her face in rivulets. She replied, "I think you just said he can stay there all day. What?"

"I'll explain everything." Brandy stood and the two walks back towards the cabin. Brandy looked over her shoulder at the still water one more time, a worried look on her face.

***

An extremely old gator lumbered across the swamp while the sun and temperature dipped. He slid silently into a greenish pond and felt the warmth engulf him. Leaves and debris that he had drug with him into the pond floated away on spiraling wakes.

A sudden movement in the water startled the gator and he submerged out of sight.

Brandy pushed the flat bottomed boat into the water and eyed Fred warily. The gator's eyes emerged again apparently returning the glare. Eventually, the gator lost interest and floated towards the other end of the pond away from her.

She tightened her grip on the wooden oar all the same and strained with all her might to listen for movements in the water.

When the last sunrays had departed from the sky and the frogs began to croak their deafening symphony she heard the sound of something or someone surfacing.

19 ONLY THE ONCE.

The fire crackled and spit. Shadows danced ecstatically on the grass and gravel. Somewhere a drunk caver sounded a turkey call. From the other side of the camp another voice responded. Brandy looked into her coffee cup and smiled.

"Look wha' I beat out Janet for!" Susan stumbled into the small circle holding a lantern over her head triumphantly. Its green base was battered and scarred from much use.

"Janet needs that more than you to find Jack if he comes vomiting in your tent." Brandy patted at the empty chair next to her, waited for her friend to sit, handed her a bottle of beer.

Susan smiled and held up the lantern for closer inspection. "I'll help 'im fin'her." Susan slurred. "I'm gonna go find Earl too. He's ove' there…think."

Brandy eyed her empty coffee cup again. "Glad to see things are definitely back to normal."

Alexander poured more coffee into Brandy's cup, sat next to her, took her hand and replied, "Indeed."

The night wore on and cavers surrounded the fire, telling

war stories. Blaine turned to Brandy, "Sooooo…" he drew the sound out "Do you cave dive anymore?"

Brandy smiled and leaned her head on Alexander's shoulder. "No. I think I'll stay in dry caves from now on."

"What about you, Alexander?" Blaine tipped a red plastic cup full of beer his way. "Do you ever cave dive?"

Alexander smiled in return, "Only the once."

EPILOGUE: 10,000 YEARS AGO.

Main time had moved on centuries into the future. One southern area of Northern America was peaceful and seemingly charmed while Yindi lay contained in a watery tomb. Alexander stood at the bottom of the pit and looked up at the glowworms. Then he turned to see a ghostly moment of time thousands of years before main time and months from his frozen time, a translucent image of Brandy transfixed by the moon and the glowworms—joyous.

He smiled, "Still there."

ABOUT THE AUTHOR

Tina O'Hailey is a mild-mannered mother of two who seeks respite in the mountains with her family, on a bluff, overlooking a wooded valley. Her education includes a BFA in computer animation from Ringling School of Art and Design. She also holds an MSCIT degree in object-oriented programming from Regis University. When not wearing flannel and jeans, she can be found wandering the halls or teaching in the classrooms of Savannah College of Art and Design.

She currently is the associate dean of digital media and entertainment arts for SCAD's Atlanta location. At heart, O'Hailey is a professor and still teaches animation and game programming every chance she gets.

Her current hobbies include writing, caving, motorcycles and baking.

Having nearly drowned at ages 3 and 11 (never told Mom about that one), she does not cave dive.

If you are interested in caving, please make sure to become educated in the sport. It is a dangerous sport where even the most nominal injury or poor weather can become life threatening.

Read more here: http://caves.org/.

Follow the author at coffeediem.wordpress.com

View other Black Rose Writing titles at

BLACK ROSE
writing ™

CPSIA information can be obtained
at www.ICGtesting.com
Printed in the USA
LVOW11s0028180418
573737LV00001B/1/P